BLOOD, LOVE AND STEEL

BLOOD, LOVE AND STEEL

A Musketeer's Tale

JENNIFER M. FULFORD

A Romantic Sequel to
The Three Musketeers
by Alexandre Dumas

THAMES RIVER PRESS

Blood, Love and Steel
A Musketeer's Tale

THAMES RIVER PRESS
An imprint of Wimbledon Publishing Company Limited (WPC)
Another imprint of WPC is Anthem Press (www.anthempress.com)
First published in the United Kingdom in 2014 by
THAMES RIVER PRESS
75–76 Blackfriars Road
London SE1 8HA

www.thamesriverpress.com

A CIP record for this book is available from the British Library.

ISBN 978-1-78308-202-5

This title is also available as an eBook

For Alexandre Dumas and Oliver Reed,
who deserve all the credit.

Acknowledgements

To everyone close to me who knows the journey behind this story, my love and dearest admiration. Thank you for your part in making this small miracle happen.

Foreword

*T*he *Three Musketeers* chronicles the friendship and adventures of an élite group of guardsmen who protected the King and Queen of France in the early 17th Century. The fictional tale begins in Paris and sends the Musketeers across France and England. Their intrigues entangle them with the spy Milady de Winter, a woman as evil as she is beautiful. D'Artagnan, the central figure in Alexandre Dumas's novel, lives by his wits and sword, learning from three "inseparables" – Porthos, Aramis and Athos – the Musketeers who befriend the young Gascon.

Each man has his own personal story. D'Artagnan falls in love and proves his intelligence and swordsmanship to earn the title of Musketeer. Porthos, stricken by the sin of vanity, searches for a wealthy benefactor. Aramis's desire for love competes with his longing to become a priest. Finally, Athos, the most serious and reserved of the Musketeers, harbours secrets from a previous life he shared with the devilish Milady. Determined to end her evildoing, Athos leads a lethal hunt for Milady. Dumas's novel ends with her execution at the hands of the Musketeers, but her death is the beginning of this story about Athos, who had at one time loved her, married her and never loved again.

PART ONE – THE FALL

"In his private hours, and there were many,
the light within Athos was extinguished
and his brilliant side disappeared into profound darkness."

The Three Musketeers
Alexandre Dumas

Chapter 1
A Duel After Dark

Paris, Early Summer, 1629

Of his many regrets, using his fellow Parisians to turn a death wish into a sport troubled Athos the least.

"A stranger might easily persuade a kiss from this nobleman's beloved wife," Athos declared, pointing to the Comte de Rochefort. "Within a week or less, I could touch the lips of his sweet Nicole by posing as a guest at their estate. Who would agree?"

With the suddenness of a cannon blast, gamblers shouted bets from every corner of the Taverne Cheval. Athos tossed his coin pouch to a grinning drunk, doubling the racket in the tavern. Before the noise died into a mild chaos, the roomful of peasants and hotheads had split the odds down the middle—half for the Musketeer and the rest for the Comte, a notorious gambler who had never lost a swordfight in Paris.

Sour-faced, the Comte tightened his fists and zeroed in on Athos across the dim tavern. Commandeering the floor of the establishment as his stage, Athos upped the ante.

"Perhaps I could persuade more than a kiss."

A few in the crowd whistled and whooped. Hatred darkened the Comte's face. The river of wine that had been consumed in the tavern since dusk fuelled the scene for mayhem.

"You've gone completely mad!" As he shouted, the Comte spitted profusely. Steely eyed, he unsheathed his sword. "But you shall not insult my wife."

Rowdy cries of approval bounced off the stone walls, and new bets flew across the dark tavern, where Athos had spent days waiting, primed for his mark. The Comte swung his sword to disperse the baited crowd, sending wild-eyed men to cower and duck behind posts, overcome by nervous laughter at the sport about to take place.

For the first time in many months, Athos felt self-assured. Every aspect of his scheme hinged on the Comte's honour and his fidelity to his beautiful wife.

"*You,*" the Comte said, drawing near and circling his sword in front of Athos, "the Devil has you in his hold."

"The Devil—or your wife," Athos said with an ironic smirk.

Too far away to lunge, the Comte aimed the sword between Athos's legs. "You have few conquests to back up your boast, Monsieur. There's not a woman in Paris who could claim you're capable."

Several in the crowd catcalled. Undeterred, Athos delivered his final insult with a slight bow of his head.

"Who could please the women of Paris while you keep them so busy? Meanwhile, your wife wilts alone in your bed." The Musketeer cocked an eyebrow. "Or does she?"

The scandalous claim reduced the room to whispers. No one had ever questioned the well-known piety of the Comtesse. As Athos had hoped, her husband lashed out with venom.

"*Liar!* Nicole is not yours to wager nor seduce!" The Comte's outburst silenced the gossip. "Your punishment is death!"

Athos bowed and headed outside for the duel of his life. He couldn't have picked a finer opponent. The Comte's reputation at fencing placed him among the best of the best. Not even in practice had a challenger gotten the better of the Comte de Rochefort. In the street duels the Comte had fought, the nobleman dispatched his rivals in a few minutes, providing no time for the Cardinal's guards to apprehend him for breaking the law. His skill favoured technical supremacy and, despite being a master himself, Athos would need every reserve of his strength to make this match convincing. Having defied death so many times before, few in the city, including those betting against the Musketeer tonight, would believe he was mortal.

Everyone abandoned the tavern for the street and torches formed a circle around the two men, both the epitome of strength. Identical in build, medium with broad shoulders and narrow hips, the two were opposing shades of physical magnificence. Athos's chin-length sandy hair hung loose and framed his grey eyes; the Comte's short, dark hair and beard matched the precise cut of his clothes.

Just as confidently as his opponent, Athos slipped his sword from the scabbard. The moonlight reflected off the blade and the damp stone pavement, adding to the illusion of entertainment.

The Comte stood *en garde* and attacked as soon as Athos faced the fight. Within the first strikes, Athos's instincts took over. Fighting was a familiar elixir. Like a shot of rum to a drunkard, it smoothed out the edges. His spirits soared with focus and resolution, for he never underestimated an opponent.

Attacking, Athos gained composure and his nerves braced for the fight. Even though he counted on — *needed* — the outcome to favour his foe, he still searched for a psychological advantage.

Athos blocked the Comte's lightning moves. A parry, a riposte, and the sequence of manoeuvres repeated in flashes of spark. Like a master, the Comte performed compound attacks with outstanding accuracy while Athos took aggression to its peak. He slammed back with overhead blows, allowing no break or opening. The Musketeer's moves matched his temperament—feverish and hell-bent.

"You can do better than this!" Athos shouted, laden with contempt. "Remember Nicole's honour!"

"You're a jackal!" Hatred rippled down the Comte's body. "A grave is in your future."

The Comte heaved in laboured bursts and jabbed at Athos's neck. Subtly, Athos provided an opening but the Comte's anger ruined his attack, and he overshot the Musketeer by several steps. Athos had no choice but to exploit the vulnerability.

Athos grabbed the Comte by the belt, shoved him to his knees and pointed the heavy sword toward his rival's gut.

Silence blanketed the street. His temperature rising, the Musketeer rendered God a fool for sparing his life. *Again.*

"You still have your sword, but what is your fate?" The Musketeer seethed through his teeth, his heartbeat quick, palms sweaty, weapon pressed to the clean shirt of his opponent. His hot words rasped out. "Save yourself. Dare me to any outlandish feat, and if I perish, you live. If I survive, Nicole is my prize."

Stilted in disbelief, the Comte gathered words and stammered. "I … I don't understand."

Athos seized the Comte's neck, jerked him to within inches of his sweat-streaked face and spoke in a heated whisper. "I'm offering you a second chance. Take it!"

The sword remained on target and, tightening his grip, Athos shook the Comte by the neck. "Dare me, for God will not defeat me."

The Comte sputtered nonsense. Athos pushed the sword through the shirt and an inch into flesh. Blood spread along the tear as the Comte sucked in air and his gut. "I have no idea what you're doing. You want *me* to dare *you*? You stand the winner."

"*Challenge me!* Name a deed before I slash you in half!"

Peering upward, neck arched, the Comte blurted an answer. "The buildings." He blinked and glanced again. "Jump between these buildings. The tavern roof, across the street to the inn."

Athos looked up. Jumping across would be suicide.

The width of Rue de Veux Chalais, a distance equal to two men laid end-to-end, separated the tavern and a dilapidated inn. Made of aging stones and powdery mortar, the buildings appeared equal in height and the span between them, death-defying.

"So be it then." His gaze still toward Heaven, Athos removed his sword and let the Comte drop to the ground.

Chapter 2
The Dare

The jump appeared to be a feat better left to festival performers or madmen. Athos couldn't have planned a more outlandish death.

On the roof of the Taverne Cheval, the bets flew again. Fourteen paces separated the tavern from the abandoned inn. Between the drunks and a new set of gawkers, wagers were made on every outcome.

"He'll miss the other side by three rods," a rogue shouted.

Another man blurted, "Five!"

"He'll reach the roof but fall off."

"He'll break his ankles and end up lame."

Heads nodded in unison when a man yelled from the back, "His luck is running out." The comment tipped the odds to one conclusion—the Musketeer would be dead upon impact.

Coins clinked from hand to hand, and several more torches were brought to the roof.

Athos peered into the faces in the crowd. A familiar lot. He wanted believability. Failing on purpose did not appeal to him, so each dare he had undertaken in recent months had to look plausible. When he had dared the Marquis de Renoir, none had questioned him. Athos had walked the full length of a mature log—barkless, greased and suspended twenty-five feet from the ground—while wearing a noose hung from a scaffold. He later had bet his winnings, two mares, that he could survive target practice by a silversmith who boasted of the accuracy of his bullets. Standing in the centre of the Jardin du Fontainebleau, Athos's luck had held out. The smithy split three pears on Athos's shoulder and more gossip spread.

Before the next full moon, he had bet the blacksmith at Le Quai de la Ferraille a new sword and a bagful of coins that he could defeat a dozen successive challengers in duels. Athos had reached six before Cardinal Richelieu's guards halted the brawl and disbursed the crowd, the size of which rivalled the last royal party at Le Louvre. Escaping arrest, Athos had drunk away his prize money at the Taverne Cheval, where he concocted his latest scheme.

Peering over the edge of the tavern roof, Athos believed he could fool his beloved Parisians one more time. In truth, he had no intention of faking the jump. His honour was of utmost importance, whether or not eternal damnation awaited him on the other side.

I'll finally be free of Milady. Unforgiven, but free.

Athos cut into the commotion. "Cast your last bets, any of you bold enough, for I shall succeed."

"Athos! Stop!"

The shout rang out from the rooftop hatch, and a lanky man in uniform rammed into several sweltering bodies and clamoured toward Athos. Through the last barrier of sweaty men, d'Artagnan heaved himself into the centre of the pandemonium.

"Tell me I'm not too late," d'Artagnan exclaimed, causing a new wave of bets behind him. Many grumbled loudly that the second Musketeer might spoil the night's fun.

Glaring, d'Artagnan forced Athos face-to-face. "I won't stand by this time."

"This is none of your worry." Athos showed no emotion at d'Artagnan's heroics.

"You failing," d'Artagnan said, pointing across, "is my worry."

"I'm a man of my word. The Comte has challenged me, and I accepted." Athos nodded in the direction of the Comte, who leaned against the rooftop hatch that led to the tavern two floors down. The nobleman stared at Athos as if he were a walking dead man who'd swallowed a poisonous pill that had yet to take effect.

"This isn't a fair wager," d'Artagnan insisted as he pushed back a rowdy onlooker. "It's suicide."

Athos shoved d'Artagnan aside, shoulder against shoulder. The impact was as heavy as lead, the same as the sickness in Athos's heart, but the younger man persisted.

"You're my friend," d'Artagnan insisted. "Stop. This is death."

"I'm allowed a running start." Athos began climbing the low-pitched roof to the ridge.

D'Artagnan dug his fingers into Athos's collar and lowered his voice. "You've become a sideshow. Has your brain worked a groove so deep nothing will bring you back?"

Athos elbowed d'Artagnan off and caught a glimpse of the Comte, who dropped down the hatch, the only exit to the tavern and street below. D'Artagnan stumbled backward and jumped into the dark opening after the fleeing man. Athos bade his dearest friend a silent farewell.

The torchlight played across the cloudy night, and the voices on the roof quieted. Athos glanced up to the black sky, and his vision narrowed into a tunnel. Touching the deepest scar on his arm, he inhaled the warm night air. The scars on his body would tell the only tale worth remembering. He visualized every step propelling him with dignity, from one roof to another. *Or to Hell.* In the silence, he launched into a run and hurled his body from its last ties to the past.

Chapter 3
The Darkness

Fearful cries echoed off the damp cobblestones on the street as the cold, wet ground drained the last of his warmth. Athos heard the far-off wails of a few men who were praying for the bleeding Musketeer to revive. In the swirl of darkness, one voice rose above the rest, chaining Athos to memories he wanted no more.

★★★

Fère. Fère, my love.

Her words float towards him as she languishes in a tub, a free-standing copper oval next to their bed. The water brims within inches of the top, and her chin rests lightly on the edge.

She hums, then speaks. *I knew you weren't sleeping.*

Resting on a fur rug in their bedchamber, he leans onto his elbows, stretches, and crosses his ankles. His bare body is wrapped only in a dewy sheet. He grabs her ring finger as she lifts a hand from the lukewarm water, and he exhales and gives way to the velvet words of longing in his throat. *I've heard it said that love is the most selfish of passions.*

His gaze captures hers. Her fair skin, her blue eyes.

He desires it all. *Stand for me.*

A melody of dripping water accompanies her rise. The sheen of her skin matches the milk-and-lavender water. Her figure fuels his most scandalous, erotic notions, every simple curve his secret to discover. Damp strands of blond tendrils cling to the nape of her neck, and droplets lick down her bosom.

In one fluid move, he stands in the tub and wraps the sheet around them, its edge in the water. It falls so he may press into her curves and explore her collarbone, neck and breasts with mouth and tongue. He places his hands on her flushed cheeks.

Do you love me?

He repeats the words and lowers kiss after kiss on her body, a reed quivering in a pond. Water spills from the tub as he descends. Her breathing quickens, and her hands find his dusty blond hair. He kneels, middle deep in water, grabbing the soaked sheet behind her thighs to pull her closer. His exhale warms her belly and causes her to quake.

Looking up, he sees a shining halo of light then nothing.

From the darkness, a wood emerges, lush and thick with moss on fallen timbers, ferns beneath towering trees and vines winding between. On horseback, he knows the dips in the land the way he knows her body. He races toward her and falls behind her superior stallion, which widens its lead. His desire to hunt kicks in, but she is far ahead. He whips harder, pursuing only hoof beats, until a blunt thud halts the rhythm. At a distance, in a copse of trees, the stallion reappears without her.

Gone.

Hah-ya!

He races toward the stallion and frantically scans the woods in pursuit, calling into the curtain of greenery.

My lady! My lady!

Silence.

No trace of her lavender lace or hair ribbon appears in the ground cover. His mind spins in all directions. Fifty rods and no sign. One hundred rods and emptiness.

The call of a crow breaks the feverish ride. He rears his horse and spots colour from her dress. Below a low oak branch, she is curled motionless at the base of the trunk. From his horse, he silently begs for mercy and rides to her, driven by shock.

Dismounting, he falls to his knees a few yards away and scrambles to the crumpled heap to lift her head, slack atop a bed of moss, brambles in her hair. Dirt soils a cheek, and blood streaks a chambray sleeve. Her limb lies half beneath her, disjointed, and he is afraid, truly terrified, to touch her.

He beseeches any force, good or evil, to save her.

Say you are with me!

She releases a slow, low groan, and he repeats each word and dares to brush her face in hopes of revival. Her body is fragile, and the limp arm is bleeding. As he takes it, one rushing breath spills from her, but she does not surface.

At the source of the blood, he swiftly slices her half-sleeve with a hunting knife. By chance or fate or God, the black ribbon tied to her arm, her symbol of mourning, is cut apart. It exposes a purplish scar on her tender skin.

A brand of the fleur-de-lis.

The unmistakable mark of criminals blazes in his eyes. He thinks he is wrong, but the evidence is real. His thoughts scatter and his insides convulse.

He rubs his thumbs over the indelible mark and presses deeply, obsessed by the truth. *Be gone like dirt*, he commands. A wave of nausea stings his throat, and he fights it back. He presses hard enough to bruise, causing a puncture wound below the mark to ooze more blood.

Backing off, his head hangs between his shoulders but he cannot feel the life in him. A howl emerges from deep inside him, one of a broken animal, of hope denied.

She stirs and her face creases with pain. Through new eyes, he sees the damage setting in. Although a few feet away, he does not reach for her.

She rasps his name. *Fère.* His stare rages with anger. She sees her mark is exposed and gasps, then recoils and flounders to find footing, which he'll never allow.

He wants her to suffer. His accusations are as sharp as knives.

What are you?! A thief, a murderer? A whore?

She clings to the oak and turns her face into its rough bark.

He bellows from the gut. *WHY? Why this? I refused to believe everything else, your secrets, the unexplained deaths around me. Everything I denied because of you.*

She whimpers and fails to answer. His thoughts collapse into senselessness.

You've deceived me over and over, and I let you.

Her muscles tense to flee.

Hatred replaces the blood in his heart, and the windows of his life shatter.

His hands move with the steadiness of an executioner. A knotted harness binds her wrists, bloodied by his rough handling. He no longer feels the warmth and tenderness of her skin. Then he calls her stallion and ties the end of the harness to the metal base of the stirrup.

She writhes and begs to be free. *No! I love you. You know I love you.*

He cannot look at her, into the place where his heart once lived and now dies. After a moment's hesitation, he slaps the backside of the horse with his open hand and shouts as if calling forth demons. Like a spark from Hell, the animal tears through the brambles, dragging her weight.

Her agony is deafening. He closes his eyes and listens, unmoved, while his soul crosses into Purgatory.

He waits until the forest is silent.

But the memory of her once-sweet voice returns, relentlessly conquering him.

Fère, Fère, my love.

Chapter 4
Recovery

"Athos. Athos."

A warm hand shook Athos's shoulder. Dried tears matted his eyelashes, and his arms, lifeless as rocks, criss-crossed a rough wool cover. Through cracked lips, Athos mustered the strength to speak. "Water."

A large hand elevated his head, and Athos felt cool metal touch his mouth.

"On my eyes," Athos whispered the correction.

The water trickled over his brow and into the sunken parts of his face.

"You've been under for three days," d'Artagnan said with a hint of relief.

A cloth softer than the blanket patted Athos's eyelids. "Try them now."

Athos worked his eyes apart to see his friend sitting beside him. They were in d'Artagnan's small room on Rue du Vieux Colombier.

"It pales to sleeping off a long drunk," Athos finally said.

D'Artagnan broke into a nervous laugh and bounced his knee. "You old devil! The herb woman wasn't certain when, *or if*, you would come out of it. I was about to send for a priest."

"No need to ever do that for me, even in death," Athos said, trying his elbow. He reached out to pat d'Artagnan's hand. "I don't suppose you have any wine?"

"Drink this water first. I'd rather you get some food down."

With the help of his valet, Planchet, d'Artagnan propped Athos to sitting and demanded that he demonstrate each muscle still worked. Convinced his limbs, neck and back could manoeuvre, d'Artagnan presented Athos a hero's feast, of which much went to the caregivers, giddy with relief. Despite a mouthful of quail, d'Artagnan told Athos he had moved only once or twice since being placed in bed the night of the jump. Blood from injuries to his cheek and hand still stained Athos's clothes. His boots, deeply scuffed at the toes, laid tossed at the bedside by his weapons.

Athos examined his scabbed face in a hand mirror. Between bites, d'Artagnan explained that after the fall, Planchet had found the herb woman to buy ingredients for a healing ointment, which were applied to Athos's right cheek and palm, scraped raw by the slide down the exterior of the abandoned inn. The wounds had begun to heal beneath the bandages. His injuries appeared less significant than many cuts he had nursed in longer recoveries. Athos tried to swing his legs out of bed.

"Oh, no you won't." D'Artagnan placed both hands on Athos's chest. "The King's physician is on his way. What do you remember of the jump?"

"Were you there?"

D'Artagnan nodded and resumed eating. "I tried to stop you."

"Obviously, you succeeded."

"It wasn't me."

"You know I don't believe in miracles."

"Oh, it wasn't a miracle." D'Artagnan stopped chewing his last bite. "The Comte took pity. He broke your fall."

"He did what?" Athos now believed his head was suffering most.

"The Comte tried to break your fall from a window at the inn. When you hit the side of the building, he briefly snagged your leg, enough to slow you down and lessen the impact. He came to check on you yesterday and demanded we send word if you resurfaced, though you're not getting any visitors today."

"Why would he want anything to do with me?"

"I asked him the same question," d'Artagnan said. "Do you remember the duel with him?"

"It's the one thing I do remember." Athos had thought it was fool-proof. He had toyed with François Rieux, the Comte de Rochefort, sovereign of the westernmost province of Bretagne, by insulting his wife and suggesting both had committed acts of infidelity. A duel ensued, but the Comte let his anger get the best of him, and he ended on his knees with Athos's swordtip on his belly. The Comte was touted as one of the finest swordsmen in France. The only better ones were his friends – d'Artagnan, Porthos and Aramis – whom Athos couldn't fight. "Where's that wine you promised?"

D'Artagnan stalled by mumbling about his poverty but eventually produced a bottle and sent Planchet out for more. Athos's servant, Grimaud, had left him during his string of suicidal acts in the late spring.

"You must admit the duel was strange." D'Artagnan overfilled Athos's cup then used the bottle to point at him. "Everyone said you out-manoeuvred the Comte, hands down. But rather than kill him, you demanded he challenge *you* to a pointless dare. Care to explain?"

Athos frowned, aware he had been exposed. For weeks, Athos had waited at the Taverne Cheval for the only swordsman who could defeat him. When that failed, the stakes had to be raised.

"I didn't want to kill him," Athos said, a sip his only solace, "just make it interesting."

"Interesting? That's what you call all these stunts of yours since the siege at La Rochelle?"

Athos took a long drink.

"I see. You're going to make me draw my own conclusions, aren't you?" D'Artagnan took a quick drink and tugged at Athos's sleeve. "That armband—how long have you hidden it?"

Athos grazed his tricep, cuffed by a band of pure silver underneath the sleeve. It clung to him after years of wear. The silver was stamped with one relief, a tiny *fleur-de-lis*.

"Don't be surprised I found it. You were near death," said d'Artagnan rubbing his own temples. "An old saying ran through my head when I saw it. *He who loves not is but half man.*"

The disappointment in d'Artagnan's voice made Athos wish he had never confided in his friend about his past with Milady, the murderous Lady de Winter, once upon a drunken night when their friendship was new. The story of his heartbreak had poured out about the same time too much wine had poured in.

Athos signalled for a refill. D'Artagnan obliged but cringed at a spill. "You know, the herb woman couldn't guarantee you would recover. What were you thinking?"

The door creaked open before Athos could counter. The King's physician, a stout, self-assured man, entered with a young woman. The second they crossed the doorway, Athos grabbed his sword from the bedside as if threatened by a Cardinal's guard.

"Withdraw, or you'll find my sword as sharp as your surgeon's knives."

D'Artagnan jumped in front of the blade. "This is the King's doctor, an honour at the request of Louis himself."

"It's not him I object to," and with a flick of the blade, Athos indicated the real offender. All eyes were on the young woman.

"She's my helper. I bring her everywhere," the doctor said, taking his nurse's elbow.

Athos sneered. "Not this time."

The physician grumbled a complaint, but Athos held his weapon until she was sent away, without much coaxing. The physician hurried through an examination and left talking to himself about Musketeer bravado. "And don't call me back if you get a headache. From the looks of it, bad wine will be to blame."

In the physician's wake, D'Artagnan unleashed his anger. "What's wrong with you?"

"Ask your doctor."

"That was the King's doctor. And why scare off his nurse?"

"I'll heal without assistance."

"Then what?" D'Artagnan pressed. "Another gamble? A stunt on a turret of Notre Dame? Why don't you challenge Cardinal Richelieu himself?"

Athos resumed drinking.

"While we're at it, why did you boast you could seduce the Comte's wife? I've never known you to romance a woman. Not even one." D'Artagnan sat in the chair by the bed and stopped Athos from taking another sip. "How long has it been?"

"Not long enough that I've forgotten."

"You allow no one in your life." D'Artagnan's shoulders sank. "It was Milady, wasn't it? Milady ruined you when she was your wife." D'Artagnan held Athos by the cuffed arm.

Athos jerked away from d'Artagnan's grip. "Your knowledge of women is based on impulse. My advice never sinks between your ears."

"When was the last time you bedded a woman?"

Athos stared at the foot board.

D'Artagnan tapped his foot. "Talked to one?"

Athos flung his cup to a corner, where it bounced aimlessly, hollow inside, much like the man who drank from it.

"Athos," d'Artagnan said, softening his voice. "You're the most ruthless swordsman in France, but you didn't get that reputation by acting like this. You've been cut from nose to navel, yet you allow your heart to bleed."

"You know nothing of love."

"You forget I've loved, too. When Constance died—"

Athos slammed a fist on the side of the bed frame. "When Constance was *murdered* you moved on to the next lover without a trip in your step."

"That's not fair," d'Artagnan said.

"Fairness and love don't co-exist," Athos said. "Deceit is a game often played by lovers. When you are on the other end of a lie, talk to me then."

"So it was Milady." D'Artagnan focused on Athos as if a target. "What happened between you two?"

"I've told you once, and once was enough." Athos looked away. As a friend, d'Artagnan was the truest kind, and Athos trusted him, maybe too much. Secrets often had a way of turning against a man regardless of who held them.

"I know you," d'Artagnan said, leaning forward in his chair, "and I can't ignore all the signs. There's more to her story than you've shared with me."

With everyone, including d'Artagnan, Athos had been purposefully vague about his past. "Useless details now."

"But you loved her."

Love or not, memories of her haunted his existence. There seemed no point in lying to d'Artagnan now. He turned his bandaged cheek into the pillow. "She was the sun, the light that made the world bloom. She was everything."

"It wasn't your fault. You didn't know she was a criminal."

"My desire for her made me blind. When her faults added up, it was impossible to forgive her or ignore the injustice. My anger—my honour—wouldn't allow it."

"So she was unfaithful to you?"

Athos looked straight at d'Artagnan. "Don't forget, she even seduced you."

From the edge of the chair, d'Artagnan flopped into the seatback and turned the last bottle upside down over his mouth, empty. "I thought executing her closed the story between you two. She locks you to the past, like that chain around your arm."

Athos allowed the message to settle over his weak body. Everything, including his friendships, ended up shaken by the mess she had made of his life.

The tension in the room eased when Planchet, gasping for air, stumbled in with two more bottles. Athos pointed to his cup on the floor and nodded.

D'Artagnan chuckled. "Don't drink too much. Monsieur de Treville wants to be the first to see you. He was the only one absolutely certain you would come to."

Chapter 5
Call to Treville

Athos despised being the centre of attention, and d'Artagnan smothered him for three more days. After many good-natured spats, Athos left Rue du Vieux Colombier for a meeting with Monsieur de Treville.

When he arrived at the Musketeer headquarters, the anticipation of a new assignment made the pain of his injuries fade. Although his appearance caused excitement among the men who gathered to spar, he returned little of it. The ongoing games of skill-building in the yard were tiresome. His recent assignments had been marginal, and he needed a better distraction, preferably a risky one.

Treville's office, with its high ceilings, dark cabinetry and displays of hatchets, knives and swords, reeked of secrecy. Confidences whispered there rarely travelled beyond its walls, and though that was a remote concern for Athos, the privacy soothed his nerves. He respected Treville for his discretion and fair leadership.

"I knew you would be here sooner than later," Treville said, pressing a handshake.

"Obviously, word of my ruin can be laid to rest."

"You appear no worse than when you were tumbling around the countryside trying to save the Queen's reputation." Treville squinted at the wide bandage across Athos's face. "Perhaps this injury will earn you more sympathy with the gentler sex."

Athos picked up a sheet from Treville's stacks on the desk and held it above the mess and let go. Treville raised an eyebrow at the not-so-subtle cue to get on with it. "Has d'Artagnan told you I have new assignment for you?"

"I thought you wanted to make sure I was still alive and able to swing a blade."

"Good, he kept it quiet, how I wanted it." He pointed Athos toward a seat, but he refused it.

"If you don't mind, I'd rather stand. It's a wonder I don't have bed sores the way d'Artagnan kept me."

"Remind me to send him my thanks, will you?" Treville tapped the corner of a map on his desk. "I'm sending you on a mission to Nantes to protect a shipment for the King. He needs it to arrive intact, and the routes to Paris have been plagued by thieves. A rather nasty band of gypsies, ambushing caravans. The shipment is scheduled to arrive in three weeks at port, that should give you time to get to your first destination and learn the details of your role."

"Not to the port at Nantes first?"

"Rochefort," Treville clipped, turning to shuffle papers.

Athos's brow wrinkled into a V. "The only trader I know from that village is the Comte I almost killed a week ago."

Treville tightened his jaw and kept shuffling. Athos clutched the hilt of his sword until his knuckles ached. He rattled off several insults at the walls, indelicate even in French.

"You send me to do the bidding of the Comte de Rochefort? This assignment has me in the clutches of François Rieux? This must be a joke!"

But the reflection in Treville's eyes assured him it was not.

Athos shouted with full force. "Your motives are wrong, Monsieur!"

Rage rushed up Athos's neck, and he kicked the chair previously offered for comfort.

"What do you take me for, a whipping post? How am I to hold my head up?"

"Hold your head up?" Treville's laugh shook the musket cabinet. "Did you forget about your wager? Every odds-maker in Paris is taking bets whether you'll seduce his wife. Or have you already come up with another ploy to get out of that ridiculous scheme? I'm trying to make this a more productive suicide, one that will actually help the King and perhaps save your deteriorating reputation."

"Send me to the Bastille instead or torture me, but don't shackle me to the Comte!"

"You've already shackled yourself. You won your bet with him by surviving. I know I won't get any credit, but I'm trying to turn this folly around. The Comte needs a particular kind of person for this job because the gypsies are becoming sophisticated. He needs an experienced swordsman, and this suits your talents. Your behaviour last week proved to everyone your vicious single-mindedness and skill, as if any of us needed proof."

"The Comte is requesting my help? I nearly slit him in two."

"That's not what I heard," Treville said with growing condescension. He punctuated each syllable. "In every account from witnesses, you provoked the Comte then showed him mercy. What I can't comprehend is *why*. You questioned his wife's fidelity and boasted you could seduce her? I can't seem to swallow that particular detail either, especially coming from you. Do you even know Nicole Rieux?"

Squeezing his sword, Athos drew it from the scabbard and rammed it into a floorboard.

"Just as I thought," Treville said. He walked toward a leaded window and lowered his voice. "You must know there are those of us who think your recent conduct is deeply troubling. You'll destroy yourself if you stay in Paris."

"Save your pity!" Athos dragged his fingernails over his scalp. "Is that what this is about—to keep me from corrupting myself? Sending me away won't detach me from … from my very person."

"This will. You'll do this because you are cornered by your own words but also because you are the most suitably skilled. Remaining here is potential disaster." Treville turned back to the room and threw up his hands. "Don't feel so belittled. The Comte has his reasons for wanting you. You're our oldest and most experienced Musketeer, and he's desperate to gain the King's favour, which you could help him do. He's an outcast at Court because he tries to live in both worlds, the aristocracy and the trades. You and he both share reputations as—how should I say it—as *nonconformists*. And he and I are confident you have no intention of seducing his wife."

With uncharacteristic rashness, Athos pounded both fists twice on the desktop. Gathering his composure, he leaned over the desk, palms down, elbows locked. "This shipment better be life or death."

"Sugar."

Athos growled. "If I hear another word, I'll shave your tongue!"

"I know you dislike the excesses of the Court, but this shipment will provide needed flourishes for visits from foreign dignitaries. The King is determined to win them over. It's politics, Athos, and sweets can manipulate many a foolish crown."

His head throbbed. "What if I refuse?"

"I cannot blame you for being resentful, but I can order you to do this. The best I can promise is that your job for the Comte will remain confidential. Everyone else will believe you are in Rochefort because of your bet, for Nicole, trying to make good on your boast. But as long as you remain a Musketeer, you're dispatched at the pleasure of my office and the King's. If you refuse, your appointment will be in jeopardy."

The pain from Athos's injuries could not match the contempt gaining ground. "Don't hang that over me. Your threat is thoroughly unconvincing."

Treville approached his long-time friend and gripped both shoulders. "Then stop these reckless ploys."

Upon exiting, Athos slammed Treville's door and stalked toward the main exit, his grey eyes cold with menace, which silenced the men he passed and dispelled any doubt of the hardness of Athos's heart.

★★★

Before dusk, Athos had put together his weapons and a few provisions for the trip, mostly dried meat and bread. He misplaced small items in the stable as he fumbled to pack, his mind questioning why the Comte would want him. Athos had handed the sovereign his first defeat as a swordsman and had publicly humiliated him and his wife with claims of infidelity.

Athos cinched the saddle strap tighter around his horse's underbelly when d'Artagnan arrived at the Musketeer stables to say good-bye.

"You're exciting him," d'Artagnan said after being jostled by the nervous horse.

"Don't pretend you're innocent." Taking the reins, Athos mounted the horse. "I know your hands aren't clean. Aramis and Porthos would never have meddled."

D'Artagnan went to fasten a buckle on a saddlebag, his eyes down. "If they knew the depth of your bitterness, I'm sure they'd abandon abbey and wife to come to your aid."

Athos angled the horse out of d'Artagnan's reach. "The Comte's involvement leaves a foul taste in my mouth."

The horse pawed the hay, and d'Artagnan tried settling the animal by stroking its haunch.

"You can't forfeit now, even if you don't care about this game over his wife," d'Artagnan said. "The Comte never dreamed it would get this far. Neither did you, but it's better to make the complication work in your favour. You help his reputation, and he helps yours."

Athos wanted d'Artagnan to disappear, a feeling he had never had about his friend in all their time together. The only way was out. In the archway, Athos forced his horse to a swift trot and ignored d'Artagnan's last call: "Be well."

Chapter 6
A Secret and a Traveling Sage

The wind gusted east as Paris's tallest spires dropped below the treeline. Athos's cape flapped over the backside of the horse, and the fresh air cooled the sting of his bandaged cheek, which he decided to leave covered a few more days.

Although his hand had healed enough to go without dressing, d'Artagnan had sent Athos off with enough bandages to last the entire two-week ride to Rochefort. Athos tossed out the bundle at the first water break.

His head pounded, not from his wounds, but from anger, chiefly because of Treville's threat. Athos's position as a Musketeer had never been questioned before and he resented being manipulated by a superior. Dejected, he decided he must go on the journey with as low a profile as possible.

He avoided inns and set up camp each night, hunting small game when provisions ran low rather than buying food in markets. The greatest disadvantage to being anonymous was he could not drink, so he passed by village taverns. Bottles were too cumbersome to transport and pouches were too small for his thirst. He had to travel sober. If he stayed clear-headed, he rationalized, his obligation would be over sooner.

With or without wine, thoughts crowded his mind. Athos was a native Frenchman, and, true to the noble bloodline, honour ruled his character. If his life came crashing down, he wanted it to happen honourably. But being French also meant *joie de vivre*. In a world which exalted life, his pursuit of death turned his back on his heritage, away from a Frenchman's passion for living, as well as honour. On the roads west to Bretagne Province, his grasp of the situation split him like a fractured boulder, and the pain sliced between his shoulders.

Months ago, the night prior to Aramis's departure for the priesthood, Athos had asked his religious guidepost whether or not God forgave tortured souls.

"A tortured soul is often a self-indulgent one," Aramis counselled.

"Perhaps not by his own choosing," Athos argued.

"Remember, God wants the sinner's conversion, not his death. Don't be so morose," Aramis told him. "You simply need another love."

But Athos refused the company of women.

Since Milady, Athos had denied his sensuality. He practiced abstinence as devoutly as a priest, who would have praised such self-control had Athos bothered to tell one. He controlled his desire for the very thing that tortured his mind. His practice was simple. He would not talk to women or look too long. His most exacting rule was he would not get too close.

He only permitted himself to admire women from afar. A mere minute or two, and the sight of an intriguing woman would allow him to fantasize on his own terms. From within. It was never satisfying; it simply laid a blanket over cloudy water.

He had fantasized about very few. Regrettably, one of his deepest secrets was an imaginary tryst with the Comte's wife, Nicole. Buried in his psyche, she inspired his most-coveted daydream.

He had seen her two years ago in Le Louvre, the royal premises. It was a humid day, and the reviewing hall was crowded by most of the aristocracy in Paris to see dignitaries from Italy, who were being presented to Court. It was a lavish, pretentious affair, the kind which drove Athos into a state of impatient boredom. In his restlessness, pure animalism drew his attention to her. Among the hundreds of women in fine heels and gowns, Nicole had captured him.

She stood opposite his regiment, across the path of the pageantry at the arm of her husband like a regal jewel on his cuff. Athos had become acquainted with François in Court but had never seen his wife. Immediately, he noticed something unique in her demeanour, different from most women of her status. She seemed as bored as him, but not in an obvious way. Less showy and more genuine, her natural poise stood out against the others. The brilliant flashes of colours from the Italian court and the crushing crowd did not dilute his impression of the Comtesse de Rochefort.

She is completely unimpressed by the event.

From his vantage point, Athos watched every move she made, and he spent the rest of the event in anticipation of every stir. She wore dark green, an unusual colour that suited the autumn tones of her skin. Her features were earthy, auburn eyes and brunette waves, loosely curled to drape at her collar and tease her skin. Her lips were as shapely as her figure and their colour finer than wine. Unlike the other women who idealized porcelain skin, the sun had coloured her with beauty more lush than a blood rose.

But other, more subtle signs made her a fascinating study. He read the tilt of her head as a preoccupied mind; her relaxed poise as a detached heart; the way she held her body next to François as an obligation of marriage. Athos watched her like a bird of prey, aware that her head was anywhere but on the intrigues of Court.

In uniform, he sweltered from the temptation across the room.

"And she?" he asked another Musketeer nearby.

"Nicole Rieux, the Comtesse? Exquisite, no? Rumour is that she suffered an unspoken tragedy that causes her great sadness. Some say she would be a nun if it weren't for her husband."

Unaware of Athos's fixation, she had arched up to the Comte's ear. Helplessly, Athos let his imagination take over—and it was he who received her warm, whispered appeals to slip away, to be alone. In his mind, he indulged her, directing them immediately to privacy, where he caressed her bare skin, his lips pressed against her neck, his mouth explored her open body beneath his heft on a canvas of sheets. He even inhaled her imaginary aroma—a tangy blossom.

Then, as if the daydream caused it, the Comte and Comtesse left, and a fog of remorse set in.

Athos had one exception to his rules about women: he would kiss the hand of Queen Anne when offered, out of regard for her position. It was a sublime conciliation. He wanted more from life, but thoughts of touching a woman always led to despair. He repressed the fantasy of Nicole, for it only led to disenchantment.

All his mind games ended in one place—down a mental black hole. Now his suffering edged him toward death.

Where will this end?

The question sparked along with his campfire. Athos watched the small blaze, and his thoughts flickered along with it. He threw a stick in the fire and wished he could sleep.

His horse shifted anxiously. In the small circle of firelight, a short, cloaked figure emerged. Athos lifted up, ready to deal with any trick his mind might play on him in the dark.

A stout man removed his hood to show a grey-black beard and full head of the same coarse hair. "Room for one more?"

"Take what you need," Athos said, relaxing back into a crouch. If Athos had a sentimental bone, it was for the meek.

The man stepped forward, lugging a bulging pack, as plain brown as his wool cloak. Clean and well-fed, the older fellow's hair lay trimmed and flat on his skull; beard clipped; his wooden clogs, newly carved. As soon as the man sat on his overstuffed bag, Athos knew he was clergy. The visitor dug a hand into his woollens and removed a handful of figs.

"I found these back off the road before nightfall," he said, nodding to one side. His smooth palm offered several to Athos, who finished one in two bites.

"Where are you headed?" the stranger asked.

"Bretagne Province."

"You must be traveling from far away. Fatigue fills your eyes."

"Mmm. At least I have a horse."

"Ah, yes, men of the faith don't often travel so well. But my legs will get me there. I'm headed for Paris to see the bishop at the abbey at Saint Germain-de-Prés. I hear the monastery there is highly revered. I'll finally earn a parish of my own, I believe. The walk is a source of pleasure, no burden at all. And you?"

"A King's errand."

"I guessed it." The man slapped his knee. "I could tell I was in the presence of a man of the Court. What are you? An envoy? A duke? Some type of diplomat?" Good-naturedly, the older man squinted in the low light.

Athos knelt to stoke the fire, which flared toward his unbandaged face.

His guest drew in a short breath. "Oh, I beg your pardon. Are you in need of a doctor?" He rose a few feet off his saggy pack.

"Far from it. And, no, I'm neither a statesman nor an intellectual. I'm a Musketeer." Declaring it always made Athos's blood run faster.

"A Musketeer! By fortune, I've never met a Musketeer. Let me properly introduce myself." The clergyman wiped his fingers across his front and held out his broad grip. "Simon Grignan."

Athos shook once with a forceful thrust. "Athos."

"My, that mark on your face, it's a mean one, and recent, I take it? Did you get it doing the King's bidding?"

"It's nothing." Athos turned the injured cheek from the firelight.

"Hmm," Grignan said. "Let me thank you, nonetheless. It's a great service you provide, defending the King, and one lacking appreciation. I know there's a blessing in my head somewhere for such work." He tapped a temple.

"Your thought is kind, but save your prayers. They'd be wasted here."

"At least your face appears better than my feet." The priest's belly got in the way as he removed his clogs. Blood stained the bottom of both feet from the toes. "Life's journeys are always tinged with pain." He chuckled, popped another fig in his mouth and offered another to Athos, who declined.

"Listen to that." Grignan gazed up toward the stars. "That noise? It's almost like a cooing, but it's an owl. Do you hear it?"

Athos listened but heard nothing. He felt an urge to mount his horse and ride out, until a chill struck his neck. *Woo-hoo.*

"You did hear it! Owls are a wonderful, night-time delight. I could spend a thousand nights in the woods and get the same thrill each time I hear them." Grignan sighed and went on without a care for Athos's silence. "I find being out in the elements feeds me, as does any testament study or meditation. It gives me a chance to get out of my head and see the world from a raw point of view. Don't you think?"

Athos shifted his weight from one knee to the next and stoked the fire again. His opinion of nature was tainted by the church, which linked the natural world to danger, sin and depravity. "I think your ideas, if not carefully stated, might put you at odds with your bishop. The mind plays tricks in spite of its surroundings."

"Oh, not so, Monsieur." Grignan's hands flew up, and his eyes widened, a clear sign to Athos that his detachment was seen as an invitation to teach. "The world comes to us in two very different ways. It comes from within us, but it doesn't end there. We need another very important part, and that comes from all around us. The air, the water, the plants, the animals. The weather and the stars. And, most importantly, each other."

Athos's ears fumed and neck tensed. "What of God? You've left Him out. To some, that's heresy."

"Of course, God is alive in all things. He's our source for guidance. That goes without saying," Grignan admitted with a few nods. "But if we close ourselves off to everything else—and everyone—our soul has no chance. We must live in harmony with the world and with others. We must have connection, Athos. Without it, we surely die."

Athos knew Grignan had aimed the subtle remark on target. The clergyman saw through him. And why not? Alone, injured and short on pleasantries, Athos wore his pain like thread-bare robes— there was nothing else to put on.

"You talk eloquently about finding connection with people," Athos said, "but until you experience the most intimate side of a human relationship, you'll never truly know about the human heart. Demand too much from it and the mind suffers with it. Your vows save you from feeling the sting of love."

Athos stood, determined to end the lecture.

Grignan extended a hand. "Oh, don't let me chase you off. I'm merely a man of religion, spouting off a few beliefs. Please, please, sit. I'll reel myself in. Your company is good for me."

Athos checked the saddle on his horse but did not mount.

"Love is a difficult thing. I'll give you that," Grignan kept on. "It sounds as if you could provide me the insight I need. What has love done to you that another love couldn't repair?"

Another love? Never.

"A fire that burns flesh once will do so again," Athos said. "Many don't learn that lesson."

"But what is it about the fire that keeps calling to us?" Grignan asked. "I would argue love makes up for its failures. It feeds the body and the mind. We need it to live. Burns, well, they heal."

"Do they? How would you know?"

The insult did not stop Grignan, who lifted each bloody foot, one after the other. "I place my love in God, and if there's anything that requires more faith and certainty, I cannot think of it."

Athos walked out beyond the firelight and stood in the dark, his thoughts stewing with contempt.

"Athos," the clergyman called. "Don't let my talk prevent us from becoming friends."

"Friends? You truly are desperate."

An exhausted sigh floated out from the campsite. Athos clinched his fists, which sent a bite through his scarred hand. Church teachings never healed his ill heart. Nonetheless, Grignan's words resounded with truth. Athos did need to engage the world rather than continue down a narrow path toward isolation, but his life seemed too far afield to reverse course.

Hearing a soft snore from Grignan, Athos returned to the dying fire. The priest slept with his head on his pack, under a drab blanket, his raw feet sticking out. The owl hooted again.

Sleep was wishful thinking. Athos guessed he was close to Rochefort, a few days by foot at most. Under the starlight, Athos packed a few items in his coat and left his horse, an animal he didn't know by name. As Athos entered the dark, the nocturnal sounds of the owl and the night engulfed him. He listened and wondered: *Where will this end?*

Chapter 7
Awaiting a Stranger

Nicole watched the road leading to her château, wishing the Musketeer would never arrive.

"There you are!" Out of wind, Hannah ducked under a willow branch and raced to Nicole. Her quick breaths reminded Nicole of a childhood memory—a younger sister rushing about for her dearest playmate. Nicole embraced the petite Hannah, whose bulging belly hindered a full embrace. When Nicole found Hannah's hands, they were still damp from chores.

"Are you worried?" Hannah followed Nicole's gaze to the road. They stood under the tall willow by the pond, the most significant natural landmark in the sovereignty.

"He's late," Nicole said.

"Like this one." Hannah patted her broad tummy. "What did the Comte say?"

"That the Musketeer may not like it here," Nicole said. "That he needs our understanding."

"My Lord knows the guest will be in proper hands." Hannah smiled up at her.

"Let's hope François is right." Nicole nodded, squeezed Hannah's shoulder, and escorted her youngest servant along the path in the field back to the house. She sent Hannah to the kitchen and returned to the library, where François sat writing at a desk. She hoped to enter without stirring him, but he motioned to her while he wrote.

"I can't wait any longer," he said. His quill scratched on the paper.

"But your patience is legendary."

"Only for you." He dipped the quill and continued writing. "This letter must remain confidential, between Monsieur Athos and myself."

Nicole rubbed her temples as if to divine the letter's contents. She opted to stare out the library window, a place where she frequently contemplated her future.

"He'll be resentful whether I'm here or not," the Comte told her, fanning the paper in the library's quiet. "He'll want to leave, no doubt."

"Please deliver your message to him in person. He's coming at your request, not mine." Her urgency interrupted him folding the letter.

"He wants nothing to do with me, I can assure you of that. So, all the better if I'm gone when he arrives. I strap him to a commitment he doesn't want. You have no history with him, so he won't blame you. He's a Musketeer after all, bound by honour and duty."

Nicole wadded a curtain fringe in her palm. "It isn't fair. He's a stranger, and I'll be alone."

"Hardly a concern for a hostess and a sovereign's wife." François straightened his coat as he stood. "I shouldn't have to stress again the importance of your role. He and his friends are favourites of the King and Queen. Adoration is not a stretch to describe their feelings. If he helps me, I'll succeed in my delivery for the King and secure an association with a legendary Musketeer. I win twice over."

From the window, Nicole spotted a sparrow skimming the surface of the pond, which she longed to run back to. The area was lush in early summer, and the willow branches swayed as if to beckon her. At a distance, the area appeared calm to Nicole although it teemed with wildlife, matching her mood. "And what if I fail? You know I've failed before."

"Your sister's death wasn't your fault. Sibonne was her own undoing." He creased the final fold and placed a drop of hot wax on the flap. He pressed the Rieux insignia, leaving the mark to harden at the desk, and came up behind her.

"Please, not another wayward soul," she said.

He pressed into her back and placed his hands on her shoulders. "I would consider your appeal for me to stay, if you would allow me back in your bed."

She hooked an arm around the drape and concentrated on the view of the swaying grasses and the reflection of the sun on the water. He wrapped an arm around her waist, bound in a sash, but her gaze was unaffected.

"Love me again," he said, hugging her waist, "and all my attempts at coercion become history. You're too beautiful for our guest to reject. You have merely one job—keep him here for a little while. Distract him. God knows you do it to me, and I've been your devotee for years."

She blocked his hand from wandering up her bodice. Instead, he dipped in and inhaled the auburn hair layered down her back.

"When, Nicole? When?" he said in a hush, and left the room and the estate.

Chapter 8
Visions and An Obligation

Other than his weapons, the only items Athos had taken from the campsite were a handful of figs. The previous night's conversation with the priest dominated his thoughts on the walk to Rochefort. By mid-morning the scenery had changed, while his ruminations continued. Men burdened with scythes and hoes crossed from dusty path to dusty path, sheep grazed, and fisherman carried poles. A rag-tag girl leading a trio of goats towards a patch of grazing grass offered Athos a sip of milk. Parched and grateful, he drank a cupful and nodded his thanks.

The goat milk was a drop in the desert. Athos rubbed glare and weariness from his eyes. The sun burned overhead.

Hadn't I just come across the girl with her goats?

She was not behind him anymore. His head listed, and the tree canopy closed into a tunnel, cooling his limbs. He tried shaking the numbness out of each hand and foot. He had finished the last of his water late in the night. He counted each step and commanded each leg to move forward.

An oncoming figure blurred in the distance, and he tilted his head side-to-side as he tried to make out the object seemingly floating his way. A gust whistled through his clothes, chilling his bones. The shape approached—a woman in a dress too formal for a peasant.

Who is she? Where am I?

Her face was obscured by the distance, but her hair was fair, her hands, delicate petals against the sheen of her skirt. Her voice, *Milady's voice*, was an old, familiar song.

Fère. I'm here.

He shook his head and covered his ears. He blinked rapidly.

Fère. Come, take my hand.

"You're dead."

Not in you.

"You're evil. A fiend. Release me." He dug his knuckles into his eyes, but her features were branded in his memory.

You loved me.

"I wish I were dead because of you."

You could have saved my life. My feelings for you were true.

"True? The *truth* is you changed my heart. Look what I've become." He pounded his chest, and the dust in his clothes powdered the air.

But you loved me without judgment. You tried to overlook my faults.

"I'm ruined. Let me be. Leave me alone and let me be!"

Milady undid blond bundles from a golden comb. Her hair spread across her cleavage, liberating her epic beauty.

You're my husband. I'm your wife, Anne. Remember? You could have saved me, Fère. It's your fault you'll never love again.

"You're a liar. Everything you fed me was a lie!" His heart raced with the force to kill, to finish her at last and free his life from bondage. Hatred stoked his will. Drawing his blade, he ran toward the radiance and flew into the air.

Flat on his back, he surfaced to find his sword missing. He scrambled upright. His clothes smelled fresh, felt clean. Milady stood in front of him, looking young, as young as his hands had been when he first met her.

Run with me! She sprinted off the path, and he whiffed the honeysuckle on her skin. His curiosity won over his resistance.

In the field, she sprinted to a lake like the one in his youth where lovers had mingled. By the water's edge, she undressed. For him. She was a sunbeam from heaven in the flesh. His arms ached to touch her. He waded out a few steps to follow her, and she led him into the water, up to his thighs, clothes and all. Her kiss was honey. Her hair, silk on his cheek. As he rubbed against her body, he felt the ring in his pocket.

She drew him under before he could place the sapphire on her finger.

★★★

Water trickled off Athos's brow. The old priest's face filled the sky. "That's it, my dear fellow. Allow me to help you up. I've been backtracking all morning to find you."

Athos's head hurt and pressure congealed behind his eyes as the smell of his sweat returned. A quick scan confirmed the hallucination was over.

"I've come to return your horse," Simon Grignan said. "I had a difficult time believing you'd leave it behind for an old bluster pot like me."

Athos was on his feet. "Keep the horse. I can walk." But his steps dragged.

"By all means, please." Grignan offered a water pouch, and Athos dribbled more than drank.

"Rochefort is still a good two day's walk," the priest said. "I couldn't let you wander off in this state in good conscience."

"I've been worse." Athos moved forward like a drunk.

"Then I'll follow." Grignan hustled to the waiting horse and took several tries at mounting. "If you could—just give me a hand."

Athos ignored him and kept walking. The horse and rider wrestled in grunts behind him until hooves trotted in his direction.

"I don't need an escort," Athos said, refusing to come about. "If you follow me, the peasants will think you're the Grim Reaper."

Athos heard the smile in the priest's reply. "I'm not the menacing one."

"Be on your way, Father. Take the horse and be on your way."

"No use of your horse, eh? I can hardly believe that of a Musketeer." Grignan trotted up to Athos, who stared at the horizon.

"You're doing a good deed for me," Grignan said. "The least I can do is returning the favour. I can get you to Rochefort and be happy to take the horse off your hands from there."

"Leave." Athos waved him off.

Grignan sighed, a rumble that ended in a small cough.

"Then promise me this," he said, pulling in front of Athos and handing him an apple. "When you return to Paris, let me be of service to you in some way, Godly or otherwise. It's the least I can do.

And I'll see that your horse is cared for by, well, by someone befitting a Musketeer."

Athos relented with an abrupt nod. He glared at the priest, who departed. Once alone, Athos clung tighter to his sword and ate the whole apple, including the core.

Chapter 9
Arrival at the Comte's Château

Villagers crammed the town centre of Rochefort. Athos could not smell the food in the street market above the stench of his body. He stumbled several times, causing women and barefooted children to scatter in the narrow streets. Shopkeepers brushed bugs from produce baskets and eyed him as a hollowed-out stranger worthy of suspicion. Wary expressions turned into closed doors.

Athos rasped, "The Comte," and a worried villager pointed the direction and vanished.

As the estate came into view over the horizon, Athos hoped for relief. He would finally face the Comte, the man who complicated his life. As was typical of aristocracy, the Comte's estate occupied the best land in the sovereignty, complete with water, woods and grazing land.

Using his final reserve of energy, Athos crossed the entrance to the grounds. The entryway was impressive—a double-wide stone archway with a turret and granite pavers. Before him stood the château, in classic French style, rising at least three stories with several window dormers on each wing. The livery and grazing field took up the far side of the main residence next to a coach house. Horses roamed in an expansive fenced yard behind the stable, where the sound of iron clanged. Athos headed toward the noise.

Inside, a flaxen-haired stableman, several inches taller than Athos, was adjusting harnesses on a wooden hook. The young man lit up instantly when the Musketeer stepped through the door.

"Monsieur Athos!" he said, unable to curb his delight.

"And you?" Athos tried to swallow despite his dry throat.

"Pierre!" he said, again too excitedly, wiping his hands down his shirt. "We've anticipated you with great eagerness."

The youth dodged out of sight, through an opening where several horses grazed. Athos heard the young man sprint and shout. "Madame! The Musketeer is here!"

After a short break, Pierre whirled back into view, panting.

"Take his horse, Pierre." Her calm voice came around the stable door the moment she did. The shadow of the eave darkened Nicole's beauty, but it was still a magnet pulling on him.

"He has no horse, Madame," Pierre said, tilting his head to one side.

Athos's memory of her was accurate. When he had first seen Nicole at Le Louvre, he had also thought that her looks undermined her virtuous reputation. Except in Paris, his eyes could wander. Here, he felt torn between desire and detachment. He wanted to absorb her beauty but also escape. The aches he accumulated on the long journey intensified – the thirst, the exhaustion and now, suppressed desire. His terrible condition was no defence against her.

Let me drink you in.

He pushed aside the urge and grabbed the dry water pouch at his belt.

Nicole spoke before the silence became awkward. "Your horse, Monsieur Athos. Is it—are you all right?"

The face from Paris. Gentle brown eyes of autumn, stunning, perhaps even more memorable than Milady's blue jewels. He blinked and nodded, and his head swam. Nicole's body faded into greyness, and the curves of her figure dissolved into a rough outline. A hiss between his ears grew into a roar. His knees buckled, and the air collapsed inside him.

★★★

Nicole grabbed Pierre to steady herself. For several seconds, the two stood bewildered over the lifeless Musketeer lying prone in the stable. Her heart squeezed into a lockbox too small for its contents. "Check him, Pierre," she said, trying to recall the last time she had experienced such shock. It had been with her sister, Sibonne. "I'll get water."

Racing toward a trough in the yard, she plunged a bucket and splashed water on her own cheeks. She tottered back with a full pail to find that Pierre had removed the Musketeer's jacket and was loosening his shirt.

"Stop." Nicole dropped the bucket. From the untied shirt front, she saw the patchwork of ruin. The Musketeer's neck and chest were covered with scars, each distinct tales of violence. Some appeared angry red. Many resembled burns, pale and smooth. The scar on his face was new. She did not dare touch any. Her hands went cold.

"His face," she said and placed her hand inches above his cheek, uncertain whether Pierre understood her hesitancy. From what she could tell, the rest of the Musketeer's body resembled an Olympian's, most likely an embattled one.

"He definitely seemed to recognize you," Pierre said, moving the bucket closer.

"But his scars."

"He's a Musketeer." Pierre shrugged. "He fights."

She scrutinized the Musketeer's torso, her hand floating above the hollow of his throat. "What should we do?"

Athos answered without opening his eyes. "Tell the Comte I've arrived."

Nicole jerked her hand away and, for a half-second, she and Pierre exchanged cautious glances. Athos came to and lifted his head. Nicole's instinct was to keep him down and find soft hay, rather than let him regain his footing. He rose as if he had never fallen.

"A problem?" Athos said, kicking up dust and averting his eyes.

She opened the space between them. Turning his back to her, the Musketeer checked himself and tied his shirt. She felt she should turn away, too, but it wouldn't erase the embarrassment he had just endured. She tried to sound buoyant. "The Comte needed to return to Nantes. He wants you to wait here and left more details in a letter, but we're prepared to care for your needs until he sends word."

His acidity would have tainted an entire well. "I was told my duties would be made clear once I arrived." He dropped to his knees by the bucket and scooped up water in handfuls, one after another. When his thirst abated, he washed his face and soaked his head.

Nicole had only one thought: *How long must I live with this situation?* It appeared decorum was not on his agenda. She took a deep breath.

"Monsieur, I'm Nicole Rieux, Comtesse de Rochefort." A quick curtsy was all she felt capable of. Athos, dripping over the bucket, didn't look up to acknowledge the courtesy, and Pierre shrugged again. She dropped her shoulders. "Pierre, tell Hannah I need her."

He dashed out, and Nicole tried the introduction again, filling her chest with air. "You should rest. You're our guest—"

"Bring me the letter." He stood up to face her and drew the sword from his scabbard.

Nicole stood still while the steely sound of the drawn weapon hung in the air. She wasn't afraid, though she thought he may have preferred it. Instead, pity welled inside her, and a buried memory began to surface. "We can offer you comfort. Food and a place to rest."

"The letter, Madame. I want the Comte's letter." He motioned the sword toward her empty hands. A line had been drawn.

Nicole backed into the doorway and awaited the old grief she harboured for Sibonne to pass.

★★★

"I also need a new horse," he said and lowered his sword. More than anything, Athos needed to escape—from the situation, from Milady, from Nicole. His lingering dizziness was an afterthought to having dropped cold in front of her. His body had betrayed him, a first in humiliation. On top of that, his conversation with the Comtesse had been the longest he'd had with any woman since his ruinous marriage.

Out. I need out. His only option was to ride to Nantes and find the Comte himself.

He locked his jaw and passed Nicole for the horses in the yard. One good horse could set right a thousand misfortunes. Unfortunately, his iciness toward her did not bring about the other desired outcome.

Nicole clutched a post at the stable door. "Are you hurt?"

The question stopped him mid-stride. If he answered yes, she would pursue a doctor. If no, he would be lying. She'd already seen him vulnerable. He jutted his chin and kept walking.

Nicole raised her voice. "The Comte has scars but far fewer. You have so many injuries … and your cheek."

There was no hiding the pity he detected in her voice. And something more dangerous only he could hear—curiosity. He squeezed his eyes shut for an instant and walked toward a group of horses.

Using his sword for support, he crouched several feet from a black horse and gently whistled.

"François is a fine swordsman," she went on, "but his injuries are minimal in comparison."

He approached the stallion, which pranced nervously, picking up on Athos's agitation. Nicole had seen more than he had wanted anyone to see.

"The Comte fights for glory," he said, "not for duty." He spoke louder than he should have.

"Your face. Does it hurt?" she asked.

He caught a glimpse of her in his periphery. Close behind him in the yard, she had inclined her head to see his wounded cheek.

"The pain has long passed," he said and laid a hand on the horse's snout in front of him, quieting the animal and searching for quiet in his own centre.

"And your other injuries?" she asked, still too close. "I'll request a doctor. Please let me."

Her sincerity broke his concentration. Musketeers rarely earned compassion. Even fewer showed it. His fellow guardsmen were too proud. Like them, Athos ignored most injuries and the scores they settled.

But Nicole was offering kindness, which he had not sought or taken from a soul in many years. A small part of him wanted to indulge it and her intoxicating company. A greater part of him wanted nothing to do with her.

"I need to know why I'm here. Instructions from the Comte." He stared downward, then back at her. "*The letter.*"

His sternness didn't move her, neither her eyes nor her body. The tension shot a streak of pain down his back, forcing a grimace. The stallion pitched to another corner of the yard and caused the other horses to whinny and scatter.

Nicole ran to a stable bell and called out for Pierre before ringing. The clanging pounded Athos's head in agony. After several beats, he locked on her auburn eyes, and she immediately ceased the alarm. Silence soon enclosed them in privacy. Every fibre of him said *look away*. In less than a minute, Pierre rushed back into the stable yard.

"Walk him to the pond, Pierre," she said. "I'll retrieve the letter."

"I don't need water," Athos said, still fixated on her. "I need to see—"

But Nicole and Pierre darted in different directions. Athos watched the young man sprint down a path to a back field, smiling and waving for him. Athos rammed his sword in the ground and took the bait.

"It's a long walk," Pierre called back eagerly. "Can you manage it?"

Athos grunted. He outmatched the young man in physical stature and, though battered, Athos's endurance returned. He shook off his aches and fatigue and caught up with the young stable hand in the tall grass.

"Ask me anything," said Pierre, who fell behind and shadowed Athos along the path. "I'm not just a stable hand and groom. I know everything about this place—and everyone in it."

The question Athos wanted answered most—*why am I here?*— was beyond the servant's station. Athos was interested in a swift farewell, not conversation. He needed no attachments or the hint of any, especially with Nicole.

Over a gentle knoll, the path ended at a pond, a smooth plane in the overgrown landscape. Cattails, brown and green grasses, red buds and sycamores grew at its edge. An impressive willow dwarfed them all and dominated the landscape.

"You'll find an opening to the bank just ahead," Pierre said, pointing.

Athos threw off his shirt and boots, hoping to cleanse more than his body. The water soaked through his sweat-stained pants to the hip, and he made a shallow dive. Some of his discomfort and doubt washed away.

I must leave as soon as possible. He would be a fool to stay in exile so close to temptation. He wanted to see the Comte, get on with the mission, and return to Paris.

When he resurfaced, Athos discovered the young man pacing among the reeds, looking restless. Athos saw an opportunity. "Pierre," he said, slicking back his hair. "You know the finest horse in the stable."

Pierre nodded, and his expression immediately brightened.

"I need a new horse," Athos said. He dunked below the surface and whipped the water off his head when he came up. Pierre stood at attention.

"I want your fastest horse," Athos said as he came onto the bank.

Pierre hesitated, partly because he was transfixed by a scar on Athos's flank. "Our fastest? For what?" Pierre's attention moved to the silver cuff on the Musketeer's upper arm.

"To ride on to Nantes."

"What?" Pierre stammered. "But you've just arrived, and not in very good shape, I might add. Are you mad?" The last words trailed off, and Pierre's jaw fell slack.

Athos passed him briskly and shoved his damp feet into his boots. He gathered his shirt and headed back.

"Wait," Pierre finally called out. "I have something you may want, but you won't find it at the house, and you can't take it with you if you leave now."

Athos kept walking.

"I make my own wine. I have a few grapevines here. My first vintage from this spring is ready to be tasted." He shouted to overcome the distance between them.

Athos paused and glanced back. *At last, a drink. Complications always clear up with wine.* "How much wine?"

"Enough to fill ten bottles."

"Then, by all means," Athos said and gestured for the budding winemaker to take the lead.

Chapter 10
A Vow and Pierre's Wine

Nicole locked the door to the library and ran her damp palms down her dress. *Had the Musketeer collapsed in the livery? Arrived without a horse?* Never mind, the questions needed little explanation. The Musketeer was as the Comte had predicted—resentful, sullen—and more. *Broken. Like Sibonne.* Like Nicole's past.

She darted for the credenza. The Comte's letter was perfectly folded and sealed, a contradiction of the mess at hand. Perhaps it would smooth over François' absence. *How can the Comte impose this man upon me?* It took only the brief encounter with Athos to understand the seriousness of her husband's warnings.

Athos lived with pain, the kind that swallowed up all good. It radiated like the moon, but unlike the cool light, his pain surrounded him in darkness. The scars on his body simply marked the evidence.

Nicole's sister had exhibited a similar aura. When Sibonne's life fell apart, her very skin radiated the hurt. Sibonne couldn't function past her losses. Nicole believed she would never see suffering like that again, prayed she would not. She shuddered, holding the letter.

He had drawn his sword? Because of her? Despite his unhappiness, he was here. He was her responsibility. She did not agree with all her husband's requests and, in fact, rejected most of them. But she had vowed to appease the Musketeer for a little while. It demanded steadfastness, calm and, above all, her boundless compassion. François deserved a small favour, and more importantly, God expected it.

She crossed herself, picked up the letter and placed her hands together. She pressed her questions upon the surface. *God, why is he here? How can I possibly help him?*

Without intending, she watched from the library window as Pierre and Athos arrived at the bank of the pond. From here, the water was the size of her thumbprint. The men were so tiny that they looked like birds against a cloud, and she could tell little about their interaction. Still, she couldn't stop from watching, and a surprising wish entered her thoughts.

I wish I were closer.

As if God had frowned, she instantly felt ashamed of her desire to spy. It must be the Musketeer's pain, she rationalized, because to anyone hurting, she was tinder to spark.

★★★

Once he learned about the wine, Athos felt somewhat less miserable. It saved him from buying liquid sustenance in the village. Having once been a sovereign, Athos knew that the smartest servants chose to grow grapes for their side income, and he gave Pierre credit for using his brain.

Pierre's meagre shelter, built of hand-sized rocks stacked head-high into a boxy shape, stood alone in a vegetable field. The dwelling, packed at the base with dirt, was erected on a barren strip. Clay joined the rocks together, and the roof was a thick layer of thatch.

"I carried the stones all the way from Rochefort. There's a place where rubble from the cliff in town falls away, and no one minds scavengers." Pierre beamed over the workmanship.

"And your wine?" Athos tried not to sound blunt, and Pierre amiably swung open a plank that served as the door.

When it came to drinking, Athos usually cared nothing about atmosphere. He would drink in a dark cellar if the need arose, and in his lifetime, the need had arisen at least once. But this was the first time he had drunk in a place so primitive.

To describe the cottage as sparse was kind, if it could be called a cottage. Dirt stirred up from the floor and dusted the sunlight from the entrance, the only source of natural light. The interior walls had been packed with dark clay, resembling the earthen floor.

A three-legged stool took up one corner, and a thin makeshift mattress, stuffed with a lumpy filling, stretched the length of a wall.

There was enough room for the two of them to stand, their heads mere inches from the ceiling. Athos noticed a candlestick and three iron-ringed buckets by the bed. The buckets were fitted with wooden tops, a cork protruding from each lid.

Pierre handed one bucket to Athos. "I can't pay for barrels, so I improvised." He reached behind the other buckets and produced two bowls carved for soup, but in this case, for drinking.

"I hope you like it." Pierre's face glowed.

The red liquid chugged out of the bucket in sloppy splashes onto the dirt floor. Pierre cursed the waste. Athos finished two pours to Pierre's one and sat on the floor near the mattress, relishing the familiar warmth the drink gave him. Pierre pulled up the stool.

"What do you think?" Pierre questioned, stock-still in anticipation.

"I think you may have something, but I won't know until I've had more." Athos held out his empty bowl.

"Well, enjoy it now. You won't find any wine in the house."

A shame, Athos thought on his third serving. He would find no pleasure in the country beyond Pierre's wine, just suffering brought on by his attraction to Nicole.

Pierre scooted the stool closer. "Would you mind if I asked you about your life in Paris?"

"What do you want to know?"

"Is life in Court as wonderful as everyone says, full of parties and intrigues and duelling?"

"All that and more," said Athos, toying with the young man, who poured another.

"And the Queen. Is Anne of Austria beautiful?"

"Queen Anne is an exceptional figure of royalty."

"So you've seen her in person?"

"I often do. I'm her servant and the King's."

"Is that why you're scarred so badly? Those marks are ghastly."

"I'm a Musketeer. I've lived with danger for more than a decade. Most don't live as long." Yet he had, against odds and himself.

"The scars I saw on your side at the pond, the deep and jagged ones, they couldn't be from a blade. What are they from?"

"The Siège de Montauban, nine years ago."

"And?" Pierre leaned in, the wine in his bowl on the verge of spilling.

"I was nearly gutted by a cannon blast and almost lost my stomach. We abandoned the siege after three months."

Pierre sipped, exhilaration shining through his eyes.

"War isn't a game of fantasy," Athos said. "Nor is Court the centre of wonder. Your wine, for instance, I'd put up against any I've had there."

After a long silence, Pierre's next question came in mid-pour. "How have you survived?"

"I don't know, but I can assure you it has nothing to do with God," he paused and sipped. "Luck or fate, I suppose, but not God."

"Are there any Musketeers who aren't from aristocracy?"

Athos immediately thought of d'Artagnan, whose poor Gascony background had not stopped his rise. "Why do you ask?"

Pierre opened his arms to the room. Obviously, his condition rooted him to austerity, at best. *But poverty is better than pain.* Athos envisioned Pierre prone and bleeding, a scene he had witnessed so many times among friends that he had become desensitized to it. At most, the life expectancy of a Musketeer hovered at a year, maybe two. Even the ban against duelling, declared by the King because of the tremendous number of fatalities, did not improve the lifespan of a guardsman. He was an exception. To his distaste, his survival had become legendary.

"You're a fool. Stick with your wine." Athos pitched his bowl toward the young man and took the three steps to the door.

"I've been practicing," Pierre said.

"Practicing what? Dying? That's certainly the fate of any novice with a sword."

"I have a sword. I just need a partner."

Many years had passed since Athos had been truly surprised by another human, and he hesitated. Pierre jumped at the opening.

"It would make your time here pass much more quickly," he tempted.

"You have the Comte to show you."

"You must be joking. I'm a servant, and he's never here anyway."

Athos stepped outside. "Show me your vines."

Pierre rounded the back of the stone cottage, where it was a short walk to the plot. Vines hung over crude T-shaped posts at haphazard distances and sagged with bunches of ripening grapes. Athos picked a vibrant grape ready for harvest.

"Here, you have potential. For yourself as a tradesman. For the fruit as wine." He raised the bluish bulb to his nose, enchanted by the smell. "Pierce its skin, and its life begins."

Athos then snatched the youth's bicep.

"*You* are best whole. Pierce your skin and your vitality drains away. If not the first time, then the next, sometimes slowly, and often without mercy." He pinched the grape and dripped the juice into the young man's palm.

Pierre pulled back and wiped the hand on his dingy trousers. "But you're alive and well. Fighting has made you strong. I should have the same chance, and if I had your skills, I could rise above my situation and be someone important, too. Look at you!"

The strong, the undefeatable, the immortal—the myth of Athos. It infuriated Athos to watch the legend grow, and it made his argument with Pierre less convincing. But reality and perception were wax and water. He had lost count of the times he had grovelled in pain for a swift end, lying in sticky pools of blood, spitting the foul fluid from the back of his throat or stumbling across the dead, half blind from the scarlet in his eyes. Without the sanctity of God or a lover or a son, he had survived.

"There's nothing noble about a slit throat," Athos said.

Pierre's retort was cut short by a horse and rider trailed by a cloud of dust.

"Pierre, what are you doing?" The horseman, a bearded, broad-shouldered man, held a fatherly bearing. "Nicole's waiting. Please, Monsieur Athos, I'm Cordes, the stable master. I'm here to give you a ride back. She mentioned a letter."

Athos was thankful for the interruption. Cordes dismounted and handed Athos the reins in a half-bow. "Leave the mare in the stable."

In the time it took Athos to mount and prepare to ride back, he watched Pierre endure a brow-beating from Cordes. Instead of cowering, Pierre returned Athos's look, signalling their discussion was not dead.

Chapter 11
Consequence of a Letter

The mare trotted straight to the livery for a bucket of feed. Athos started to calculate the distance he might make before dark. Less achy because of the wine, he felt he could ride all night. He entered the yard to pick the best horse and found Nicole exactly where they had left off—a safe distance away. A scrappy yellow tabby prowled around the hem of her dress.

"I brought the letter." It was not in her hands. "Did the water help? You should rest. The ride from Paris is difficult, even in a carriage. And, by foot, I cannot imagine—"

"Why am I here when your husband isn't?" He loaded his voice with contempt.

The cat tucked behind her and leapt out of sight.

"The Comte's business takes him away on short notice. You were late. He said it may be several weeks before he needs you." Not a hand fluttered or quivered. He wondered if she ever faltered under disrespect.

"Several weeks," Athos repeated. He inhaled a lungful of straw-scented air. Patience was in his nature but being chained was not. *And on a shackle controlled by a woman, no less. This woman.* Nicole Rieux, Comtesse de Rochefort: the woman who, in one chance sighting in Paris, had corrupted his mind.

By any standard, she deserved notice from the opposite sex. Well-proportioned, firm contours along bust, waist and hips. Bronze, lucid eyes. Soft hands for give-and-take touch. Her beauty was natural, like that of chestnut trees on a rolling hill.

But he also saw in her, as in every woman, a beautiful deceiver.

She picked up the cat, which had wandered back. Rather than wilt under his glowering, she looked poised, like a painter's subject, which she probably had been. She modelled respectability in her pose, as straight as his sword was sharp. He doubted that she ever made a room feel cold.

"It seems odd the Comte would leave you alone with a strange man," he said.

"Monsieur, the Comte leaves you in capable and appropriate hands. We have every comfort you could need."

Such a useless exchange. She was the only link to the pitiful man who summoned him here, yet her response was flat, giving him no indication of François' intent or a clue to making the delay tolerable. She controlled the message, the comings and goings, the menu, all his care. With a little tension, leaving would be easy.

"After the letter, a bottle of wine will do," Athos said.

"We don't keep wine in the house."

"You said you had every comfort. Ask Pierre to send his. He shows promise."

"You drank his wine?" She reacted exactly as he'd hoped, disapproving and irritated.

He hid his pleasure. "There's not a château in France without a bottle for guests. Several bottles."

"We rarely entertain." In one long exhale, she seemed to release her frustration. "You must feel out of place here. I'm sorry. Along with the wine, is there anything else you require?"

Her expression softened and cast pity. She'd played the higher card, and it stirred his discontent like a bear baited on a chain.

"The letter," he said, seething underneath. "I want the letter."

She pointed to a bench behind him. He snatched up the letter and read:

Monsieur Athos,

It's odd how fate can change, yet if you receive this letter, you are bound by your tongue. The boldness of your words and actions binds you to me. I should have let you die, but now you are beholden, obliged twice over. You must ensure the King receives his sugar in my name, and you must make all of Paris believe you've tried to seduce my wife. How did you put it,

'Within a week, I could place my lips on sweet Nicole's.'? And your brashness—so public! Your reputation teeters in the balance. Had I not seen an opportunity, you would surely be dead.

The odds-makers favour your winning my wife's affections. But I wager mightily against your success. No doubt, a small fortune shall be my reward. There's much the foolish gamblers do not understand about your ways with women, yes? And, what makes the irony of your boast much sharper is the Comtesse herself. As you shall see, my wife will greet you with all the grace she possesses. But she's an island: exotic, mystifying and clouded from every angle. I'll retrieve you soon from exile. Please save your energy. I need it for my enterprise. You owe me your life.

François Rieux
Comte de Rochefort

Athos crumpled the letter on his brow. He now had proof. He was the pawn of a gambler. Athos had handed the Comte weighted dice: the aristocrat was a guaranteed winner.

How could I have allowed this?

"Did he upset you?" Nicole was right behind him. He had no time to move—she was too close. "What is it?" He heard her step even closer.

She's right next to me.

His dignity trampled, he had nothing to lose, and instead of leave, he turned to face her, daring to feel desires he once wished were dead.

"Monsieur?" She stood still. Her dusty brown eyes shone with compassion. For the first time, he heard her steady breathing.

Why did I single her out in Paris? For reasons that a lifetime of exploring wouldn't satisfy.

Nicole's features triggered every urge he had spent years repressing.

Just one touch, perhaps to her cheek. A brush of her hair.

Dare he think it, *a taste of her lips.*

"Are you well?" she repeated.

"Don't give my behaviour a second thought." He said it as much to himself. "All I need is wine."

If only he could convince himself that would do.

"Are you certain?" She hesitated, and her hand protectively covered her silken throat.

Let her go. He begged his body to obey.

He closed his eyes, backed away and gestured *be gone*, sending her out of his heat and the stable.

Her scent remained, the fragrance of fresh air, the outdoors, clover. The taboo smell of a forbidden road. He was tasting sweetness again, like a speck of honey on the tongue. The deliciousness of living in his flesh. He had tried to detach himself from it forever.

Impossible.

The tryst he had conjured with her in Paris was a delusion. In her presence, reality stood out like a drop of water on a rose.

She's real and much too close.

Chapter 12
The First Lesson

At a pace fit for battle, Athos fastened a small supply pouch to a fresh horse. Just as he began scrounging for a harness, Cordes showed up, pitchfork in hand. "Shouldn't you be inside?"

Athos hurried from bin to bin. "I'm riding out to Nantes."

"Now? You only arrived hours ago." Cordes scratched his beard.

Athos grabbed a clean bridle and bit hanging from a stall post and threw it forcefully into Cordes' body. Stunned, the stable master fumbled until the equipment hit the ground. "As you wish," he managed.

Athos knew the journey to Nantes would demand far less endurance than his most brutal tests. Yet after the Comte's letter and his close encounter with Nicole, he would have preferred war.

A few possessions, a pallet and pack of provisions would provide more comfort than he had known at the sieges of Montauban or La Rochelle. In both conflicts, his regiment had suffered weeks with only stale bread for rations; cannonballs rattled his broken sleep; men moaned in constant agony because of their open wounds. He had endured the severe injury to his side for countless days with neither a blanket nor shelter.

In comparison, the trip to Nantes would seem a jocular hunting trip. On a fresh mount, Athos galloped through the arched stone entrance, adjusted his sword and did not glance back.

He would have time on the road to decide what to say to the Comte. François could not force him to stay in the country. Athos had his limits. The vile letter tucked in his saddle bag had overstepped a boundary. Because his commission was a royal request, delivering sugar to Paris was all Athos was willing to do. François could not demand he go on with the phony play for his wife's affections. Although he disliked losing, Athos chose to forfeit Nicole. He couldn't win and had no intention of trying.

Within a mile, the tallest buildings in Rochefort were within view. At the same time, the clopping of a swift horse came up from behind him.

"Monsieur, Monsieur!" Pierre called above the hoof beats. "I demand your attention!" He circled in front of Athos and laboured to regain his breath. "Please, don't leave. I know you're disappointed by the wait, but staying here could be good. A few days can't hurt."

To his surprise, Athos had underestimated the impression he had made on Pierre and the impression the youth had made on him. It charmed Athos to be pursued by a servant. Pierre's attempt to salvage the situation was genuine, although unsalvageable in Athos's estimations.

"I don't expect you to understand," Athos said. "It has nothing to do with you."

"But it does! You're the only guest we've had in many seasons. We never see anyone from Paris, and now you wish to dash it all because of your impatience," Pierre said, spitting out the last few words.

The insult stung. "Chasing after your guests doesn't get your horses fed."

Athos tried to ride around him, but Pierre produced a sword from an inconspicuous sheath at his side. Pierre's boldness called to mind a young d'Artagnan.

"Save your battles for when the stakes are high. You've got nothing to gain here but my anger."

"Prepare to defend yourself if you wish to remain on your horse," and with that, Pierre charged the short distance toward the Musketeer.

The lesson the young man needed meant a fight. Athos drew his sword and deflected Pierre with a robust block, disorienting him. Athos jumped to the dirt path and motioned for his challenger to do the same, but the young man pulled on the reins.

"You said you wanted a lesson," Athos said. "Now is the time for one. Unless, of course, you've changed your mind."

Pierre jumped off of his horse, once again full of himself.

"The first rule of swordsmanship is to expect anything from your opponent." Athos put his sword back in its scabbard. "And secondly, never assume you know the full motives of your challenger."

"Take out your sword!" Pierre demanded. "We've only just started this duel. Or, is that how you do it? You run away from every challenger, even a seventeen-year-old. Maybe that's why you've survived so long, by running off like a coward."

"You haven't heard a thing I said." Athos lowered his centre of gravity and waved Pierre closer.

"You cannot fight without your sword!"

Athos circled closer with his arms outstretched. Pierre stared and shuffled into an awkward stance.

Athos pointed at the young man's eyes. "You're frightened."

Pierre huffed. "You're unarmed. How can you fight?" But the strain in Pierre's voice suggested the obvious: bare-handed.

"Try me."

Nothing was left for Pierre to do but charge. The exhilarating rush lasted a few seconds. Defying the abilities of the human body, Athos arched in a mercurial move and grabbed the hand on the sword until Pierre cried out in agony. In a single manoeuvre, Pierre was disarmed.

Still in motion, Pierre stumbled onto all fours, his back to the fight. His disjointed tumble made him vulnerable. He hurried onto his feet and struggled to regain balance. When he turned around, the sword tip was pointed at his throat.

"If you had truly angered me, you'd be dead," said Athos, not a bit winded and his aim steady.

"That wasn't fair! You know I'm inexperienced. This was no lesson—it was a drubbing," Pierre said and backed away.

"But you won't do it again."

Athos turned for his horse. Within a few steps, Pierre slammed into Athos with all the anger the previous failure had ignited. The two fell hard on the dirt path, and the sword landed under their bodies.

Pierre pushed Athos's shoulders down with his forearms and kneed him in the lower back.

"I'll let you up if you promise to stay."

Pierre's triumph lasted less than a gust of wind.

Athos inched from the ground and grabbed Pierre's thigh. The instant he unbalanced Pierre, Athos grabbed the sword beneath him. Teetering on his shins, he blindly swung the sword backward, striking Pierre's side in the soft flesh under his ribs. Pierre's sudden stillness was worse than the red on the sword.

Athos flipped over and watched the blood spread like dark wine on the white shirt. Pierre clutched his side, and soon the young man's hands were covered. Pierre's eyes glazed, first with novelty and then in horror, as he blinked at his soaked clothes. Ashen, he fell prone.

Athos flung off his jacket and shirt and pressed the latter onto the wound. He had swung out of frustration, a huge mistake. When the blade went in, he had reared back, hoping it had not penetrated deep enough to kill. The depth of the wound was deceptive. Death tended to be capricious—for one man, a cut might be fatal; for another, a minor scratch.

"You won't die," Athos said and applied more pressure. "I'll see to it. You'll survive."

Pierre used what little energy he appeared to have left. "Who are you?"

Then he went under.

Chapter 13
Her Tempting Request

As soon as Athos carried Pierre into the foyer, the household turned upside down. Athos was pushed aside to a corner. Within minutes, a mild hysteria developed and Nicole arrived in the midst of it. Without flinching or fainting at the sight of Pierre's wound, she took charge and directed the staff to carry Pierre upstairs to a second-floor bedroom. Servants bounded to and from the kitchen and jostled up basins of hot water and clean rags. Under her command, the emergency became a well-oiled triage.

Servants started accusing Athos of murder. Jeers grew to shouts. Cordes came close to cocking Athos in the jaw before Nicole calmly stepped between them.

The stable master yelled over Nicole's shoulder. "You and your sword, out!"

"Let me." Nicole placed a steady hand on Cordes' chest until another burly helper pulled him into a corner. Athos followed Nicole outside, where the air felt cooler and thinner. He buttoned his coat all the way. His nerves were calm, but he was stunned by the outpouring of care for the young man—the peasant Prince.

"Save your explanation for later," she interrupted his thoughts. The lines on her forehead deepened, but her hands were steady. "May I inspect your sword?"

Athos thought *no*, but he levelled the weapon out for her. Clean. She nodded. As of yet, he had not seen her react emotionally.

"I have little time, so I'll be blunt," she said, keeping her distance. "You'll leave your sword and your pistol at the door. You are forbidden to bring them inside or handle them on the grounds. You will not use them for *anything* while you are here."

Athos simmered over the exaggerated punishment. The request pinned him like an arrow to a target. "Have you seen your servant's sword?"

"I know it was probably Pierre who did the provoking. But he didn't wound himself."

Athos half nodded before she started to go. "Any other demands?" He wanted more time with her, if only a second or two.

She looked him straight in the eyes and said with genuine concern, "Cope, Monsieur Athos. Simply cope."

He would have dropped to his knees had she asked.

Turning away, she held the door for a few seconds. "You're not harmed, are you?"

"Not this time."

"Please, forgive Cordes. He's the best of men but very protective of Pierre. We all are."

The formidable front door groaned shut, and Athos marvelled how she had removed the stinging arrow from his ego.

A doctor arrived within a half-hour, and Athos returned to an empty foyer, defenceless. A maid offered him a clean shirt on her way upstairs. He held back from asking about Pierre's whereabouts. Athos had become a pariah.

He was alone for a long stretch. Forgotten. Extraneous. No one requested his help, and he felt it would have been senseless to offer it. Even *he* reviled his actions, despite using restraint with Pierre. Athos had not swung his sword with full force. He had been reckless yet not overly aggressive. Or so he thought. He had wanted to clip the edge of Pierre's overconfidence, but Athos rued the results. He had acted out of carelessness. A swordfight required unflinching decisions. This time, Athos had let his casual attitude about death get the better of his skill.

Idle and restless, he skulked around the first floor, surveying the château and checking doors. As an outsider, if all he could gain was an impression of this place, *an impression of her*, then the solitude was worthwhile. In any case, the household was too preoccupied to keep an eye on him.

In the long corridors and unlocked rooms, the art and décor favoured birds or plants. The popular hunting, fishing and gaming themes in

Paris had not migrated to the walls or upholstery in the château. The place was full of black-and-white drawings in charcoal. Row upon row of them. In the library, he carefully examined one piece, a sketch of a nesting dove. Behind the dove, a woman's hand reached out to stroke the creature. A rosary dangled between her fingers.

A standing clock clanged in the hall outside the library. Seven o'clock. Three hours had passed since the assault.

He returned to the base of the stairs, feeling agitated again. It was too quiet, no shuffling feet or cries of suffering. Keen to any sound, he stood statue-like until the half-hour chime. Then a plain plebeian scurried from an upstairs corner toward the stairs. Starting down, the servant clung to the farthest handrail and dropped his head to avoid eye contact with Athos.

Athos grabbed the servant's wrist when he reached the last tread and blew off like a pistol. "What do you know?! Tell me, how is Pierre?"

The trembling man shook his head and scurried through a narrow doorway toward the kitchen.

Athos pounced on the stairs, taking the steps three at a time. He started in the direction everyone had gone but him, down a wide corridor flanked by a floor-to-ceiling window. He paused at the view of the oncoming dusk and quieted himself to listen again, to inform his next move, but no sign came. He turned another corner and at last saw a dim light from a tight passageway. At the end, an alcove opened.

In the nook, he found a high-backed chair next to a door carved with twisted ivy. On the chair's flat seat, a single candle burned in a tall candlestick. By the chair, bloody water and rags filled a white ceramic bowl on a pedestal. The door, recessed several feet, was closed.

He debated trying it. Athos wanted to open it, but resisted. A brazen entry into the room was out of the question. Instead, he leaned in and listened. To be sure, if the outcome of Pierre's wound had been fatal, grief might spill into the alcove, but no words, whispered or otherwise, came from behind the wood.

He paced a few moments and stalled at the end of the hall. He squatted in the shadows with his back against the wall and kept vigil.

Although steady on his haunches, he ached from his cross-country journey. It seemed days since his arrival, but darkness loomed on only the first night. Sleep would have been welcome. But for the moment, he needed to stay alert and put off leaving. The consequences of his actions were too brutal.

How old was I when I first felt the blade? Twelve, he remembered. His teacher, an elderly guardsman, cut him deeply above the knee.

"Athos! If you're so careless in your defence again, it could cost you your leg," the old man had admonished.

Athos reacted with anguish and adulation. He bandaged the wound by himself and pranced around his father's estate showing even the lowliest lackey his limp. Having earned the badge of injury, Athos's pride swelled. The milestone placed him closer to manhood.

That same day, he stuffed hay into a burlap sack to make a fencing dummy and hung it from an old oak in the sheep herder's field so he could try his lunge, grinning through the pain. But after dark, alone in his room, the throbbing wound tortured him.

For many fitful nights afterward, he begged for God's mercy, one of the few times he had done so in his life. If he had known the number of more severe wounds he would accumulate as a man, he might have ended his affair with blades then and pursued academics, his other passion. But healing made him forget, and he had headed into manhood with his scabbard firmly at his side.

Athos believed Pierre possessed the same strong-headedness. Pierre had wasted no time in asking Athos, a stranger, to indulge him—by showing him the ways of the sword. Pierre's yearning to change his life was sincere. And naïve. Steel could further a man's status and bestow honour but at the expense of innocence. Like Athos's first wound, the one on Pierre initiated the young man to the brotherhood of combat.

The bedroom door began to open, causing the candlelight in the alcove to flicker. Nicole emerged from the other side. She pulled the door closed and stared at the candlestick on the chair. A sigh rattled her lungs. The front of her ivory apron was streaked in blood. Her face was spotty from tears, and she frowned. She grabbed the apron, bunched it in both hands and pressed her forehead into the dreadful splotches.

Athos stayed against the dark wall and observed her. She cried for several minutes before her breathing evened out. She leaned against the doorway and began to whisper. The faint words had a familiar cadence. Slightly louder than the ticking of a clock, the chant was unmistakable.

The Latin prayer fell from her lips. With her eyes closed, she made the sign of the cross, continued her spiritual murmurs and ended with her head buried again in her apron.

"He'll survive," Athos finally said from the shadows.

Nicole jerked her head up. "Athos? You frightened me. Please don't lurk in the dark." She picked up the candlestick and cast light in his direction. "Yes, Pierre will survive. You must have known. His injury is serious but won't be fatal."

Her momentary surprise passed, and she crumpled into the chair, her shoulders bent forward.

"Rest will help both you and Pierre." Athos kept to his crouch.

"Explain to me what happened. I don't understand." Tears began to well in the corners of her eyes. "You struck a novice. A stable hand. His delusions of swordfights are dreams of a boy. He's only had a sword for a few months. Didn't he tell you?"

Athos stood but remained in the dark. "He chose to keep that detail to himself."

"Tell me, in your words, what brought this on? The letter?"

"Madame, I can't deny responsibility for Pierre. He tried to stop me from leaving. I think it hurt him to see me go so soon. Pierre thought he might intimidate me. Obviously, the lesson ended badly." He glanced at his feet. "Please, how is he?"

"A bandage was insufficient. The doctor stitched several inches. It was very painful." She drew a shuddered breath. "For us all."

She grabbed a rosary from her pocket. "I still don't see how this could happen." Her voice hardened, and she lifted her shoulders. "He'll need round-the-clock assistance. You could tend to him at night. Stand guard, as it were. That's what soldiers are trained to do, isn't it?"

Athos leaned into the light. His breathing became shallow. He studied her body language in the illumination. *Soft but strong.* Deep inside, he knew the immediate needs of Pierre were not the only reason why he would stay.

"I'll remain here until the Comte sends for me or when you no longer need my help."

"Thank you." Her shoulders fell again.

He walked into the low light, straightening his stiff joints. His personal tug-of-war and mistrust of women seemed far off, if only for this moment. Being with her in the candlelight soothed his chronic psychosis. He caught her concealing a quick glance of his upper body. His scars were safely hidden underneath the borrowed shirt.

"Why do you continue being a Musketeer?" she asked, quieter than before. "Haven't you fulfilled your duty to the King by now?"

"It's my life. I live to serve the King and Queen. I'll remain a Musketeer until my last day." *Or until madness has its way.*

Behind Nicole, the door opened and a petite young woman stepped out. In servant's attire, she had an angelic face, but her cheeks were puffy and eyes were red.

Nicole rocked the girl in her arms. It was an embrace saved for the most beloved of family. Separating to speak, they kept their hands wrapped together, just above the girl's pregnant belly. Athos marvelled at their closeness and at his tolerance for standing so near two women, unheard of since his vows of celibacy and distance. He could not understand their whispers, yet they piqued his senses.

"He'll be all right." Nicole brought the girl's head up. "Hannah, this is Monsieur Athos." The two turned out, and Nicole wrapped her arm behind the girl, whose body tensed. Hannah immediately stepped back and whispered into Nicole's ear for several seconds.

"Go on now," Nicole told her. "Rest until I call for you." Without hesitation, the young woman disappeared down the dim hallway.

"Your familiarity with the servants—" Athos began.

"Hannah works in our kitchen." Nicole's face shone, and she watched the departure of the servant longer than normal.

"And what did Hannah say about me?"

"Why do you think she spoke of you?" Nicole turned her attention to him.

"Because she whispered to you."

"She's frightened of you."

"That can't be all she said," Athos said, testing his newfound boldness.

Nicole became entranced by the candle, which was almost spent. "She thinks you're not an ordinary man, that you are to be feared, and that you are also—" she paused, "*striking*."

The fine hair raised on his neck. He became a human tuning fork waiting for a beat. Athos wanted to cross his false boundary, corner Nicole in the doorway and demand: *And what do you think?*

She seemed to read his mind.

"However, I think you've come to us wounded and exhausted and don't care to be idle here. At the risk of sounding rude, you seem to have little patience for the situation you're in, and you dismiss people interested in your comfort. But if you continue to be a danger to others, including any more of my servants, my tolerance will end."

He probably deserved worse. If he presented a real danger, he wondered if she could keep him in check. She returned the rosary to her apron pocket. Her grace mesmerized him.

"But you're willing to stay for Pierre," she added, "and for that, I'm very grateful."

Her eyes softened into pools of liquid copper, and an unusual ripple of contentment ran through his veins. He might enjoy testing his will power on her.

"You seem to be forgiving me," he said.

"I know Pierre." She glanced back at the door. "You're not entirely to blame." She moved aside, signalling he should enter Pierre's bedroom. "If you would, please. The doctor will return in the morning."

"And what of tomorrow?" Her whereabouts suddenly seemed important to him.

"Tomorrow, we start fresh."

Chapter 14
Nicole's Letter

Nicole wondered when she had last been up at midnight. It was not the clock chimes that made her question; it was the silence after the last bell. She heard no birds from an open window in her bedroom. Not a single ostentatious whippoorwill or an annoying starling. Not even an owl. Without their calls, her spirit folded inward.

Which had upset her more in the cascading events of the evening? Athos's dreadful condition upon arrival and the sight of his scars? Or Pierre bleeding from a wound too long and too deep?

But she had maintained her evenness. She could do that. Practice had made it possible. Her hand must be steady to write the message her lips could not utter.

She shuffled around on her untidy desk. Stained with charcoal and smears of ink, the stacks of half-finished drawings on her desktop covered the writing surface. It was difficult for her to see the work as anything but a product of her half-hearted life. She cleared enough space to write. From the top drawer, she retrieved the inkwell, a quill, and a sheet of stationary stamped in gold leaf with a flamboyant R.

She threw a sideways glance to the corner bookshelf. She needed all her strength for what she was about to write, and the framed Madonna sitting on the shelf gave her courage. She brought the palm-sized picture to her lap and let out a strained sigh.

Of the many gifts the Comte had bought her—more aptly *peace-offerings*—this one touched her the most. The artist who had painted the cream-skinned Madonna captured the essence of the holy mystery in her eyes. Their colour perfectly matched the robin's eggs that Nicole monitored each spring and summer in perches she had placed across the estate. She visited the nests daily until just before the hatchlings were ready to fledge. After their successful departure, she would gingerly pick the remnants of eggshell from the nests and place them in an old lace box in her drawer. In the fall, she scattered the shells on Sibonne's grave. It was a small tribute to a sisterhood long gone.

The Madonna was a touch too comely to be hung in a chapel, yet it added to her mystique and increased Nicole's fondness of the gift. Because of her beauty, this Madonna defied the orthodox, and to Nicole, the image reflected her own. Nicole found strength in faith while another part of her craved earthly delights. In the image, *her eyes* alluded to the pursuit of life's pleasures, not the sanctimony of salvation. The small painting expressed a different view of the way things could be.

Tonight, Nicole had to give up control of the way things had become. The letter was the only appropriate answer. She tested her quill on a scrap then wrote:

Dearest François, I have failed in your request. Return to me.

You have my every favour. My heart is yours again.

Faithfully, Nicole

The Musketeer was far too reckless for her to deal with, which resurfaced many bad memories. *And warnings signs.* She could not be held responsible for his actions and engaging him any further might lead him to discover what had happened to Sibonne.

How could Athos and Sibonne be so much alike?

Equally troublesome, Nicole was out of practice with proper societal rules.

She did not follow many—particularly barriers of status. Within the cocoon of her small, familiar staff, she cared for each servant as an individual. Athos seemed to care as little about pretence as she did. She brushed aside expectations of her status by refusing to entertain aristocrats or travel to Court. The quiet of the country suited her better, and the Comte eventually stopped complaining. He returned home less frequently each season. She wilfully allowed his absences to continue, but it led to stinging consequences. She felt unloved.

Not that François ever gave up wanting her. More intensely than ever, he challenged her cool rebuffs. His ventures in trade, low-brow by society standards, were not for fortune alone. In fact, she knew they were not for fortune at all. They were lavish gestures to gain her favours. *Bribery.* Art, books, finery. He had outfitted the estate in a fashion that rivalled any Duchy. Recently, he had resorted to giving money to the poor in an attempt to spear her heart with one message—he would never give up trying to win her affections again.

After the initial awkwardness of their arranged marriage, she had enjoyed the intimate part of their life together when it was whole. The idea of love-making frightened her at first. She and Sibonne had spent many nights on an empty guest balcony discussing how a man might be, especially following Nicole's arranged marriage to the Comte.

"Mère says she doesn't remember the first couple of times with father." Sibonne revealed the secret one starless night.

"If Mère made such a statement, she did so to protect us." Nicole blushed. "And when did you hear such intimate details, Sibonne? Your propriety crumbles daily."

"Oh, you know I don't talk so candidly with anyone else." She playfully elbowed her older sister's soft waist. "And I overheard her tell our cousin, right after her engagement."

"Sibonne, eavesdropping is a sin—"

"I say making love must be an act without equal. Why do so many poets write of it and artists envision it and songs express such longing?" Sibonne hugged herself. "Oh, to have a lover!"

"You're mixing up love with the consummation of a marriage."

"Consummation?" Sibonne belly laughed. "Is that what you're calling it? It's sex, Nicole. You're going to have sex with François Rieux and more than once."

But Sibonne's secretly procured wisdom from their mother held a thread of truth. The first month after Nicole's wedding was unremarkable, and her mother and father were no longer alive to lean on. François assumed her father's sovereignty, and she respected her new husband and grew to appreciate his attention, in and out of their bedchamber. Nevertheless, wedlock left her nothing to tell her sister about the throes of love-making except a bland generalization: "It's as you suspected." Sibonne had stalked off unsatisfied.

Then two years passed, and no heir arrived. François' anxiety for a son overwhelmed her ability to relate to him. Her confidence deteriorated to self-doubt, and the nature of their intimate life changed. François did not criticize or pressure her, but he grew impatient. He came to her more often yet connected less with her emotionally. She retreated to her art. Then, while Nicole lived in a haze of discontent, Sibonne disappeared.

In contrast, Sibonne's love of Remi, a blacksmith's son, was profound and all-encompassing. She fell for him knowing Remi's status would prevent them from marrying. But Sibonne had found love and passion—two qualities missing in Nicole's marriage. Sibonne knew ecstasy while Nicole had not. A chasm developed between them.

Nicole then shattered her sister's trust. Remi and Sibonne ran away. Nicole tried to assure herself it was not jealousy that caused her to disclose their whereabouts but concern for her sister's welfare. Nicole was wrong. Sibonne's separation from Remi destroyed her will to live. François' involvement in the sordidness made matters worse.

When Sibonne died, François was unrepentant. Nicole wished she could forgive him, but no amount of prayer or personal exorcism helped. She wanted to wash her sister's blood from his hands. And her own. She couldn't, and therefore, she wouldn't allow him close. He was a red coal to her tender skin.

Nicole lifted the picture of the Madonna and stared back. *The eyes.* The Musketeer's grey eyes told her much. He suffered from a tangled, awful circumstance. He wore his sadness like a family crest across his solid, handsome frame.

If Nicole knew his history, she worried it might make her care too much and place her dangerously close to a hypnotic flame. The way he looked at her, in the few times they'd been alone, was hypnotic. *And striking.* Hannah's description of Athos was correct yet incomplete. He was more than striking. He was haunted, mesmerizing, intense, bold. Nicole's curiosity for a person had never been stronger.

She propped the Madonna on her desk and folded the letter. She needed to send it, as an escape.

Chapter 15
An Unusual Household

Athos found Pierre asleep in the Royal suite, the elegant chambers every aristocrat prepared for the King of France or his entourage. The likelihood of a visit was miniscule. Nonetheless, noblemen spent fortunes on the possibility. Athos had not seen as grand a suite as this one anywhere else in France. The silk piping on the furniture and curtains, the gold-threaded facings on the mounds of pillows, the thick cables gathering the drapes from exotic lands, the plush wool rugs and every curve of crown moulding reeked of privilege.

Like most sovereigns, the Comte showcased his wealth in the Royal room. The wood shined with polish, and the furniture created a sense of precision, each piece complementing the next, to swallow a guest in refinement. Athos likened it to a tailored jacket—wearing it made a man's head grow. To harbour a servant here flew in the face of convention. Athos had never stayed in a suite fit for a King.

In contrast to the room, Pierre lay shrivelled and pasty in a canopied bed under a silk coverlet. His eyelids, sunken and purplish, meant he had lost a good deal of blood. Athos placed his palm inches from Pierre's nostrils to feel if he was, indeed, alive. Warm air brushed his hand. Recovering from a blade wound could sap the toughest man's strength and use up stores of energy quicker than disease. With practice, Athos had been able to sew his minor cuts. It always drained him. He fared better at his own doctoring after a bottle of wine.

Athos was drawn to a red velvet armchair across the room near a tall window. The sunrise would come soon, and his stomach ached with hunger. The apple from the priest had been his last meal, and thoughts of his conversation with Grignan lingered: *What has love done to you that another love cannot repair?*

Nicole presented a problem. She was enthralling and alone, placed before him like a shaving of chocolate on a silver platter with a card that read *Yours for the Taking*. But she was not his, and he could not take her anywhere—into his arms or deeper into his mind.

Unannounced, a male servant quietly pushed a serving cart into the room. Athos ate what was offered: broth, bread and dried fruit. Afterward, another gift arrived with the same servant.

"Madame requested you have this." The servant bowed, opened the bottle and left. His request for wine was heeded after all. This vintage, Athos discerned, was not from Pierre's harvest.

Madame requested you have this.

The wine warmed his belly and dissolved his tension. However, it did nothing to stop the provocative images of her. Being close to her had revived his vigour. And it was not just her physical beauty. Grace shone through her every move. Her appeal radiated from inside. She placed compassion above status. The average aristocrat would have boarded a wounded servant in a shack and withheld the doctor's fee from his tenancy wages. Instead, her staff stood by for Pierre's every need. How far her compassion extended, he did not know. The mystery intrigued him; he wanted to find out.

From his seat by the window, Athos estimated that the assault on Pierre had happened relatively close to the château. Someone must have sent Pierre to stop him from leaving.

"You didn't answer my question from yesterday." Pierre's voice ended the perfect silence in the room. Athos had sat in the quiet for several hours.

He kept staring out the window. "On the contrary, I have a question for you. Who sent you after me?"

Pierre cleared his throat then groaned. "Even that hurts."

"You'll need to get up and move soon."

"First, you cut me down, then you tell me to get up and heal. What else, my liege?"

"Tell me, who ordered you to come after me?"

"But you haven't answered my question. And I asked first," Pierre said.

"Refresh my memory."

"*Who are you?*" Pierre laboured to swallow.

Athos could tell that Pierre, pale and weak, was not ready to move or hear a truthful answer. "When you have lived as long as I have, doing what I've done, a man can lose touch with … acceptable ways of interacting."

Approaching the bedside, Athos made the sign of the cross. He did not say a prayer with it. The symbolism was enough. Although weak, Pierre was rapt by the Musketeer's gesture.

"I forgive you," the young man whispered.

"So easily? I still need to toughen you up, I see."

Pierre's laugh turned into a grimace. "How did you do it? You have so many scars. Did any of your wounds truly stop you? This is killing me."

"It's how often I've suffered. Familiarity can numb the pain." Athos rubbed a scar on his palm. "Take hunger. Your first empty belly can be unbearable. But the next time, it's not as difficult because you know what to expect. With a blade wound, it's the same."

"Frequency doesn't dull every experience," Pierre rasped. "I doubt I'll ever tire of being with my lover."

"Ah, you've been with a woman? And my treatise doesn't apply?" Athos studied Pierre for signs of lying. He only saw boastfulness. "I suspect you're too new with women to know. Are you sixteen? You'll need more than lessons in swordplay."

"Seventeen, Monsieur, and I cannot imagine ever tiring of making love to my Hannah."

"Her baby is yours?"

Pierre nodded, careful not to move anything but his head. "You've seen her?"

"I think she's very young, and you, too, to be having an affair. Who knows of this?"

"Everyone. Nicole allows it. The baby is mine," he confessed. "I love her. Nicole lets us stay together, and I thank her every day. Hannah and I are better off together."

"Nicole allows it? What about the Comte? The church?"

"Nicole is our shelter. She's like the Madonna. Her compassion is bottomless." Pierre spoke louder and faster. "And not just for me, but for everyone here, and all the living things in her world."

Athos lost the thread of the conversation. *Compassionate? And completely out of the ordinary.* "You still haven't answered my question. Who sent you after me?"

Pierre lowered his volume. "No one wanted you to leave. You're our guest."

In any other situation, Athos would have pressed for a better answer. "For a servant, you're treated like a king."

"Nicole wants me to live in the house, over the Comte's objections. I prefer my cottage."

"Probably a wise decision, if the King were to visit."

"The King?" Pierre's laughter shook his body until he clutched his side in pain. "Don't you know? The Comte isn't liked in Court."

"A wealthy outsider, yes. Except wealth excuses many missteps."

"He's the butt of jokes in Paris," Pierre said. "I think this mission of yours is a chance to improve his standing. It will please the King."

Athos dug his fingers into his brow.

"You don't want to do it, do you?" Pierre asked.

Athos answered only with a sour glance.

The young man sighed. "If only I could be so choosy."

Athos moved toward a picture on the opposite side of the bed, another charcoal image. It was larger than one he had seen with the dove. It was a landscape of the pond from the bank, where Pierre had taken him. The work appeared to be by the same artist. No signature, similar to every charcoal drawing he had discovered the day before.

"Do you care for that drawing?" Pierre asked.

"There are several like it downstairs."

"They're Nicole's. That's her favourite spot, under the big willow at the pond. She draws and watches birds from there, almost every day, when the weather is good."

Athos rubbed his face with both hands, which smelled salty. Exhaustion tore at his shoulders. He needed another chance to think and to drink.

"I'm certain it's a boy." Pierre's comment drew Athos back to the bedside.

"When will you know?"

"The baby is due any day. Do you have children?"

"No, none."

"Then you have that in common with the Comte."

The Comte and his wife. Athos couldn't hold back his inquisition.

"François is in Paris often, rarely with your Madame. Why?"

"She's put off by Court. She is too attached to the church and her pursuits here," Pierre said proudly. "She loves the estate and the freedom she has to do what she wants. The Comte gives her plenty of leeway. Although his absence doesn't do her any good."

"She's unhappy about it?"

"She wants children. If she had children to fill the house, she'd be happy."

Athos narrowed his eyes and opened his arms. "And what's the meaning of you being placed in this room?"

Before Pierre could answer, the door gave way and Hannah peeped in. The oncoming sunrise was intensifying the reds and golds in the room. She shielded her eyes from the glare and hesitated at the door.

"It's okay. He knows," Pierre told her.

She rushed to the bed and gently laid her bulging middle near Pierre, careful not to jostle him. She swiped his forehead with the back of her hand and kissed him carefully, once. She kept her lips near the corner of his mouth and continued to sweep his reddening face. The blood in Pierre's cheeks was a good sign, but Athos left, for witnessing the two lovers was more than he could bear.

Chapter 16
A Tortured Encounter

Outside the King's suite, a faint thumping side-tracked Athos in the hallway. He followed it until he rounded a far corner where Nicole stood before a mirror, clutching a rag, swirling it repetitively across the silver frame. She worked with more anxiety than purpose, digging with each swipe. She could not steady the mirror. It bumped the wall, left then right, as she polished in small circles. But polishing was not the point.

Athos hung back, recognizing her exasperation. And lusciousness. Nicole's body moved freely underneath her dressing gown, a thin garment that would please any lover. The light-weight fabric outlined her figure, and her auburn hair was undone, tucked from her face by combs. Over and over, she ran the rag. Over and over, she ran her problems, deepening the grooves of trouble. Although her body was a siren, he sensed her disquiet. She was trapped in a current beneath a layer of ice, searching for an opening.

Perhaps she needs a lifeline …

He was sure she did not feel his presence until he laid his hand over hers, firmly halting her motion. He immediately regretted his impulsiveness. But not because of what she might think. His skin came alive. He was touching a woman again by choice, and the pleasure of her warmth and sweetness of her scent made his body tingle. A familiar, forgotten pleasure ran through him. In the mirror's reflection, he looked brash, her face beside his. His dark stare was countered by her brown-eyed apprehension.

"You carry a burden," he said, afraid to breathe the moment away.

His body was within inches of touching hers. He shoved down the thought and shored up his dwindling discipline. He released her hand and gave them room. Her body posture relaxed. When she came around, her sleeve gently grazed his forearm like a lick of flame. He felt an invisible fire coursing in the air between them. Connecting eye-to-eye seemed too dangerous. He concentrated on the rag in her hand.

"The strongest rocks can splinter, Madame. Don't worry about Pierre."

"Why aren't you with him?"

"Hannah took over," he said and cautiously glanced up to see a tiny frown.

She crossed her arms over her front, and she stepped to the side. "Please go back to him."

Bewildered by her continued concern for a servant, he decided to stay put. "He's fine. I can't say the same of you."

She locked her jaw and hardened her stance. "You should be with him. You made a promise. Hannah has other duties."

"Are you infatuated with Pierre?" he asked, risking the insult.

"That idea is as well-conceived as your attempt to leave." Her forcefulness demanded eye-contact. Athos chose to look at his reflection.

"You're upset because I've hurt Pierre, and now you must trust me with him."

"I need you to live up to your agreements, to me and to my husband. That's all."

"And this," he said, claiming the rag, "is your way of coming to terms with the circumstances?"

She backed into a doorway. "Seeing Pierre hurt brought on bad memories."

"I understand," he said.

"Do you?"

"Memories can be demons." He returned the rag to her, again within reach of her warmth. "But indulge one piece of wisdom. Let the demons go."

Then he reluctantly bowed to her wishes and left. But from around the corner, he listened. She stayed a long time by herself in the quiet.

★★★

After Athos departed, Nicole repeated the words she had written in her letter to François over and over in her head.

I have failed. Return to me. I have failed. Return to me.

Even prayer would have fallen short. She faced the mirror, overwhelmed by questions.

What kind of love can both uplift and destroy a life?

Is it possible to save someone from self-destruction?

In the mirror, she smoothed over her lower lid, trying to wipe away the encounter with Athos. Her wrinkles looked pronounced, evidence of years of guilt for her part in her sister's death. Her thoughts spilled over into memories of Sibonne and her lover Remi, whom her sister had loved more than life itself.

Nicole shuddered. She rarely allowed herself to think of it or the cover-up that prevented Sibonne's melancholia from disgracing the family name.

With the introduction of Athos to her world, a wedge split Nicole's usual grief. *Yes,* he had experienced pain like her sister. *Yes,* his scars showed that he courted death. But the man in the mirror tonight had reached out to her and relayed a message below the surface: *You, Nicole, spellbind me.*

Her next thought bordered on sin.

Does he spellbind me?

She touched her cheek and blushed in the silver filament of reflective glass.

Chapter 17
In Search of Her

Athos established a routine. He wandered the house and grounds by day to soothe his insomnia and returned to Pierre at dusk. He didn't bother to settle into his guest room and had not seen Nicole since their encounter at the mirror, several days ago. She had been conspicuously scarce. Impatient to see her again, he decided to visit the place she loved. The willow by the pond. *Her willow.*

Off the bank, he found a narrow cut in the tall grass that led directly to the tree. The entire area grew wild except for the path. During his short dip the first day, the massive tree had impressed him. Its canopy swayed with age. Being late summer, it was in full leaf, and the wind aimlessly brushed its branches across the ground and the water's surface. Like a veil, the branches formed a secret shelter that he entered uninvited.

Inside, there lived a delicate tranquillity. This was her refuge. She brought herself here to iron out the bumps. A half dozen paper cranes ticked back and forth from string tied to low-hanging limbs. The paper had faded. The brightest crane, red flecked with gold, seemed recently folded.

Smooth, palm-sized stones ringed the border inside the canopy, and a few twinkled with mica. A larger flat rock met the water near the trunk. Standing above it, Athos saw tell-tale signs of a careful hand that had snipped away boughs to create a view of the pond and fields beyond it. The view, bountiful in its green hues, was as carefully framed as the art in the house.

Charcoal scribbles decorated the flat rock. She was left-handed. He darkened the tip of an index finger with coal dust and slipped a leftover black nub into his pocket. The rock drawings were crude—half of a beak, an ill-proportioned wing, a spindle of cattail. The stone was a wasteful use of charcoal. But the sketches were more whimsical than the finished ones on display in the house. This was the artist's experimentation.

If she sat on the rock and looked out, her feet had to dangle in water or crisscross the rough seat. Either way, she probably tossed her shoes aside, along with her stockings. How many petticoats had she ruined with coal? It didn't matter to the person who sat here. The stillness mattered. It fed his desire to find her.

The sun was at its highest point, and the light reflected sharply off the water. Across the pond, the breeze blew a field of wild bushes. Until then, he had missed the white spot on the horizon. A bonnet, just above the grass line. Someone sat in the brush on the other side of the pond, facing the field.

Athos tore through the veil of leaves and searched the bank for a path. The sounds of frogs and insects ratcheted and covered his footfalls. Swiftly, he picked out a trail, ignoring brambles that stuck to his shirt. At fifty yards, glare hindered his line of sight, yet the hat was a beacon. Slowing to a crawl, he began to make out a profile. He needed to risk a bolder move. He held his breath and peered over grass for a split-second.

Immediately, a bevy of quail flushed out of the grass.

"Oh, please no!" Nicole moaned when the last birds scattered. The bonnet sank below view. Hunkered down, Athos heard the shuffle of paper.

Nicole stretched up with a stool in one hand and a satchel on a shoulder. She shaded her eyes in the direction of the birds and weariness weighed on her shoulders.

Athos came clean. "You tire quickly."

She grabbed the kerchief around her neck, and the black on her fingers soiled a corner. "Do you always approach by surprise? You have the gift of a hunter."

Her levity made him relax. "I didn't intend to disrupt your drawing."

"Well, today's session is over."

"Your subjects?" He wobbled a hand to mimic the birds.

"A disadvantage of wildlife. Did Pierre tell you I draw?"

"He's talkative for a patient."

Nicole pivoted toward the main house, and Athos followed, choosing not to close the gap. "You've been avoiding me," he said.

Her momentum broke momentarily. "It might appear that way, but no. I have no need to keep you at a distance." She wiped a trickle of sweat on her temple with the back of her hand. "I suppose Pierre also told you I keep to myself."

"And that you care for being outdoors."

"If I can draw a few hours a day…" she trailed off, her eyes on the horizon, as if another bird might catch her attention and keep her outside.

"You're very productive. The walls in the house are a tribute to your work."

"I've been drawing for more than fifteen years. A few of the sketches turn out well. The Comte has them framed in Paris as gifts."

"The highest form of compliment."

A graceful shrug suggested otherwise.

"Why birds?" Athos asked.

"They're excellent subjects. At rest, they're still for long stretches of time, which is ideal for drawing, and their feather patterns are easy to reproduce. People are much too complicated and impatient."

"I agree."

Nicole glanced over her shoulder and caught him staring. "I take it you have little patience."

"For drawing?"

"For people."

"If I sketched and had to choose between birds or people, you and I would have something in common," he said.

"I'm convinced you don't have the patience for either."

"The last time we spoke," he chose his words carefully, "it was your patience that seemed thin. I hope I didn't cause your fit of housecleaning."

She re-adjusted the strap of her satchel and scanned the horizon as she walked. "I worry about Pierre's welfare. He's so headstrong."

"So much so that it sends you off polishing silver in the night?"

"He's wild," she said. "Very much like a Musketeer, from my observations."

A fine parry, he thought.

She pulled her skirt smartly from a sticker bush and waited for Athos to close the distance between them. In the breeze, a few strands of hair from under her bonnet caught on an eyelash, tempting him to untangle them.

"Actually," she said, tucking her chestnut hair, "you might be able to teach him self-control and give him some necessary defensive skills. He needs to learn how to use his sword. Would you teach him?"

"I'm under very strict orders by the head of this estate to disarm," he said and pretended to draw his sword, which had been commandeered by Cordes days ago.

"I'll return it, all your weapons, if you promise to teach him. However, you must agree the sword will only be used to teach," she said.

"I will—with one condition of my own."

She dropped her head. "That you leave of your own accord."

"I wish to watch you draw." He could tell her eyes widened though she did not look up. He pressed his caveat again. "You should allow me this one favour, seeing that I'm confined here until your husband sends for me. It's a small token, under the circumstances."

"I—" Her cheeks reddened. "I believe—" Her tongue failed her. "I'm not worthy of an audience."

He didn't care whether he was bold or improper or broke his rules. With a fingertip, he tilted up her chin. "I doubt that very much."

Abruptly, she spun toward the sunlight and asserted, "Your weapons are stored near my horse's stall. Cordes will show you where. I'll draw tomorrow an hour before dusk. Meet me at the willow." She glanced back. "And don't scare the birds again."

Chapter 18
A Second Lesson in Blood and Steel

At Pierre's bedroom door, the hallway clock struck half an hour after ten. A servant shot Athos an exhausted scowl, a minor demerit for being late. A neatly folded pair of pants and a fresh shirt were left for Athos in the red armchair.

The room was cool, and Pierre appeared pinker in his slumber than the night before. Setting aside the fresh clothes for later, Athos sat in the chair and removed the charcoal nub from his pocket. Perhaps this was used to draw the picture over the bed. To be close to her, watching her draw seemed an honourable compromise.

"You look different tonight," Pierre said sleepily.

"You do, too. Have you tried moving?"

"You should have seen me earlier. I was hurling insults, but my body moved fine."

Athos chuckled.

"You laugh?"

"Don't take it as a bad sign."

"I believe something has happened since last night," Pierre said.

Athos enjoyed the starlit window. "Tell me, how do you arrange trysts with your lover?"

Pierre's answer was flush with ego and longing. "The words of Desportes."

"A true Frenchman. You have access to books of his poetry?" Athos pressed a finger to his lips. "Let me guess, Nicole not only taught you to read but also allows you to use the library. I'd like to know how you lay the footwork for your meetings with Hannah. From the looks of your cottage, you sleep alone."

"I must keep up some degree of morality." His slanted brow revealed cunning. "We write notes, exchange whispers, and much can be told by the body."

Athos had to admit Pierre was more sophisticated than his age. "But where do you take her?"

"She has a small room in the servants' quarters. It's difficult to go in and out because of everyone living there. We also meet in my cottage, but it's cold in winter and hot in summer. By far, my favourite place is the chapel." Pierre pointed toward the window. "You can see it from where you sit."

The four-square structure was built alongside the turret at the gate. On either side of the black door, cross-shaped windows opened to the yard. Those, and a stubby spire on the arch above the door, were its only religious markings.

"You meet her in a chapel? To perform ungodly acts before God?" Athos shook his head. "I know I'm not an upstanding example, but your soul is surely damned."

Pierre glazed over with what must have been images of past deeds, even in marriage a sin in a house of God. "It's beautiful inside the chapel, dark at night, except for candlelight. It's quiet and usually empty. There are only four pews, and they're all covered with cushions and very fine fabric."

"I assume Nicole has no idea what's been done on them," Athos said.

"We're careful not to involve her or anyone else. Despite what you may think, we observe some rules. My feelings for Hannah are pure. The expression of my love is wholesome in my mind. She's my one and only."

"You live recklessly," Athos declared. "I don't know whether to pity you or be jealous of your ignorance." He wanted to pass on a more serious lesson, but his own history was so poor that he considered it not worth the words. "Be careful. Your life is just beginning."

"I live for her," Pierre said.

"Still, in the eyes of many, especially the church, you're dangerously out of bounds. Your actions involve others whether you want them to or not." He wished to say: *Many sacrifice for you to rear a bastard.*

Pierre smiled. "Nicole will pray each of us into Heaven."

The remark filled Athos with scorn, for his own salvation was out of reach, and Pierre represented the start of another failure.

"On your feet. Show me your strength." Athos motioned for him.

Pierre didn't budge. "I've been round and round the entire floor several times. You can ask the others about my progress."

"But not with your sword." Athos brought two swords from behind his chair. Dressed in only thin trousers, Pierre jumped to his feet and struggled for balance.

"You seem too quick. Let's see you with this." Athos threw a sword, which Pierre caught clumsily. "Ready for your second lesson?"

"If this was the first," Pierre rubbed the bandage around his middle, "then, of course I am."

Athos put several feet between them while the tip of his sword dug into the thick rug. "A sword is the extension of a man. Your entire being is present when you use it. You become the essence of power, grace and history. Or you buckle from the weight."

"This isn't heavy." Pierre cut the air with his weapon. "Yours, however, is very fine. Is it custom?"

"Made especially for duelling."

"Since that's been banned, you might as well let me take a turn with it," Pierre said, boldly stepping forward.

"The weight itself—" Athos swiped the tip between them, "—isn't from the weapon. It's the weight of experience that you bring to bear on your opponent. Your skill, your determination, your character are your trio of tools. If you lose one of them, you've lost everything. You, Pierre, lack skill."

"But I have determination and character, so I'm well on my way."

"Only if you apply them soundly. When you attacked me, your emotions got in the way."

"So you'll teach me skill and shore up the rest." Pierre pulled back his shoulders. "You must admit, I have determination in cartloads."

"Are you certain there's no Gascon in you?" Athos asked.

"Quite." Pierre inspected the weapon and readied an *en garde*. "How did you come by my sword?"

"I simply asked. Now, *en garde!*"

Pierre's stance showed Athos a great deal about his pupil's raw quality. His grip, his centre of gravity, the position of his feet and the looseness of his free arm meant Pierre had the finesse needed to advance quickly from beginner to serious challenger. Although determination might carry him, stoking that coal was dangerous. A thin line separated from wilfulness. Sheer will would help him live longer, but wilfulness sacrificed caution.

"Gather your wits," Athos said. "I can already sense your overconfidence. If you start your fights full of glory, it will blind you to the strategy of your opponent. You have to think three steps ahead. *Attack, defend, attack.* Watch my sword, my shoulders and my balance to learn my advances and block them. After my third advance, if you survive that long, you'll be able to spot my weaknesses and exploit them."

Athos might as well have been shouting from the bottom of a ravine because Pierre lunged before the instructions were over. In a slight of hand, Athos blocked the attack and gripped Pierre by the forearm.

"You weren't listening. You listen, you *live.*"

"Damn you, Athos! Let me finish my move!"

Laughter curled from the Musketeer. "Is that what you'll ask your first opponent? Why don't you simply propose he stand still? He's just as likely to do that." Athos resumed being serious. "Pierre, you must think. If you can't keep your head, then it will roll from your shoulders as plainly as I speak."

The young man's chest caved. Pierre couldn't stand the criticism, and Athos blamed it on immaturity. If one skill was to be taught, it had to be control. Bravado alone would leave Pierre vulnerable in a fight.

"You need a focus," Athos instructed. "You must think of one experience that calms you rather than excites you. From this calm, you attack. Think of your opponent as a headless dummy."

"This focus, could it be a person?"

"It can be anything. A constellation, a lute playing at a street fair, water pouring from a pail, the hum of a stranger…"

"Or of a loved one? What's your focus?"

Athos had already released Pierre to sit. By the window, Athos listened to the wind vibrate a pane.

"A starless night, away from people and fire and earthly distractions, only a black moon." Athos ran a hand down his sword and heard the phantoms only he could hear—the fatal cries of mortals. "You may choose to live by the sword, but it will never steer you toward light."

"Show me."

And Pierre listened. A flame burned through his eyes, bright with purpose. As a teacher, Athos demanded focus. Early on, he slapped Pierre with his blade directly on the binding of his wound. His pupil took it, disguising the pain as concentration.

Athos moved the large furniture to the edges of the room, widening the area to spar. Pierre learned basic footwork and simple compound attacks. He quickly learned a feint, a tactical trick to start an attack on one side then switch without warning.

"You can feint many times within a single attack," Athos encouraged, growing pleased with the demonstration as the night drew out. "If you can do it well, your mark will have no idea where to parry."

Although charmed by Pierre's quick study, Athos was a reluctant role model. He had never taught blade work before, leaving instruction to the guildsmen and master teachers. They promoted it as an art form, unlike men of his kind who used it for killing. With Pierre, he felt as if he were scheming to steal a child and stamp him with a bittersweet mark of hubris.

"You're bleeding through." Athos let down his guard. Pierre's performance hadn't suffered.

"And you stink." Pierre cut the air diagonally as well as Athos's sweat-stained shirt, impressive even for an old hand.

"*Touché*." Athos acknowledged. "Tomorrow, I'll show you the *pris de fer*, the taking of the iron."

Pierre settled back in bed, and Athos changed into a fresh shirt, using the torn one to mop up his sweat. He had lost track of time.

Indeed, the days and nights were running together. Commonplace for him. But instead of drowning in remorse, he was able to quiet his mind.

He sank into the red velvet armchair, savoured its comfort and fell asleep.

★★★

The sound of a moan woke him. The light of dawn coloured the King's suite in a hue similar to faded parchment. Murmurs drifted from Pierre's bed. The covers were drawn, and the pillows were thrown off. Hannah, her bulge covered by a thin camisole, straddled Pierre, flat on his back. They were both naked from the waist down. They whispered candidly, swept up in love-making, unaware Athos was awake.

He resisted the need to move, to exhale, to blink.

"Thank God you're mine." Pierre arched his hips between Hannah's legs and his hands gravitated to her breasts. Their rhythm continued. Her long hair teased his chest, and her body undulated as they tripped across the sun. Athos was scorched in their path. He tingled in empathy, powerless to avoid the heat filling the room.

"Pierre." Hannah locked her fingers behind Pierre's neck and kissed his collarbone. "Pierre, now."

The release came within seconds. Their bodies, joined by sensuality, reached the pinnacle for several heartbeats before burning out. Sighing in satisfaction, Hannah folded into a half-moon over Pierre's lax centre and murmured lines of love. Athos remained as still as a wall sconce.

"That didn't hurt, did it?" Hannah asked and rubbed Pierre's bandage.

He kissed her palm. "I never knew pain could be so pleasurable."

Pierre closed his eyes the instant she closed hers.

For several minutes, Athos sat frozen across the room until their breathing deepened. When he stood, his head and body pulsed. Pierre and Hannah rustled in drowsy bliss. Part of him was ashamed for staying, but he also raged with new life.

There was truth in the act of love. For years, he had wanted to believe he could live without the touch of another human being, but it was a faulty philosophy. Refusing love in his life would push him to end his life. Time did not soothe his pain; solitude did not; risking death did not. One person could. An untouchable woman who expected him at her side by day's end.

Chapter 19
Circle of Grass

When the sun reached the horizon, Athos met Nicole under the willow. She appeared serene at first but frowned as soon as she caught sight of the weapons at his waist. He wore them to show he appreciated their return. Instead, he realized that they drew a line, possibly a necessary one, between him and her.

Nicole, in a plain dress, dark vest and bonnet, carried a satchel of sketching supplies. She set out in the waist-high grass and goldenrods toward a grove of trees. He fell in line behind her on a path through the foliage. She led them to a flattened area beneath the trees, no bigger than a modest flowerbed. Once there, she pointed to a barkless branch in a sycamore where a large, crude nest fit at a crook.

An owl, she mouthed.

It took a while for Athos to see the majestic head of the creature because the nest was camouflage, and the owl, motionless.

"Noble," he whispered.

"I've never seen this kind of owl on the estate before. Its eyes are pitch, and the feathers have markings I can't identify. Thankfully, he, or she, is at rest."

Sitting, she gathered several stiff papers and a stick of charcoal from her satchel. Soon she was flicking her head from paper to bird. Athos felt as if he had faded into the background.

He wondered why she had not backed out. He didn't sit too closely, not for need of distance; he simply wanted to see every nuance of her joy. He was as concentrated on her as she was on the owl.

Such beauty. No matter if she's out of my reach.

"You study people," she said and stayed on task, alternating between the page and the bird. He could see her sketch from an angle. She had completed the outline of the owl's body.

"I'm not used to living by society's rules," he said, unashamed. "You don't seem to worry about your standing either."

"I'm married to a wealthy man and attend Mass and confession faithfully. What others think of me, especially those at Court, isn't my concern. I lead a good life away from gossip and politics."

"Fortunes can change," he said.

"If I were penniless, I would still have my faith. If I were faithless, all the wealth in France would be of no use to me."

And so he watched and accompanied her for three afternoons. The owl cooperated every day. Each afternoon began the same. An unspoken greeting under the tree, a walk through the grass, a descent into the circle, to be isolated by nature. Their conversations were sporadic but intense. The quiet, even more so.

"You don't talk much," she said on the third afternoon in the circle. She began cross-hatching the breast feathers. The joints in her fingers were white from pinching the coal. "Don't you enjoy the company of others?"

"About the same as you."

"Fair enough," she said, straightening her shoulders.

He regretted his dusty social skills. "Like you, I don't care much for society. My socializing has been with drunks in taverns and headstrong men."

"Men like my husband," she said with a reticent smile. She glanced for his reaction. "I imagine Pierre must remind you of people you know. Truthfully, if given the freedom, I'm certain he would fit in much too easily in Paris." Her smile disappeared.

"He would also learn more about the world."

"His life is here." She pressed the coal, and it splintered.

"He'll never be more than a servant here," he said. "It doesn't get much worse."

"He could die violently. You know Pierre wants to be a Musketeer, which is death itself." A breeze ruffled her bonnet ties.

"Duelling is the certain use of harm for uncertain outcomes. War is the same. They both equal pain."

"You worry about things you know little about, Comtesse."

His challenge called for a rebuke. Instead, she disarmed him. *Again.* "Call me Nicole."

"Nicole, then." He nodded. "Does losing a loved one to old age cause less heartache than losing a man to a sword? His people still grieve. A person is responsible for his own afterlife, and it doesn't matter if his death is violent or not."

"Losing a loved one is devastating," she said. "Violence makes it unbearable."

"Not everyone has a choice," he said.

"Why is violence necessary?" She crinkled the corner of her drawing. "I think powerful men are arrogant and shouldn't decide other men's fates."

Athos got quieter. "Does what I am bother you?"

The grass blew lazily toward her, and she looked away from him. "It's natural to fear violence. Death is final. Salvation is the only answer."

"I'm a Musketeer. I live with death and violence. It requires many sacrifices of mind and body. Salvation is a luxury."

"It's a necessity. It's your *soul*," she insisted.

"God doesn't live at the tip of a sword."

She placed a hand over her drawing. "Is God in your heart?"

"He was once, a very long time ago."

The pink in the sunset faded behind her. "Perhaps, He still is."

If only she knew. *He is not. You are.*

Because of her, he was falling in a new direction instead of to the grave. She was salvation. A blasphemy to the Church and everyone else.

She sharpened her coal with a tiny knife. "Will you share with me what happened to your face?"

"I fell." A half-truth. He thought he saw her tremble.

She broke the tip of the coal with the knife. "In a duel?"

"A dare."

"You wager?"

"It's one of Paris's most treasured pastimes," he said, picking a stem of clover, trying to let the tension settle down. "You must have heard about it from François."

"He shares few details of his trips to Paris with me, and news is slow to travel here. My contacts in the city are more tied to the church than to gambling." Her next question took him off guard. "What has been your most prized winning?"

In a heartbeat, he thought: *You. You are my most treasured prize. I'm here with you, seeing the beauty of life again, my bloody past losing its hold.*

"I outfitted myself for the war at La Rochelle playing dice."

"When you fell," she said, placing her slender fingers near her cheek, "did you win that time as well?"

"Gloriously so," he said with a faint smile.

"And what did you win?"

"This moment with you." It was true, and he did not want to lie. Still, his bluntness charged the air between them, and his immodesty stopped her questions and drawing. A wind played, and a twig snapped. The owl swivelled its head in each direction and flew off. She fled, too, parting the curtain of grass in the direction of the bird.

"Wait—" A breeze tossed his word aside.

Hold on. She needs distance. I intimidate her.

Her footfalls quickened in the grass and grew fainter.

"Nicole." He desired her name across his tongue. It plucked his heart like a chord, and, abandoning discipline, he plunged through the grass after her.

The path opened to a moss bed along a stream, and trees on the bank created an invitation to the water. Their shade chilled the air.

She must be here, following her bird, shaking off my intensity.

Under the canopy, he closed his eyes and listened. He heard what she must hear, the lovely solitude. He also heard what she could not. His blood pounding a message: *Find her.*

He checked each step along the stream's edge, watching for slippery stones and soft spots. He ran like a boy in search of a lost playmate; he felt abandoned and needy. He hopped from rock to rock. He slipped ankle deep then outran the humility. The soft bank slowed him down, yet his neck grew damp. His optimism waned. The forest swallowed him whole.

"Nicole!"

Athos ran faster and checked everywhere for signs. *How could she disappear?* The stream grew wider. His lungs burned, legs burned, need burned. His body heat suffocated him.

When he saw her on the other side of the stream, his heart slid to a halt.

She seemed far away, in another part of her mind. Quick breaths came from within her. She leaned against a sturdy sapling, whose branches dangled over the water. She rested her forehead on a low limb, took a deep breath and lowered her soft brown eyes to the creek.

The stream bubbled like laughter. The trees became tall walls, and the leaves formed an ornate palace. The wind swirled into a mass of warm bodies.

Le Louvre. His first daydream of her was coming to life.

The grass beneath him became marbled floors and a royal cavalcade echoed in his ears. This was Court. Nicole was here. Beside him. She was *his* and no other's. He succumbed to her request for privacy. *Be with me.* Under his influence, in a sea of sheets and sweat, her entire body was his, easing his pain. Nicole was his remedy to madness.

Nicole looked up from the creek. Her eyes ran up the length of him and seemed to gleam with pleasure. Just long enough. She hugged her centre and called his name.

"He is lost," she said then, and the dream was gone.

"The owl, you mean." His high was unshakeable.

"Our time is over. Walk me back."

He trailed closely behind on the path. When they arrived at the entrance of the château, she told him the drawing would be complete the next day.

★★★

As soon as dusk settled, Nicole slipped out to the chapel to sort through the chase. She tried not to admit she had been running away from him, but had she? When she heard him chasing her in the woods, her relief had vanished.

She was good at running. She outran Sibonne her entire childhood. Nicole's sprints brought hot cheeks of shame to her sister. It exhilarated Nicole to watch the land zoom by. She skilfully took quick turns and maneuvered the creek like a snake between the elms and oaks.

In her afternoons with Athos, his demeanour confounded her and stirred dangerous feelings. She was treading on porous moral ground, and her prayers in the chapel sounded weak.

Forgive me Father, for I have sinned.

Was it a sin to be in his company? Her flawed life seemed frailer near him.

Athos raced after her in the woods with the same determination that probably propelled him to bloodshed. Yet he was lost, and she worried that rescuing him from his course could send her down the same path.

The chapel grew darker when she recalled looking up at him from the water.

He opened her heart with a forbidden key.

In another time, another place—another book with a different story—she might have allowed herself to fall. And for a moment in her most cherished place, the woods, she had let him think she could fall. *It's possible. We're possible.* She had shown her feelings for an instant too long before she spoke the real certainty.

"He is lost," she repeated in the smothering silence of the chapel.

Her prayer was in vain.

Chapter 20
Clipping a Swallow

For Athos, that night with Pierre dragged slower than a funeral procession.

"You're distracted," Pierre said after he disengaged the sword from Athos in a half-hearted spar. "Are you upset with my progress?"

"No, simply thinking of other things."

"What could distract you here? Watching the grass grow?" The questions fell on deaf ears.

"If you were unable to be with Hannah," Athos asked, "what would you do?"

"You're asking me for advice on love? I thought you said I was a fool?"

"Never mind. My mind is wandering," Athos said.

Pierre soon crawled into bed. Before passing into sleep, he spoke up. "To be with Hannah, I'd make a deal with the Devil himself."

★★★

Athos arrived at the willow earlier than usual. Nicole's warning that it might be their last time together in the field agitated him. Like gun powder in a pistol, it primed him for desperate measures. His tongue was the hardest to control.

"Any other woman would be intimidated by a man staring at her," he said minutes after they sat down in the circle of grass.

"It doesn't bother me."

"It should."

"You wanted to watch me draw," she said and blew dust from the drawing. "That means you study me, my work."

"You could have put a stop to it well before now." His eyes narrowed with reproach.

"You act like the owl when it hunts. I've watched this owl hunt, in daylight when necessary, with supreme focus."

"Was that what you were up to yesterday? Observing your predator?" Athos pointed to the nest.

"Like you, he doesn't stop until he's satisfied."

"By instinct," he said. "But prey does not take up nest with its hunter."

"I am not prey." Her lips tightened.

Athos frowned, and she gruffly shoved her hands into her satchel.

"Here," she blurted, offering paper and another stick of coal. "Today, you try."

He was dumb-struck. "I'm not an artist and have no desire to be one." He stretched out more cat-like than before and left the paper sitting on the grass in front of him.

"Try. Once," she insisted.

"Give me an incentive."

Her cheeks turned pink. "What kind do you suggest?"

"Draw me."

"No." She grabbed the supplies and repacked the satchel with all her things.

"Am I so hideous that you cannot draw me?" Athos rubbed his chin and crossed his ankles.

"As I've explained, I don't draw people. I haven't drawn people for many years, and I don't wish to start now." She glared at him. "Why did you want to watch me draw?"

He conceded that he deserved a little boiling push-back. The careful boundaries of good behaviour were becoming as smudged as the charcoal on her fingers.

"I wanted to see what you get from this distraction of yours."

"It's not a distraction. It's art." She forced it out, but he didn't budge. "And I gain meaning and connection with the world."

"You sound very much like a man I met on my way here." The priest Simon Grignan would chuckle to see Athos now, but only if

Nicole had been eligible. Even a liberal priest could not excuse an infatuation with a married woman. "He was a priest, the man I gave my horse to on my way here."

"You gave your horse to a priest? You spoke with a priest?"

"It's more accurate to say he accosted me and rambled on about connecting with nature. And people."

"You feel no ties to either, do you?" She practically glowered. "You could have simply asked me *why* I draw."

"And you had a choice to say no—to this." He pointed first to himself then to her. "You chose to let me in."

He anticipated her astonishment, and in fact, enjoyed it. Ultimately, he was pushing for a reason, to test her tolerance, and by chance, find favour in her good graces. Better still, a place in her arms.

I may never have another chance. I'm a crawl away.

He leaned forward, watching for signs that she wanted the same. Her disbelief became apprehension. She parted her lips and froze, then her gaze averted behind him. That's when he heard the hooves. At his back, twenty yards from their circle, a stag towered above the swirling grass. His ears and tail were still. Scarred by territorial battles, its short-haired haunches twitched from flies. The larger-than-life creature snorted and pawed and looked straight at them, antler tips pointing toward the sky, then down.

In slow motion, Athos removed the pistol from his belt.

"What are you doing?" she said, low but urgent.

The animal grunted. Athos aimed.

"Athos! No!" The pleas rolled from her gut.

She lurched before he could take his hand off the trigger. In an awkward roll, her momentum shoved their bodies into the grass. His pistol discharged as he slammed sideways on the ground, and the weapon fell forward. She landed on her back next to him, her eyes on the clear sky, the light fading to grey. The massive buck jerked and bounded in another direction, making the ground thunder, before the animal disappeared.

"Nicole!" Stunned, Athos was at her side. "Are you struck?"

Her eyes were glassy.

"Nicole!" He trembled, afraid to touch her. "Did the bullet strike you?"

"We don't hunt here. I don't allow it." Her expression was blank, her stare unfocused.

Athos cradled her head and felt the beginnings of a knot. "Are you struck? Answer me!"

"My arm. It's cold."

With battle-tested skill, Athos found the bullet mark on her sleeve. He tore at the entry point. The bullet had ripped through the soft flesh on her shoulder, in and out, and left a wicked, bloody gash.

How could I?

He removed the bonnet from her listless head and folded it into a crude bandage, using the ties to wrap her arm, once, twice, three times. He shifted her into the crook of his arm and draped her across his lap. He had no choice but to press the wound.

"No, please!" Her face creased. "You're hurting me."

Before he could whisper solace, she lost consciousness.

He stifled the urge to cry out.

No! Not you. Not you, too.

Tender in his arms, the woman capable of healing him bled by his hand.

Forgive me. Forgive me.

Feeling exposed and vulnerable, he tightened around her body, the events spinning wildly in replay. The act was perilous, if not also punishable. The sound of the pistol could arouse alarm. He couldn't be found with another bleeding body, and even as a Musketeer, he was ill-prepared for this kind of mistake.

I've shot an innocent. Understanding will be in short supply, especially after Pierre.

Darkness began to descend, but her body radiated heat. He had to try. Lifting her easily, he scrambled to the pond. Carrying her was comforting. At the edge, he took the kerchief from her neck, doused it in the water and dabbed her brow and cheeks. It didn't revive her.

Please, please come to.

He tried again and wiped the sticky blood around the makeshift bandage. Dousing again, he pressed the cool kerchief onto the bump behind her head.

Nothing caused her to flicker.

His thoughts sped through several plans. He needed discretion, an isolated place to take care of her. His ability to cope bordered on insanity. But he was not insane, and she was alive. Whole. Warm in his arms. In a flash like heat lightning, his chaos turned to calm.

She inhaled and exhaled. Then again. And again. He listened for her heartbeat and called upon reason. *She's hurt but will survive. This harm will pass, and along with it, so will this moment.* He had the chance to absorb her beauty without hiding his true feelings, and no one would ever know. Including her.

Beyond understanding, she was in his arms, ones that had suffered for years in emptiness. He traced the sun streaks in the deep brunette framing her face. He combed her hair between his fingers and cupped her cheek. He brushed his lips on her forehead and discovered her scent, a blend of clover and coal. His scar grazed her expressionless cheek.

Dare I touch her lips? Steal a kiss?

The Devil preyed upon his will. Pierre's declaration tolled like a bell: *I'd make a deal with the Devil himself.* Like once long ago, Athos seized the temptation.

"God help me," he uttered and dipped into oblivion.

Hidden in the grass under a darkening sky, her lips yielded, but the kiss was not returned. It was a one-way connection. Imperfect. He pulled up quickly and searched for a reaction. None came. He felt delusional and misguided. His liberties needed to end, for she deserved the best of his intentions, every ounce of them. Fate had its limits.

With a new plan, he began a short, secret trek out of the grass, carrying a gift of chance and misfortune in his arms.

Chapter 21
Confidences in the Cottage

Inside the door of Pierre's cottage, her head swept away from his chest. He laid her on the rumpled mattress, and she grimaced, holding her arm like a broken wing. The darkness was disorienting, and he lit the candle by the stool and placed her satchel by the door. He had doubled-back for it, careful no evidence was left behind.

"His cottage?" she rasped.

"It was the closest place to take you. It might be better if you lay on your side."

Gently, he helped her over and checked the bandage. "You've stopped bleeding."

"What happened to the stag? Did you hurt it?"

"It fled. He escaped unharmed. I wish I could say the same for you." He couldn't look at her. He took the damp kerchief from his pocket and wiped dried blood from her arm. "The bullet didn't lodge in your arm."

"And the owl?"

"It flew away. I promise, you're the only one hurt." He nodded toward her injury. "We must keep the bandage tight."

He rewound the strings of the bonnet to even the pressure. She sucked in and tensed.

"I never thought I would be cared for by a Musketeer," she said, wincing.

"Hmm. Your head may ache from the bump and your arm will hurt for several weeks. Once it's healed, it will probably look like a minor burn."

"Branded by a bullet."

He had shot Nicole on the same shoulder as Milady's brand. The irony was small recompense for his behaviour. He shoved down the memory of the fleur-de-lis, along with Nicole's handkerchief in his pocket.

"You may be dizzy from the bump and confused from losing blood, Madame. I hope when you realize what I've done, you remain as light-headed and don't send me away."

"You'd like to stay now?"

Judging from her pallor, his diagnosis was correct. Why would she want him to stay unless she was completely out of her mind? He tossed a worn blanket over her.

"Remember, I'm the same guest who first hurt Pierre and now you, after suggesting you flirt with unfamiliar men." He smoothed the lumps from the blanket and realized she might not remember most of their conversation later. "Of course, I'd like to correct my mistakes. Please allow me to make up for my errors. I pledge my service to you, as well as Pierre."

She bit her lower lip. "Why did you shoot?"

"It's too close to rutting season. I've seen lusty stags trample men twice my size. Frankly, I can't fathom why François would allow his lands to go wild."

"I asked him to. The animals deserve a sanctuary."

"But wild animals are meant to be hunted," he said. "Of course, respect them, but also know them. The owl has talons that could snap the bones of your fingers or wrists. No wonder the stags come right up to you. You pose no threat."

She pulled the blanket to her chin, and he immediately wished he could take back the tirade. Thankfully, he spotted Pierre's wine and drinking bowls at the end of the bed.

"This should lessen the pain." He offered her a bowlful.

"My head cannot think as it is."

"I know I'm still earning your trust, but a few sips will take off the edge. Please, let me help."

She murmured yes, and it allowed him close again. He lifted her head and brought the bowl to her lips, avoiding eye contact. He wasn't sure his intentions could remain pure; it would take a mountain of will to stop his desires from spilling over. As she drank, the crescent shape of her mouth reminded him of the kiss. If possible, he would touch her lips again and let the Devil and God battle for his soul.

After three sips, she paused, and he reluctantly settled her down and poured himself a drink.

"Why do you find wine objectionable? It's nourishment, a cure for sickness, a gift of life," he said, courting a lower-key conversation.

"It clouds judgment."

"Every Frenchman knows it soothes pain."

"Which kind in your case? Real or imagined?" She mouthed *no* to another sip.

"I won't deny it's a comfort to me. A cure for incurable ailments."

"If you'd like, I can be a safe place for you to share your troubles," she said.

"And I thought I was the caregiver." He glanced at the door, hoping for continued privacy. "I think offering you a confession at this moment might be unwise, though you seem to offer shelter to many things. Your birds, wildlife—and young lovers. Do I look like I need sanctuary, too?"

Her legs shifted restlessly under the cover. "It's a Godly act to offer comfort and refuge."

"Right now, I'm not the one who needs them," he said.

"My head is spinning."

Athos placed the back of his hand against her forehead, stopping short of a caress. "You're slightly cool. Rest. We can talk about my life when you're better."

She closed her eyes and made the sign of the cross. As she prayed, he realized that in her ordinary world his actions must have been bizarre and probably tossed her into chaos. Nevertheless, she had shown him mercy in *her* moment of need.

He watched her chest rise and fall. The chance that he would be this close to her again was as unlikely as taking a second kiss. She was wholly unaware of her beauty, a mortal creature capable of immortal pleasures. Real yet touched by the divine. A Venus, Aphrodite or Athena.

He wondered how the Comte made love to her, if he selfishly swam in her exquisiteness or if he was mindful of her wants.

Athos suspected she longed for an intense, sophisticated coaxing from a lover. It was the only kind of love Athos ever wanted to make.

She whispered an Our Father.

"Your devotion is infectious." His thought was impromptu, as was the next. "Could you ask God to forgive me for hurting you?"

"I forgive you," she said, eyes soft. "Of course, God will, too, but you live very far from His influence. It's troubling."

Athos poured himself another drink. "My relationship with God is clear cut."

"Clear cut in that you live outside His grace."

"And how do you know that?"

"Your own words. '*God does not live at the tip of a sword.*' And because you asked *me* to request His forgiveness." She paused. "Do you pray?"

"Have you a plan to make me start?"

"My faith isn't influenced by others, and neither should yours," she said.

"Perhaps, but I find your religious practice riddled with exceptions. Indulge me," he said, pouring wine into both bowls. "As one of the faithful, have you sought forgiveness for allowing Pierre's affair to continue? For his baby to be born outside the church?"

She cleared her throat and took her time answering.

"Pierre is like a son. He came to us when his father died. Pierre was ten and had no mother. He and Hannah formed an attachment very early on as playmates because they were the same age. She was really the only one here for him to be young with."

"There are ways to channel youthfulness."

"I did. I began to teach them reading, writing, art."

"He told me he could read," Athos said. "You truly don't care a wisp for convention, do you?"

"Teaching him served a purpose. When he came to live with us, you can imagine his head-strong nature in full bloom. The Comte and Cordes couldn't satisfy his energy, always running tirelessly in search of fun. Every day, he looked for ways to engage his playfulness, and Hannah tagged along when she could. I did my best to step in, but it was only a matter of time before they discovered each other—in more inappropriate ways. I take responsibility for letting it happen."

"You seem determined to keep them together, but you can't shoulder all the blame."

"They love each other." She clenched the blanket, squinting with pain. "They need each other, and when the baby arrives, they should be together. They should be married, but he's impetuous. Neither François nor my priest will consent to their marriage."

"I suspected you might have tried." His eyes moved across her to the dark cottage walls. "So you are their sanctuary."

"The arrangement is flawed."

It demanded his truthfulness. "It's blasphemy."

She sank deeper into the bed. "The subject is an ongoing dispute with my confessor."

"But you confess it? That's true devotion," he said. "Your honesty is your failing *and* your virtue. In my mind, there's no faith without honesty. Truth, in many ways, can be divinity."

"It's impossible for me to understand God's purpose," she said and touched her shoulder. "I indulge Hannah and Pierre but cannot alter God's will."

"That's your confessor speaking."

"You say there's no faith without honesty," she said. "The reason you drink—it concerns honesty, doesn't it?"

He peered into his cup to mask his surprise. Her accuracy was uncanny. "Dishonesty, Madame," he said after a drink.

"Please call me Nicole." She reached out from the covers, her hand a token. He wanted to lay it on his cheek and bless it with a kiss. Instead, he tightened his jaw and placed the wine in her grasp. She was learning more of his history than was safe, calling him out of a dank, slippery cave.

She sat the wine on the floor. "Someone—someone dear to you—dealt with you dishonestly. That's it, isn't it?"

"Some time ago."

"It's the reason you reject God."

He smirked, finished his bowlful and pretended to pray, his hands flat together. "God is life," he said. "So when life itself leaves you, so does God."

"You only deepen the divide with your sarcasm," she said.

"And you ask too many questions." He wanted her to stop before his shame became transparent.

"The dishonesty must have been unforgivable, something you couldn't live with," she said. He thought the statement distilled his pain too simplistically. As she waited for a response, her curiosity turned into a sad, blank stare.

A long silence followed, and he rechecked her wound. "This will hinder your drawing."

She pretended to sketch on the blanket with a finger. "Perhaps that's best. It distracts me from more important things."

"Saving people's souls?"

"I'm not a saviour, Athos. I need to concentrate on my own faith."

"And how will you return to the house injured without an outcry for my head?"

"Hannah will see to me."

"What will you tell her?" he asked.

"Only what's necessary."

Placing his future in her hands demanded complete discretion. It required her to gloss over the accident or hide it, even jeopardize her faith.

"I don't want you to compromise yourself," he said. "You shouldn't sacrifice for me. I'd sooner depart." His last words were less truthful.

"You tried that once," she said.

He detected a hint of mischief in her tone. "I won't run from my responsibilities."

"Don't leave then," she said.

It was so irrational. She was downed like a clipped swallow and party to a sketchy plan to help a God-forsaken man. And, she had easily zeroed in on the source of his misery. There was no logical reason for her to want him to stay.

Unless …

He could only wish.

"Then I place myself in your hands for safekeeping." He nodded. "However, you must allow me take you to Hannah safely. Can you ride?"

Within an instance of her nod, he raced to the stable for a horse. On any other day, such energy would have come only from peril. Now, it came from care. He quickly saddled a horse in the dark and sped back to the cottage in half the time. It didn't matter. The tiny room was empty, except for her charcoal sketch of the owl, adrift on the bed.

Chapter 22
Aftermath of the Accident

The next morning, Athos asked a servant to show him to his guest room. His night with Pierre had been uneventful, and Athos stayed quiet. He wanted time alone.

On the long walk to his room, Athos passed no fewer than a dozen door alcoves, behind which he hoped Nicole was healing in a suite full of lush fabric, soothing hues and a bed designed for royalty. Unfortunately, he could not enter to offer comfort, and her injury would cause significant discomfort. Experience told him as much.

His room was much smaller than Pierre's, sparsely furnished and painted in a watery blue. None of Nicole's artwork hung on the walls. An ink drawing of Queen Anne dangled over a bedside table, but it was too flowery to be Nicole's.

Low to the ground, a large four-poster bed with an embroidered coverlet and a matching canopy was the centrepiece of the room. Two straight-backed chairs and a round table were grouped near a corner fireplace. A pillared glass bowl filled with apples stood in the centre of the table. A vertical window, not much wider than his shoulders, overlooked the livery and coach house. He swung the window as wide as its hinges permitted.

Solitude set apart every corner of Nicole's world. Her rejection of society's rules made the estate an island, like her hideaway in the willow. She created a place to live in peace at odds with the outside.

Yet trouble wove through her world like a silver spider web. A pregnant housemaid. Young, unmarried lovers. A distant husband. Athos sensed in Nicole a hidden anxiety. But for no apparent reason, she was at ease with him, a brooding stranger. Nicole showed undue kindness to an outsider with whom she had only a vague connection. He had infiltrated the refuge of a beautiful, married woman. Or rather, she let him in.

He inhaled the breeze from the window, recalling each syllable she spoke in the cottage, every expression she cast, the cascade of her brown hair, his hands handling her body.

Despite the accident and her flight from the cottage, Athos was not remorseful. He felt connected. He and Nicole shared a secret, and he had her drawing. The reason she ran away was simple—she felt something for him and could not confront it.

On top of a dresser sat a ceramic wash basin and a few thin linens. He smelled of moss and sweat. He wished he had groomed himself before their last rendezvous. It wasn't in his upbringing as a young nobleman to be unpresentable. Later, when he became a Musketeer, he cared little if women found him dishevelled.

He disrobed and scooped water from the basin onto his face. With a hunk of soap, he vigorously scrubbed his head and dusty blond hair, ears and neck, making the water cloudier with each rinse. He repeated across his chest, middle and forearms.

He grazed the silver cuff on his upper arm. It lived on him like a birthmark. Over the years, it had become such a part of him that he often forgot he was wearing it. Now, it trumpeted a nasty message. A woman had ravaged him once.

How could he compare Nicole with Milady? Nicole was a pristine river. Like a warm current, she soaked him in pleasure and brought on a long-abandoned sensation. *Desire.*

He didn't want the feeling to end. He wanted the rush all over him.

Never mind the shadow of sorrow.

His human spirit demanded a new course.

He dried his hands and pulled Nicole's kerchief from his pants on the floor. It was a token of redemption. The fabric, wrinkled and spotted with blood, was a delicate talisman. He pressed it to his mouth and smelled the slight aromas of clover and coal.

She's been in my room. It smells exactly like her.

She may have sat in a chair and pondered what it might be like to watch a man sleeping—a man other than her husband or a wounded young servant. He ran a hand across the covers of the bed and lingered at the pillow, thinking she might have done the same, seeking the warmth of his body.

He laid the kerchief on the pillow. Surrounded by Nicole's mist, he soaked a towel in the rinse water and ran it hard down his buttocks and legs. Would she, seeing the basin, have imagined him washing?

He pictured her by the window, a fine strand of bronze hair across her face, her expression fearless. She had been with a man before. She would stare at his body. Instead of Nicole being the centre of attraction, he would stand objectified. Honed by swordplay, he would bathe as if performing a visual concert for an audience of one. The cut of his torso would shine with water, and his soapy palms would glide from collarbone to groin.

Soon, a subtle look or a rapid breath would unite them. Shedding silks and ribbons, swimming in vulnerability, their bodies would tangle across his bed in pure hunger.

Get a hold of yourself!

He threw the towels to the door and fumbled to dress. Washing his body had accomplished the opposite of cleansing his thoughts. All he could hope for was to be in her company. But like his visions, the opportunity to be closer to her was beyond his control.

More than anything, he wanted to see her again—to issue a better apology, to walk along the pond's edge, *to watch her live.*

★★★

Nicole's carriage, a gift from the Comte, was covered from ceiling to footboard with the finest imported velvet, a Parisian commodity. The textile appeared black in the early-morning darkness, but Nicole relished its true colour, a smoky lapis. She usually rode in the carriage alone and for one purpose. Confession. Her priest, Father Audric, expected her most Saturdays at the hour after dawn.

She rode the carriage to her church, Notre Dame de la Tronchaye in Rochefort. She visited the church more than any other place. She had been married there and was a devoted attendant at Mass. Cordes drove her to its doors and few other destinations.

The most pleasurable part of going to church was her entrance. Although she dressed exquisitely, it wasn't the clothes that she liked most, for no one was inside the church but her priest. Of all the money François had spent to reunite them, his lavish generosity toward the church touched her. His gifts were evident in every corner, from balustrade to altar. The most ostentatious gifts were three towering stained-glass panels depicting Adam and Eve, the Crucifixion, and Moses. Nicole usually disliked bold displays of wealth; however, she approved here. Ironically, François' ego and desperation were also on display every time she opened the doors.

Nicole approached the confessional with a dry upper lip, her outward calm due to years of practice. She concealed her churning emotions and the burning pain on her shoulder by focusing straight ahead.

A heavy, gold-threaded curtain separated her from Father Audric. He was her only confessor, a diminutive man with soft hands. He had become the priest in her church about the time Pierre arrived at the estate as an orphan. Her history, daily rituals and pastimes were as familiar to Father Audric as the Psalms. He cleared his throat. She began with the sign of the cross.

"Bless me, Father, for I have sinned. It has been more than a week since my last confession. Our guest has arrived, and I—"

"The Musketeer? I hope that means you will bring him with you tomorrow. Tell me his name again?"

"Athos."

"By all means, make Athos welcome in this house of God."

Nicole heard an inkling of pleasure in the priest's invitation.

"I don't think he'll accept an invitation, Father. As delicately as I can say it," she paused, "he presents many difficulties."

"François wanted you to make his stay comfortable."

"Yes, but he's troubled and estranged from the Church."

"He's Catholic, isn't he?"

"Of course, but his faith suffers because he's deeply wounded inside."

"We're all wounded in some way. Gently lead him back. You're an example in the eyes of God. "

"Except that he questions my faith," she said, tightening her hands together. "His curiosity is insatiable."

"He already knows of the situation with your two servants?"

"He and Pierre have become friendly."

"Yet another reason you shouldn't allow Pierre to stay. He's a servant and needs to be treated as such, not to mention separated from your servant girl."

"Athos asked me why I allow Pierre and Hannah to continue."

Father Audric huffed in frustration. "Even a wavering soul sees your mistakes. Nicole, you must put an end to their intimacies. I demand again that you send the girl to the Carmelites. If you allow this to continue, God will punish you for it."

"I believe He is punishing me. I'm troubled for another reason. I promised François that I would preoccupy the Musketeer until he's needed, but there's a shadow over Athos, and though it seems to be fading—it comes at my expense."

"What do you mean?"

"It's—it's the way he looks at me, as if he is drawn to a light."

"A light? I trust you've done nothing to bring this about?"

"No, I've indulged neither impure thoughts nor actions." She made the sign of the cross. "I'm certain—I've done nothing improper. He's not coercive, and I have interacted with him decently. He's simply drawn to me."

"How do you know this?" Father Audric sounded right against the curtain.

"He's unable to hide it."

"Or it could be you're seeing something that isn't there, casting your own depraved thoughts onto him. Detach yourself from his company at once. Clear these gnarls from your path. Send him to your husband. *Immediately*."

"He could be redeemed. I know it's possible."

"This entire state of affairs deeply troubles me—it's developed so quickly."

"There's something else." Nicole cleared her throat. "I'm not certain what it means or whether it's a sin, but I had a dream. It came to me after the Musketeer arrived. I can't explain it, but in the dream—Athos kissed me."

Father Audric yanked the curtain aside and stood straight as a staff. His mouth turned down at the corners.

"Abomination, Nicole! These details you give—his lack of faith, a shadow of darkness, and the possibility of impure thoughts. Toward you. Perhaps by you. And, your apparent enchantment! This situation, without question, *is wrong*. You sacrifice your salvation and your relationship with God."

She looked down. "He reminds me so much of my sister."

"Your sister was misled by a vagabond whom she thought she loved."

"Athos told me he was deceived by another," she said softly.

"You must bring him here. I must see him. And let us pray God is merciful on you both."

Nicole closed her hands together. Father Audric covered her head with one hand, administered the prayer and ordered her penance. "As soon as I've seen this Musketeer myself and he's departed, you will prepare for your pilgrimage. It's long overdue."

She could not move. Father Audric blessed her and retreated briskly to his study as she struggled to whisper.

"With the help of Thy grace, I will sin no more and avoid the near occasions of sin. Amen."

Chapter 23
Truth and Lies

At mid-morning, Athos awoke famished. This hunger was different—welcome and driven—sending him to the kitchen.

A portly woman punched and kneaded a sticky lump of dough on a butcher block. A basket of eggs, a pile of peeled apples, and two pitchers of milk occupied the counter, which ran the length of the room, cluttered by utensils, rags, and bowls. The stocky cook pounded and pulled the dough, dusting the floor around her hem with flour.

"You had to eat again, eventually." She concentrated on the pliable ball and not on the guest. "You're too early for the bread. The first batch is still baking. Make do with the pears."

Athos found a large wooden bowl of pears and a knife. He cut slivers of the fruit, which seemed sweeter than remembered. The kneading continued, and Athos leaned against the counter to eat and watch the cook while the smell of baking bread filled the room.

As he wondered how he might find Nicole, he glimpsed the tail end of Hannah's skirt sweeping into the pantry. Hannah was probably the last person Nicole had seen the previous night. Hannah was Nicole's confidante but was afraid of him. After a few minutes, he knew she was hiding.

"Make sure the lid on the flour bin is tight in there. We don't need any more mice," the irascible cook called.

He wanted to know how Nicole was feeling. Perhaps he could coax some information from Hannah. If he was lucky, he could read Hannah like a limerick, short and simple. From all accounts, she was the most innocent person in the household, despite her dalliance with Pierre. And besides, Athos was starting to enjoy being around women again.

Hannah, however, was plastered to a corner.

"There's no need to be frightened," he reassured, careful to stay at the pantry door.

She shook her head. He tried to empathize because her impressions of him were as troublemaker and worse, but he wanted information.

"Please," he said, closing the door with a shoulder, "I'll not hurt you."

"You slashed Pierre without so much as a .... a ... a blink," she stuttered. Fear locked her in place.

"And what does Pierre think of me?"

She balled her fists. "You're a murderous scoundrel."

"Are those Pierre's words?" Grinning would ruin any progress, so Athos dropped his head and played the apologetic rogue. "I'm concerned about him and have apologized. I hope you can accept my regrets as well."

"I told Nicole not to send him after you. *Begged her.* And I suffer the consequences." She was on the verge of tears.

"You did, did you?" It fell to the innocent to reveal the truth. Pierre had skilfully avoided giving Athos this information as handily as he hid his trysts with the young mademoiselle trembling by the spice jars.

"Nicole said Pierre was the only one who might convince you to stay," Hannah said.

"Perhaps she was right."

"You felt obliged to stay only after you hurt him!" She nailed the point again. "If you hadn't helped Nicole after her fall last night, in my opinion you'd be better off gone."

"Her fall?"

"Didn't you see it?" Hannah flattened her hands across her apron. "I thought you were at the willow when she fell off the branch?"

"Not exactly."

"Well, nevertheless, Nicole—and I," she blushed, "are grateful you helped her last night. It's a miracle she hasn't fallen from the branches before now. I can't fathom why she wants to draw from up there."

"Puzzling, isn't it?" But he wasn't paying attention to Hannah anymore.

Nicole sent Pierre. Then lied about the accident. For me.

Nicole's virtue was slipping with every passing hour. Her willingness to keep him here and shield him from the worst made his body thrum again.

"Where is she now?" Athos said, braving two steps. "Is her arm better?"

She tilted her head. "Oh yes. I replaced the bonnet. At least you didn't lose all your wits." Hannah made sign of the cross. "She's gone to confession."

To cleanse her soul of its winding turns? What keeps her from telling Hannah the truth—unless it's impossible to defend?

Cordes blustered from the kitchen. "Hannah!"

She skirted by Athos nimbly. He grabbed a shelf for balance.

"Nicole's waiting for you," Cordes told Hannah. "She wants to go to the chalet."

"Should I be concerned?" Athos emerged from the pantry, hearing the opportunity.

Everyone in the kitchen erupted in unison: "No!"

Athos caught Cordes' arm before he could pass. "I don't imagine you'll tell me where you're taking her?"

Cordes looked Athos up and down. "The hunting chalet. On the farthest corner of the Comte's land. She goes there on occasion. It's not out of the ordinary. Just a quiet place."

Quieter than here? "Could I be of use?" he asked instead.

"No," Cordes said, wrinkling his brow. "The trip will be brief. Tomorrow is Sunday, and she never misses Mass."

The cook at the butcher block, whom they all called Duchy, wrapped a hot loaf in cloth for the trip. Even surrounded by the delicious aroma, Athos felt swept aside as the kitchen emptied.

★★★

Tangled thickets sprawled across the road to the chalet, catching the coach's wheels. The ride usually took an hour, but this trip required extra time to clear the foliage. Nicole didn't mind the delay.

The quiet inside her precious carriage and the promise of isolation at the chalet calmed her nerves. Hannah rarely came along, but Nicole wanted the company. Still, she didn't encourage any conversation until Hannah started twisting at hairpins.

"Is there something bothering you?" Nicole finally asked.

"The Musketeer. He came to the kitchen before we left."

"That's curious," she said. *And complicated, if he spoke to anyone.* "What for?"

"He was hungry."

Nicole began to smile but turned away to keep her satisfaction to herself. Hunger meant healing.

"His appetite can't be what's upsetting you," Nicole said. "What is it?"

"I wasn't very kind to him." Hannah frowned and spun a ribbon gathered at her neckline.

"I know you're upset with him because of Pierre. It's natural to blame him. But I imagine Monsieur Athos never heard insults as sweet as yours."

Hannah fanned her face. "I suppose you're right. He didn't seem to take my accusations too seriously. I thanked him for helping you."

"You spoke of me?"

"He asked about your wound," Hannah said, less tense than before.

Nicole laid a hand on her bandaged shoulder, which burned. A bump in the road increased the sting.

"He wanted to escort you this afternoon," Hannah said.

"That's very considerate."

"Considerate? I wouldn't describe him that way," Hannah said with a sour pout. She parted a carriage curtain. "He's … peculiar. Always trying to push people away but attracting them at the same time. I'm still wondering why he helped you."

"There's a shred of compassion in him. You'd have to agree he's very attentive to Pierre."

"You always see the best in people."

"If that's how I'm judged then I pray my faults may be forgiven, at least in the eyes of you and everyone else I cherish." Nicole managed a meek smile and let candour overtake her better judgment. "I haven't been as honest with him as I should be."

"You, dishonest?" Hannah's head bobbled with another bump. "About what?"

"I haven't told him everything he should know, everything he deserves to know."

"About your sister? Why would she matter to him?"

"Her story is very similar to his." Nicole looked out the window toward the treeline. The chalet was close.

"Why do you want to relive that past? I've never understood why you return to reread your journal from those days. I'd want nothing more than to forget about it."

"I find new meaning in it every time."

"Does that lift Sibonne any closer to Heaven?"

"No, Hannah. It never will." A pang of sorrow welled inside Nicole, and she rubbed an eye, wishing it away.

Hannah touched Nicole's hand. "Whatever you keep from him, you'll set it right. I'm not the best judge of whether he deserves it. Your honesty is angelic."

"If only that were so," Nicole said with a note of futility.

Cordes shouted to the horses, and the carriage slowed down. A heavy canopy of trees loomed over the final stop. In their shadow, the temperature dropped noticeably.

The chalet was a striking alternative to the main house—rugged versus refined. The Comte built it for hunting excursions the year she married him, but he allowed her to use it more frequently after the loss of her sister. Besides Cordes and, on occasion, Hannah, none of the other servants were allowed, especially Pierre. The steeply pitched roof, shelter each year to only a few determined guests, represented sanctuary to Nicole. She never shared this idea with her priest. She'd lost count of all the trips over the years since Sibonne's death. Too many to remember.

From a secret kitchen cabinet, she unlocked a thick, leather-bound journal. While Hannah and Cordes took up chores, she retired with the book to her private quarters, the largest musty bedroom. At a small oak desk below a window, she read the inscription, a part of her ritual.

Nicole, You are a steadfast sister. A lifetime of love shall be yours. Sibonne

The journal, Sibonne's gift to Nicole on her wedding day, fell open to the same entry. Nicole wanted to close the book. Reading it brought on regret mixed with finality. For her, pursuing truth often ended that way. She read the journal to comprehend her failed marriage, to understand her withdrawal from the world, to rethink the choices she had made against her faith. She was pulled to the journal to find meaning. Again, she sought an answer—why was she drawn to Athos? Because his soul was as identical to her sister's as one heartbeat is to the next?

She sped through the rereading but absorbed every detail. As the sunlight angled sharply into the nearby window, she devoured the entries one by one until the pages turned blank. Nicole lit a row of candles at the desk, and with each wick, the light penetrated further into the room and into the past. She flipped to the back flap and found, in its safe place, the charcoal drawing of Sibonne, the last one Nicole ever drew. The picture depicted life in pain.

She often drew in trance, replaying her history all the while. Sibonne was her touchstone once, before she ran away. In her absence, the months of worry had fractured Nicole. After relentless pursuit, François brought Sibonne back to the world a completely different person. He had found her bed-ridden, recovering from childbirth. Her lover had fled with the baby, and Sibonne had refused to speak.

Nicole's memories of Sibonne's young lover Remi were spotty. Nicole had met him once or twice. A blacksmith's son, Remi was lanky and a tease, and his personality complemented Sibonne's passionate nature. Both were too clever for their own good. Nicole was struggling with her own marriage, under pressure to have a child, so she had missed important details of Sibonne's blossoming relationship. Sibonne fell in love while Nicole's home-life worsened, and one day without warning, her sister fled Rochefort with her lover.

At the time, Nicole did not know Sibonne was pregnant. But, in hindsight, she understood why Sibonne didn't tell. How could her sister share such a secret when Nicole was trying desperately to produce an heir? Nicole pondered the question over many drawings.

Nicole wished Sibonne had opened up when François brought her back. Instead, she withdrew. She had every reason to; in a single stroke, she had been separated from her baby and lover. Facing such a blank future, Sibonne refused to connect with anyone or anything. So Nicole began to draw her, and it provided the tiniest opening between them because Sibonne watched the black lines become art, become her.

During that short period, Nicole realized Sibonne was broken. She had loved Remi profoundly, and life without him was a phantom existence. Like a midnight wind against a windowpane, Sibonne passed into a life of emptiness and dark. Compared to the depth of that love, Nicole's relationship with François was emotionally shallow.

In the candlelight at her desk, Nicole closed the journal as a nagging idea came into focus. She understood why Sibonne had thrown everything away, soundly rejected consequence to follow a path that jumbled her head but ignited her soul.

Love is irrational, sudden and impossible to resist.

To Nicole, the thought was a savoury morsel wrapped in a bittersweet medicine.

In the desk drawer, Nicole found a slender stick of coal and a curled-up paper. She sketched and smudged, scratched and remembered, trying to get the vision close to likeness. The image pestering her mind burned to come out. She blew coal dust and darkened the ovals to the exact shade and emotion.

Grey eyes. An ever-lasting hunger.

How could it be so? Defying her conscience, she yearned to look into those eyes again, feel the weight of his stare on her body and indulge the longing she had never felt for anyone before him.

Chapter 24
An Urgent Reconnaissance

An hour before dusk, Athos decided to follow the trail to the chalet. He had resisted all day, and his logic was exhausted. He couldn't think of any good reason to wait. He would be able to tell instantly if she had left because of him.

His horse shook its mane at the first hard jabs, but soon, the two were flying. He rode at full gallop, pushing his horse more aggressively than when he had left Paris, where the tight passageways kept his pace constrained. Without buildings and pocked streets, they sped down the path and flew over strewn foliage. The speed invigorated his purpose.

Discovering her feelings meant everything. His behaviour had not repulsed her. Nevertheless, he risked an even greater quandary. Nicole was a creature driven by virtue, and corrupting her would be the handiwork of dark forces, not an honourable soldier of the King. Uncovering her feelings endangered the moral decency of them both.

Under a chilly canopy, the woods surrounded him as he approached the chalet. The horse breathed heavily, and he tried to quiet it. Inside, the lights were saffron, lighting the tiny place like a lantern. Knocking was not an option.

He tied the horse to a tree far enough away that a whinny would get lost in the chill. The late summer temperatures did not pierce the thick overgrowth. It was truly a surreal place. The trees were tight around the chalet, forming a barrier of whispering green that stretched into the sky. It smelled of damp hay and faded flowers.

Before he had time to decide on an approach, footsteps came from a cluster of trees near the back of the chalet. Cloaked, Nicole was walking through the saplings. The oncoming dusk hid him from sight. She ducked under the overhanging limbs and side-stepped through thickets, then she was gone.

Squinting in the waning light, he began to trace her route. The dark worked against him; sound had to be his guide. He matched her footsteps from a distance to cover his pursuit, but her brushing footfalls played games with his ears. Fearing he might lose her, he abandoned stealth and patience. His feet landed with small explosive crunches. One step faster and he would be racing.

"Athos?" she called, nearer than he thought.

"Why are you running away?" he asked between quick puffs of air, finally seeing her silhouette between two trees.

"I'm not running away."

"Then why are you here?" He opened his arms, not sure whether she could see the concern on his face. "Why did you come to this chalet? These woods?"

"I could ask the same of you."

"I'm here because of what happened last night, because you are injured and because I caused it. And now I'm afraid you're running away. *From me.*"

As always, Nicole remained faultlessly steady. Though hooded, her words were strong. "I know they may seem connected, but I have other reasons for being here."

He needed to see her brown eyes. "How is your shoulder?"

"Hannah tended it very well."

"Yet you sacrificed the truth for me." He inched closer. "You lied to Hannah."

"Hannah is judgmental. I decided the details weren't necessary."

"You didn't just omit details. You changed them. Why would you be less than truthful with her? It must be for some other reason." He closed the space between them to a few feet. "The only conclusion I can draw is that you're keeping your feelings hidden. From her. *From me.*"

"This isn't my hiding place, Athos." From beneath her hood, she attempted a small smile.

He stepped closer, wanting to remove the cover. "Then why are you here if not to distance yourself from me? There seems to be no other explanation."

"Not to an outsider." Then unpredictably, from under her cape, she slid a warm palm into his. "Come with me."

The light, smoky and purple, heightened her sudden touch, which was infused with heat. She took the lead, and small landmarks began to appear on the path. A knotty log, an arch between two trees. And then a paper crane. And another and another, until the trees became background. The cranes blew gently, tottering from string, hanging in droves from low branches.

"Your cranes," he said, making no attempt to conceal his fascination. He walked into her but stepped back when she let go of his hand and dropped to a knee. Her attention focused on a round stone at the foot of a subtle rise in the moss.

"I buried my sister here seventeen years ago." From the side, the cloak hid her face.

He lost all clarity. "This isn't a cemetery. It's not holy ground."

"The way she died wouldn't allow it. Still, many don't know the truth."

"Why are you here? To mourn? Why now?"

"When my life becomes confusing, I drift back to the past. Her history, my history."

"Tell me *why*."

She laid a hand on the gravestone. "She was very much like you. She loved someone completely, and lost them because of betrayal. It changed her. Broke her. She refused to live."

"How did she—" A cold sweat covered his brow.

"The cliff in the village. Many people to this day think she fell."

He saw his own deadly ledge in Paris. The feeling he experienced before leaping off the tavern roof pricked him again like a thousand thorns. He could not describe the overwhelming pull of the edge, the compulsion he felt before the jump. Now, standing near Nicole, the pull was to her.

"I was responsible for her death." She stood and gathered her dress. "She ran away with her lover but left me a note in secret to reveal where they were hiding, and I selfishly gave the information to François to bring her back."

She kept her eyes on the stone and its engraving: *Sibonne Tremon. Beloved Sister.* "I betrayed her. I should have let her live in peace.

It was the biggest mistake of my life." Then she said, not to the grave, but to him, "I do not wish to make it again."

The hood fell back to show her pained expression. "Athos, I know why you're here. You're here because you have been trying to take your own life."

Athos felt the smarting radiate from the base of his neck. "The Comte told you."

She didn't need to nod or answer. A rush of blood loaded his veins and boxed his mind. "You've been trying to save me, too." The words stung his tongue. His disbelief triggered a reflexive need for his sword. All the clues made sense. She wanted to save him, not love him. "You've known all along."

She stepped back, but he grunted for her to halt. His thoughts darkened, battling for ground—her misdeed against his need to be with her. "You're telling me because you can't stand to lie anymore."

She nodded. "Because you're hurting—"

He scrambled to her, imposing the force of his entire being in a single move. He grabbed her wrists through the cloak, catching her from buckling. "But you're lying about something else, too. You're lying to yourself. You *know* you are."

She twisted her hands. "Please, Athos. I'm sorry for concealing what I knew."

"It's amazing how one lie can lead to another, isn't it?" He could smell coal and clover, a temptation like none other, transforming his emotions from derision to desire.

"You deserve the truth," she whispered, eyes closed and body inflexible.

"Then tell me the truth, Nicole." He brushed her cheek with his lips, skin coveting skin. "Is it so hard to say?"

Then he paused over her lips, his anticipation more seductive than the moment before winning a duel. "Say it, Nicole. Tell me you feel what I feel. Tell me you love me." He pushed his lips onto her mouth, and he felt no inkling of hesitation from her. Her reaction was not to hold back. She responded equally, laying aside self-control, and countered with power. His first stolen kiss by the pond paled to her surrender now. If anything, she savoured the release, too. Her lips were not like he remembered a woman's.

They were softer, fuller, sweeter. Milady had been so young when he first kissed her. Nicole was a mature woman. To Athos, it was the difference between cinder and inferno.

The cover of night made him bold, and his hands discovered warmth and willingness inside her cloak. She became a night-blooming jasmine, radiating from his touch. She opened to his roaming hands, reversing any doubts he had about his advance. She was inviting him in. In awe, he relished her vulnerability and held her tighter. Her reaction told him everything she was powerless to say.

He dropped his mouth to her throat and kissed it with each whisper.

"You're water to a stone." The years of his celibacy were a mockery in the circle of her body. "Even the most solid are worn away."

He tilted her head to see her radiance. "Say it. Let me live."

Her lips were red and wet from his boldness. "Athos, you ask the impossible."

"I ask the sacred."

She fell into another kiss but just as quickly pushed back, trepidation racing through her eyes. Then he heard it, too. Something, or someone, approached in the woods.

Chapter 25
The Family Secret

Heavy footsteps crushed the undergrowth. Athos knew better than to trust the encroaching dark. He hastily let Nicole go and backed off, damning the interruption.

"Your body tells me everything," he said, a few steps from her, "and soon your words will do the same."

Athos's abdomen ached from the separation, but he put more distance between them. He never left her eyes, seeing for the first time that her self-control had fully deteriorated. She pulled her hood over her face and hid the feelings he knew filled her heart.

"Nicole!" Cordes' voice, typically deep and sober, sounded shrill. He still hadn't spotted them as he yelled from the tree cover. "I'm sorry to disturb you, but Hannah … there's … she's … It's the baby's time!"

Cordes stumbled over a fern before he found them. He eyed both curiously when he realized Athos was also at the gravesite.

"Monsieur Athos? We left you at the château, no?"

"I thought Nicole might need me."

"Did you say something about the baby?" Nicole redirected. "Is Hannah in labour?"

"She thinks it's time, Madame," Cordes' characteristic calm was outweighed by urgency.

Nicole flashed a look to Athos, and both blurted, *"Pierre."*

Cordes and Athos, coachman and outrider, soon raced from the chalet. Athos rode ahead of the carriage to reach Pierre and Duchy first and prepare them to leave. He arrived just as the waning daylight turned to dark.

Urged out in the courtyard, Pierre argued adamantly with Athos about riding in the coach.

"I nearly beat you at our last sword lesson wearing this bandage," Pierre protested, refusing to follow Duchy inside the carriage. "I'll get there much quicker if you let me ride my horse!"

"It's time to start thinking more of others and less of yourself. You won't do Hannah and your new-born any favours by needing as much care as they do when you arrive," Athos said, unclipped by the protests. "Besides, when will you ever see the inside of a carriage again?"

"I've seen plenty!"

Athos shoved the youth in, by then convinced there wasn't a single spot on the estate too sacred for Pierre's sexual liaisons.

"How will I be of any use tonight anyway?" Pierre shouted from a coach window as the rig lurked to a start. A lantern on an exterior hook rattled as Cordes picked up speed. Pierre refused to relent. "I just need to be handy when my namesake is ready to duel."

Using his sword, Athos swatted the door near the tips of Pierre's fingers, despite the fact that the squabble was helping Athos stay focused. If he allowed his thoughts to go where he most wanted, he would have out-distanced the coach. His soul could have flown back to the chalet without a horse.

Nicole's heart is mine. As imperfect as the world may be, she is mine.

★★★

Duchy barred the men from the chalet. Half-heartedly, they opted for various distractions in the night air to endure the wait. It was too dark to fence, so Athos and Pierre arm-wrestled until pain got the best of the young challenger.

"Have you ever held a new-born?" Pierre asked Athos.

"No, though a christening is quite enough of a spectacle to get the idea," Athos said, his mood light. "What will you do now, Pierre? Your plate fills tonight with immense responsibility."

"To be honest, I'm not sure."

Cordes chuckled, sitting on a stump and carving a small spoon out of a piece of soft wood. "You'll get used to it. My first was a ghastly terror, but the next three, well, let's just say, you get used to it." He tossed the tiny spoon to Pierre.

After several hours, the three wandered off in different directions. Athos found refuge at the back of the chalet where a curtained window was outlined in lamplight, most likely where the three women toiled. He tried to imagine their labour, but his mind was wrapped around the kiss in the forest. Nicole had responded deeply. Inside, she probably huddled near Hannah's sweat-streaked brow, offering supportive words and a cool rag, thinking little of the man who had compromised her faith with desire.

She's in her element. Surrounded by the people she uplifted, this place was hers. He was a misshapen key. Against every principle, except one, she had reached out to him. She had been swayed by love.

The front door creaked open. He sprinted around the corner to find Nicole stone-still in the quiet. When she saw him, her expression was a mixture of relief and fatigue.

"Where's Pierre?" she said, hugging her shawl around herself.

"He and Cordes have gone off to wait. Is it over?"

"Yes, the baby is here. Healthy and hungry."

"You must be pleased."

She nodded. "I have a new member of my family."

"*Your* family?"

"Pierre is my sister's only son," and without warning, she faltered, white and listless. Athos caught her before she reached the ground.

"Does he know?"

"I've never told him," she said. "Is he far from here? Don't let him know. I don't want him to know."

The warmth of her body hours ago had disappeared.

"Why are you telling me this?" he said in a low tone, instinctually checking for unwelcome ears.

"I don't know." She blinked and gripped her shawl. "You'll do the right thing. Just find him." With help, she stood up and leaned on the door. "Bring him here."

Athos scoured the nearby woods, whistling and shouting. Cordes came first from the direction of the coach. They redoubled the effort. Knowing little of the lay of the land, Athos mounted a search from the only path he knew, the one to the grave. It seemed shorter this time, and he came to its end with a foreboding feeling.

Pierre knelt at the headstone, engrossed by its engraving. He looked serious and puzzled. "Who is Sibonne Tremon?"

Do not let him know. Compelled by Pierre's confusion, Athos extended an arm. "I think the answer you seek can be found elsewhere."

"Do you see? This is my family name. This woman died the year I was born."

"I've never held a new-born, Pierre. Tonight, you are blessed with the very thing that moves men to pursue noble causes. Come, meet your daughter."

"A girl?" Pierre finally bolted up from the ground. "I have a daughter."

"Waiting for her father." A ripple of sorrow came with it. Athos knew the chance he might have a child was as likely as beating loaded dice.

"Have you seen her?" Pierre stood, the gravestone a distant concern.

"Not yet. Let's go see her together."

The cottage was warm from a crisp fire in the hearth that filled the room with a feeling of security. Everyone surrounded Hannah and the baby, both swaddled in blankets, propped up on a loveseat next to the fire. The baby's face peeked out from her wrap. Pierre froze in wonder until the child wiggled.

"I like the name Sophia," Hannah chimed to him.

"It's Greek, like the name Athos." But Nicole did not acknowledge him when she said it.

Look at me. Let me know you are mine. Even a glance would be a small sign that their kiss held equal importance in her heart. "Sophia means wisdom," he said.

She nodded once. A subtle reaction, if anything. Only he noticed the self-consciousness weighing her down. She clasped her hands in her lap and tucked in her elbows. She never looked up.

A numbing sensation started in his legs and crept into his stomach. He stepped out of the firelight and into the shadows where he could watch her more blatantly. Light from the fire flickered across her profile. Pierre picked up the tiny bundle that was his new daughter, and Nicole smiled weakly. Her attention soon turned again to the flames, not to anyone else, especially Athos. Her affections were shielded, and he'd only created the need to reinforce the armour.

Athos backed up to the door. Except for Nicole, the others laughed at the new-born's delights, and he slipped into the night. *Alone again. As it should be.* Inside the idle carriage, he pulled the curtains shut, removed his weapons and coat, and waited.

Chapter 26
A Carriage Ride

The birds started singing long before daylight when the coach door opened.

"Such faithfulness." Athos spoke lower than a hush, stretching a hand out to Nicole. "You won't miss Mass, even on a birthday."

She settled quickly into the opposite seat, closing the door fast before Cordes could suspect anything. "You left us last night, again without saying good-bye."

"When were you planning on telling Pierre about his mother?"

"Thank you for keeping my secret." Her brow wrinkled with worry but evened out with the first jerk of the carriage.

"I found him at the grave," Athos said. "He wanted to know if the Tremon in the ground was his namesake. There's no keeping it from him now."

"I've put it off too long. François doesn't want him to know. My husband objects to transferring any privilege to a bastard relation."

"You seem to conspire frequently with a man you rarely see." Athos shifted his weight in her direction. "How do I fit into your plots?"

Warily, she crossed her arms at the waist.

"Am I actually needed in Nantes?" Athos asked. "Or was that a lie to get me out of Paris?"

"My husband *does* need your help. He has plans for you. I swear, your stay here is temporary."

"Why isn't he here? He left you alone to deal with me."

"François believed you would reject him or worse," she said.

"Then you knew what came between us in Paris. How I provoked him."

"He told me about your state of mind, like my sister's," Nicole said. "I haven't meant to cause you pain, only to offer peace and perhaps distract you from your suffering. It's been a poor attempt at healing. I'm sorry."

"Sorry?" His distaste for the lies might pass, if he could heard her speak her heart. "For concealing what you knew about me? Or being untrue to *your* heart? You don't love your husband, do you?"

He pinched a pleat at her knee. Her hands fidgeted above the fold, and a quiver ran down her.

"You don't love him," he said, the confidence clear in his voice. "You know it and have lived with it for a very long time. Your marriage and your faith are at odds."

"He was involved in my sister's death." Her frankness came in a flood. "He was acting honourably, but he took no pity on her or the young man she loved. If he had used restraint, it may have ended differently. But she's gone, and I can't bring her back. It's hard for me to overcome the blame I feel for his role. Or for mine. I search myself daily for any seed of forgiveness. And one day, I will forgive him as I should."

"But you don't love him."

She twirled her wedding ring under her glove and after a long breath looked toward the window as if she could divine the future. "He loves *me* dearly. I'm his shining prize. He was taken with me long ago, by desire, and no less by the position he secured in marrying me … the same year my parents died."

He knelt at her feet. "You could have grown to love him. You didn't."

He reached for her shoes and removed them, testing her tolerance of his freedom. She rested her head on the seat cushion and allowed the gentle liberties, the scandalous strokes. He caressed her ankles and slowly moved up her calves. He grazed his lips across her skirt at the knee.

"We share more than a kiss. We share a shaken faith. I think my salvation is impossible," he said, reaching behind her knees, "as adamantly as you deny the feelings in your heart." He felt goose bumps through her stockings.

"Wait," she said, reaching down. "What you are saying may be true, but I'm not yours. *I am anything but free*. I'm simply a woman, not an ideal wife or the perfect Catholic. I'm a woman struggling to keep her family together. See me for who I am—flawed but trying to live honourably. You're a stranger who has seen my life's impossible knots. I'm not sure how, but you did.

"You," she traced the scar on his face. "What do I know about *you*? That you are hurt inside and out. That someone you loved betrayed you. That's all I know. How can I truly love you if that's all I know?"

He squeezed her calves, and she took him by the shoulders.

"You're damaged so painfully that you throw God and people aside. You're a sceptic of any care. You're a casket, filling with water, chained on all sides. How can anyone bring love into a life as locked away as yours?"

He rose up abruptly, flattening against his seat.

"Let me see your hands." She grasped his wrists and turned his hands up and over, inspecting the old wounds. "These are the hands and the body of a man. No more, no less. You're not a fiend or a monster, unworthy of love, and you're not cursed. You're a man who has suffered in unspeakable ways and now wishes to be free."

She pushed his sleeves above the elbows and gently rubbed the scars. "And these marks of valour, they are the mercies you sought." She stopped when she felt the silver cuff on his upper arm. She drew back the sleeve and sighed.

"A fleur-de-lis." She touched it with a fingertip. "You're not a criminal either."

He shoved down the sleeve, and she inched away. A silence hung between them like the ghost of Milady in his dreams. He felt exposed, no veil to hide behind. Her assessment of him was accurate. Inspired truth. She settled back into her seat and looked away from his shame.

She knows me better than God.

His reverence for her grew. He knelt before her again, as if taking the sacrament. He leaned up, stroked her cheek and took a kiss.

The taste of her lips spilled the tension in his chest. She granted him the freedom to flee the pain. The freedom to touch her.

She set limits without speaking a single word. She guided him to lips, neck, wrists, but no more, and he treated them like fragile glass. Summoning his immense will power, he resisted pushing her for more. He yearned to burn past the barriers but was careful to honour her boundaries. The blaze within him torched a mass of bad memories in a pyre.

Their breathing became synchronized, rumbling through them and tempting a height beyond purity. Yet he felt more pure in Nicole's arms than at any moment since his last confession, so long ago. The carriage rolled on, and Athos confessed. *I love you. I am in love.* Over and over, intent on honesty, on imprinting Nicole with his fierce longing. In her eyes, with each declaration, he knew he sealed his future to hers.

By the time the coach halted at the mew stiles near the church, the taut rope of his self-control was on the verge of snapping. "You know this is a sin," he managed to say while burying a kiss on the sash beneath her chest.

"But not adultery." She placed her lips to a scar on his open palm.

At the staging area, Cordes dismounted, and from the drawn curtain, Nicole quickly asked him to run an errand. "I'll only be a moment," she told Cordes.

Making another sweep of her neck, Athos remarked on her coolness under pressure. "You behave as if you've been a mistress before."

"Come in with me."

He jerked back instantly, astonished. "To Mass?"

"If you leave the carriage now, Cordes will be gone and you can walk home after Mass. We can sit in different pews. No one will know we're together."

"This," he said, pointing down, "is beautiful folly." Then he pointed out, "That, is certain Hell."

"It doesn't have to be that way."

"Nicole," he said, clipping her chin. "I haven't practiced my faith in a decade, and I've drawn you completely off centre. Now you want to drag my damned soul into your church? I would ask what has come over you, but I believe I already know the answer."

"You're not damned."

"And you have yet to say to me the one thing I want to hear most." He kissed her again. "I'm in love with you." Another kiss. "Let me hear you say it, too."

She bowed her head, as in prayer. "You admit the most intimate feelings for me, but you keep something close to you, something that separates you from others. Your life is clouded in pain. You lock it behind iron. Please open up, Athos, and not just about your love for me."

She squeezed his hand and waited. Finally, she turned toward the door. "Come inside," she said, "and let me in. Let God in." She opened the carriage door and stepped off. His arms fell back to his sides, and he sat dead-still. She paused several seconds before closing the door as gently as a lid on a coffin.

Chapter 27
Her Prayer and His Confession

She dipped the tips of her fingers in the holy water at the stoup and walked solemnly to a pew. She began a silent prayer as she made the sign of the cross.

Dear God, What has come over me? I feel glorious and frightened all at once. My hands tremble but my heart flies. I am straying, but I feel I have dug up a pearl hidden in the deepest ocean inscribed with my name. It is the water's depth that scares me. I beg your forgiveness but at the same time offer you my thanks. Blessed be the mystery, the wrong and the right. I will never truly understand. Show me the way.

★★★

Athos left the coach and approached the entrance of Notre Dame de la Tronchaye as the choir inside began Mass. The thick doors represented a passage he had never intended to cross alive. He gazed up at the pale sky while a faint wind nipped his shirtsleeves. He needed an inkling of composure.

A starless night, away from people and fire and earthly distractions, only a black moon.

He stealthily pushed one side of the double entry. Its dark iron hinges swung open without a sound. He found a vacant pew near the back. No one turned to acknowledge him, not even the baby thrown over a shoulder three rows ahead, who was fascinated by a mote of dust.

He last visited a church for Porthos' wedding, and Athos had not taken communion. Inside Nicole's sanctuary, he was reminded of a deep snow he had travelled through on a mission for the King—beautiful—but menacing. The grand designs of a church were purposeful—to calm the masses into thinking all the circumstances and drudgery of life changed upon entering. His purpose was to soothe his soul in another way.

He scanned the back of the heads. No Nicole. Sliding to the other end of the empty pew, he resumed his search until he found her. She was not sitting near the front, as Athos would have guessed, but four rows from the back by a group of older women. He was near enough to see her eyes closed in prayer.

What am I doing? He fought for an ounce of sanity. She was devoted to God, but he couldn't help returning to the recent hours when her baser human qualities surfaced. She was as real, weak and yearning as he was. He wanted her more. He wanted every fragment of detail. Being near her, even in church, fed his self-indulgence, though here the barriers were much thicker than the sash around her body.

Father Audric began the sermon.

"In Revelations, Jesus redeemed His people and made them priests like Himself before His future fulfilment in glory. As the scripture says 'He is coming amid the clouds and every eye will see Him, even those who pierced Him.' For the faithful, this seeing is the completion and the acceptance of Jesus. For the unbeliever, it is the judgment and lament.'"

Emptiness filled Athos's lungs. Nevertheless, he waited for communion with a stillness rivalling death. He wanted to see her receive. She rose for the ritual, followed the faithful line, crossed her body, and summoned peace as the bread of life mixed with her blood. A lifetime had passed since he had done the same, but he knew the feeling well. It was a melting oblivion, like her skin on his tongue, fortifying his body with salt and the impressions of salvation.

Without a doubt, my soul is damned.

She might contest it, say it wasn't so, but to sit in a house of God, without a splinter of reverence—desiring a woman bound to it—sealed his damnation. She was a devotee; he would never be one again.

Why does she want me here? To remind me of my wrongs? To bring me back to God? He dug his nails into his palms and waited for more singing. Athos believed no one knew he came or left.

Outside, by the carriage, Cordes scratched a sideburn, appearing more astounded than the previous night when he saw Athos at the grave. "I'm beginning to believe you are a spectre," Cordes said, shaking his head. "I don't suppose you'll tell me how you managed to get here?"

"I need a horse."

"You're lucky I have my three best. Take the mare," Cordes said, beginning to rework the harnesses.

"And what do I tell Madame?" Cordes asked toward the slump of Athos's back.

"Whatever you like."

Athos walked the horse up the cottage-lined street and turned a corner. Flower boxes decorated window sills with day lilies that drooped in the heat. He walked toward an open end in the street and took a turn down an isolated alley.

His mind overflowed with images. The grave, her kisses, her face lit by the chalet's firelight, the tight seam at her waist where he sinfully placed his mouth. And the stained glass. The jewels of her church, pure inspiration in one set of eyes, useless idolatry in another.

The tunnel-like alley echoed with ordinary sounds. Children laughed from a second story as a maid threw basins of grey water from a low window. Doors opened and closed. Feet pattered. Life went on. The bells of the church rang.

Over his sagging shoulders, a voice travelled down the narrow street. "You came into my church." She stood at the alley's opening.

He slapped the horse's haunch. "How did you know?"

"Our priest."

"He told you a stranger had come inside?" he asked.

"He said my guest might be in need of his host."

He did not return her smile. "He knows about me? About us?"

"He knows who you are but not what has passed between us." She searched in his eyes for approval. "Father Audric asked to meet you."

The nail marks in his hand throbbed. "Is that why you wanted me to come to Mass?"

"No, Athos. I want you to be whole. It's one way of making you heal," she said, approaching him full of purpose. "He actually knows very little."

"Including your true feelings."

"I'm confident I can handle those," she said measurably lower.

"And what should I to say to your priest? That I'm in a one-sided love affair with one of his most devoted followers?"

"Tell him the truth about your life," she said. "Ask for forgiveness."

The horse whinnied and danced, and Athos shouldered the animal to a standstill. When she came within reach, she dangled her fingers under his, playing them like a trickle of water.

"Nicole, I don't believe in the power of God to save me. I've been truthful about my feelings for you. Now you ask for more."

He grabbed her fingers, trying to coax her closer. She resisted.

"I want you to let go of your pain. You must unburden your conscience." She glanced over her shoulder. "He's waiting."

At the end of the alley, a figure covered in clerical robes moved into view. The small-framed man with thinning hair waved once to Nicole. She meekly waved back.

"You couldn't keep from telling him my story," Athos said, mesmerized by the man standing in the way.

Her eyes hinted slightly of anguish. "He's my confessor."

The priest waited.

The thought pained him: *She wants the truth out, and this is her answer—a man of the church, a confession.* Bile tainted his throat. Believing there to be no other escape, he yanked the horse around and began a dignified march toward the crossroads.

"Madame Rieux." Nodding, Father Audric chose the path of least resistance. "Pleasant to see you again. And will you introduce your guest?"

"Father Audric, this is Monsieur Athos," she said.

The priest clasped his hands and nodded more to the side. There seemed no loftiness about him, unlike the men of the cloth Athos had known, particularly Aramis.

"What were your thoughts of this morning's Mass?" Father Audric asked in a cautious inflection.

"Father Audric," Athos began, "have you ever served men in war? Priests simply take confessions on the battlefield, often at the sides of fallen men. Confessions are rampant from the dying, the wounded, the sleepless and the drunk."

"No, I can't say—"

"I find it comforting that absolution may be sought at any moment." His eyes went to Nicole.

"Athos," she said, a subtle hitch in her voice. "There is privacy—"

"No." He looked back to the priest. "Confession is critically important to men in need, at any time, at any place. Wouldn't you agree, Father?"

"It's certainly an important part of devotional life," the priest said, perplexed.

"There's no forgiveness without it," Athos said. "No freeing of the soul, no room for the heart to grow and heal. When will you take a confession? Any time it is offered?"

"I'd say, yes, at any time."

"Then hear mine. *Now.*"

"What?" Father Audric tugged at the slack in his robe to step forward. "You want to offer a confession? Here in the street?"

A clattering wagon crossed behind in the main road.

"Athos." Nicole shook her head slowly, but it signalled only fear.

Athos knelt before them, his jaw set. "Forgive me, Father, for I have sinned."

"This is quite unorthodox, Monsieur," the priest said flummoxed. "This is no battlefield, and you appear as healthy as I am. We're only a few blocks from the church, and your confession is a private matter, not for the ears of a female or anyone else for that matter." The priest's eyes darted from windows to doors.

For once, Athos craved water instead of wine. "I confessed the day before I wed a woman I loved so immensely my life changed forever. If there was any sin in my love for her, it was that I loved too much. I devoted myself to her happiness and pleasure, and I vowed to God to give her my name and fortune, which I did willingly and without expectation."

"Athos—" But with a raised hand, Father Audric stopped Nicole from going on.

"I was her disciple, and my desire for her consumed my consciousness. It was what made her downfall my complete undoing. You see, she was a branded woman." His pitch strained. "And for a brief moment, I contemplated living her lie without question.

I loved her beyond reason, but it wasn't enough. My honour stood in the way. It was drilled into me, and I couldn't forsake it, not even for her, my magnificent, beautiful mistake, Anne. Her deception shook my honour at its roots, and I changed into a foul-hearted rot of a man." He searched for words, his eyes darkening.

"She and I were alone in the woods when I discovered her most despicable secret. A brand on her left shoulder. A fleur-de-lis." He clinched the silver cuff under his shirt, pulsating with history. "She had hidden it from me, and I exploded with hatred because of the traitor she was to my devotion. The brand was the breaking point of my trust. She never admitted to any of her lies. Ever. And there were many."

Athos went from the priest's pale face to hers. "So I bound her wrists and lashed her behind a stallion. I damned her to what I knew to be an immoral death. For many years, I couldn't remember what I had done, only that the pain of her deception ruined me absolutely. I—I still have her blood on my hands."

He squeezed his palms, the visions clear only to him.

"That's when it happened. That was the moment of my separation." He looked at the priest. "I loved her so much I abandoned God; for when she fell, He abandoned me. So I picked up the sword and went to my King. The single virtue I had left was honour, and with it I believed I had the ability to crush the memories that poisoned my heart. I fought without fear. I took the sword and pistol to my bed.

"And many times, I used them and felt no remorse. I decapitated men, pulled bowels from flesh, severed arms and feet and blinded undeserving rogues. The entire time, I accepted my ruthlessness as an ugly result of what I had become.

"But blood has given me little comfort. I've never upheld the blade as anything nobler than agony. This heroism marking my body," he said, slapping his chest, "is a charade. Each old wound equals pain and underneath each one lives an unconscious wish to die. But that realization—that dawned on me very late in this life."

He bowed his head and lowered his voice. "My journey, you must know, was torture. Enough to break any man, but I endured. Until I saw my wife again. I discovered her alive last year. She had survived my brutality." Near tears, Nicole leaned into the priest, who clutched her waist to steady them both.

"She had survived my mindless revenge, and her beauty wasn't spoiled. Not outwardly, but inside she had changed into a demon, a woman named Milady. She was a creature of hate. During our separation, her cruelty had been magnified. My rejection had sent her deeper into malevolence. Perhaps if I had offered her forgiveness, she could have lived a different life. I could have lived a different life. But I didn't. My heart hardened. She lived to seduce a young man I considered my son, and she devised a plan so devious it ended the life of the Duke of Buckingham."

"The Duke of Buckingham?" the priest asked, articulating each syllable.

"The very one. Her fiendishness spread beyond the crimes she was branded for. But the damage to us was done long before her return. My life was waste, as was hers."

A long moment passed before Athos spoke again.

"Father, is there a penance for the greatest of sins? Voracious desire, hate, loss of faith and guilt that wipes away your mind?" Athos searched intently in Nicole's eyes—for her forgiveness. Neither Nicole nor the priest were able to speak, let alone comprehend.

"And yet, I live. And, unbelievably, I hope. Hope is a puzzling human trait. It remains inside us whether life gives us beauty or injustice."

Distant street noise echoed in the alley. The three held still.

"What happened to her?" Nicole asked, barely audible. Athos rose from his stupor.

"She had killed Buckingham, so I wasn't alone in her pursuit. The swath of her destruction dug her grave. Ten men were in agreement. We hunted her, and then beheaded her. I arranged and witnessed the act myself."

He backed away and stuck a hand under the nose of the horse, which snuffled and nibbled the empty palm. Then he grabbed the mane and swung up without benefit of a saddle.

Nicole took a step. The priest waved his hands. "I forbid it, Nicole."

She hesitated. "Where are you going?"

His heart whispered a tender good-bye. "The truth is yours now. Unfortunately, it's also still mine." He moved the horse to within a few feet of her and handed over a letter from inside his coat. The wax seal was broken, and recognition dawned in her eyes. The letter from the Comte to Athos, now entrusted to her. Athos tapped his mount and disappeared around the corner.

Chapter 28
Without Resolution

The wind from an imminent afternoon storm carried grit into Athos's face and stung his eyes. His tongue and lips were dry. He felt spent and powerless to control the trembling, but he rode on.

He gave the horse free reign. His destination was pointless, now that his fate was not rigged to any real purpose. When his senses returned, Athos realized the mare had brought him to a fitting end. The pond by her willow.

After a long drink, the horse grazed in the nearby field. At the pond's edge, Athos let the water soak his boots. A dragonfly zipped along the surface. From a patch of cattails, he dislodged a stem, dug a thumb into the brown comb and separated the spores. A puff fell away and another and another, aimlessly, until the clumps disappeared underwater. He crumpled the stalk and squeezed it in a tight fist.

A stagnant aroma lifted off the water. He knew it well, the stench of decay. He sunk his hands into the shallow mud, and the water splashed a lament. The mud covered the imperfect scars on his palms and fingers and backs of his hands. His whole being craved the cover.

He had gambled that dragging the truth into the sunlight might make it evaporate or smooth over its imperfections. He was mistaken. Sunlight also had the propensity to burn. He was scorched to a crackling black.

He burrowed his hands deeper into the soft mud. If he stayed a few careless seconds underwater, the pain would cease.

At the abyss, he caught his reflection in the water, fell to his knees and wept.

***

A firm squeeze returned Nicole's swirling thoughts to the church. She sat in the front pew. Father Audric emphasized the end of their prayer with a purposeful hold on her icy hands.

"A-men," he said in two distinct beats.

"Amen," she repeated.

"Be ready by noon tomorrow to leave. I'll send my valet to escort you here, and then we shall leave on your pilgrimage." He studied the glass window depicting the Resurrection. "You understand I forbid you to continue to be in his company."

"Isn't there a prayer of forgiveness for him?" She gaped at the same window.

"Your compassion is truly limitless." The priest, brimming with calm, headed in the direction of his study. "It would take eons of prayer to absolve him."

"He simply loved the wrong woman."

"A woman sent by the dark angel himself," Father Audric countered. "A most extreme test, which he didn't pass. Nicole, leave him be. Gather your wits and belongings and leave him to God."

When she returned to the carriage, her stomach ached. It was because of her that Athos came into her church. Because of her, the horrifying confession spilled out.

Cordes waited, having arranged the coach to manage without the horse he gave Athos.

"Cordes, what would a man do if he found himself hopelessly lost?" Nicole was not expecting a useful answer.

"Ask for directions?" He shook his head. "Well, perhaps not."

"Lost inside," she said, fatigued. "Lost inside."

"Oh, now that's a different matter entirely but not at all difficult to answer," Cordes said, giving her a hand up. "He'd drink."

Chapter 29
Anointment

The door to Pierre's cottage lay flat on the ground like a ship's plank. Nicole's determination withered at the thought of crossing into the lair, where the only wine on the property could be found.

"Athos?" she finally called out.

A dirty hand grabbed the door frame before Athos stuck his head into the sinking afternoon light. He squinted.

"Ah, Madame, I hope you brought more wine. There's very little left for you to join in the party." He ducked back into the shadow, and she recovered her courage.

It took several seconds for her eyes to adjust, but the interior was always barren, and the décor had not changed. Athos sat on the stool, reclining on the opposite wall, his shirt untucked.

"How much have you had?" she asked.

"Not enough to forget."

"Athos, you confessed."

He grunted. "And received absolution?" He waited for a response. "Your silence tells me otherwise."

"It went straight to God's ears," she said.

"And to yours. You don't need to appease me or pretend my life is salvageable."

"I wanted to make certain—"

"Make certain I didn't hurt myself?" he asked bitingly.

"Assure you that you simply loved the wrong woman."

Despite the drinking, he stood straight up and kept his balance. "I'm doomed to repeat the same mistake."

"How do you know you love me? Perhaps it's only my concern for your well-being that makes you feel the way you do."

"How does a doe know its mother? A bird, how to nest? Instinct." He raised his opaque cup to swirl the wine inside.

She became conscious of her every breath. He moved defiantly closer.

"You know, I've seen you before," Athos said, "in Paris. You attended a parade of Italians for the King at Le Louvre."

"That was several years ago. My last trip. I don't remember seeing you."

"I couldn't keep my eyes off you," he said. "But, I know what you are thinking now. You're thinking I could have had any woman there that day. And, you're probably right. They were perfumed and beautiful—perfect, truly—and many were flirting with Musketeers. But you stood out. You were different. You're the one I chose." He brushed a hand down her jaw.

"Chose?"

"To make love to in my mind." His whole hand cupped her chin. "You see, after Milady, the one sin I've avoided is seducing women. I've had no indulgences of the flesh to confess. Only impure thoughts of them. Impure thoughts of you."

"You've had no lover, no mistress?"

"Never. My wife's deception shattered my trust, along with the rest of my life."

Nicole sat hard on the dirt floor, out of reach of his caressing hand.

"No affair of any kind?" she asked.

"Not—a single—person."

"Until now," she whispered, the pieces falling into place. He had never touched another woman. Never held one. Never kissed another's lips. "Until me."

He crouched, looking straight into her. "You're the first I've allowed."

His expression searched for understanding. *And permission.*

"May I?" he asked, touching the buttons on her neckline one by one. She closed her eyes and felt the tiniest pressure on her throat as he undid the first.

She swallowed for air. "Your hands are dirty."

"Hope has saved me again. Here you are, before me. What am I to make of that?"

She opened her eyes as he pulled a kerchief from a pocket and rubbed wine on his muddy palms.

"My handkerchief?"

"And your blood." He rubbed the darkest marks on the cloth and placed it on the petite mattress. He stared at the bed. "Are you afraid? Afraid to be with me?"

The buttons tightened around her airway, and a sudden surge of desire pulsed through her. The smell of wine on his breath deepened the intoxication of her yearning. "It's not a question of fear. I'm not afraid of you, but what would be the outcome of us being together? You know the answer."

"My immortality," he said, "the one outcome blood and steel couldn't give me."

"And my fall." The real truth, she thought. Yet she knew he was also right. Surrendering to him completely could end his spiralling decline. His confession in the street had been the testimony. On his body lay the evidence and, possibly, the answer to the question ripping at her heart: Should she give in to desire and love him? Or not?

She gently tugged his loose shirttail. "Show me how you've suffered. I must see it."

Uncharacteristically, he hesitated. She saw he was ashamed because their fate might rest on his bare skin. He ran both hands roughly through his sandy-coloured hair, contemplating the inevitable, then quickly pulled the shirt over his head and tossed it to the door. She thought she was prepared, but tremors started immediately in her stomach. Trembling, she covered her mouth.

"My God," she breathed.

His torso was a hieroglyph of pain.

On his side, a gash of mismatched scars ran over and back in a gruesome jumble. It cut a permanent indention into the flank of his physique. She realized it should have been a mortal wound, whatever the cause, which one in a thousand men might survive. Months of agony to heal. She attempted a gentle pass over its unevenness but quickly brought her hand back to a large teardrop at the corner of her mouth.

The scar was the worst of many.

"Now you see me for what I am," he said.

Nicole felt immersed in his pain. It was her chief virtue and flaw, the ability to empathize but the inability to distance herself from the anguish of others, and Athos was like no one before. Here before her, she saw why. He needed healing of a deeper dimension. She cried for both the extent of his injuries and her growing feelings of love. They could only lead to compromises in her faith and fidelity, for she could not deny her heart was defeating reason.

He wiped her tears and placed her palms on his chest. He rolled her sleeves to the elbows, tracing the soft undersides of her arms. She allowed him to guide her soft touch over the injuries—from his neck to the band of his trousers. She understood many of his scars had never been touched before, and with her tears, she anointed all that were bare.

"Tell me you desire more, too." He said, when she buried her forehead into his chest. Nicole heard his heartbeat quicken. She clutched his shoulders, her knuckles white. A rain had begun in the field. The smell of the storm made her long for a blanket, for warmth and privacy. He rubbed the small of her back and waited a long time for an answer. In their embrace, she cried softly.

"It's all right. I ask more than I should," he said. "But I need to go. You know I can't stay. I'll be in my room tonight but only tonight. If you want me for any reason, come to me. I'll wait until dawn and leave without fail. You've done more for me here than you know."

He kissed her forehead, pressing deeply as if for the last time, reached for his shirt and vanished into the rain.

Chapter 30
Her Decision

The rain dampened Athos's clothes before he entered the grand foyer. He was dizzy and exhausted and saw no one on the long walk up to his bedroom.

It was dusk. His bed was crisply tucked, and a basin of clear water sat on the sideboard. He wiped droplets from his hair with a towel and washed his hands, finally removing all the dirt.

No fresh clothes were laid out. Ambivalently, he sat near the table in his wet shirt and pants. Grooming in anticipation of her was unnecessary. He had asked her to disregard her faith and take a road of lesser integrity, and he was safe in assuming she would choose higher ground. Her declaration in the carriage confirmed it: *I am anything but free.*

Her choice to let him go was pure Nicole. He still felt connected to her whether or not she threw away everything to be his lover, his saviour. She had not been repulsed by the sight of his body. Quite the opposite. She had mourned over it. She had been deeply touched by his pain. Nicole lived on a higher plane, and he could admire from below without harm. Less fulfilling for him on Earth, but little devastation for her in Heaven.

I love her without prejudice.

Under his sleeve, he firmly took hold of the silver fleur-de-lis cuff, and it came off painlessly. The silver band dropped to his wrist, and he rubbed the grooves of the imprint. For many years, he wore it to remember the wickedness of love. It had been Anne's wedding gift. After her fall from grace, he stamped it with the fleur-de-lis to signify her evil. In the glow of Nicole's care, its time had passed. He tossed it to the bed, where it skidded and fell to the rug.

A month ago, trouble like this would have sent him pacing into the wee hours for solutions. But she was not a problem to be solved, and he could not fight reality: Nicole would reject him, and accepting this, a wave of grief buckled his stomach. He sprawled toward the bed in misery and collapsed into a fitful sleep.

Athos's head jerked up when a hall clock chimed one in the morning. His clothes were dry from body heat and stuck to his skin. His mouth felt doughy from Pierre's wine, and he longed for another drink. He had new memories to suppress. At least wine might cloud his mind from wondering: *What if? What if on the other side of my door, she waits for me? Am I a fool to let the night pass?*

At the door, he stood motionless. Maybe on the other side was a place beyond description or a new destiny. He let a minute pass and opened the door. The hallway was empty. The moonlight from his bedroom window should have been the only light except for a golden sliver from a door left ajar—directly across the hall. He glanced left-to-right and went to the light.

The room was small, half the size of his bedchamber and accented in dark green. There was no bed; it was the sitting room of a suite. Shadows played from a four-taper candelabra at the centre of a round table. A lit fireplace heated the area, but the logs were turning to ash.

He was not alone. Nicole was asleep at a writing desk, her head and arms a paperweight on a pile of sketches. Her loose auburn hair splashed across the desktop and down her back, feathering her pale dressing gown. Leaning against her credenza was the shameless letter from the Comte, the stake Athos had used to end his confession.

She knows she was my pawn. In light of the tenderness she had shown him, using her in his cat-and-mouse game with the Comte was unforgiveable. She probably had wept reading the letter and had allowed sleep to take away the hurt.

He knew he should leave, but watching her sleep relieved his regrets. Though he had wronged her, she had given him as much as she could. Still, he wanted more. Look, he thought, from the beginning she boarded me dangerously close to her after all. This was her bedroom suite. Her most-private self. All a few steps away from his room. Shelves of books lined two walls, and her drawings decorated the rest. Frame after frame of charcoal drawings hung square and true.

He went back to her, noticing a plate of cheese and olives neglected to one side. Then his gaze caught the miniature painting near her inkwell—an intricate coloured sketch of a sky-eyed Madonna. The virgin's odd expression seemed to yearn for something beyond her grasp. *Apropos. Even a Madonna can depict life's mysteries.*

He laid the back of his hand on Nicole's cheek and whispered good-bye. A few weeks ago, he was running from her. Now, it took immense effort to leave. In the hall, he closed her bedroom door and stared at his own. It was black in the darkness, another passage into a bleak chapter of his life. *I will never see her again.* Crossing the hall, he tried shaking off the thought when a soft glow from behind him overshadowed his sadness. Light flickered as her door opened.

He stood in the shadow of his door, unable to look back. "I'm sorry I woke you."

"I need to tell you something." She sounded frail.

"About the letter?"

"François' letter seems irrelevant now. There's something else I need to say. I'm leaving tomorrow at midday on pilgrimage."

He clutched the doorframe, keeping his back to her. "Where are you going?"

"Father Audric is making our arrangements. He hasn't told me yet."

"He believes that I've corrupted you." He dug his nails into the wood.

"You're a man like any man, just as susceptible to sin as anyone, and I'm a woman who cares too much for the pain of others. He thinks it's dangerous for me here."

His hands ached. Helpless to the urge, he faced her. "You could have let me go without telling me this. Why are you?"

"I wanted to tell you at the cottage. I've needed to go away for some time to set myself right with God. You understand the complications in my life. They're more than the product of the last few days and your arrival."

"But my confession brought on his decision."

"You were intensely forthcoming." She stepped closer to him. "You showed something I've never seen in another person— complete openness. I never thought I would know your whole history. You described your life story so candidly, understated the tragedy of it. I believe you have been more honest than I have, maybe in all my life." Then she became reserved. "Forgive me, Athos."

He caught a handful of her dressing gown and closed the gap between them.

"I should be apologizing to you. The only words I want to hear you say are still in your heart. Say them. Let me leave knowing the truth."

He traced her lace collar with a gentleness that completely opposed his racing thoughts. "You could wait for the day to be different," he continued, "or God to be gentle, but it drags down every part of you. I can feel it. You live in this world, not in the hereafter. I love you, Nicole. Please tell me how you feel before I'm gone."

"It's impossible." Her voice was full of misgiving. "I can't allow myself to love you. How can I?"

A stone formed in his throat, and he brushed her lips with a thumb. The decision was in her hands. "I have detached myself from the good in life for too long," he said, "and so have you. I don't want to live like that anymore. I want love."

He let go of her gown, allowing her to step back towards the safety of her room. From the doorway, she looked behind her— at her pictures, the papers, the textured fabrics and colours, the Madonna. He saw she was at the bridge of before and after.

"If there's a prayer for such a moment, I don't know what it is," she said and walked straight to him. His kiss was fierce, and he entwined their hands, sending a tremor between them. They stopped kissing long enough to enter his room.

In the dark quarters, his kisses landed everywhere more freely. She smelled of musk and ecstasy. Soft and supple under the thin gown, her body made his entire being vibrate. The shifting fabric over her skin was a ribbon beckoning to be untied. He lifted her arms delicately, as if butterfly wings, and circled around her once, so awestruck that he didn't realize he spoke.

"You are the sun, splendour, deity."

"Not a God, Athos. A woman—" She scarcely completed the sentence, "—in love. I'm in love with you."

They were the words he had waited to hear. They were her last in the ripe second before he opened her gown and dropped it to the floor. He pressed into her back and wrapped an arm around her waist from behind. Using a few conscious breaths, he summoned all his patience to enjoy her slowly. He kept her hands from sliding back between his thighs and murmured his intent. "Let me take my time. Our time." Her perfect curves were exotic against his clothed body, heightening her glory. Eyelids closed, her head fell back on his shoulder to succumb to the game of his wandering. He wanted to experience every nuance of her body, connect with it in his way, before taking her to his bed.

He used the tips of his fingers like a downy feather to caress down her front. He painted her with the ease of a master—neck, breasts, hips, every tender rise. He conveyed his gentleness and desire with a steady hand. Her hands floated above her and into his blond hair, arching at his touches. She moaned *please*, wanting him to be as vulnerable as she, until he quietly shed his clothes and let them fall. He kissed her nape, and she turned to meet his body full on.

It was a dive into a waterfall, splintering the ice encasing his history. His soul sang: *Freedom*. Clinging to her, he moved them onto the bed.

There, he followed her desires. She searched for his pleasure points effortlessly. Each pass sensitized his skin. None of the scars mattered; her hands healed them. She drifted across the length of his body, from his throat, to his middle, then to the hardness below his core. Seeking consent with gentle strokes, he ventured between her legs, and her arousal intensified at his touch. She was silk, smooth and slick.

Soon, neither could endure more exquisite torture and raw need took over. In an instant of mutual abandon, their bodies joined. Inside her, the surrender had never felt so right. They moved in harmony—their pulses, their muscles, their sighs. His strength tensed the cord of her pleasure to the brink. Sensing her body about to crest, he roared her into an auburn flame and pushed them over one beautiful peak.

He found wholeness in her arms. She was not like old memories. She erased them. In the afterglow, she curled around him and whispered, "I love you." He memorized that moment—her skin against his, the shape of her breasts, her belly rising and falling. The brutality of his life faded away.

In the next quiet hour, he played her with a fingertip. He skimmed from her crown to the curves of her lips. He traced their beauty with a figure eight of infinity, teasing her to part them. Then he used his finger as a quill to paint the gloss offered by her tongue. Her mouth became a rose wet with dew. He let his finger skim downward, naming the parts of her body along the way.

Chin. Throat. Hollow of neck. Heart. Belly. Navel.

And lastly: *Eden.*

She coyly squirmed and hummed, then noticed his arm, free of the silver cuff. She touched the imprint left behind.

"You took off the fleur-de-lis. Will this mark heal?" Her question was as light as her touch.

"Tonight, it heals completely."

Chapter 31
Finding a Way to Farewell

Throughout the night, he meandered over her body. He wanted to learn her.

He read the curves of her skin like a virtuous man studies the Bible—hands running over each line with regard, turning the delicate pages with care to enhance the reflection, absorbing each scripture and holy passage.

His wandering created moments of great stillness and captivation. They exchanged simmering gazes. He combed through her hair with his fingers and listened at her breast to her innermost essence.

Then the heat between them surfaced again like wildfire. He found her burning past any doubts. She experienced boundless bliss in his heat. It wasn't forged from hurt or vows or blood or lust; it came from acceptance and vulnerability.

Just before sunrise, they began a deep conversation and talked of soulful ideas, her creativity, his love of Paris, the poets they prized and a fantasy of walking outside together, hand-in-hand, free of shame. As the skies lightened, she passed into sleep. Athos watched her in peace and contemplated the secrets of fulfilling slumber.

Hungry, he left her to nap and retrieved the plate of food from her desk along with a single taper. He sat cross-legged in bed next to her and watched the sun come up from the small window. The sun, her body, the food. Each added to his completeness. Her willingness to love him knitted his world together.

Halfway through his tiny feast, she sleepily snuggled around his back. "How long has it been since you were with a woman?"

"Many, many nights." But instead of sorrow, he felt very little sting and smiled intensely at her.

"Your smile is worth a thousand days under my willow." She kissed his thumb and licked the oil leftover from an olive then ate a piece of cheese from his palm. "How were you able to resist women? The way you made love to me, Athos, I can't imagine you spending many nights alone."

"I simply lost my appetite. Women represented emptiness, and I had no hunger for them, mostly." He ate another olive. "But I believe my cravings have returned."

He laid the plate on the floor and stretched on his side behind her. Over her hips, he criss-crossed a path below her navel and teased the tuft between her legs. "From what I discovered last night, it has been quite a while for you, too."

She lifted her head and turned to him for a brief kiss, after which she crossed her arms over her bosom. "I've never veered in my fidelity."

"I know." He nuzzled her neck. "I promise to safeguard your heart, until my own death."

"Or, until the unforeseen." Her eyes twinkled with tears.

"I didn't mean to upset you."

She made him lie in front of her. He could see she loved the look of him. The oncoming light was kind to his injuries, even the impossible indention on his side.

"How did you get this?" she asked, touching the spot.

He recognized she was changing the subject, trying to hold down the tears. He nuzzled her earlobe. "Ask Pierre."

"You'll be in charge of him when I leave," she said.

"Please don't go." It was a subject he was avoiding, too, though inevitable.

"Athos, I can't change the course of events."

"We just did." Her tears finally came, and he hugged her. "But we're together now. Love me. Don't think." Despite it all, his heart was tranquil. He was a changed person in every sense. He nestled himself near her ear and bore witness. "You have freed me from a darkness that surrounded my heart for many years. I thought it was unbreakable. Now, I owe you everything. My debt is impossible to repay."

Her breath was sweet on his lips. "Where does this go?"

"We head into the future together. I'll live it with you in my heart, and hopefully someday, by my side."

She shook her head. "I'm tied to my duty, my faith—" she shuddered, "—my husband. You cannot be with me. We cannot be together, and we separate today, probably forever. From now on, you and I are a fantasy."

"Nicole." He laid a hand between her breasts. "You are in my blood. I cannot take you out of me, *ever*. You'll live inside me until the end, and nothing, *no one*, will shake you from me. And I will not be shaken from you."

"It's remarkable. You have undoubtedly changed."

"Through and through." He smiled at her again.

She bit her lip. "Please promise me you will protect Pierre. He's impractical and shamelessly ambitious. I couldn't live if any harm comes to him. I trust you to take care of him."

"You have my word. Besides, his hands will be preoccupied, which is more than I can say for mine."

He kissed her cheeks, taking the salt from her tears as sacrament. He made love to her again, and try as he might to live by his words, the tenderness came with unwelcome pangs of sorrow. His lovemaking was more desperate, more final, and it moved her to a height that humbled him to witness. In the penetrating rays of the morning light, she soared like a bird in a strong wind, tempting fate to catch her.

Chapter 32
Departure

The household staff was morose as Nicole's trunks were delivered to the courtyard. Cordes had prepared the carriage, and the waiting began for the priest's summons for the pilgrimage. Nicole decided to wait in the chapel. Before the luggage was collected, she asked Athos to stay in his room as long as possible, then meet her in the sanctuary for their good-bye.

In the front pew, she dabbed tears, staring at the four candles she had lit at the altar. One for the new baby, two for Hannah and Pierre, and one for her lover. The three left behind at the chalet would forgo a hurtful parting.

When she had gone looking for Athos after his street confession, her intentions had been simply to provide the solace she offered to anyone hurting. But he was different. She had not stated her feelings for him before then because she had not wanted to admit them. The complexity confused her. He had recognized her love, and in his determination, he showed her it was worth the risks. She had contemplated backing away, but in reality, she needed him as much as he needed her.

He proved to be an open-hearted lover. In the night, he carefully followed her lead and took time to match her emotions with the physical highs. He approached her as if he was a child given a precious toy, gratified and rapt, but always focusing on her pleasure. He never seemed out of sync with her level of passion. From quiet to extreme, he respected her feelings with every stroke. And he wasn't doing all the work. He showed immense satisfaction at her forwardness to fulfil his pleasures, using all she knew of love-making to please him. He was a substantial man, tantalizing in his physicality.

She wanted him to leave behind the past for one unmatched night. And possibly never again.

A cool hand landed on her shoulder, and she grabbed it without thinking. "You know an owl is as light as a feather." Her candles flickered. "Its bones are hollow, and its wings are filled with air. Can you imagine the freedom, the sheer weightlessness of flight? I envy the freedom."

A soft nudge kissed her crown.

"Be with me," she murmured.

The Comte circled in front of her. "It's the only reason I am here."

Part Two – The Unforeseen

"Dust to dust, ashes to ashes," Aramis said.
"Man is born to sorrow; happiness lasts but a day."

The Three Musketeers
Alexandre Dumas

Chapter 33
Her Reversal

A commotion in the courtyard drew Athos to the chapel entrance within seconds. The door gave way as he pushed. Regaining his balance, Athos saw the outline of a man in the faint light of the sanctuary. The Comte looked hard-ridden but smug.

"Athos, how good of you to wait for my return." The Comte's expression was a cross between arrogance and elation.

Athos tried to read whatever story lie behind the surprise. "What choice did I have in the matter, François? I'm here at your request."

"From what I can tell, not very happily." The Comte stepped aside. Nicole clung to the back of a pew.

"You knew that when you brought me here." Athos dug his heels. Facing the Comte was inevitable, but with his unexpected return, Athos's confidence drained away, fearing the acts of the previous night couldn't be hidden. He fought his pessimism. In an army of men, surprise tactics could annihilate good morale after weeks of good fortune.

"Your letter stated you were going to send for me," Athos said. "Have plans changed? It's me you have come for, yes?"

"Our plans haven't changed," the Comte said, then pointed to his wife. "But Nicole's plans have. She wanted to spend a night with me before you and I embarked on our venture. She sent for me."

Try as he might, Athos could not disguise a long glance at her: *Why?* Her quick response abated his fears.

"You'll have to confront the priest, François. He wants to leave within the hour on a pilgrimage. He demands it. That's why I'm here, awaiting his summons to depart."

"Then I shall have to persuade him to wait." François wrapped an arm around her middle and brushed past Athos. "No doubt, he'll see the benefit of our reunion, if only for tonight. He's a practical man and knows the virtues of a strong marriage. One night won't set back your salvation."

Athos knew she could not look back or give the slightest indication of their shared disbelief. A weight dropped onto his chest. Heavy-hearted, he leaned against the chapel door after François and Nicole left. He ached watching her disappear, arm-in-arm with his nemesis, into the tomb of the house. The fickleness of fate or the wrath of God, he could not pinpoint which, placed control beyond his reach. The sharp reality weakened his spirit by half.

He found François and Nicole in the foyer with the Comte's entourage. Servants collected small bags and belongings from his three men, all much younger than Athos. No introductions were offered, and though they appeared spirited, they soon retired upstairs. The Comte began boasting about how quickly they had made the trip from Nantes. He had pushed them three days and nights with little rest. Showing scant weariness, he fired off instructions to a group of servants—prepare food, restore provisions—while Nicole, dejected, sat in a side chair. Her blank stare morphed into resignation when the Comte issued a final command: *Waylay the priest.* Athos watched him ink the message and send a servant boy on the mission. Slapping Athos on the back, the Comte pulled him into the library and produced a flask.

"You're wise to bring your own," Athos said, regretting he could not reassure Nicole before being drawn to the room.

Engrossed in a drink, the Comte sputtered before remembering his manners. "Why, yes, you've learned the house rules, I see. I'll send out for a demijohn. I can tell you've survived your stay here well enough. Here," he said offering the flask, "no animosity?"

Pride smarting, Athos played along. He took a drink and François' handshake. The wine tasted like vinegar.

"So tell me, my Musketeer friend, is my bet safely won? Did she reject your kiss?" Wearing a shrewd smile, the Comte rubbed his hands together, making Athos wonder whether the winds or the pigeons had delivered the night's news.

"I doubt anyone would believe if I had won."

"Take a share of the winnings?" François asked, completely frank.

"Not even to pay for my burial."

François went from one corner of the room to the next, half smiling, inspecting the walls and Nicole's art as if he had never noticed them before. Athos returned the flask, and the Comte emptied it. "I have you to thank for my sudden visit."

"How's that?"

"You must have frightened her, that streak of Satan in you. If your mood here was as terrifying as when we last met, I'd understand why. True, you were out of your mind in Paris. You look more cool-headed now."

"A fraction." Athos let him hang onto the delusion by reclining in a chair, but his interior monologue ricocheted like a gunshot in a mausoleum. *Why return now?*

"I must admit, it's a mystery to me you're still here," François said, throwing the flask into an empty armchair, "especially after my letter and the confounding circumstances of this place. It's a triumph to your honour that you stayed as long as you did. You're truly one of a kind, Athos."

"Why are you here then? Obviously, not for me."

"Well, we do have business to take care of together and soon. Sadly for me, we must leave tomorrow. Early." His eyes narrowed. "But yes, I have another reason for being home. What did you learn about me in my absence?"

"That every convention here seems turned on its head," Athos said.

"Exactly and to a degree that I haven't been able to rectify in many years, until perhaps now." François' smile reflected self-satisfaction. "Nicole wants me back."

"I know she has rejected you."

"In more ways than one." François' bearing suggested a long-tended hurt, but he rebounded with curiosity. "But, I'm wondering. What did you do to bring about her reversal?"

Athos chose his words carefully. "It must have been accidental. Don't rush to thank me for the favours."

"Did you learn about Sibonne?"

Athos nodded.

"One look at you and I could see Nicole crumbling at the similarities. I'm afraid you were at a disadvantage on all fronts. In fact, I stand somewhat humbled by your stamina, enduring my wife's sadness as well as my lack of directions. But your work for me will make up for it. I'm completely confident of that now, and you'll be well compensated. We'll ride to Nantes at daybreak." He headed for the door, fatigue sapping his posture. "I must excuse myself. I'll need my strength if tonight promises to be a memorable one." Before leaving, François smiled. "I'll make doubly certain the wine is sent to your room."

Athos rubbed his stinging eyes. *She's giving in.* It was his fault. Thankfully, he was not the one suffering fatigue. A window of opportunity had opened.

Athos dashed to the foyer, but Nicole was gone, likely to seek a hiding place. The kitchen clanged with activity. Dinner for four extra men was an hours-long process, and preparations had begun as soon as the travellers arrived. Athos tried there first, hoping a clue to her whereabouts might be dropped like a crumb of bread.

Duchy, resembling an egg in a top-to-bottom white uniform, raised an eyebrow. "You'll be served in the formal dining room with the rest of the men. My better judgment questions why."

Though completely devoid of hunger, Athos dipped a finger in the buttery mixture Duchy was stirring with a wooden spoon. He hummed at the taste. "And did you happen to see any mice scramble this way, by chance?'

"I tend to ignore the ones with rings around their fingers, as should you," she said derisively.

He faked a smile, knowing his charms could crack the shell of any egg. "Certainly you have more than a delicious morsel of food to offer, Duchy? You are the lifeblood of this place."

"Your flattery is useless on me, Monsieur," she said, rapping his knuckles with the spoon before another finger touched her mixture. "Now be gone with you."

Desperate for an answer, he leaned into her side, using every bit of randy persuasion he could muster. "But you, of all people, know how important this is. You're not a dispassionate woman."

Her eyes darted to the pantry, then to him, and back to the pantry. Trying not to jump to the door too soon, Athos bowed. "I'm certain that if given enough time, we could become mutual admirers."

Twisting a handkerchief, Nicole leaned against an onion bin in the pantry. Hot pink patches splotched her face. Athos locked the pantry door with the wooden lever. A quiet lull emptied their hearts.

"What have we done?" she asked. Her body listed sideways, and he gathered her in his arms. Her back was damp with sweat, and she smelled like worry.

"Has he laid his hands upon you yet?" He veiled his disquiet by stroking her hair.

She began sobbing into his shoulder. "Not yet."

"I accept the blame. You reached out to him because of me, because of what I did to Pierre, because of my insufferable behaviour."

"After you struck Pierre, I was afraid of what you might do next, and … and because I began to feel something for you, in spite of everything."

"That's what you were thinking the night I saw you at the mirror."

She nodded and rubbed her forehead against his chest, making his heart race.

"It would help me if I knew how long it's been since you were with him. As man and woman." He hated asking, but it would tell him how resolute the Comte might be in seeing her promise fulfilled.

"Several years. I can't remember exactly. I don't have any memories of the last few times we were together."

His heart sank. He closed tighter around her, trying to reassure but feeling helpless.

"I'll provoke him," he said finally. "I have many reasons not to disguise my anger for this situation."

"No! No, Athos. I won't watch him kill you."

"He didn't kill me before."

"What?"

"You still don't know the whole story of how I ended up here."

"I believe God works in very extraordinary ways." She wiped tears on a cuff and reclaimed some calm. "This is my doing and my responsibility. And I'm positive I can put him off one more night. One more time."

He lifted her head. "How? A man doesn't take rejection of that kind lightly. He's your husband, and you've refused him too many years. The loss of intimacy can eat a man's soul. He won't stand for it, and he could force himself on you. My cornering him into a fight is the only way."

"Let me try. Please let me try first." Her face was stern with determination. "I have an idea, and if it fails, do what you must. But let me try another plan. You'll know what to do, simply give me a chance. It could save you from getting killed."

Her lips were warm. He felt his kiss must relay his approval, though he had doubts about trusting a plan he knew nothing about.

"Tell me what you are thinking," he said. "How will you stop him? I can't let myself imagine him with you. Not after last night. I won't let it happen. I would rather be whipped to death by the Cardinal."

"You'll see. I promise. But we can't stay in here together any longer. It's too dangerous." She moved to the latch, but he caught her.

"I think I've given away my feelings for you." His kiss lingered at the corner of her mouth. "Even Duchy sees my love for you."

"She'll keep her suspicions to herself for me, but only for me. Don't worry about her. Just don't try anything. Let me go for now. Only for now."

Nicole's composure was passable when she left. To recover, he needed more time alone to ruminate, amidst the garlic braids and salted meats, in hopes that whatever she planned kept their newfound love intact.

Chapter 34
A Disrupted Dinner

As promised, François sent a bottle of wine to Athos's bedroom. It sat unopened on the round table.

Although tempted to drink, Athos wanted to stay clear-headed. Staying sober didn't work either. Desperate for a solution, he paced the afternoon away upstairs, tormented by scenarios of how Nicole would stop her husband, the man driven by a false promise. The Comte wanted his wife, and there was nothing Athos could do about it.

His pacing intensified as his options shrank. Her physical surrender was the Comte's priceless reward, and Athos honestly couldn't think of any excuse to keep a starved lover from a promise like hers. A feigned sickness wouldn't be believable; her stubbornness would crumble under strong hands; and the thought of her husband's unwanted lips and skin against her body made Athos choke in revulsion. Her offer to the Comte was worth a King's fortune.

Finding his sword near the bed, Athos concluded the situation demanded violence. The only way to stop the course of events was to provoke the Comte again as he had in Paris, by affronting the nobleman's ego and picking a fight. He didn't fear the Comte. Athos could deal with the risk and even gain some pleasure from a duel, except that a second match now put him at a distinct disadvantage.

I want to live. To breathe, feel light on my face, love her.

Despite the obstacles between him and Nicole, life had new meaning.

Athos drew his sword and reviewed it in the sunlight from his bedroom window. He knew of no finer weapon to live or die by.

Untested in battle, it was a prize unto itself, perfectly balanced and etched with an intricate royal motif. In contradiction, the weapon symbolized his desire to die because he had commissioned the piece in Paris during one of his darkest days to duel to the death. For Nicole, he would use it to live.

He changed into a freshly ironed shirt and donned his doublet, which had been brushed, the buttons polished. He tucked his pants into his boots, spit upon them and rubbed them clean of dust. He smoothed his hair into place with a damp hand and buckled his weapons at the waist.

Downstairs, the aroma of roasting quail greeted him before the dinner guests arrived. Servants flitted to and from the kitchen. One came in to polish the carved wooden panels by the buffet while others replaced misshapen tapers in two candelabras on the banquet table. Several bottles of wine were uncorked.

The Comte and his men arrived from the airy back porch looking wind bitten and introduced themselves as each stood behind a chair around the table. There was a sinewy soldier named Vachon Demoncheaux. He was handsome in a ruddy way, sporting curly brown hair and large, round eyes. Vachon held himself in a manner that suggested he never backed down from a fight. He came with his younger sibling, Henri, who took after his brother's looks, yet carried himself more confidently. The third man, Camille Duschanne, medium and sturdy like Athos, seemed the most mature and statesmanlike. A redhead, he was the only one to offer Athos a handshake and hung on to Athos's hand an extra moment.

"Your accomplishments are well known to us all, Monsieur," Camille said with a broad grin and claimed the next seat, standing behind it on formality. "You'll have to tell us how you came to be in the company of François. It's far beyond my understanding."

The Comte took the jab lightly. "Be thankful, Camille. You're a fine marksman, but Athos and I are the better swordsmen."

"I can hold my own," said Henri, who bumped his chair into the table, anxious to sit. "Still, because you're a Musketeer, I'm glad you side with us."

"It might be helpful if I knew what side that was," Athos said.

An uncomfortable quiet forced François to answer. "I'll explain after dinner."

Athos only nodded and stood at a place next to Camille and across from Henri, both of whom scrutinized the table, over-decorated with vases of day lilies and crystal. Henri whispered across the centrepiece. "A little overdone, don't you think?"

Silence followed. All eyes went to one place setting, unclaimed at the end. The Comte, fidgeting as he continued to stand, drummed his fingers on the back of his seat, until, perturbed, he shouted for Duchy. When she appeared, she bowed and crossed her arms over her pristine apron.

"Duchy, why are we waiting? Where's Nicole?"

"Pardon me, my Lord. I was instructed to give these to you as soon as you called for me." Duchy placed two letters on the table next to his spotless plate.

The letters were almost identical. The paper—size, colouring, fold—matched precisely. Yet from an angle, Athos could tell one was sealed, the other opened and slightly rumpled. *The Comte's letter to me.* A tingle ran up his back.

The Comte silently read the recipients' names on each.

"One for me," he said and lifted the sealed one. Askance, he looked to Athos. "And one from me to you."

The Comte broke the seal on the unopened letter and within seconds squeezed his eyes shut. He carefully refolded the letter and placed it by his plate. He raised the second letter in his own handwriting and spoke, each word ringing louder than the next until he was shouting: "Who the Devil gave her this!?"

Duchy cringed as François whipped the letter across the table. It landed on the plate in front of Vachon, who picked it up and scanned it greedily.

"François," Vachon said, the grin of a bully growing on his face, "the bite in your own words now seems to be turned back on you."

The Comte grabbed Duchy's elbow. "Who gave her that letter?"

Athos remained calm and silent.

"I … I'm only the messenger." Duchy bent fearfully.

"What's the meaning of this?" Henri interrupted, grabbing the letter from Vachon's loose hold.

"My wife won't be joining us. Someone has stuck a knife in my back." The Comte came close to shouting again. His hatred shot straight to Athos. "The letter intended only for *you* has slipped from your hands."

Athos leaned on his knuckles toward the head of the table. He welcomed a fight. It was his to claim, and deep down, he was thankful for the outright blame. He didn't count on Nicole's plan taking a sudden turn.

"It didn't slip from his hands." In the doorway to the kitchen, Pierre stood wearing his sword. "It slipped from mine."

Athos's instincts called on him to intervene. He wanted to do the fighting, not sacrifice an amateur. But Pierre stuck out his chest and stood rock-hard behind the Comte like a strongman awaiting a stomach punch.

"I also delivered Nicole to her priest today," Pierre said, nose in the air.

"You thankless ... miserable ... bastard!" François cursed and lunged simultaneously. He punched Pierre in the eye with a solid fist and suffered an equally hard punch in return.

Camille, befuddled by the whole exchange, wedged himself between the two, grabbing the Comte's lapels. "François, step back. He's a sapling, hardly worth it."

As Camille struggled to deflect François, Athos reached Pierre, pulled him to a corner and shook sense into him. He transferred in one serious look: *This does Nicole no good.*

"Get out!" the Comte shouted. "Get out Pierre, or I'll throw you out!" Fuming over Camille's strained shoulder, the Comte hurled a string of saliva toward the fearless youth.

Athos clasped Pierre by the shoulders and used as much authority as he could muster. "Leave. Now."

Pierre heeded and took to the kitchen. Trying to evoke the same confidence, Athos addressed the others. "This matter is closed. Nicole is gone. Apparently, she's in the priest's hands now."

"Not for long." François motioned for his men to leave and started for the door, but his authority eroded when the brothers erupted in laughter.

"You two make quite a pair," Vachon interrupted between sucks of air. "What a show!"

"Unbelievable," Henri said, smiling broadly, still in possession of the tossed letter.

"A little enlightenment would help," Camille said. He was the first to sit down, commandeering a bottle for company.

"It seems," Henri explained, directing the story to his puzzled companion, "that François and Athos are entangled in a bet in which the Comtesse is the prize."

"You wagered your wife, François?" Camille asked.

"Her affections," Henri corrected.

"I did no such thing." The Comte glared at Athos, who reciprocated.

"It's written in black and white. According to your letter, you took Athos up on a bet that he couldn't steal a kiss from your wife," Vachon said, snatching the letter back from his brother, "which is hardly less objectionable to the woman involved."

"Your letter twists a knife into a wound," Athos said.

"Save your righteousness," the Comte said. "Don't lay the blame on me after what happened between us in Paris. The fact that I only used a letter to condemn your behaviour is proof of my restraint. The embarrassment I suffered in Paris justified more than ink on a page."

Amused, Vachon bit into a pear from a centrepiece bowl and poured wine in everyone's glass. "Nevertheless, it seems the insulted party has fled."

"She won't be far. Duchy," François called, turning to the cook, huddled by the side of a china cabinet, "how long ago did she leave?"

"A little over an hour. Two, at most."

"Hold on! We don't know where they're going," Camille protested, finishing a glass and visibly fretting about the rest of the meal. "At least let us eat."

François ignored him. "When we return," he instructed the old cook, "I want Pierre and his things to be sent to the blacksmith in Angers." With acrimony, he added, "He's expecting him."

Chapter 35
Telling the Truth

A bruise forming over his eye socket, François sent his men to ready the horses. They continued to protest for their dinner, but he pacified them by promising to return before midnight. The search for his wife, he reassured them, would be swift.

Duchy complained as well. "Where's Cordes when you need him?" Then she returned to the familiar confines of her kitchen, leaving François and Athos alone.

Athos tried to hide his growing self-assurance. He marvelled at Nicole's bravado, her clean strike at the bull's eye. She gambled that François would not dare kill Pierre, her blood relative.

"She doesn't bend," Athos told his rival.

"I see your time here wasn't wasted."

"Other than remove the veils of your life, there was little to do."

François found his riding gloves in the foyer and yanked them on. "You must be thinking 'Isn't he pathetic? Excessive wealth at his fingertips, and the treasure he wants most is locked in a tower guarded by God.'"

Athos gave an honest reply. "Some obstacles are much greater than God."

"Yes, Athos, your example gives me a dash of hopefulness. At least the archangel doesn't ride me to the gates of Hell." The Comte cast a shifty smile. "We'll still leave tomorrow for Nantes. Until then, your charge is to get the boy to Angers. Be quick about it."

Athos followed the Comte to the front door. "You squander his talent, sending him to ram iron and shoe horses."

"What talent?" The Comte stopped at the threshold. "Getting the help pregnant?"

"He's become skilled with a blade."

"Let me guess. His teacher?" He swept a hand toward the Musketeer.

"You could benefit from another outrider. He shows promise."

"I'd rather scald my ass in oil."

Athos knew his next suggestion would be audacious but worth one try. "You could be done with him another way. Vouch for him to Monsieur de Treville. Send him to Paris, where he'll live and breathe peril as a Musketeer."

"Only to meet him again later, in a dark tavern, itching to pick a fight? Look at what that's got me." The Comte pushed the door wide open.

"You know his baby has been born."

"A boy?"

Athos shook his head.

"Small miracle," the Comte said, lifting his head to Heaven. "Someday, I'll give thanks to the Holy Mother that there's not another swinging blade named Tremon running loose."

No sooner had the Comte left than Pierre rounded the corner. "He persecutes me! And for what reason?"

"You challenge his authority."

"He's a blackguard," Pierre seethed, also suffering a black eye.

"One who controls your future." Athos paced the granite in the foyer.

"And what is my future? I'll be shackled to a hot pit of coal by the end of the day."

"It was bold of you to take the blame," Athos said, heading to the kitchen.

Pierre stomped to a halt by the banquet table. "Only a miracle will save her now."

"Pierre, we'll play our cards. She's out of his clutches for the moment. Right now I must know where the priest is taking Nicole."

"But she's only an hour into her escape. He'll soon catch up and drag her back."

"Where is she going?" Athos asked insistently.

"The abbey of Saint Germain-de-Prés."

Paris. Athos ignored Pierre's continued protests.

"Athos, she's doomed. The Comte will seize her from the priest's hands, I'll be banished, and you'll be on your way. Nothing will change!"

"*Everything* has changed." Athos collected the two letters from the dinner table and barged into the kitchen, where his entrance interrupted the clean-up. Duchy reared up from the butcher block when Athos darted toward her. "Duchy, can I place my trust in you? Ask a favour for Nicole's sake?"

A little wild-eyed, she wrinkled her eyebrows together. "Only for Nicole."

"Then empty Pierre's cottage. Everything in it, what little there is. Every item must be burned or hidden. And, as far as anyone is concerned, I've left for the time being to escort Pierre to Angers."

"As far as I'm concerned, that's the best place for you, too" she said, not the least bit apologetic.

"You're not taking me to Angers, are you?" Pierre asked, following Athos as he rushed outside toward the stable. "You leave Nicole high and dry."

"She has her protector."

"Cordes? He won't defy the Comte for Nicole, no matter if his true allegiance is to her."

"I don't mean Cordes."

Pierre's eyes narrowed with recognition. "Father Audric."

"A source even higher than that." Athos worked at double the pace to saddle his horse stall-to-stall by Pierre. "But we shall ensure He doesn't fail."

Before mounting, Athos took the reins of both horses, though Pierre protested. Athos struggled not to lecture. "You need to say your good-byes. It may be a long time before you see Hannah and your daughter again. You have precious little time."

"What's to become of me?"

Pierre's innocence struck Athos hard in the chest. "Only God knows."

Pierre disappeared instantly, and Athos pulled the letters from a breast pocket. He remembered all too well the letter from François. In the letter Nicole left her husband, the script was as beautiful as the drawing he had watched come to life.

I am better off in the hands of God, than with a man who wagers on my fidelity. My walls become a fortress today. Farewell – Nicole

She could have easily addressed the letter to him. Because of his actions, Athos was accountable for the present mayhem, and it started by wagering that she could be unfaithful. But he hadn't truly known her then, and his intention had been to bring on his own death, not soil her honour. Still, he was responsible, the troublemaker. As it turned out, his poor behaviour made no difference to her. She understood that he had not intended to hurt *her*. Giving thanks, he took the tiny nub of charcoal he had found at the willow and wrote two short messages on the blank flaps of her letter.

Pierre was quiet on the ride out. At the fork in the road near Rochefort, Athos chose the route to Paris. They galloped in the oncoming dark, and Pierre pulled ahead.

"Reel in your bravery," Athos called, reading the Pierre's body language as a desire to test swords against his oppressor. "I want to catch up with them only after the Comte has reached the carriage. Otherwise, we invite a fight."

"And?" Pierre said, revealing his intentions.

Athos rode up beside. "That's not our goal."

"You want the Comte to catch her?"

"Of course not," Athos said.

Pierre's horse veered skittishly, sensing the anxiety of its rider as plainly as Athos did. Pierre's suffering equalled that of a son being ripped from his mother's arms, of a man abandoning a daughter and lover, of an uncertain future.

Athos felt deeply sympathetic. "I want her to leave and find safety. I understand her situation with the Comte is much like yours, bitter with no love lost."

The younger man huffed.

"Did you read the letter the Comte wrote me?" Athos asked.

Pierre stared ahead a few moments. "You used Nicole to provoke the Comte, but I don't know why. Who was she to you? Or François? Isn't Paris full of beauties and their protectors? Why did you pick the two of them when there are so many?"

"It was a means to an end. I know that probably doesn't make sense to you."

"You're a nobleman, right? You come from privilege and advantage?"

"I once held a sovereignty, true. People knew me as Comte de la Fère."

"Why then? Why have you chosen this path?"

Athos smiled kindly at Pierre, riding in tandem, feeling an affinity for another man he had not felt since the bond of the Musketeers. "Maybe I should explain."

Although focused on the route, Athos told Pierre his story. By repeating it, a gentler version unfolded—his inexplicable love for Milady, her assault on his heart, his rejection of life, and finally, his flawed pursuit of death. He talked of violence and honour in service of the King and the numbness in that duty, which helped him survive. He ended by describing the fateful jump from the roof in Paris. Athos astonished himself, telling it again in plain words. The sorrows hurt less. He wasn't seeking approval or forgiveness as he had in his street confession for Nicole.

Pierre listened without interrupting. A long time passed between them as the road stretched out, evolving into a path of transformation rather than risk.

"You're a different person now than the day you jumped from the tavern," Pierre concluded.

"You're wiser than your age. I should have known."

"I think I know why you're healed."

Athos had no response, for he had kept his love for Nicole bound to his heart.

Pierre pointed ahead, encouraging them to speed up. "She deserves to be loved as deeply as you appear to love her." Then Pierre spurred on his horse to forge the way, and the shadows of the treeline covered his tracks.

Chapter 36
Pursuing the Pilgrim

To Athos, the road back to Paris looked different. Backtracking was a skill he often used as a Musketeer, but on his journey to Rochefort, he had not memorized the rocks and trees and milestones because of his discontent. Now on his way back to Paris, his neglect intensified the urgency of catching up to the fleeing coach and its precious cargo.

Athos did not want the Comte and his men to know he was behind them. Athos's confidence in Nicole's plan was high. He would let her scheme play out if possible. Still, he needed assurance it was working and, if necessary, he would step in. He represented the last barrier between Nicole and her husband. Either way, he would see her one last time.

Pierre rode ahead, cocky as ever. After more than an hour, Athos pulled astride. "We may be close." He took the lead and abandoned the road for the brush.

Pierre dropped behind, confused. "What are you doing?"

"Staying alive. You didn't think I was going to charge up with you in tow? I'm here to see her plans work. I'll stop him if I must."

"You mean *we'll* stop him," Pierre asserted.

"No, Pierre. I will stop him. I'm saving you from Angers. I am *not* involving you in an ambush."

"So you didn't mean it after all?" Pierre looked insulted.

"Mean what?"

Pierre jerked his horse to a standstill. "That I should be sent to Paris to become a Musketeer. You knew the Comte wouldn't support me in that effort. If you truly thought I was ready, you wouldn't keep me in the wings now. There's more to me than you know."

"Pierre—"

His rant was unstoppable. "I've been studying swordplay since long before your arrival. I've been sneaking to the village for years to find partners, even without a blade of my own. Nicole never knew."

"Pierre, listen to me." Athos scowled. "This isn't the time to test your capabilities, which I'm confident are adequate enough to help you survive most contests of steel. But you need time away from the confines of Rochefort and your life there. You need to grow and learn of the world and its ways. I'm giving you that opportunity. I risk a great deal to steal you away. I take on that responsibility willingly, but I need you to recognize the danger. And to cooperate. You'll have your time. This isn't it."

Pierre stared at the ground. The young man would face even greater tests than swallowing bitter reality, but Athos showed pity and gave him the lead to push through the gnarly woods.

The bank slanted sharply, and as they descended, they lost sight of the road. Pierre was the first to hear noises ahead. They halted in a ravine, tied their horses to a spindly beech tree and crawled to a flat boulder that overlooked the road by a few feet.

Below, an argument was well underway.

Father Audric stood outside the coach, dwarfed by the mounted men. He grimaced sternly at the Comte. "You should be coming with us."

"Pilgrimages are reserved for the devout. I'm only asking you to postpone the trip a day or two. There's no harm in my request. You know how little time I spend with Nicole." The door of the carriage was closed, and from above, Athos could not see in.

"You, of all people, know the importance of this journey," Father Audric said. "It will cleanse her, improve her moral and upright standing. I object to your patronizing, but that doesn't change the circumstances. She's a woman, more prone to contamination and impressions. This will benefit you both. You'll see."

"It will, Father, but not today." François dismounted and gave the horse to Vachon. "Nicole, come out."

The brothers exchanged bemused glances in the quiet, which egged François on. "Nicole!" He pushed Father Audric to the side, and tried the door to the carriage. It was locked. "Nicole! Open the door."

"Just drive the damned contraption back home," Vachon said, stifling a laugh.

François pounded on the door with the force of a blacksmith's iron. "Nicole. Unlock yourself."

"Seems to me she's been locked up quite nicely for some time," Henri said, rejecting a reproachful look from Camille, who was trying to calm his horse. Father Audric made the sign of the cross.

"Cordes!" The Comte slapped the coachman's boot. "Turn around. We'll escort you home. Father, you'll have to ride with Henri since it appears you won't be welcomed inside the coach again." Henri groaned at the punishment.

But before the Comte remounted, the door slowly creaked open, and a determined voice declared: "François. Come inside."

François appeared blindsided, like he had been spoken to in English. He paid no attention to Vachon and Henri, who were too juvenile to pass up a few whistles and jeers. Henri called: "Should we leave you two love birds alone?"

All at once, a response emerged from the carriage as François shut the door behind him.

"Cordes, move ahead. Do not turn around." Nicole called from inside. "I need to speak with my husband in private."

★★★

Nicole sat in the middle of the front bench. She wore dark traveling clothes, including gloves and a flat hat, her brown hair swept up snugly underneath. Not an inch of skin was exposed, except for her face. She pursed her lips and burned him with an unforgiving stare.

François fell back into the opposite seat. "You made a fool out of me in front of my men."

The carriage swayed on the pitted road.

"You are perfectly skilled at that without my help."

François lost all evenness. "Why do you continue to mock me? I've done nothing but bend to your wishes for far too long. I've let you take complete control of my own estate. I continue to endure your rebuffs of my generosity, and I'm starved of any pleasures of marriage. Nicole, you … *this* …. is intolerable! I won't stand for it any longer!"

"Did you win?" Her question floated like a goose-down feather on a breeze. "Did you win your bet?"

François loosened his collar with two fingers and jutted his chin. "Is it any surprise?" He steamed with arrogant righteousness and began unbuttoning his jacket. "It's sheer stupidity for anyone to question your fidelity. But, I have to tip my hat to the Parisians who love a good gamble. Did you know the odds were against you in Paris? More bastards believed Athos could seduce you, and I wasn't about to let an opportunity for easy money pass me by. I knew better." He laid his folded jacket on the seat and untucked his shirt. "Your fidelity, however, will no longer mean your chastity."

She watched him remove his shirt and place it neatly over the jacket. She had not seen his bare chest and arms in years, and their strength was shocking. Fear welled inside her.

"You wagered on my name, François. My reputation. What you did was more offensive than any wrong I may have committed against you. Where's your honour?"

He unbuckled his weapons and let the belt drop to the floorboard. In a lightning move, he grasped her hand and pulled off a glove, dispelling her resistance with little effort. In a blink, both gloves were strewn to the floor.

"François, this isn't the place." In futile glances, she sought an escape she knew did not exist. Only woods passed through the slits of the drawn curtains.

"I will make it right." He shoved his body next to hers, forcing kisses on her neck and chest and finally her mouth. The kisses were hard and relentless, unlike his careful approach in years past. Recoiling from his mouth, she struggled for air, her nose pressed flat against his face, the musk of his lust filling her throat.

"Let me go. François, not here!" She sounded like a trapped rabbit, squealing in a vice.

He groped with his pants. Undone at the waist, he flattened her on the seat and pressed down, invading her mouth again. He pulled and twisted the skirt above her thighs. She was losing; her penance had come due.

"Take me back home! I promise I'll live up to my duties as your wife. Just take me back." A tear dropped to the velvet cushion. Undeterred, he pulled down a sleeve from her aching shoulder, and the air between them chilled.

"What's this?" He sat back immediately. The bandage wrapped around her upper arm was dotted with dried blood.

"I was injured."

"What?"

"I was shot. It was an accident."

His nostrils flared. "You were shot?"

The words sounded so improbable; even she had difficulty believing them. But now the truth was out, thrust into the open, to stop his assault. She was jeopardizing her secret and the person she loved.

"You were shot by Athos." The Comte was not asking a question this time. "What in God's name has gone on between the two of you?" He withdrew into a seat corner and gaped at her dishevelled state, then his own. Her hands trembled adjusting her sleeve, and she all but wept to see he was coming to his senses.

"You asked me to detain him, François. He tried to leave the estate twice, and the second time, I intervened personally. A stag came upon us and … and it was an accident."

The carriage slowed down. "My Lord!" Cordes shouted from outside. "There's a rider-less horse blocking the road up ahead. It looks like Pierre's."

François appeared confused—until the name Pierre sank in. He hastily fastened his pants, replaced his shirt and weapons and jumped out. Nicole watched from the open door. The horse, a distinctive brown mare with white-tipped ears, idled in the roadway. Pierre's saddle was empty.

François, grumbling, walked around the carriage and corralled the horse. His boots scraped to a halt when Athos rode up.

"Lose someone?" François asked, his sarcasm unchecked.

"Pierre took off when I stopped in the village for a drink."

Nicole covered her mouth. Athos avoided glancing at her through the open door.

"This is a God-forsaken day." François grabbed hold of a wheel and shook it so vigorously the axel vibrated. "Then we shall find him."

François mounted the loose mare, demanded Cordes take Nicole home and turned to Athos. "You come with me."

The Comte's bluntness sent Nicole to a new low. Athos was wise in the ways of men and would have heard it, too. Her husband's tone had the sting of a hornet—Athos's story was in question.

Before breaking into a gallop, François peered into the open door of the carriage, draining Nicole's spirit with his intense eyes. "We'll take up where we left off once the boy is found."

Chapter 37
Usurping a Carriage

Nicole fumbled with her gloves but ultimately surrendered to the shudders. She yearned for her sister's rosary, packed above the carriage in a trunk. She prayed to Saint Gennadius for mercy. In her lap, her gloves were damp with tears.

I am married. I must submit. The idea bumped inside her mind as her head bobbed from the ride. Cordes could not find a wide spot in the road to turn around, and he drove slowly, making the dips in the road more pronounced. She couldn't hear the search party for Pierre at all. The canopy of the trees became thicker, and the carriage grew darker than the fading indigo sky.

"Whoa," Cordes said, drawing out the command. "Madame, you have a tag-along."

Pierre was just a foot from the cover of dense trees. Nicole called his name too loudly at first, then remembered—*he's a runaway.* "Quickly, inside."

In the shelter of the carriage, she instinctually checked him for harm. "How did you get this?" She touched the black eye. He laughed and shrugged off her care.

"I'm not hurt, except for this." Pierre passed a hand over the side where Athos had cut him. "And it's healing."

"He's looking for you. They all are. Why did you come here?"

"François banished me to Angers. Athos saved me."

"Angers?" Her frown deepened into physical pain, until gratitude for her nephew set in. She gave Pierre a fragile smile. "So you didn't run away as they suspect? Athos brought you here?"

Pierre smiled impetuously. She squeezed her eyes shut. "What is he thinking? You'll be severely punished if you're found. Whipped or worse. You must hide."

"We're going to hide together. We just have to convince Cordes to help us."

Though her husband's assault was fresh on her mind, Nicole realized Athos's gamble might pay off. An opportunity to vanish had landed at their feet.

Cordes argued with a ferocity that turned his face several shades of rose.

"Absolutely not! I have orders to turn around and return home, and I'll do that as long as I sit at the seat of this coach." He ground his bottom into the bench. "You've severely miscalculated. Now get back inside, both of you."

"Cordes, the Comte insists on sending Pierre away to Angers, for good," Nicole said.

"Well," the driver's face mellowed a bit, "I've been telling him for years to watch his step, and now see where his headstrong behaviour has gotten him?"

Nicole stopped Pierre from reaching for his sword.

"Don't even try it," Cordes said and snapped his mouth shut.

"I'm still your superior," Nicole said, venturing into authority delicately. "You're also bound by your duty to me, and I'm not going back."

She kept quiet an extra moment then began walking down the road alone. Pierre threw up his arms. "You know she means it."

"Madame!" Cordes' plea was scornful and desperate. "Madame, please don't make me choose."

She pivoted to a stance. "I won't. Just leave us the carriage. Pierre will take me on my way. Tell them he overtook you on the road and forced you off. He's already a fugitive. Please, Cordes, bear the shame. It's so little to ask."

He sat and scowled. "It's against every drop of sense in me. And I'd do this for no one else but you, Nicole. Especially not for you." Cordes pointed at the smug young man. "You have no idea the consequences you're courting. God save you." He jumped from the bench and began marching back with his shoulders squared, struggling for an ounce of dignity. After a few yards, he looked back at Nicole. "I hope whatever you have in your head is worth this foolishness. Godspeed."

Nicole did not feel endangered by the speed Pierre demanded from the team, but fear stabbed her chest all the same. *How far must we travel to feel safe? Where will we go? What if they catch us?* This mutiny could be Pierre's last. He shouted assurances to her from the driver's seat. She fell back into the once-comforting carriage bench, aware of a foreboding she could taste. A bitter slurry of doom.

The getaway took shape in the moment. The plan was no plan. The seconds bled into minutes and the minutes into the eternal spin of time. Every jerk in the carriage's balance or whip of leather signalled alarm. The end. A disaster of her own choosing. Her achy fingers clutched the cushion, and the velvet fibres turned to needles. The dark would make no difference. It concealed her escape but was no hideaway. She knew François would pursue them like a nocturnal hunter determined to feed.

A mellow patter of rain fell on the roof. Enough to smell and hear and interrupt her misery. A change in the wind whipped a damp curtain across her face. The raindrops quickly doubled in size and speed. They blew through the window, pounded the ground and hammered the carriage roof, increasing in severity by demonic proportion. The water kept coming. Thunder rolled. Flashes turned night into day.

At the peak of the tempest, Pierre squalled. It rattled her from the harrowing storm. Nicole thought he needed help, but after several more eruptions, she realized he shouted in victory, not in need. The downpour could have easily drowned out his cries of conquest. In disbelief, she thrust her head and shoulders out into the elements, the driving rain stinging her face. His features a blur, Pierre stood, face upturned, hair in a tussle, shaking a defiant fist and slapping the reins madly. Though he struggled to make headway in the torrent, he was crowing in elation.

"God is with us, Nicole. He's the rain! The storm! We're saved!"

Chapter 38
Dangerous Ground

"The ravine and ditches are flooding!" Vachon was livid. The search party converged at a landmark in the road, where Father Audric waited, grumpy and soaked. In agitation, Vachon nearly knocked him to the ground with his horse. "If Pierre is on foot, he's not going very far. This storm is too treacherous. I can barely see as it is!"

Water was pouring off of François' leather hat. Trying to act impassive, Athos hunkered under his own. Athos had ridden alongside François during the entire reconnaissance, partly because he wanted to prevent the Comte from discovering the fugitives but also because he sensed the nobleman wanted to keep an eye on him. He and François were the only ones who didn't seem ready to call off the search.

"Come on, François," Henri blurted in the downpour. "We've got bigger boys to deal with soon. We can't start back to Nantes in the morning tired and hungry. It'll cripple our plans. We'll catch our death out here."

Camille, the steadier hand, pulled alongside and made a more common-sense appeal. "You have what you came for. Your wife is on her way back. That's the prize. Not the boy."

François grunted and peered down the road, as if the fugitives he'd been chasing might suddenly appear in the flashes of brilliant lightning. Seeing nothing amiss, he reversed course and headed toward Rochefort. Each horseman fell in single file behind him. Father Audric rode Pierre's horse, and Athos drew up the rear, considering it a miracle that no one noticed the carriage had never turned around.

The long ride back was quiet and miserably wet. The rain eased up near the village, enough for François to talk without shouting. "I need a drink before we get back. Anyone care to join me?" He looked straight at Athos.

The consensus was to seek relief at Rochefort's only tavern, Le Vignoble, and wait out the rest of the storm. Basically, to get dry and drunk. Beaten by the weather, Father Audric excused himself to church quarters, not once taking exception with Athos's involvement. In context, Athos was where he fit in most, among men of swords and severe causes.

Two large fires, one in a centre pit and another in a corner fireplace, heated the tavern. They comforted Athos despite his worry about the other end of the road. He wondered whether Cordes had decided to take up Pierre's and Nicole's cause or fight against it. Athos had told Pierre as they plotted, "Appeal to his good-nature."

Athos sat at the table closest to the fireplace, while the brothers and Camille opted for the bar with its buxom young server. For several drinks, François sulked at the open front door before joining Athos by the hearth.

François took the only other seat at the table. "You know, we have more in common than most men."

"Yes, we both have the tendency to bring out the worst in people."

François' laugh sounded strained. "We both allow passion to dictate our choices. For me, I'm determined to reclaim my wife. You," he pointed, wine still in hand, "pursue honour like the Devil pursues the damned."

"Perhaps because he pursues me. I've escaped without harm so far."

"I'm curious. What do you think of her?"

"Your wife?" Athos paused for a drink, but his mind was chasing after an answer. "You want my opinion? That will only get me in trouble."

François refilled his glass and studied the liquid. "You've been alone with her for several weeks. Enlighten me. What do you think of her?"

"She's as you said in your letter, an island, mystifying, clouded."

"Then explain to me how you shot her."

The air in the room evaporated. Athos hated walking into traps. "I wanted to hunt, and she got in my way. Before I could stop my shot, the bullet caught her shoulder."

François took a sip and leaned closer. "She said you tried to leave, and she was injured attempting to stop you."

"I assumed I could find you in Nantes with little trouble. You can't blame me for my impatience. Or hunting a stag."

"And Pierre, I hear, dragged you back once. But the second time, she came after you."

"She was doing what you asked, keeping me here for your plans. That's what you asked her to do. Occupy me to satisfy you."

"She hasn't cared about satisfying me in years." François shook his head and clamped his jaw.

"Nicole also recognized how much Pierre admired me. Her care for him is no secret."

The shadows in the tavern darkened the Comte's brow to black. "Yes, and there's the matter of Pierre, the other piece that puzzles me. Why are you still here if you let him go?"

"He left of his own will." His glass empty, Athos picked up the bottle between them, finishing it in a single swig. "But if that's what you'd like from me," he said, wiping his chin with a sleeve and getting up, "you don't have to ask twice."

Though spirited men relished a fight, Athos wanted no part of one now. He headed for the exit, certain he would not be offered a second out. Everyone in the room startled when a chair hit the floor behind Athos and split into pieces at the Musketeer's heels.

"I expect you to be ready at dawn." The Comte stood in the line of attack. "Leave now and I'll have the entire province out hunting you with hounds and fresh horses, and I won't give up as easily as I did with Pierre."

Athos pushed through the tavern doors. Outside, he took a deep breath of the cool mist and started for the horse stalls. Perhaps the Comte would track him, perhaps not. If there was to be any escape, the opportunity was prime.

The ostler, a pre-adolescent pitching hay to the animals, became frustrated when Athos demanded he switch tasks.

"Just one horse," Athos said. "Only mine."

The boy stiffened, straight as a post, then pointed toward the tavern. He scurried out of the yard, dropping the pitchfork with a hollow thump. The sharp end of a sword nudged into Athos's spine.

"The truth, Athos." François wheezed at the rain that blew inside the shelter.

Athos raised his arms. "I've told you the truth."

François pressed the blade. "Why didn't you flee with Pierre?"

"Follow the logic." Athos talked as rapidly as the words would come, though his coolness was powerfully intact. "I'm still obligated to you, and I live my life by my word, you said so yourself. Pierre was disposable."

"An ordinary scoundrel would have fled after shooting a man's wife and helping his servant escape."

"But I'm not an ordinary scoundrel. I'm a Musketeer, and I stayed because men like you and me don't back down in the face of impossible circumstances."

The rationale was his only chance, but it depended on François believing in their shared characteristic: abiding honour. In the terrible silence before a false judge, Athos spun around. François' hand was shaking; Athos's claims were causing doubt. François' shoulders fell, and the tip of the sword dropped to the hay as he stumbled backward.

"But now I've lost Pierre, and it will cause me to lose her."

"She told me Pierre was her nephew."

"And the only reason I keep him around. Even Angers was no punishment. I just wanted him safe and out of the way, so I could have her with no distractions. She's all I long for. Every day. Every single day of my life." François sat on a mound of hay, the mist matting his dark hair. "Tell me. Tell me why you provoked me in Paris. I've wanted to hear it directly from you, but it could be that I didn't want to know at all. It was a woman who broke your spirit."

"I was much younger and taken in by foolishness."

"Women make men fools."

"For many years, I've believed that love is a lottery whose prize is death."

François dropped his head to his knees. "Nicole resists me. You probably know. She blames me for the death of her sister. It doesn't really matter what actually happened. Her sister would have taken her life despite my actions, whether or not I pushed."

"Pushed?"

"Not literally. She leapt to her own death, but I destroyed her will to live. I wanted Sibonne to disclose the whereabouts of her bastard child, so I told her I had killed her lover. Remi had run off with the baby when I came too close to finding Sibonne, so I thought she would direct us to her son rather than live empty-handed. If she thought Remi was dead, I deduced she might tell us the child's hiding place. She didn't."

"If she *thought* Remi was dead—?"

"Sibonne's lover is still alive. Pierre's father is alive." The men locked eyes. "I've been searching for Remi for seventeen years. The last seven years I've hunted him purely for Nicole's sake, in order to reunite him with Pierre."

Athos contemplated a thousand repercussions. François went on. "When Pierre came to us at ten, Nicole suspected he was blood right away. She kept it from me for a few weeks then finally confided her suspicions when I questioned her concern for the boy's welfare. Of course, I didn't believe her. But she couldn't be persuaded. She knew it. His features, his hands, and of course, his mischievous personality, all pointed to his identity. By the time he turned thirteen, his looks confirmed it. In our hunting chalet, there's a portrait of Sibonne and Nicole as young women. Their resemblance to Pierre is unmistakable."

"But you'd been looking for Remi before Pierre came to live with you—to kill him."

"Out of vengeance. When I allowed Pierre to stay, Nicole softened up to me for a while, but it didn't last. Once I understood my wife's devotion to him, I decided my only chance to regain her love was to bring Remi back. Reunite son and father. It was fate that I hadn't killed him already."

"Fate?" Athos's throat was dry. "Not a merciful God?"

"God, mercy, faith, have nothing to do with it. You and I, for instance. You picked your fight with me at a very fortunate time. I'm closing in on Remi. I'm certain of it. He lives with the gypsies roaming the provinces between Nantes and Paris, stealing from port caravans to make do. I would recognize him only at close range, but he'll be good with a sword, and that's where you come in."

"You think I could capture Remi without killing him."

"As easily as I could. He may try to intercept our caravan of sugar on a certain dangerous section of road, and we can capture him or another gypsy and ask for a trade. Remi, for another man's life."

"Do your men know?"

"They've been instructed to defend our cargo but not shoot to kill. That's all. The gypsies won't have guns. They'll come after us with cunning and brute force, and you're familiar with both."

Athos stroked a nearby horse, streaked with salt. He didn't want François to see his downturned face. "Does Nicole know Remi is alive?"

"Of course not." He answered quickly then stood, kicking clumps of wet hay from the bottoms of his boots. "I need Remi's safe return, or I have nothing. If she knew I'd lied to her sister, it would be over. If I have him, then the lie doesn't hurt as much. I can convince her it was a mistake. Otherwise, I'm certain she'll abandon me. She's already left me in spirit."

"Bringing Remi back to Pierre makes you a hero. You take credit for their reunion and then release Pierre from your care once and for all." Athos understood, but his experience taught him that well-laid plans rarely worked. "You could fail."

"The alternative is to live a hollow existence, trying to undo what cannot be undone and continuing to live outside her grace. My life with her is a failure." François leaned against a crossbeam and peered into the wet darkness.

Athos saw himself in François, the mirror image of his state not long ago. Agony mixed with futility. No future worth comprehending. The juxtaposition tore through Athos like a cleaver through a carcass.

François cleared his throat. "Love is a lottery whose prize is death," he said, toying with the cadence. "You say you know that kind of death."

"The evidence is etched across every inch of my flesh."

"And yet you live," François said before gathering his horse. "Be ready to leave at dawn."

After the Comte left, a half-drunk Henri flailed into the yard. "Are you two still at each other?" He shrugged, took a gulp from his bottle and handed the last sip to Athos, who drank it and braced for the night's finale.

★★★

It was past midnight when Athos and the rest of the search party returned to the château, hours after François. As they dismounted, a series of macabre wails pierced the silence, sending a chill into the night air. From a back balcony, a man was howling into the dark clouds. Everyone but Athos remarked on the obvious suffering. Then a series of shots rang out. Traces of gunpowder, like super-bright fireflies, skimmed up the corrosive sky. Cordes, disoriented and still soaked, opened the front door.

"Nicole is gone," he said. "Pierre took her."

Chapter 39
New Pages

A thos lingered in the dank air while the others turned in. He preferred space rather than sleep. Inside her chapel, the darkness filled the aching gaps between his bones. He lit a single candle and watched the flame become a solid teardrop. He knelt at the place Nicole came often and whispered a prayer.

God our Father, thank you for her. I owe her my soul. I feel whole again. Her absence doesn't diminish my recovery. How or why my turnaround has happened, I don't understand. Living these new pages of my life is not frightening. The future is feather-light in my hand. The story being rewritten, across tattered scraps, is miraculous. Is it you? God, if I come to know if it is you, will it matter? I ask nothing but this: Look kindly upon her. Forgive her. She needs your mercy, more than I ever will. She is one of your most faithful, imperfect as she strives to live your example. She is your compassion on Earth. Look kindly, I beseech you, for she creates the good you seek on Earth. I ask your forgiveness, for her, for us, for now and evermore. May she see me through such merciful eyes.

★★★

Anxiety reduced Nicole's body to a wilted heap in the carriage. She nodded in and out of sleep throughout the night until Pierre broke their journey. He looked full of unspent energy when he revived her. Behind him, the bluish haze of dawn peeked through the curtains. "I've found a place to stop. You need to rest."

The small inn was unfamiliar, her last trip having been years ago. The inn's sign was illegible, and the landmarks surrounding it barely constituted a town. A shed for a seasonal market, a trough and stakes for horses, a rickety row of houses and the smallest of hand-laid stone churches were the landmarks she glimpsed from the carriage window. She let Pierre make the necessary inquiries and readjusted her clothes and replaced her hat to make a decent entrance. Not that she cared about impressions, but these small vestiges of her upbringing never died, regardless of whether her life recovered from the consequences of recent events.

The coolness of the morning took her breath away. It would be autumn soon, and the change meant the dying season. How could she live through another fall and winter with a new weight on her heart? Irrevocably, her old life was gone. Adjusting to the new one would require more time than she had before the fields went fallow.

Had she fallen in love with Athos? If the pins jabbing her insides were any indication, she needed no other signs. She knew she had never felt this way for François or anyone else, so comparing it with her past was impossible. Her only reference was Sibonne, and the results of her sister's relationship left Nicole feeling empty. Separation from Athos trampled the notion that a life together would prevail.

Inside the inn, near the top of the steps to her room, she couldn't go any farther.

"What's wrong?" Pierre said, hefting a trunk behind her.

"Go get him."

"Athos?" He struggled to maintain balance.

She let her eyes answer. He flicked his head sideways to the privacy of the room, and she found the sense to take heed. As soon as they got inside, he unloaded his arms and his tongue.

"Usually, it's me who makes the poor decisions," Pierre said, unlatching the trunk and digging inside. "There's no way we're going back there."

"Take a fresh horse. I have money. Please, go get him for me."

"I can see you're worried, but we have it all worked out. There's a plan." His hands stopped searching in the trunk, and his eyes flashed with mischief as he lifted up her sister's rosary.

"This is a plan?" she asked, taking it. "To pray? To commandeer a carriage and hide in ramshackle inns in hopes we can outwit my husband?" The bile in her throat stung. "I need to see Athos."

Pierre stepped back and sat loose-limbed on the edge of the flimsy bed. His face beamed with pure wonder. "My soul be damned."

"Don't speak such words." She glanced around the room, certifying their privacy, except from the ears of God.

He let out a short laugh. "Don't say such things? Look at you. Never, never in my wildest dreams or upon the life of my own baby girl would I have believed this. This!" He thrust both arms out. "You two are in love."

"Did he admit—?"

"Not as recklessly as you have just revealed your affections for him." This time he laughed from his heart and slapped his knee. "I'm happy! For the both of you."

"How can you say that? It breaks my faith with God and my vows to François."

"How can you care for the Comte anymore? He's the reason we're here."

"It's my duty. I'm married to him whether I love Athos or not."

"Oh, don't start getting confused about your feelings, Nicole. You're definitely in love with Athos. Here." He manoeuvred her in front of a vanity mirror. Her eyes were bloodshot and pronounced by dark circles, but the trials of the night were small compared to the intangible ember of life shining beneath her fatigue. It made her happy, and suddenly, very sad.

From behind her at the mirror, Pierre's smile began to wane. "I may have little experience with love, but I know it can be as painful as it is joyous."

"I'm sorry you had to leave Hannah and the baby behind," Nicole said. "I didn't say my farewells to them. Did you?"

"Athos made certain of it." Pierre started for the door before she could reach out.

"What is the plan?" she asked.

If it had been any simpler, time would have spun backward. Backward to when Father Audric was escorting Nicole to Paris himself. The same course was to be followed. Athos had calculated that François would hunt for Pierre, so he had waited at the side of the road until the search began. As soon as Athos had distracted

François, Pierre was to commandeer the carriage for one destination, Paris and the abbey of Saint Germain-de-Prés, the original goal. There, Pierre told her, she would find refuge in the monastery with a sympathetic priest.

"Athos gave me a letter for him, a priest named Simon Grignan," Pierre said. "It asks him to give you sanctuary."

"He mentioned him once." She put the letter to her lips, then in a pocket, and twisted the rosary around her hands. "What about you?"

"Another letter." Pierre puffed his chest out. "I will go to the headquarters of the Musketeers."

Nicole tightened the rosary around her index finger. Any protest at this point was useless. "And what will you do there?"

"Make a name for myself."

Her body fell across the bed, her back to the young man. So much had happened in forty-eight hours that her thoughts compressed in pain. She mumbled her guilt. "You don't even know who you are ..."

"Then tell me." He was at her side, searching for answers in her eyes, unwilling to hear *no* this time.

It took her an hour to explain seventeen years of secrets. Hearing the tale of his family, Pierre's self-confidence about his Musketeer plans faded, inch by inch. When she spoke of Sibonne's death, Nicole broke down several times to cry and required Pierre's arms for comfort. He gave it, albeit with blank eyes. She knew he hid the worst of his feelings. The story of his past was hardening him, and the process crumbled her optimism regarding Athos's careful plans.

"I have letters for you," she said. "In her final days with me, Sibonne wrote you letters. I never read them. At first, I thought of destroying them, but I couldn't. Then, because of a secret plan I haven't deciphered, you came to us. Remi and Sibonne must have made an arrangement for you to be placed in my care if they were both gone."

"Where are these letters?"

"With my journal. At the hunting chalet."

He stared out the window. "Near her grave."

It took her a moment. "I'm sorry."

Pierre left her clinging to the bed covers. It was almost midday. He looked around the tiny room, and his hand gravitated to the pommel of his sword.

"What now?" she asked.

"Rest. Eat," he said without inflection. "Then, move on."

Chapter 40
Separate Journeys

S tretched out on a pew, Athos rested his eyes in the chapel. When Camille touched his shoulder the next morning, he sprang from the bench as if snapped by a hair-triggered trap. Camille laughed. "Do you always sleep in strange quarters so tightly wound?"

"You assume I was asleep," Athos said, his joints aching. He checked himself and inventoried his weaponry.

"Whatever the case," Camille said, fighting a smile, "our journey is about to begin."

Athos walked to a cross-shaped window by the chapel entrance. Outside, Cordes was assembling the horses. Henri and Vachon were fencing in the shade of an eave. By the light, it appeared to be only a few minutes after sunrise.

"What of François?" Athos asked.

"He says you and I are to accompany him to Nantes. He's sending the two others to track Pierre. What's his obsession with the servant?"

"I believe it's an obsession with his wife."

"And you seem mixed up in it somehow. How did you dare win her affections while working for her husband? Though I usually try to avoid intrigue, you'll have to shed some light on that story soon."

"We'll have plenty of time for catching up." In the night, Athos had decided against escape. Following through with the Comte's job would give Nicole a necessary advantage. If Athos disappeared now, the Comte would hunt them all. If Athos stayed, he'd be an insider. Athos watched as the Comte exited the house and approached Cordes, who nodded in the direction of the chapel.

Athos checked and found the candle he'd lit the previous night for Nicole's protection had burnt out.

"Where's Camille?" the Comte asked Cordes, which Athos overheard from the chapel window. The stable master pointed toward the chapel, and Athos nodded for Camille to take the lead outside.

The Comte waved the two over. "Take charge of the extra horse, Camille. It's your job to keep up with the provisions. Cordes is staying behind. Someone will need to be home when Nicole is returned."

The Comte called to the younger men. "Henri! Vachon!" The two brothers, sweat glistening on their foreheads, stopped their swordplay. "It's important you keep Pierre alive."

"What for?" Henri challenged, assuming a haughty pose. "He's just a rat, and a dangerous one, if I know the type. Kill him so you won't have to shackle him. You have sovereignty."

"And as sovereign, you'll do as I say." Unafraid, the Comte claimed the centre of the circle of men.

Bumping past his brother, Vachon bowed to the Comte. "I'll take care of it."

"But you must pledge to compensate us whether or not we bring him back alive," Henri said, behind Vachon's protection. "Otherwise, you send us on a useless mission."

The Comte mounted his horse, tightened his leather gloves around the reins and tapped his heels. "You have my word."

Athos felt invisible and was uncertain whether to take comfort in it. He was the last rider to leave the courtyard, and Cordes stopped him before Athos rode out.

"Monsieur, do you know? Do you know what I think you know?" His plea sounded more like a cry of relief than a question.

"Rest easy, Cordes. The light of her God is upon us all."

★★★

Nicole's back ached from the rough side road Pierre had chosen to take to Paris. Though she had eaten and rested, her mind and body were spent. She lacked coherent thoughts. The only certainties were the journey and the arranged destination.

When Pierre broke for the midday meal, he argued they should abandon the carriage. She suddenly gained a renewed attachment to it, despite the near-miss she'd had with François in it.

"I can barely handle the journey as a passenger," she said, her eyes sore from crying and broken sleep. "I don't think I could ride on horseback the rest of the way."

"Do it for Athos," Pierre urged. She frowned at the terrible unfairness of the demand. He retracted. "I'm sorry, Nicole. But we must find a quicker way. I don't think François will give up looking for us. This mode of travel is too slow. The side roads are too rough and poorly marked."

Pierre walked ahead, farther than she could see. She knew he was right. If they were to escape, she needed to shore up her fortitude and cling to the chance they were given. She owed him and Athos.

When she acquiesced, Pierre jumped in the air and let out an adolescent yelp. She took what little joy she could from seeing him act his age. In short order, he drove the carriage into a small opening in the woods and detached the horses. Then, acting as if he had used it a thousand times, he pulled out his sword and began swinging. He hacked at the ground cover to use as camouflage for the coach, but his strokes had the signs of a more experienced swordsman.

"Where did you get that?" she asked, standing within arm's length of the weapon.

"This?" Pierre lifted the sword to the sky. "It's Athos's sword."

He has given Pierre his sword!

Pierre turned the weapon in the light. "Athos said it was a superior tool to defend you."

Nicole watched him swing the weapon like an expert, trimming the laurels and vines and slashing brush with every swipe. Its sharpness was murderous. Still trying to grasp the meaning of the gift and Pierre's skill, she helped drag the debris to the carriage. When it was sufficiently disguised, Pierre took the end of his shirt and ran it along the edge of the sword. It gleamed, a marvel of craftsmanship. He set an odd-shaped rock near the carriage's hiding spot as a landmark.

They had no saddles. Pierre assured her they would buy the best at the next village. She tarried at their departure.

"Must it be a complete loss?" She gazed at the vine-covered carriage, ashamed of her selfishness. For the first time she could recall, Pierre responded as if she needed a lesson. "It's a ball and chain to two people in a hurry."

It didn't take long for her to remember why horses were one of her favourite animals. The freedom and power of the ride invigorated her, and she vowed to begin a new drawing of a horse as soon as they landed safely in Paris. They purchased equipment late that night at another unfamiliar destination, and her feelings of loss subsided. She awoke before Pierre the next day, feeling the same sense of purpose the sun brought with each new morning. *Renewal.*

Chapter 41
Not As The World May Seem

The men rested at eight-hour intervals. Camille held the lowest rank and always took first watch. They rotated as sentry, Athos taking the next guard, then the Comte. By the end of the second day, it became rote. No one spoke beyond necessary directions. Rapport with the Comte was tenuous at best, and their exchanges were rare. To Athos, it indicated the Comte was embarrassed for admitting his failed marriage—or more troubling—that he wanted no more to do with Athos for the complications he'd brought on.

Who could blame him? Athos had shot his wife, let Pierre escape and ruined a promised night of passion, and possibly, reconciliation. And that was the more digestible version of events.

On the journey, the Comte seemed deep in thought. Athos caught François taking stern assessments of him as they wove between forest and fields. The Comte was a smart man, having amassed a fortune by more than brute force alone. His suspicions of an affection between Athos and Nicole might surface. Athos's future lay on time and quicksand. He couldn't have slept in the most feather-filled bed.

The night before reaching Nantes, when François fell under the spell of sleep, Camille broke the stalemate. "You two are far from being friends."

Athos was watching the fire with long stretches between blinks. "A luxury on this mission."

"So, if I have the details right, you bet him that you could seduce his wife? And he agreed? That makes no sense. What were the stakes?"

"My agreement to come on this trip." For now, Athos believed muddling the details was justified.

"Did you make any inroads with her?"

"Her piety made her a mountain to scale."

Camille smiled. "So, you lost, and now you're helping François capture a gypsy and deliver sugar to the King. Do I have it right?"

Silence implied Athos's acknowledgement.

"For some reason," Camille said, "I don't think you truly wanted to sleep with her. I may be a simpleton when it comes to Court and the scheming that goes on there, but you strike me as someone who could easily find soft companionship."

"You have a right to be jealous," Athos said, hoping an insult might end the conversation.

"Ah, it must have been the challenge. You were bored, and Nicole was an intricate lock to pick. You wanted to test yourself with the most devout. God knows she's beautiful enough. So, now that you've lost, who's waiting for you back in Paris?"

"If I named them all, you'd be shocked."

"One, just tell me one. The prize, the sensuous treasure beyond all others. Let an old married man live." Camille grinned with anticipation.

Athos didn't return it. "First, you're not old. Secondly, wanting to live another man's life is a fruitless game. And lastly, I'd sooner die than divulge my one."

"You're a man of great honour, Athos. She must be quite desirable. I appreciate that. It's a shame you and he don't get along," Camille tipped his head toward the Comte, who breathed out in short puffs. "He's a lot like you, you know. His dalliances are a little less secretive, but only a little."

Athos quit his fire-induced stare. "What do you mean?"

Camille brushed his jacket and leaned back on his pallet. "He has a lover."

A waterfall might have drowned Athos more humanely. The revelation took him under by fathoms. Camille sat up again, moving into Athos's line of sight. "Athos," he snapped his finger, "you, a Court player, can't be shocked that one of your own keeps a mistress?"

"I … I didn't know." *Nicole doesn't know. Could she?* "Who?"

"Mademoiselle de Montpensier. Geneviève. The second cousin of Henry the Fourth."

"An affair with a royal." Athos repeated it, but not to continue the conversation.

"Scandalous, isn't it? If François suspected I'd told you, he'd be furious. He's adamant about keeping it quiet."

"Of course." Athos took a long look at the sleeper. "Discretion can mean the difference between life and death. How do you know?"

"When he hired me two years ago, I arrived earlier for my duty than he expected. Early, as in, the break of dawn. I caught him leaving a room in the inn where he stays in Nantes, and she was half-dressed following him out."

"Where does he meet her?"

"Nowhere in particular. In Paris and Nantes and other places. I try to stay out of it."

"Did he leave her behind to return home this time?"

"If I had known this subject would engage your tongue, I would have mentioned it sooner."

Athos rattled himself out of interrogation mode. "I assumed he was still in love with his wife."

"Oh, he is. I do know that." Camille nodded with the certainty of a death sentence. "He's deeply in love with his wife. He speaks of her only in reverence. Frenchmen may claim they love every woman they bed, but Nicole is special. And, as you've probably discovered, she gives him no outlet for his affection, and that can drive a man insane."

It can, as my life could prove. Before Camille tired, Athos pried for more information. The Comte had been seeing his royal for several years, perhaps three. She saw no one else and had turned down the proposals of several dukes to remain François'. He kept the affair secret by bribing anyone who knew. Camille's wages were padded to keep him tied to the Comte's every whim. Athos finished probing when the fire lost its flame, and Camille fell asleep.

Athos wandered away from the campsite and churned over the discovery. He had done more than insult the Comte's honour at the tavern in Paris; he had split the hair. François had fought Athos to uphold his wife's reputation but also to repel rumours of an infidelity. In complete ignorance, Athos had insinuated the Comte was an adulterer. No wonder he had wanted to question Athos right away upon his return home—to ensure his secret was still safe. *Safe from his wife.*

In one sense, if Nicole knew of her husband's affair, it would be good. She would have justification for rejecting his advances. But like the underside of a week-old carcass, it smelled rank. Athos hated knowing. He hoped Nicole had no knowledge of François' infidelity. Better for her well-being. For selfish reasons, Athos also wanted her decision to love him untainted. He wanted her love without spiteful motivations.

The complexities of their situation were heart-wrenching. All he and Nicole could hope for was distance from her husband. If the Comte found Nicole, the consequences would be harsh. Athos and Pierre might be implicated; the sordidness of the affair could be made public. She would withdraw in disgrace. For the first time, Athos roiled over their choices. Any future between them would catch many lives in an unsavoury stew.

But Athos was committed—to her, to love. The commitment lessened the risks and the loneliness. He hoped, during their night of surrender, the one promise he had made to her was clear: *I'm yours, Nicole, for the rest of my life.*

Chapter 42
The Crossing

By day four, the Comte complained every hour about the group's pace. Underfed and grimy, Athos lagged farther behind. There was no point in winning the Comte's favour. Athos could feel his contempt hillsides away.

Beyond a cross-hatch of dirt roads, Nantes appeared on the horizon. From a distance, activity at the docks appeared meagre. Athos expected the curves of the waterway to be swollen with boats of every size and duty. He recognized Venetian and Dutch flags right away; the humidity and low breezes wrinkled the colourful insignias in lazy folds.

Children with dirt-stained legs ran barefoot from corners to beg for coins. Their arms and legs were brown from the sun and thin from the hardness of living by fishermen's castoffs. Peasants hunkered and stared while mothers scrubbed clothes in the dirty water filling their washbasins. Men argued amid the stench of fish and brine. Stalls gathered flies on heaps of filmy, silver catches. Athos forgot about his own filth with each switchback into rows of shops and houses. Some were dismal shacks stricken by poverty, no doors or furniture. Other homes and businesses were examples of better fortune, bedecked with glass panes and flower boxes. The streets narrowed, and dust whipped through the tunnels of buildings and constricted alleys.

The Comte, seeming no happier since their arrival, cantered through town until the mossy odour of the river overpowered the stench from the ditches. At a T-juncture, the street opened to the piers, bustling with men and cargo. Athos and Camille stopped on the Comte's orders, and he disappeared on foot into a crowd of tanned workmen swarming to and from planks of vessels roped to shore. Canvas sails and crates weighed heavily on the dock workers' backs. Horse-drawn carts loaded with parcels and duffles swayed past.

"I think we beat our time on the return trip," Camille said, removing his hat to wipe sweat from his hairline.

"So sugar is our cargo?" Athos asked, sceptical of the plan. Being kept in the dark about the details of the mission ran counter to Athos's training, but he hadn't wanted to press François for details, lest he risk a fight. Prior to Nicole, he considered his life disposable. On this journey, though, life was precious. Every move mattered.

"The bait." Camille's eyebrows shifted up.

The appetite for sweets in Paris had grown with the appreciation of art and cultural diversions. Honey was good; sugar was better. It also became a lucrative underground commodity, desirable to the wealthy. Chocolate, an indulgence in Court, required sugar.

Athos appreciated the Comte's business acumen and how it rewarded him handsomely. François was an educated risk-taker. His market consisted of the privileged class, which may have looked down upon him, but the sacrifice was a smart gamble. As distasteful as it was in France, the English believed commerce was an admirable way to make money. The Comte probably forgot the snobbery in Paris when the port workers treated him with respect here, despite their lack of finesse.

Near the passage where Athos and Camille waited, two mules pulled a flatbed of rectangular boxes stamped *Produit de Haiti*. Several yards back, the Comte exchanged words with a captain, whose uniform was cut too high at the waist and exposed a hairy underbelly. They started arguing.

"This won't be enough," the Comte said, dragging a hand through his hair. "You owe me more mules. That's a quarter million *livres* of sugar we're hauling."

A twitch that had started in the captain's cheek went double-time when he spotted Athos and Camille outfitted for a fight. "But you have an extra horse with your team. Use it." The captain scratched at his waistline.

An encroaching horde of loud sailors crowded the Comte in passing. The noise and unresolved argument caused an uptick in the captain's facial spasms. Out of frustration, the Comte let the captain go and harnessed the extra horse to front the mules and threw the horse's saddle and bags onto the cart. He frowned at the motley arrangement. "Camille, you take the lead. Head us northeast, out of the city." Then to Athos: "You're in the back with me."

Camille whistled and shouted to clear the streets as they lumbered ahead. With the addition of the bulky cargo, it took longer to get out of the city, and the sun began casting afternoon shadows. The crowds and narrow streets hampered the caravan, and it jerked and struggled along. A few times, Athos recruited passers-by to angle the cart around corners, and at one point they all had to work a wheel from a sinkhole. The most direct route, in front of the Cathedral of Nantes, was clogged with chunks of granite and masons. This time the Comte's complaints, directed miserably into his own collar, seemed justified.

Athos kept quiet but grew anxious. He wanted to know what to expect outside the city. *Where will the gypsies attack? Are we placing ourselves in danger? Should they forfeit the sugar to track Remi?* After the last vestiges of the city passed by, his patience ran out.

"You leave me in the dark," Athos said riding up next to François. No response.

"How am I to assist you if I don't know what we're doing?"

The Comte yanked on his reins and fumed with frustration. Camille rode past, saluting them both. For the first time in several days, the Comte looked directly at Athos. "There's a channel crossing over the Loire at Bellevue. It will require three trips to get the sugar across the river. The wagon and horses will go first with Camille, then I'll take half the sugar across, and after that, you and I will take the last half. Camille will stay on the far side to wait for us. It's a shortcut but a notorious point of thievery. At any other time, I would direct my men to travel two days away to avoid it, but we'll cross and tempt Remi to strike. If luck is blowing in our favour, Remi and his band will try ambushing our caravan there." His voice dropped. "I make the first attempt at him. You fight the others, by pistol, sword, whatever means you see fit. I don't care if we kill them all, but we cannot, *must not*, kill him. You must only pursue Remi if I am unable. Do you understand?"

"I pursue him if you're wounded or dead."

"Only if."

"What's my incentive?"

"Your life."

The consequences stabbed Athos but he showed no duress. "How will we know him?"

"Do you know Pierre?" The Comte's sarcasm was palpable. Athos nodded, and the Comte's mouth curled on one side. "Then you'll know Remi."

Several miles before the channel, the mules needed rest. The men divvied up a hunk of stale bread and a sausage. The road followed the river, so Camille watered the animals and replenished the water stores. The Comte scratched calculations on a crate of sugar with a white rock.

After another hour, they arrived at the channel crossing to find the dock deserted. Athos estimated sunset was less than an hour off. On the glassy surface of the Loire, the flatboat floated midway between destinations tethered by a rope spanning the banks, a haul of a hundred fathoms. Their side of the river was thick with bluish moss; on the other side, reeds blocked the dry land. In slow motion, two pull-men headed toward the bank, grabbing the rope hand-over-hand with gloves stained by river scum. On the pier with barely room to move, Athos waited with the flatbed cart and team.

Once the boat docked, a pull-man, forearms bulging from endless trips, took the Comte's fare and directions as if handed marching orders. The crates were stacked on the bank, and the mules and horses were guided onto the boat with the empty flatbed.

As the boat launched, Camille lodged a boot between spokes of the cart's wheels then waved and called from the bobbing craft. "Make haste, noblemen. Don't waste your time making friends."

For Athos and the Comte, it was their first time completely alone since the night Pierre and Nicole had fled. The awkwardness between them seemed thicker than a thorny bramble.

"Have you confessed recently?" The Comte asked, his back to Athos, who watched the boat gain distance.

Surprised, Athos ran a hand down his throat. "My soul is intact. And you?"

He looked back. "Before I returned to Nicole, yes."

Athos's spirit dropped, anchoring his tongue. The Comte had wanted a clean start with Nicole. As long as the Comte lived, Athos could never attain such freedom. *For love, Nicole and I must live a lie.* The shadow of François would always hang over them.

It was strangely validating, knowing that Nicole was worthy of the love of two men. The wrongs between her and her husband were the central conflict in the drama. Ink on a script. And Athos was a character, written in by a mysterious hand, God's perhaps, at any moment to be blocked out. His time seemed borrowed onstage, and the next page might place him in peril, far from the arms of his love, who was directed onward.

"You never fully answered my question," François said. "What do you think of her?"

Athos stood at a juncture. The crossing represented the end of an obligation. François might overshadow Athos's hope for the future, but once this work was done, he would never be beholden to the nobleman again.

"I can say this. She's worthy of your torment. She's as close to a Madonna among men as there may be. A Madonna, with earthly eyes, who lives in a world of pitiful mortals. That's what I sincerely think of her."

François didn't look at Athos again.

Camille landed the craft safely across the river, and the oarsmen returned the boat. All hands loaded the first sugar crates. In carefully balanced stacks, the boxes were placed fifteen paces long and chest high, all the boat could handle. François stared at the other bank, the point vulnerable to possible ambush. Neither shore felt safe to Athos, who was left behind as François delivered the first load to Camille.

From his vantage point, Athos watched François hurry through the unloading and help pull on the way back. Flush from exertion, François' face was streaked with sweat and river grime. Once everyone had loaded the last crates onto the craft, Athos jumped onboard, and the boat swayed under his weight. Still breathing heavily, the lackeys pulled first. Athos's boots slid while seeking a spot at the back of the boat near François. They crouched like two gargoyles over a precipice, entranced by the swirls in the wake.

Athos counted rope pulls. Twelve … twenty … thirty-two. Then *thwap*. The air parted. The whir was unmistakable. Only an arrow could cut the wind like a knife. The pull-men broke their cadence.

"Look there!" one shouted.

But a succession of thumps on the crates at Athos's back kept him still. Two, three, four arrows lodged in wood behind him. A splash came from the front, and the mass of a pull-man bumped the boat's underside. Athos heard the man gurgle for help just before his body floated by with an arrow lodged in the soft tissue near his heart. Blood darkened the water in a winding line from the point of entry. Two more arrows sliced the red depths where Athos unsuccessfully reached for the dead man. From the front: "Abandon ship! Abandon ship!" And another splash sent the boat rocking.

François braved a glance. "Our last man's jumped! We have to pull."

"They're attacking from my side!" Athos shouted to François above the splashes of the fleeing boatman, who was thrashing the water like a startled goose. "Can you see the shore? What's happened to Camille?"

Athos squatted behind the Comte, who took a second look around the protection of the sugar crates. Arrows cut overhead, striking the water between the boat and the panicked swimmer until one met its fleshy mark, and the second pull-man went still.

"Who do they think they are? Robin Hood?" François blurted.

Instinctively, Athos and the Comte grabbed at the slackened tow rope, still threaded at the helm. In one yank, they wrapped it around the cargo to the safety of the rear.

"We're getting our wish," François said. "Damn the saints! Arrows aren't what I expected." Athos matched François' rhythm, gripping and pulling in guttural heaves. Teaming up, they tugged the rope, though it caught at the box corners, causing their boots to slip with each pull.

François threw an arm across Athos's chest. "We need better leverage. We need to pull from my side of the boat. As long as they attack that side—" François pointed, but his expression was more telling. His plan didn't guarantee survival. They were too far away to meet the enemy with swords. Pistols, their best protection, meant Remi could be shot.

"On three," Athos pitched in, but they both moved at two and planted themselves at bow and stern, crouched low, hauling rope like souls climbing from Hell. Arrows on the other side penetrated the wood and water.

Camille was nowhere in view. Onshore, the cart was unmanned, and the mules and horses were panicking. Their transportation sat vulnerable. François' certainty drained away. Athos pulled harder.

"Just keep up—" but Athos stopped in mid-tug when he spotted Camille. On the bank, he was gagged and roped, manhandled by a trio of men covered in black, their heads and faces hidden under dark brims. Another bandit in black with a tall bow walked into the open and loosed an arrow. For a split-second, Athos thought *jump*, before the tip buried into his shoulder.

Ripping the flesh between his chest and arm, he convulsed and blood sprayed François' back. Athos whipped backward then forward, landing on François and sending them into a skid. Athos flailed for traction, reaching for anything—François' bloody shirt, a wrist, a belt. They tottered like a jumble of loose fruit in a basket. Athos's leg slipped off the boat, but François caught him and violently swung him upright, jamming the arrow. Athos screamed, and François cursed. "Damn it, move back! Move back!"

A second arrow missed François' head by the width of three fingers. Their eyes met, and Athos saw the veins in François' temples bulge with a crude need for survival. Using a shoulder, François shoved them back to safety.

They ended in a heap behind the crates. When Athos landed, the arrow twisted to a point that almost made him black out. Scrambling up, François propped Athos to his good side and bent over him. Blood covered their clothes and gloves, soaking them through. François threw his gloves into the water and wiped his hands down his pants. Arrows sprinted above in chaotic directions.

"Your fighting arm is injured." François' nostrils flared; blood was everywhere.

Clenching his teeth, Athos sought focus. "Push the arrow out."

"It won't make a difference." François squatted and touched the quiver.

Athos inhaled in short gulps. His head rang. The blood on his skin felt familiar—warm and costly. "It's not fatal. Push it through."

François watched in silence. When he spoke, he sounded far away, and his words began to melt together in Athos's ears. "It may not be fatal," François said, "but it makes you lame."

"Do as I say! Push it through!"

François came face to face. Athos blinked faster. His vision blurred. With each pound of his quickening heart, Athos struggled, beat upon beat, against failing. Down, under, away. "For God's sake, push!"

François was stone.

Athos steadied himself against a crate, grabbed the quiver and pushed, grinding tendons and muscles. He arched, and his body shook. Pain coarsed downward in wave after wave. He wailed and pushed again, making his hands and the quiver slicker with blood. The tip tore deeper, scraping past bone, but the arrowhead stayed buried. François gaped and put what little distance he could between him and the horror.

In a final pitch, Athos rammed his body forward, hammering the arrow's blunt end on the deck. A sadistic crack snapped the air. The flesh on his back and the shirt punctured, and out poured crimson. The arrowhead jutted from his shoulder.

Completely limp, his sight failed, but he held on and spit out: "Break it off."

"Why? You can't fight now, and that's all I needed you for."

"You'll be dead as well," Athos rasped. "Listen, they're swimming for us." But Athos didn't know if the echo was the gypsies or the flood of darkness rushing in. He could only make out a wisp of François' voice.

"Give me your last confession." François sounded cold. "You need to confess. You've been where you shouldn't have. You've seen the blue-eyed Madonna, haven't you?"

Athos blinked erratically, the blindness complete. With each dip of the boat, his awareness rocked away. Athos yearned to feel secure. To bathe in Nicole's warmth. His last wish was to remember.

Brown, he recalled. *Nicole's eyes are brown.*

His body went under, and the chill of the water seeped in.

Chapter 43
Moments of Black

The current surged around Athos's body. The magnetic rush of the river pulled him through algae clouds and past slippery limbs. The water stung his shoulder and surrounded his heart. In the murk of the Loire, the fleeting promise of life was replaced by suffocation. A lifetime of memories gushed by, every regret and redemption. His head bobbed once to the surface, and he reached for a mirage in the rising moon. Instead of the light of hope, he touched the hand of God.

★★★

"Step back!" Pierre shoved Nicole from the window. "They've found us."

The street was grey as she peered over Pierre's shoulder to watch the scene twenty feet below. Vachon and Henri dismounted in the early-evening quiet of Le Mans.

Nicole squinted, but the feeling of oppression wouldn't budge. She and Pierre had ridden for days with precious little rest. They fell in exhaustion at any odd inn when the alternative routes took them too far off course. They decided on the small place in Le Mans because it was tucked in an out-of-the-way quarter of the city. Still, she was hunted, and the trackers mocked her getaway.

From the second-story room, they saw the men speak to the youngest ostler. Pierre steadied her. "I bribed the boy, but he won't hold for long. If they've found us here, it's useless. I'll have to divert them so you can escape."

"Escape? I'm incapable of going on alone. We have enough money to buy fresh horses. If we leave from the back by the tavern, we could succeed together."

"And if they find us together, we'll both be detained or worse. I can distract them, without violence, and you'll have your horse and an opportunity. Believe me," he said and squeezed her shoulders and kissed her forehead, "you can do this."

She saw manhood in him; it was calculating and brave. She nodded, and he glanced again to the road below. Pierre checked his weapons and stood by her.

"The ostler will take their horses. I'll go to the stable and hide them and ready yours to ride. I'll bring a lamp down there," he pointed to the corner of a leaning building, a long stretch down the street. "When you see me swing the light, leave. Head toward me, northeast. And don't look back."

Alone, she clung to her damp clothes. She had rinsed them by hand along the way to stave off the stench of sweat. They were all the clothes she had since her trunk was left on the abandoned carriage, and now, the accoutrements from her former life seemed frivolous. For years, her daily existence had been as smooth as glass; the shards of her new life were jagged in comparison.

But her faith stayed whole, and she prayed often. They were not prayers of fear but praise and gratitude for wholeness. Love made the jumbled puzzle complete. Athos was right. Her life meshed with his despite the unknown. Still, she checked and rechecked her course: Will God bless this love? The possibility catapulted her forward.

She retrieved the small purse containing the remnants of her possessions: several coins, Sibonne's rosary, Athos's letter to the priest folded into a leaflet of Psalms and one drawing from her previous life. She fitted her gloves, hooked her cloak and waited for the signal.

Suddenly, it came. The lamp swung. Pierre's face was obscured by a hat. She slid into the hall and down a second stair, away from the activity at the front. At the landing, she looked toward the tavern archway for unwanted stares. She darted to the rear exit, the creak of a loose floorboard her only regret. Outside, she tightened her cloak, rounded the corner and checked again for the lamplight at the checkpoint. Pierre was gone.

The stable felt like a crypt, closed off and cold. Several stalls were empty. Her saddle was on a horse she didn't recognize. *The work of a shameless Pierre.* She couldn't be mad at him for swapping for a fresh one. It was probably a better trade for the other owner. Her horse was a beauty but too fatigued to push on. Still, a strange horse, a dim night and a lack of lamplight increased her fear.

Residences and shops lined the roads through Le Mans, but she rode at a slow gait. She wanted to be the portrait of calm, though without an escort she looked out of place. Her skirt hid the trousers Pierre had loaned her to wear. Glowing windows helped light the way through the narrow roads until she came to the highway, parting her from possible danger and Pierre, her last connection to home.

She urged the horse to run at top speed. The moon reflected off the rocks and tree trunks and gave enough light to see. Yet, it was a bizarre sensation, flying down a strange road, guided by intuition. The journey inflamed her independence. She bent to the horse's ear and whispered: *Fly.*

She outran time. The hills climbed and fell. The horse ploughed through the dirt softened by rains and cool nights. The moonlight grew stronger; her eyesight grew keener. Somewhere under this sky, Athos, too, rode toward a shared destination.

Around a switchback, the road dipped. Her horse stalled and pinched at its bit, then danced in confusion.

"Whoa," she said in a hush. "It's okay. It's okay." But the hair on her neck spiked. Something moved up ahead. Her heart fell. "Hello?"

From the shadows, a figure on horseback sauntered forth. It blocked the way. Ominously, the horse and rider cantered in her direction.

"I need to pass," she said, determined to sound confident.

Thirty feet away, the rider kept coming. The light was too low; the face was a dark hole.

"And I," the dark man said, "need to find a runaway wife."

She slapped the reins and spun. The gelding responded like fire in wind. Nicole found rhythm fuelled by fright. Her heart thumped in time with the beating hooves. "Ho! On!"

A thundering demon on horseflesh charged from behind in a stampede of death. A bevelled blade flashed. The steel slapped the clips at her boot, and she veered sideways, her horse losing momentum and courage.

"No!" She bellowed, lacking the nerve to look back, to meet the eyes of the Devil. "No!" The sword streaked in the moonlight, pumping in and out of her periphery.

Give up and I die.

She yanked hard on her reins, and the chasing mass passed by in a streak. She leapt from her horse and landed stiffly but on foot. She scrambled into woods. A thorny vine ripped her seam, and she cried in bursts and bunched her dress into a ball. She kicked and kneed, clawing a path. A bramble slashed her neck, and a thin line of blood bubbled up.

Three more stretches to safety. Two more leaps to freedom. One more heartbeat and away.

Until heavy hands grabbed her waist.

Chapter 44
Pierre's Triumph

Pierre pulled the hat over his ears. From a shady corner, he watched Nicole sneak to the stable and waited to make sure no one followed her. Watching her disappear triggered a feeling he didn't expect, that of a bowl scraped clean of its last meal. She was gone. His touchstone for everything solid was engulfed by the night.

He was also angry. He had hidden it from Nicole, but the story of his parents had soured his gut. It wasn't fair of her to have kept it a secret for so long, season upon dull season at the château. He was a bastard. The son of a suicidal woman. An aristocrat gone mad. His mother's history mashed his future to pulp.

For years, he had polished his dreams of escape from servitude to a fine lustre. Perhaps from wine profits. More boldly, from his skills as a swordsman. Now that he knew his past, the game had changed. He could never be free of his family history. Had he just been a blacksmith's son, climbing from the bottom would be hard but doable. Now, the cruel truth was in his possession. Madness ran in his blood. He needed to rise to a height so grand he was untouchable.

His horse was tied to a stile several lanes from the inn. He wasn't leaving yet. He was waiting. Waiting to fight and begin rebuilding. His reputation began tonight.

The inn remained quiet, as did he. He had not been this composed when François punched him in the eye. Pierre understood his hot-headedness usually worked against him, but of the numerous irritants in his life, François topped them all. The history between them stunk of mutual hatred. When Pierre came to the château to live, François made certain that Pierre knew his boundaries.

The week of his arrival, in front of the entire staff, François pissed on Pierre's shoes. The sting of indignation grew from there on.

So he rebelled. He ran amok in the chambers and secret passages and pastures and played the entire staff with his charms. Nicole stood by him. Early punishments from François, severe whippings and beatings, were short-lived. And soon, so was the Comte's time in the country. It was as if Pierre's rebellion had been devised and executed to rid them of the sovereign, and it had worked.

A few tavern patrons stumbled from the rough doors below the inn in Le Mans. Voices and laughter from inside floated into the street. It would be easier to simply join them, Pierre thought. Be happy with an ordinary life. Embrace the birthright of the common man. He smirked. *I'd rather shrivel and die.*

The drunks passed, and another man crossed into the street. Alone, the figure appraised every object in the vicinity from a static point in the open. Then he pulled his sword from its scabbard.

"Come out, Pierre. I know you're out there." The shout echoed. A light from an upper window grew brighter, and the face of the man lit up. Pierre's first real challenger looked pleased. "Pierre. Show yourself. I know you've been here and have our horses."

"You flatter me, Vachon." Pierre wanted to toy with the nerves of the Comte's young henchman. "Remember, I am but a sapling and hardly worth it."

Vachon smiled toward the shadow where Pierre hid. "Those are Camille's words. I know you can fight."

Pierre came forward, sword drawn. "You sound certain."

"I take every man with a blade seriously. Even my brother. That's why I'm still alive."

Pierre circled to where the light was more to his advantage. He knew death was possible, but the rush in his blood offset the risk. "A duel, then. If I win, you swear to our safe passage."

"I'm afraid it will only be for *your* passage. Henri pursued your Madame with a fresh mount." Vachon jingled a heavy coin purse.

Pierre's throat tightened. *She's doomed.* "You'll never catch her!"

Like a gladiator, Pierre lunged. His sword rattled as it struck steel. The vibration numbed Pierre's hand. A response came quickly. Vachon attacked, ripping into Pierre's overcoat. The sword snagged in the heavy folds, and Pierre grabbed the end with the fabric and twisted. But the bounty hunter curled his wrist and thwacked the side of Pierre's leg, bringing him to one knee. On his shin, Pierre scooted and swiped low but missed.

Vachon stared down maniacally. "You're pathetic. I've killed a dozen men with this sword. Tonight, you're thirteen."

The soliloquy gave Pierre time to get to his feet and remember. *Focus. Attack. Defend. Attack.* His will dug in. The blade was perfectly balanced. As solid as he could make it, his assault punctured Vachon's bicep. The challenger doubled in pain and clinched the wound.

"Don't give up so easily," Pierre said.

"Damn you!" Vachon flung out with a lunge, but his strength was visibly depleted. Pierre swooped aside and skillfully avoided the blade. Vachon rushed him again, but the lunge was weak. Pierre chopped once, and the weapon fell to the ground, stunning Vachon and sending him sprawling for his sword.

Pierre stomped on Vachon's wounded arm and bore down. Vachon's cries peeled through the street. Pierre refused to let up and ground his heel into the cut directly on the bleed. After a semi-conscious wail, his aggressor passed out.

Pierre left him in the street and took his horse. Towing his own, Pierre galloped through the passageways of Le Mans toward another rendezvous with triumph.

★★★

Henri reeked of wine. He buried his face in Nicole's hair. "You smell as good as you look."

Nicole elbowed his rigid side and struggled for air. His arms encircled her waist more tightly.

"If you calm down, I'll loosen up," he said from his messy exploration of her neck. She dropped an arm. "That's it," he nearly cooed.

Nicole made a dry weep. Henri led her from the thicket by the wrists and planted her between the horses, caged by animal flesh.

"You're as fine as any horse I've seen." He slapped the salt-streaked neck of her horse, making Nicole shudder. "Possibly as fine as any woman I know, too. Men must gape at you. It explains why the Comte goes to ludicrous ends to retrieve you. Maybe I should thank him for the job."

Nicole felt sick. Sweat soaked her back and the night air stuck to her skin like a damp glove. "Please, let me go. I'm on pilgrimage, God's calling."

"God has infinite patience. Your husband does not." He grabbed her purse and handled its weight. "A few coins?"

He ripped into the small bag and dumped Sibonne's rosary to the ground. Nicole tried reaching. "Not what I'd recommend," he said, kicking it away.

He pocketed the money and unfolded the drawing from the Psalms before dropping the tiny booklet to the ground. A smile slowly formed. "This explains a few things." He dangled the charcoal drawing of Athos in front of her. His eyes shifted between her and the drawing. "Spending time in artful pursuits? Or making up for an empty bed?"

He crumpled the picture and stuck it under her horse's nose. The animal sniffed and nipped the creases until the ball of paper rolled off Henri's hand.

"If you're so quick to take Athos into your tender mercies," Henri said, "then perhaps you wouldn't mind one more." He grabbed both of her elbows and glared at her chest. "Once ruined, always ruined."

"Let me go!" She twisted, but he held fast and buried his mouth in her bosom and inhaled. In a flat second, he wrapped the lead of the horse around both of her wrists tightly enough to burn. He groped her breast and attempted to kiss her open-mouthed. She bit his lip. A slap stung her cheek.

"You've got no place to go." His words were hot on her neck. "This won't take long, and I dare say, it will surpass your Musketeer." Rough hands forged up her skirt. Her belly ached. Tears dampened her lashes. He fumbled with Pierre's borrowed trousers tied to her middle. She wanted to cry for help but knew it was futile. She fixed on a star in the sky and summoned blackness— the power to block out her entire body. *Never feel. Never think. And never remember.*

His mouth and tongue were thick and determined. He tasted of wine and garlic. And then blood. Blood on his lips. Blood in her mouth. *Impossible.* His body grew slack, and when she realized why, she shook at his moans. Blood oozed from the corner of his mouth. His last moment was an abrupt seizure. He landed on her like soaked laundry and dropped sideways. Then she saw the sword, half buried in Henri's side. It reflected the moonlight, and in the gleam, Pierre pulled it free.

Chapter 45
Athos and the Gypsies

H unger tore at Athos, and his throat ached from thirst. He roused for what tasted like bread and water and repeated the ritual in a haze, never fully aware of his surroundings. He could tell his clothes were dry, that a fire snapped, and the air was still as night. And then another night, and another. He slept and floated between memories of being underwater and his body losing heat. Gentle hands on his skin warmed him, and conversation broke into his drifting. *A Musketeer*, the voices said, *a Musketeer*.

"Are you awake?"

Athos squinted. The fire burned a few feet away, and the heat forced his eyes shut.

"Are you a Musketeer?" The tongue was French but gravelly.

"Water," Athos murmured. It scraped his throat to speak and induced a fit of coughing. Athos clutched the soft hand holding the cup and nodded twice for more.

"You can hear me, can't you?" The inquisitor was not the one offering water. Whomever spoke was more forceful, a man off to the side, where the light of the fire didn't reach.

"Yes, I'm a Musketeer."

Several whispered conversations began immediately. The exchanges were excited and quick and then were silenced.

"Why were you delivering sugar?"

Athos shaded his sight from the glare of the firelight. He could barely lift his head, and his shoulder throbbed. He couldn't feel his arm. "Who are you?"

"There's no authority out here, especially not the kind that might rule a Musketeer. Whether you cooperate or not, you'll be on your back for many more nights." The speaker came into the light, though his outline was all Athos could make out. He was slender and wore a cape with a sword and a bow to one side. Athos was too weak to stare.

"Did you shoot me with the arrow?" Athos's head swam, and the throbbing made him nauseous. He shuddered and vomited, too frail to do anything but turn his head. A second wave made his skin clammy and his head list. A cup pressed his lips, and Athos let the cool water dribble in. A rag ran over his face and mouth, and he smelled the fire for the first time.

He heard the caped man come close. "Can you feel anything?"

Athos wanted only to breathe, not to answer questions or resolve his whereabouts.

"If you can't feel your arm now," the man loomed above Athos, "then you may never again."

Intense pressure on Athos's elbow caused his eyes to snap open.

"Good," the slim man said, a flint of a smile growing underneath his beard before he quit pressing Athos's arm. "There's life in you yet. You are far from Paris, and you're alone. Your kind usually don't travel that way."

Athos swallowed saliva and a billow of hickory smoke. "The King can direct us as he pleases."

"The bandits would be thrilled to know they downed such a prize."

"Then you must feel satisfied, being the villain who attacked me." His head pounded even from a few words.

"Far from it, your lordship," the stranger mocked. "We try to keep the bandits from the shipments."

The heat from the fire filled the crisp air. It was too warm to stay awake or feel the breath going into his lungs, so Athos lost the battle of words to his body's need to heal.

★★★

In the pale light before sunrise, Athos woke. The fire was ash and closer than he remembered. He felt his cheek, thinking it was singed, and craved another drink of water, but none was near.

He lay in a glen of trees, an enclosure of green, yellow and red. Under lumpy woollen blankets, other sleepers clustered by the cool firepit.

A woollen scrap covered his lower half, and a bandage tightly cinched his chest and shoulder, which wept amber through the dressing. He remembered the blood. He remembered the clamp of the arrow. He remembered the fall into François' back and clamouring for cover. He remembered François' disgust, the refusal, *the push.*

Athos inhaled deeply and tried his uninjured arm, which was whole but stiff. The other, his right arm, primary for swordplay, he couldn't move.

Athos cursed and focused. The fingers, wrist and joints felt fused into a lead spike. Nothing responded. François was right: *You are lame.* Lame, Athos thought, but alive and very much keen of mind.

He used the good arm to push up. Blood rushed into his temples, and his ears rang. When the threat of the blackout faded, Athos bent his knees and sat up silently. He counted a dozen slumbering figures beneath covers. No one moved. Horses snorted from the woods behind him. He was weaponless, shirtless, shoeless and weak.

"Think hard about your next move."

Athos recognized the voice. From behind, the cloaked man strolled out of the woods. The morning light cast a distinctive twinkle in the fellow's eyes, making them bold and familiar.

"I can't flee," Athos said, turning to the dying fire.

"From the look of you, I don't think an injury has stopped you before." He came into the circle of the encampment.

"What good is a wounded Musketeer to you? I'm defenceless. You probably disarmed me yourself, whatever name you go by."

"I'm Reginald. And you, *you* are a most remarkable specimen of man." He stuck out a gloved hand.

Instead, Athos threw the blanket over his injured shoulder. He couldn't stand looking at the dead arm.

"It's not entirely useless," Reginald said, nonetheless friendly. "You felt me grab your elbow a few nights ago. But you're right that you don't have the strength to leave, not yet."

Reginald produced a leather pouch and handed it to Athos. It sloshed in the transfer, and Athos coughed after the first swallow.

"Too soon for wine?" Reginald found a second pouch among the sleepers and handed it over. Athos kept drinking the wine then took the water. Reginald knelt on one knee and smiled.

"Your body tells many stories." Reginald nodded to Athos's flank and the mark of near-death. "Care to share a few?"

Athos squeezed both pouches empty and tossed them back. "What do you want from me?"

"Information."

"You know I'm a Musketeer safeguarding a shipment of sugar. I have nothing else to tell."

"Who were you transporting the sugar for, besides the King? Who brought you to the Bellevue crossing?" Reginald's blue eyes narrowed, and he switched knees on the ground.

"A man I owed a favour. Now I'm free."

Reginald drew his sword between them. "His name, Monsieur."

"François Rieux, the Comte de Rochefort."

Reginald spun to standing and jammed the blade into its scabbard. Curses licked through his clamped teeth. Athos nodded to himself. "Friends, are you?"

"Why are you in his company?"

"I owed him my life."

Reginald spit into the ashes and a quick sizzle played out. "You bargained with the Devil himself."

"As did you, it seems."

Reginald stepped on a coal and twisted his boot heel. "Not with him. My bargain would have never been with him. He's every foul human trait twisted into the form of a man."

"In most respects, I agree."

"Your patronizing won't win you any favours." Reginald picked up a rock and threw it aimlessly into the woods, causing a small animal to scamper. "You're working for him, building his fortunes and taking up his causes. You allowed his greed to flourish."

Athos listened but was studying his captor's profile to determine his age; the features were too tortured, and his beard disguised the cleaner lines of his face. "As I said, I owed him my life, but I don't any longer."

In one motion, Reginald's sword was at Athos's throat. "He would have told you about the chance for an ambush. He didn't need a dead Musketeer. You were his protector. You know more than you're admitting."

Defiantly, Athos grazed the stubble on his chin with the blade. "I was his second. He would have sooner hung me than ask for protection. I had no choice. He needed me to keep his target alive."

"The target being a gypsy?"

"A man the Comte hunts," Athos said. "A man known as Remi."

Reginald dug the sword tip into the white coals. A nearby sleeper shifted under a blanket. Another snored. "I haven't heard that name in many seasons."

"You know him." Athos started to see a resemblance to Pierre.

Reginald nodded. "The gypsies say that Remi shares the Comte's past, present and future. If Remi could, he would kill him."

Athos scanned the sleeping company. "Where is he, this man Remi?"

"Your body may be afflicted, but I'm not as easily fooled by your cunning, Monsieur, Monsieur—?"

"Athos. My name is Athos."

"Athos, what will you do with your freedom from the Comte, if that's in fact the truth?"

"Is this what you call freedom?" He looked down at himself. "I'm captive and defenceless."

"We have no intention of keeping you," Reginald said.

"Then why save me if not for ransom or revenge? If you didn't hurt me, as you want me to believe, what am I to you?"

"Confirmation. And since it appears you'll survive, perhaps you can also be a messenger." Reginald scanned the sleepers. "I'm sure the gypsies would like to send this Comte of yours a message."

"From you—or Remi?"

Reginald laughed, stirring a few of the others. "If you knew Remi, you'd know he wouldn't send missives by injured soldiers. He would take any chance to slice your partner in two."

"Then why hasn't he?"

Reginald's good humour evaporated, and his jowl muscle flexed. A sleepy younger man placed a hand on his shoulder. "Father, is it as you thought?"

Reginald glanced back and nodded but only just. He glared at Athos. "As soon as you're able, these men will provide you a horse.

As for the message, the Comte needs reminding. The circumstances that may have bound one man, don't bind another." Reginald locked forearms with his son.

Athos shook the blanket off and moved like a puppet to get to his feet. Reginald and his son were joined by a few other men as an audience. Though bandaged at the shoulder, Athos had to act quickly to keep the arm from flopping.

"I think this Musketeer would be good company in a fight," Reginald said to the others, who snickered. "Too bad you belong to the King."

"I know of a young man who doesn't, one who feels just as Remi does about the Comte. He's learning his way, the way of honour, of men and good deeds, such as your effort to save me. You could offer him help. He's on his way to Paris now, to be free."

Reginald acted as if nothing were said, exchanging jibes among the growing group of rousted men. Athos knew Reginald was listening though he acted distracted. Reginald pointed in the direction of the horses in the woods, and his son left the circle.

"And this Pierre," Reginald said, "who is he to us? If he's wise, he'll forget the past and pursue his freedom, help or no help from a band of gypsies."

"He knows nothing of his past. He's innocent. But it makes his life unhinged, and he longs for a better future. If he were to know his past and know it well, his path might be different. His life might be different. Men are not men when their past is buried."

Reginald grabbed a pack and shoved a stray blanket inside. "Men are not men when promises to the grave keep them from honour."

"Tell Remi this young man is his own blood." Athos ran the words together to seize the open window before it closed. "He's bold and fiery and will do better in manhood if the past were his guide. He needs to know who he is."

Reginald turned his back to Athos and bowed his head. The sun had risen, and the warmth of the light replaced the dead fire. Reginald shielded his face from the new day.

"What would a son think of a father who handed him over to the enemy? Nothing less than a traitor." Reginald squeezed his temples. "If this young man needs a foothold, tell him he can't undo past mistakes, whether they were made by the heart or by the head. He will always be Remi Tremon's son, if in name only."

Reginald started for his horse too quickly when his son led two mounts from the woods.

"Heal fast, Monsieur Athos," Reginald said. "Like most Frenchmen, the gypsies are warm-hearted until the food runs out."

A few men chuckled and began tending a new fire.

Athos trusted that his legs could withstand the challenge. He reached the pair of horsemen as Reginald climbed into the saddle.

"Tell Remi that Pierre is no longer a boy," Athos said, faint from the exertion. "He's a man. A father. He has a daughter. A baby named Sophia."

A wrinkle or two smoothed from Reginald's crow's feet. He was as still as a rock. "When?"

"She was born this month."

Reginald looked to his son, and after a long pause, jabbed the horse with his heels. Letting go, Athos wavered on his feet. Before disappearing into the trees, Reginald called back. "Tell him where you found me, Monsieur. Let him decide."

The camp quieted after they left. Another offer of water brought Athos back to his spot. His stomach knotted and he rubbed his shoulder, then laid it on the cool dirt and willed it to heal.

Chapter 46
Meeting a Priest

For Nicole, arriving in Paris was like a curtain drawn open. The light was brighter. The noises were crisper. The activity, vibrant. While she had idled away in the country, Paris had thrived. Seeing it again after two years inspired her to want to know the future, impossible as that was.

She drew a blank about her last trip. Even good memories would have paled in comparison to her new knowledge of what had happened the last time she was in Paris—Athos had fallen in love with her from afar. She stopped her horse for an instant to ask God for strength, then she cantered onward.

Though she was worried about Athos, any positive change in her state of mind was welcome. Henri's death clung to her conscience. She would live forever with the image of Pierre killing a man. Paris lessened her burden because of its colourful shops and goods, foods and new faces. It made her feel the way she needed to feel to survive—hopeful.

Pierre had not spoken much since burying Henri by the roadside. Nicole had offered the prayer, but her involvement in his death kept her words short. She was culpable. If she had not fled her husband, no blood would be on her hands. The taste of his death flattened her appetite.

She wondered if Pierre wanted to be free of her. He kept riding ahead, leaving her alone for long distances. She allowed it because she was certain by then that no one followed. But privately, she lamented that he was growing distant, wanting to be his own person, fulfilling his life's dreams.

Inside the city, Pierre sped up their pace, and once, she thought he smiled. She remembered her first trip as a child inside the walls of France's jewel. The newness of the experience, leaning from the carriage window, young and free.

"Pierre, I could show you a few places you might enjoy, if you'd like," Nicole called over the clatter of a potter's cart.

"Just get us to the abbey." His dismissal thudded against her heart.

The abbey at Saint Germain-de-Prés was a milestone, an architectural stalwart that had withstood medieval siege and religious politics. The tower, the highest point in any direction, was impressive on its own. The monastery and church sprawled across an entire neighbourhood, just outside one wall of the city, and the abbey's occupants lived inconspicuously behind the cut stone and iron barriers.

Pierre left her at the wide, arched entrance so he could find lodging. She had never been inside the church because she had always attended Mass in private chapels at the invitation of dignitaries whom her husband courted for influence. Her anticipation grew to see its marvel and feel its history. It would be good to commune with God and re-orient her mind, but her feelings bordered on anxiety, too. She came to her destination a different woman. Her sins followed her across the threshold.

Inside, her knees locked when the door rumbled shut and vibrated over the amplified silence. The air was waxy and moist, and the cavernous interior made her breathing sound louder than a choir. Believing her presence was ear-splitting, she covered her mouth and nose and dodged into a nearby side chapel.

In the dim alcove, she came upon a life-sized statue of a man in robes. At his feet was a crow. The bird's face, upturned to the saint, seemed to pose a question. To Nicole, the question was obvious: *What next for me?* It chilled her. Often in her life, she had been the questioner, except that she had asked her questions of God by sketching birds. Art was her inquiry into life.

The statue fascinated a man seated in the quiet side chapel. He turned his head and noticed her. He resumed gazing at the statue and, without breaking his contemplation, whispered, "What's the bird thinking?"

Nicole looked side to side but found no one else near. "Am I disturbing you?"

"Oh, no, please. You're not disturbing me at all." He popped something in his mouth and began munching loudly. "It's a ponderous question, don't you think? The bird is asking something profound of Saint Benoit."

"That may be true. I think animals can communicate with the holy, but this is an artist's creation, and who but the artist could say what the bird is thinking."

The round man patted the pew beside him, and she accepted the invitation to sit. He offered her a handful of pistachios and dug out a rosary from the folds of his clerical robes. "I do believe the bird's question is the same as ours. That sounds muddled," he whispered, grinning on one side. "The question in the bird's mind is the question we each ask of the higher authority. We may adjust it from time to time, but the essence is the same, and it hits us like a diamond chisel when we're quiet."

He nodded and lifted his eyebrows to evoke a response. Nicole sent him a timid smile and felt safe. "My bird asks, '*What's next?*'" she said. "'*What's next for me?*'"

The priest took her closest hand and bowed his head. "Then you have come to the right place."

★★★

Simon Grignan's hands were warm. His stature was solid and his way, disarming. As soon as Nicole passed him the letter from Athos, she left her doubts behind. He unfolded the paper, read it silently and took a few steps toward the statue to rattle his throat.

"Well, you've certainly arrived with a purpose." He walked briskly to a side door. "Please, come this way."

The door opened outside to a covered walkway adjacent to an expansive meditation garden. Hedges lined the passage and deterred wanderers. Empty benches in the garden sat against the seasonal bounty, late summer blooms and trees heavy with fruit. At the end of the walkway, a one-story building with tiny square windows stretched through the garden. Inside this wing of the abbey, the hallways were wide and the doors along the corridor were closed. At an L in the hallway, another sequence of doors began, and at the building's terminus, the priest led Nicole to an open room.

It was a library, no bigger than a stall for horses, with a rough bench and a hand-hewn table of beige wood. Grignan deposited her on the bench and pulled up a chair with a worn red cushion.

"Tell me, is Athos well?"

Nicole wiped the back of her hand across her cheek. "When I last saw him, two weeks ago, yes. He was whole in body and mind." She looked down.

"And you?"

"What can you tell from the letter?" She shot him a troubled look.

"His letter advocates for your privacy. He writes here, 'Keep her under a cloak of secrecy.'" Grignan folded the scrap of paper and stared at her ring finger. "Monasteries are not hiding places, Madame. You're married, is that correct?"

She nodded. "My husband and I are estranged."

Grignan made a short, exasperated snuffle. "I must admit that I'm a little confused." He placed the letter on the table.

"I need sanctuary." It spilled out of her. "I came to Paris on pilgrimage, but in truth, I need distance. My marriage is tenuous, and my husband will search for me. I'm not ready to confront the situation I find myself in ... the situation *we* find ourselves in."

"You mean you and Monsieur Athos?"

"He shouldn't be blamed," she pushed on before he could interrupt. "Please, Father Grignan, he spoke kindly of you as a man of learning, far beyond the stricter teachings of the church. You left an impression on him. When you see him again, you'll see he is changed."

Grignan coloured but tried to downplay his pride. "I'm a man of the faith, Madame. I adhere to the church's principles as devoutly as anyone who dedicates his life to God. I simply try to be open to other interpretations, if only for the sake of argument."

She felt flush as well. "Can you help me? Help us?"

He tottered onto his clogs and went to a shelf where he zeroed in on a slim volume. Handling it with care, he flipped to the end, pointed and read:

"O cunning Love! with tears thou keep'st me blind.

Lest eyes well-seeing thy foul faults should find."

Grignan chuckled then laid the book beside her. "The man who wrote that wasn't a religious man, and he was English." His tone became serious again. "Madame, I'll help you, but I harbour concerns for your wholeness. I believe, very soon, you should confess."

She bent into her lap and cried, bringing the priest back to her side. Grignan patted her back and read aloud from the book until the light changed in the room. He said the sonnets were written by a man named Shakespeare who had experienced overwhelming love and betrayal. The poems quieted her, and after many tears, she knelt at the priest's feet. Like the bird in the statue, she submitted to God and asked her question: *May I be forgiven?*

★★★

Pierre seemed cavalier when Nicole told him she was staying at the monastery; he had found lodging near the Musketeer base. After word of her accommodations, he fidgeted in his saddle.

"Please, Pierre, don't be angry with me."

His expression was cold. "We've come a long way. I thought this journey meant freedom for me and for you. Somehow, that's not what I feel."

Nicole peeled his hand from the saddle horn and held it against her cheek. "Promise to forgive me and also your parents, especially your mother."

He stared ahead.

"If nothing else," she said, "remember that anger and a sword make a dangerous pair. Hannah and Sophia need you. We all need you to stay safe."

She squeezed his hand before he let go and backed the horse into the street. She muttered, "I love you," but he never returned the good-bye.

★★★

Within a week, the sunlight from Nicole's small window became her only companion. She rarely saw a monk in the wing where

Father Grignan put her. Meals were brought to her door. It seemed to her a place for castaways or recluses. She didn't mind, for she spent the days in penance and in recreating the events prior to her arrival. Often, the wings of her imagination carried her straight to Athos.

She wanted to write to him and give assurances of her safety. And she wanted to write Pierre and make good her misjudgement. She couldn't do either. She did not know of Athos's whereabouts. In peril? In pursuit? In Paris or in the clutches of her husband? For Pierre, she struggled with the right words: *I am ashamed. It was wrong for keeping the past a secret.* The right words didn't come. She should have told him his lineage from the beginning, regardless of the Comte's wishes. Her mistake would hinder his dreams.

Grignan appeared at her door after the evening meal one night. His shoulders slumped.

"Madame Rieux, I must ask you. Is your path becoming clearer with time?"

She offered him a seat and returned to the desk. Her quill was dry. "How long have you known you wanted to serve God?"

"From a young age. Ten, I think. I was good at preparing the communion." He grinned like a new altar boy.

"Did you ever fall in love?"

Grignan's cheeks pinked, and he coughed into his hand. "My attentions were elsewhere."

Nicole tightened her shawl and stood by the window. Her insides felt constricted. "In the view of the church, my choices are limited. I'm married. My attention may be elsewhere," she checked his reaction, "but my options are few."

Grignan locked his hands together. "Madame, are you familiar with the teachings of Thomas Aquinas?"

"Of course, but I can't recite him."

"He was a great man and a deep thinker. He believed in certain qualities of real things."

"Real, as in flesh and blood? Of the body?"

"Yes, in a way," Grignan said. "He believed that all real things have transcendent properties of being. Their properties are truth and goodness. And most definitely, he thought that all things have a final cause and, therefore, a purpose."

"A purpose for living?"

"A purpose of being," he nodded. "So, if we live by Thomas's teachings, we have a purpose in existence. Apply his idea and you'll know if your life measures up."

"But what about sin? Sin is evil, and when we commit sin, we stray from our purpose. Isn't that what the church teaches us? How can we honour our purpose when sin has been committed?"

"I believe you must answer the first question." He stretched from the seat. "Madame, what is your purpose? How do you pursue truth and goodness? How is it manifest in your life?"

Her head thundered. Her life story tumbled about, beginning from childhood: chasing her sister in the fields; playing dolls and silly games; learning to care for kittens and catching frogs. With her father, there were walks; with her mother, doting education and refinement. She absorbed the love they gave, and in her adulthood, it flowed generously from her to others. Love connected the beads of her life. Despite any walls, she loved the people within her sphere of influence. She even cared about François, though their union held no passion.

"Ah," Grignan said. "I can see you know what your purpose is."

She pinched the bridge of her nose to ward off the faintness. Grignan offered a cup of water.

"But I have sinned," she said. "You heard my confession."

"It's called the problem of evil, and wise men have contemplated it for years and will contemplate it to the end of time."

He poured a second cup for himself. "Thomas Aquinas considered it, too. He believed that God allows evil to exist so that good may come of it." He paused for a drink. "When you arrived, you told me that I would find Athos to be a changed man. You did, didn't you?"

In her mind, Athos's voice resounded: *You have freed me from darkness. I owe you everything.*

"He ... he has found light again." Her voice trailed off, disbelieving the beauty of the paradox—his change had come because of love, though it was a sin.

"And if he knows love, then he knows God." Grignan tapped her knee. "You, Madame, have led another to God. Take solace in such goodness, despite the troubles that bind you."

The priest soon left. Exhausted, she laid on top of the bedcovers. The night bore down, her energy waned, and her mind wandered to a peaceful place. She was walking to the pond, skimming the grasses with her outstretched arms as they brushed her clothes. The sun crossed below the horizon. The water smelled clean, and under the willow, she found Athos.

Chapter 47
The House of Treville

Pierre sat in his room for two days, pouting and ashamed that he lacked the courage to present Athos's letter to Monsieur de Treville. Being in Paris was exciting and disorienting. Both the stench and the sweet aromas of city life wafted into his upper window. Below, he saw merchants and aristocrats bartering in foul tempers. Children raced about in neatly ironed attire behind women in dresses so wide that the streets seemed to shrink at their passing. The women were the most fashionable and the most beautiful he had ever seen. It occurred to him, in a state of mild disbelief, that Nicole and Hannah and a few others at home were the only women he had ever known.

He read and reread the note to Treville:

M. de Treville, I present to you Pierre Tremon of Rochefort, Bretagne. He could do well under your wing. I vouchsafe his ability and will return to his mentorship as fate will allow. In duty, Athos.

Pierre wished Athos could present him in person, introduce him as the swordsman he knew he was. During his short time as Athos's student, he had strengthened his sword-fighting skills to a respectable level. Sparring with the Musketeer had become the highlight of Pierre's day and even began to rival his time with Hannah, who was miserable from the pregnancy. In fact, the last night they had slept together made him want to reach for the sword all the more—to make a name for his child and make Hannah a Musketeer's wife. She was oblivious. Because of her simple nature, she never questioned him about the ambition fogging his mind.

The skills Pierre wanted to learn from Athos encompassed more than swordplay. He wanted to know every aspect of society: how are personal favours given and received? What intrigues can advance a man in Court? How does one gain an audience with the Queen? It beguiled Pierre to be in the company of a man so close to royalty. Athos was Pierre's route to destiny.

As were Pierre's conquests of Henri and Vachon. When tales of his exploits became public, respect would follow. Pierre regretted he had shown Vachon mercy. Henri was an easy kill. Watching him manhandle Nicole sickened Pierre much more than the blood that later gushed from Henri's gut. Death was fascinating and macabre, how swiftly life ended from the thrust of a blade.

At all hours, Pierre continued to watch the street from his room. One particular afternoon changed his attitude. A nobleman wearing a rabbit-trimmed jacket slapped his servant to the ground. The young man was about Pierre's age. The aristocrat spoke harshly and left the peasant on his knees. Before getting up, the servant spat on the ground where the man had stood. Pierre secured his weapons and left with his letter.

The house of Treville buzzed with activity. Dressed in his cleanest clothes, Pierre appeared humble. In all aspects, he was dull in comparison to the Musketeers in Treville's chambers. Men in fanciful jackets and trousers bobbed about with spikes and chains, daggers and spears. Leather dummies became targets when real matches were scarce. Pierre gawked as one guardsman defeated four muscled men in a row at arm-wrestling. The winner passed over Pierre for other opponents.

A valet pointed him to an upstairs office suite, where Pierre presented his note to a male secretary. A few seconds later, the secretary motioned him in. Behind a desk, a uniformed officer, whom he supposed was Treville, looked up at him, back down to a logbook and resumed writing.

"I have Monsieur Athos's sword, if you need further proof," Pierre said and went for the sword.

"Please keep your weapon at your side." The man had his head in the book. "I have your letter of introduction, and that's enough."

But the conversation stalled, and the officer kept writing. Pierre began to squirm. "Am I to stand here—?"

"Quiet." He scribbled on. After several broad strokes, he laid the quill aside.

"I'm Monsieur de Treville. Tell me about Athos." Treville leaned back in his chair and folded his arms.

"Monsieur Athos?" Pierre expected the questions to be about his own fate. "He's with my Lord, the Comte de Rochefort." Then he smiled. "But Athos made it possible for me to be here."

"I surmised that much," Treville said picking up Athos's letter. "And he thinks you're worthy to be a Musketeer."

Pierre grew an inch. "I pledge my loyalty to the King."

"Yes, yes." Treville sounded annoyed. "But Monsieur Athos, is he … well?"

Pierre thought Treville's questions impertinent. "Do you mean," Pierre asked, "has he suffered any bodily harm? Not in the time I was with him."

"Let me rephrase." Treville came around the desk. "Is Athos in a mood that … that is light?"

Pierre's eyebrows shot up, hoping his answer would end the matter. "Why, yes. He's in love."

Treville sat abruptly on the edge of the desk. "Say that again, young man."

"He's in love, though I cannot tell you who she is."

Treville's laughter bounced from dark panel to dark panel, filling the room with a spirit that broke the tension. Pierre began laughing, too, mostly to relieve his own nervousness. The secretary returned to the room befuddled but bearing another message, which he whispered to Treville.

"By all means, send him in," Treville responded loudly.

A lanky soldier marched in wide strides to Treville and bowed. He then turned to Pierre with a broad, open face. Treville slapped the Musketeer on the back and blustered: "D'Artagnan, this is Pierre Tremon, the newest friend of our dear Athos. Monsieur Tremon brings us good news." Treville winked at Pierre. "Athos is in love."

★★★

"Here. Keep us happy until dawn!" D'Artagnan slammed several coins on the bar of a neighbourhood tavern, La Plume et Pointe. The barkeeper slid the coins into an apron pocket.

Placed in the care of the Musketeer by Treville, Pierre followed d'Artagnan to a well-lit table. D'Artagnan was determined to celebrate the news, and Treville had returned to his logbooks, smiling. Pierre's impression of Musketeers, foremost as serious men, was soon shattered by d'Artagnan.

"I see you favour the brunettes," d'Artagnan said as Pierre stared at a handsome woman laughing nearby.

Pierre nodded and checked whether d'Artagnan saw the woman send a brash air kiss in his direction. "There are too many to admire."

"So take your time and find the right one."

"I'm promised to another, and I'm a father."

"At your age? Married?"

"Not yet. My sovereign and the village priest refuse to allow it."

"Ah, good for you. It won't be a complete sin then to sample the Paris treats." D'Artagnan grinned toward Pierre's new admirer. "Now, start from the beginning. I want to hear everything about Athos."

Pierre sipped his wine and muddled through the story of meeting Athos. He showed d'Artagnan his wounded side, which was healing into a long scar. He talked of the evenings spent rattling blades in the bedroom, blatantly testing swords in the luxury of the château. When his story turned to Hannah and the baby, he lost his train of thought.

"Will you make me a Musketeer?" Pierre cringed at his own immaturity, but he had heard no promises about his future.

"I can't make you a Musketeer," d'Artagnan said. "Is that what you're here for?"

Pierre ground the bottom of his cup into the table. "I'm here to change my fate. The Musketeers are my fate."

"You'll have to fight."

"I already have." Jubilantly, Pierre retold the escape from Le Mans and his defeats of Vachon and Henri. When he paused, d'Artagnan laughed, making Pierre feel small.

D'Artagnan waved off Pierre's poor attitude. "Not that those aren't important, but the fighting you'll need to do will be in a regiment with other men in combat. My time came at La Rochelle. I was a young man of simple means and was first assigned to

Monsieur de Essartes' guard. When I had demonstrated my abilities there, I rose to the ranks of Musketeer."

"But the French aren't in any wars right now, are we? What are my options if not the battlefield?"

D'Artagnan poured more wine. "The French are always on the verge of a fight. Between the Spaniards and the Protestants, we'll never have a moment's rest. Treville is making assignments now for another attempt to push the Huguenots from Montauban, so it could come sooner than you'd like. Service in the field will earn you the King's emblem. Duelling, on the other hand, will make you a notorious criminal and possibly land you in the Bastille. Or dead. I don't know which is worse."

"The Bastille?"

"The Cardinal has convinced the King to decree duelling an offense punishable by imprisonment. No one listens, but take care because picking a fight might land you in a place worse than death."

Again, the limits on Pierre's opportunities came as a blow. The rest of the evening and on into dawn, he was as attentive as tree bark. He drank, but the wine coated his throat and stomach in bitterness. The small steps he'd taken to freedom felt miniscule, and his impatience simmered. The women sauntering in and out of view were the only diversion.

Unbelievably, he sat in the company of a Musketeer and would soon be assigned a position higher than servant. But the longer he sat, listening to the merriment in the tavern, the less he felt uplifted by it. He blamed his father. He blamed his mother. But most of all, he blamed the Comte de Rochefort.

Chapter 48
Recovery and A Friend

A clamour started at dusk. Athos had spent the day exercising his good left arm, where his reflexes were fluid. His right was in constant pain, and it still wouldn't move. He humoured the gypsies, who found his determination to heal as entertaining as a troubadour.

Athos was resting when the commotion spilled out from the surrounding woods. A small group sent to the nearest village for provisions returned with an unusual find.

Announcing the discovery, a burly man with a head like a cannonball, whom Athos knew as Guere, swore in the direction of Athos. "Haven't we got our hands full with one lame swordsman?"

The gypsies had rigged up a gurney with a horse blanket and bamboo shoots. Across it, a man curled on his side.

"Camille!" Athos scrambled on his knees across the dirt. Camille was quiet and wheezed irregularly. Sweat dampened his forehead, and his cheeks were sallow. "Bring him water!"

"You know him?" Guere said, poking the fire. "Then you can take care of him."

Athos urged Camille to receive water, but nothing went in. "Give me the wine," Athos said, wedging a bottle through Camille's chapped lips. The wine drizzled out one side and prompted a quick choke.

"Enough," Camille said. His throat sounded dry, and his face was sunburned.

Athos motioned to one of the women, and she opened a small wooden chest.

"Left for dead," Camille said and weakly peeled back his jacket, where blood had dried on the breast lining. The stain near his chest was damp. A bullet had pierced front-to-back, at a location identical to Athos's injury. Without thinking twice, Athos unwound part of the bandage from his own shoulder and began to dress Camille's wound. Camille winced and recoiled in pain.

"At least you can move it," Athos said, stopping at the armpit. "That's more than I can say."

Unfazed by the comment, Camille fell back limp. He took water, and the healer woman covered his sunburn with ox lard. The men in the camp lost interest and took to cooking dinner. Athos sat by Camille through the meal and the fall of darkness.

The night was moonless, and Athos couldn't sleep. Hour after hour, he listened for any change in Camille's rough lungs. How many days had Camille been forsaken? Five? Six? Death might be close.

At the quietest point in the night, Camille rustled under the covers, and Athos bent to his friend's mouth with water. Camille managed several long drinks.

"How long has it been?" Camille said, his voice a scratch in the air.

"You've been asleep for several hours," Athos said.

"No. How long—in love with Nicole?"

Athos laid Camille's head on the pallet and turned toward the fire. "When did you know?"

"When François surrendered onshore."

"He spoke of it?"

"He cursed her name."

"Did the gypsies kill him?"

"They released him for the sugar."

"And you?" Athos asked.

"Shot. I should be dead."

"Thank God you're not," Athos said, rubbing his own wound and feeling useless. "Rest."

"Your arm," Camille said.

"Don't worry, my friend. God is also kind to me." Athos raised his good arm and clinched a fist, a silhouette in firelight. "I'm ambidextrous."

In a few hours, the sun rose in a ball of burnt orange. Athos remained at Camille's side, wondering if his friend would deal with the pain as a Musketeer would, conquering it mentally. Athos's shoulder and arm, wrapped immobile, throbbed in dull pulses, but it was a distant concern. He was growing restless; he needed to reach Nicole before the Comte did. His dread smouldered near the flash point. If Vachon and Henri had not found Nicole, the Comte would hunt her with the bloodlust of a wolf on the scent of a fresh kill.

Camille awoke mid-morning, appearing more lucid. "Water, then a word."

Athos carefully positioned the spout to Camille's mouth. "I must leave today, Camille. I'm strong enough, and my heart demands it. I regret I won't oversee your care, but these are kind people, and my obligations are to her. You seem to have survived the worst of it."

"Go to her, but I caution you, the Comte is filled with evil now. His heart is destroyed."

Athos stayed through breakfast, feeding Camille rye porridge and attending to personal good-byes with everyone who had helped him. The mood was light, in peculiar contrast to the cloud forming over the ridgeline.

Chapter 49
To Destroy a Man

A mist covered the wrought iron gates of Paris in droplets. Pierre counted the lines of water to pass the time, waiting at the city barrier of Quinze-Vingts. The moist air and wine filled him with buoyancy. After his night of celebration with d'Artagnan, he had kept on drinking. The entire day and the next. Out in the elements, he gulped from a bottle in the dark, and with each subsequent drink, he looked more and more the part of a destitute beggar, hair sticking out in stray patches and wet clothes sagging on his frame.

Wine provided the perfect fuel for the courage and stamina to wait out his nemesis. The entrance at Quinze-Vingts gave Pierre a faultless advantage. There were nooks and walls to hide in and around, and very little foot traffic passed in the street through the open gate.

Pierre's idea had taken shape when d'Artagnan took him out carousing. Unbeknownst to the Musketeer, Pierre was calibrating the details of a plan with each sip of wine. After Nantes, the Comte would more than likely ride to Paris to find Nicole if she was not returned home. The Comte would station himself at his apartment and search every niche of the city for her. In well-disguised conversation with d'Artagnan, Pierre learned of the closest point of entry to the Comte's residence. He planned to wait at Quinze-Vingts until he froze to death.

The odds were poor he'd run into the Comte. But Pierre had nothing else. No Musketeer billet. No commission. No Hannah. No Nicole. No spiritual foothold. And for hours in the drizzle, wet to the skin and hungry in the belly, freedom reigned.

A rumbling started beyond the wall, and his neck tensed. The lumbering of horses and wheels increased in volume, and when he dared to peek, he spied a cluster of bobbing lanterns. Five horsemen in riding outfits raced their horses at full gallop toward the passageway. The piping on their jackets and studded cuffs sparkled in the moonlight. A carriage, gilded with golden foil and symbols of royalty, raced directly behind them. Pierre stepped from the wrought iron for a clearer view. A uniformed coachman whipped the horses, and the team travelled with a percussive tailwind.

Four more riders followed the speeding coach, and one slowed down to knock the hat off Pierre with a brazen sword. "Show your respects to the Queen, Monsieur," the horseman yelled, and then was gone. Pierre had stood a shoulder's length away from royalty.

Recognition of his destiny, of providence, overcame him. "Long live the Queen!" And by shouting, he reaffirmed his purpose.

His head filled with possibilities. To achieve greatness, he just needed a push, and by confronting the Comte, he dared to start down that path. He had two goals: gain his freedom from servitude and humiliate the man who had spent his life humiliating him.

The hours tested him. A few carts and vendors rambled through the entrance, and Pierre ran out of wine before he heard hooves on the street again. It was a single rider in the night. Judging from the silence between each clop, the horse was tired. Pierre braced against a limestone column, pants soaked and buttocks cold. Little did he know that what happened next would define his destiny.

He straightened his body upright. Though sleepless for two nights, he wasn't tired. He felt brave from the wine. The rain was gone, and the clouds moved in rotund clumps, allowing stars to shine through the grey. Pierre inhaled the musk of his body and called it pure stamina. If he pulled off a surprise, the ambush would be his life's greatest achievement.

When he heard the leather of the saddle, Pierre made a quick assessment and knew immediately he'd beaten the odds. On the horse rode the Comte de Rochefort, and his face in the nightlight was pinched and grave. *Distracted.* And, therefore vulnerable.

In a silent burst, Pierre lunged for the Comte's sword and flung the weapon from its scabbard into the street, where it skidded into a puddle, assailing the quiet. In the same instant, he grabbed the reins and punched the Comte's thigh to stun him. The horse whinnied and pitched but Pierre held tight. Off-guard, the Comte kicked his assailant, but Pierre climbed up one stirrup and wrestled the Comte off-center and onto the street. He landed on his back with a rough bellow, and Pierre dropped to his feet, leaving him in charge. The horse ran off.

Pierre pointed his sword between the Comte's legs. "If I knew better, François, I'd help you up. You can blame my bad manners on my upbringing. If you're not nice to me, I may piss on your boots."

The Comte pushed up on his hands and frowned. "Take that ridiculous sword … "

Pierre kicked the Comte's crotch, and then relished the cries of agony and his rival's realization that the steel threatening his manhood was far from ridiculous. Pierre turned the sword over a few times. "Magnificent, isn't it?"

Doubled over, the Comte glared at the piece. "That's not your sword," he sputtered.

"It's in my possession, therefore it's mine."

The Comte curled tighter but managed to speak. "You haven't the vaguest notion what you're doing."

"I'm doing what I should have done a long time ago. Grant me my freedom, or I'll cut you through." Pierre pressed the sword into a crease at the Comte's belt.

The Comte swatted the sword with his forearm and spat. "You're a coward. You fight like the gypsies, shamelessly sneaking up on their victims. Frenchmen fight with honour. There's no honour in you, and there never will be."

Pierre flushed and moved the sword to the Comte's throat. "I won't hesitate to kill you if I have to."

"Then do it, but you'll never know for certain whether you were good enough. You'll never truly know if you were a better swordsman than your most hated enemy, and you'll wonder about it the rest of your life. Satisfaction will never be yours."

Pierre hated him more in that moment than in all the previous years combined. He was being played, and he loathed it. He also agreed what the Comte said was true. He wanted to know if he could win, and the only way to find out was a fight. Pierre swung his blade wide, motioning the Comte to find his weapon. The Comte scrabbled up, went for his sword and returned armed. His posture exuded an entirely different command. His body was outlined in black.

"You're the lowliest creature on Earth." The Comte's steadiness was unnerving. "Your father is a bastard. Your daughter is a bastard. You are a bastard. And if God were here presiding, his judgment would be this: Damn the Tremons, for their lives are meaningless."

Pierre launched first. In a loose rage, his hatred exploded into madness. He hacked with one blow after another, forgetting lessons and techniques, reason and restraint. The Comte blocked wave upon wave of Pierre's hate. Holding the sword two-fisted, Pierre rammed it overhead, which sent sparks skyward like tiny prayers to Heaven, and again, and again, until his arms ached for a soft opening to bury the blade deeply into the man crushing his will.

Pierre's life flashed with each useless surge. The Comte deflated his confidence as he had his entire life. The Comte was not attacking; Pierre saw he was calculating, letting the fuse fizzle into a dud. Panting and sore, Pierre pointed the sword at his enemy's heart, but his hands shook. Sweat dripped into his eyes. The wine had flattened his energy. He had been fighting himself rather than the man from his past.

"*En garde*." The Comte lunged. The attack was as Athos had taught – the level-headed wait and win. In a feint, the Comte disengaged Pierre's sword and sent it flying into the air. It somersaulted and landed with a chilling ring, like a chime for a final meal.

"Lie down." The Comte manhandled Pierre by the shoulder. "I said, lie down."

In shock, Pierre dropped cross-legged on the damp ground.

"All the way," the Comte said.

Pierre shut his eyes and forced his body prone. The ground smelled of putrid human waste, and a tower bell rang. Dawn drew near, and his heart cowered.

"Pierre, look at me." The Comte hovered overhead. "Good, now tell me where she is."

Pierre swallowed back the stickiness in his throat. "You intend to kill me."

"Not if you tell me where she is."

"And sentence her to the same doom."

The Comte dug his sword into the ground inches from Pierre's ear. "If you tell me where you have hidden her, I'll swear to your freedom. If you don't, you're dead."

Pierre squinted to see the sky behind the Comte's head. It promised to be blue in the coming light. He could tell the colour would rival the wildflowers near his vineyard back home, be bluer than the summer tones of the pond and truer than the glint of Hannah's eyes.

So he watched it dawn. He saved his life—his pathetic, miserable life—alone and prone at the gates of Paris.

Chapter 50
Retrieving a Swallow

Nicole sat at the statue of Saint Benoit and his bird. Her room in the monastery had begun to feel small, so she had started attending late afternoon Masses and finished her evenings with the saint.

A note to Pierre she had sent three days ago had not been answered. He was proficient at writing, but the city would be a powerful distraction. He loved distractions, and Paris was a trove. The nights were seductive, and the days were full of characters and captivating activity. She left the roaming to him, preferring the abbey's peace. She prayed frequently.

Her last conversation with Father Grignan several days before had ended sooner than her curiosity would have liked. She came to know him as she felt Athos knew him. An open-minded, humble priest, who was sensitive to life's realities. He suggested a book about a group of nuns known as the Ursulines, who advocated that women should be religious teachers. He asked her to keep the book to herself, and she agreed. He was unconventional, but a man of faith in body and soul.

For several days, Nicole's evening meal grew cold while she attended the statue. When a monk made the rounds to lock up, she was usually the last to leave the church sanctuary. Today was the same. After she heard the front entrance lock, she retired from her meditation and headed for the breezeway. As she reached the side door, a pounding erupted from the front of the church, and the startled monk returned to the main entrance with a large key.

Nicole stiffened. François' voice boomed from behind the heavy enclosure.

"Let me in. I'm a patron of the church, and I demand you open up!" The pounding continued. Nicole shrunk behind the door to the monastery and stifled a cry. She sprinted through the breezeway and lunged into the monastery's corridor like a heavy wind.

"Father Grignan!" She had never been to his room. "Father Grignan!"

A monk appeared in a doorway, pushing his hands down to signal quiet. "Please, Madame, this is a place of tranquillity. Whom do you seek?"

"Father Grignan, who gave me sanctuary here. Please, I must find him."

The monk shuffled down the hall and waved for her to follow. Five steps into the meditation garden, on a bench, Grignan sat hunched over, apparently asleep.

"Father!" In her haste, Nicole pushed Grignan off-center. "François is here. My husband is here. I'm not ready. I cannot see him yet. Please, please intervene."

Grignan shivered, throwing off his nap. He scratched his head and blinked, then took her hands. "Nicole, tell me this. What will more time do? Are you certain time is what you need?"

She calmed the shakes by locking her fingers and checking the periphery. "I don't know. I'm confused. I'm not ready to let go."

"Let go of what?"

"Of Athos."

He nodded and dug a rosary from his pocket and handed it over. "I say you must be honest with yourself. Be honest about your life. You can't avoid your husband forever. In church doctrine, separating a marriage is troublesome and complicated. Can you find it in yourself simply to speak with your husband? Learn his mind as well?"

"Please talk to him for me. I'm not ready." She dropped her head to see only the garden path. Golden leaves covered the ground.

The monk returned. "Father, a man is asking about your … your friend." He glanced at Nicole. "He seems a little agitated and, after the last disruption, another is not welcome."

Father Grignan closed his eyes and made the sign of the cross. "Nicole, I'll talk to him, but I won't prevent him from seeing you.

You're his wife." His joints popped as he rose from the bench, and his clogs knocked in staccato on the walkway.

"I could stay in your room?" She considered dropping to her knees, but it seemed too much. She wrapped the rosary around her hands instead.

"My dear," Grignan looked back, "you already are."

***

In her room, *Father Grignan's room*, she poured a cup of water. It smelled like sulphur, and she couldn't drink. She had no idea what she would say to François. She couldn't lie anymore. God already knew her story, and handing over the truth to Him was the more important event. Except it didn't feel like that now. It was François who was on his way. She might as well be branded.

The air from the tiny window removed the smell of sulphur, and her nausea passed. She pressed a cheek to the sill and inhaled again. Of course, Grignan would be so generous. He stayed in the monastery at the church's behest, and soon he would be dispatched to a new parish. Selfishly, she hadn't noticed how generous he had been, but it touched her. Now, she was in his hands, and he was in her prayers. A knock interrupted her message to God.

"Madame, it's Father Grignan."

Her air fluttered out, and she balked at the door. Asking for God's help, she opened it to find Grignan in front of her husband. François' eyes went straight through her. He was thinner, and his clothes, though neat, hung poorly. He looked hungry—for food and answers. His virility had been replaced by contagion.

"Madame, your husband requests an audience, which I am obliged to give him. You do understand?" Grignan wanted her agreement, but the caution in his voice made her think twice.

"Father," she said, taking his hand. "A moment?"

"No, you may not." François crowded the priest.

Grignan repositioned his broad body to block François and nodded to suggest that Nicole should invite them in. She took the only chair in the room. Inside, the two men remained standing, and the door was closed.

Grignan started with a tentative *ahem*. "The Comte and I have discussed the circumstances which brought you to this place, and he believes the best course of action is for you to spend the remainder of your time in Paris with him."

"No." She crossed her arms.

François smirked and muttered an indelicate response.

Grignan redirected: "Madame, your pilgrimage—"

"Your pilgrimage is a farce," François said.

"So is our marriage." Nicole straightened in the chair and decided to stick unless forcefully removed.

"But you're mine, according to the church, this precious haven of yours." François rolled his eyes.

"May I make a suggestion?" Grignan asked.

Nicole and François simultaneously blurted opposing answers.

François closed in on the priest. "It's my opinion—"

"Perhaps you should wait a day," Grignan interjected and stepped back.

"—that you're no longer of use to my wife." François seized the priest's collar.

"François, let him go." She jumped up and grabbed François' wrist. "Let him go, and then we can talk. *Alone*."

François released his hold, and the priest angled out of the way to leave. "I'll be right outside."

François shut the door. "Sit."

She didn't. "Why do you think you can treat me so poorly?"

His laugh ended with a push, and she landed off-kilter in the chair.

"Me?" He was trying to keep his volume even. "Treat you poorly? You're the Comtesse de Rochefort, one of the wealthiest provincial wives in all of France. You reject society, gifts, lawful expectations of your husband, and I'm the offender? Your life is on the brink of change, my love, and it's my pleasure to assist."

François began to stroke her shoulders. "This is how it shall be. You shall gather your belongings and accompany me to our Paris quarters. You won't contact the priest or anyone with whom you travelled to Paris." He hissed his final demand into her ear. "And finally, you shall tell me the truth. Everything. Every detail you confessed to God."

She turned from the heat of his breath, straining her head to one side. "And if I refuse?"

"Then I shall kill Pierre, just as I did his father."

Her eyes stung. "Do you have Pierre? Please, François, no."

He went to the small bed in the corner and reclined, arms behind his head. He crossed his ankles and smiled sideways. "The gossip is that Pierre is a free man clinging to a dream of becoming a Musketeer."

"You have freed him?"

"Why, yes. Why do you look so astonished? I may place you in prison, but I don't wish to be his captor any longer. I will kill him if you defy me, but I'll always be grateful to him for helping me find you."

Nicole held down a sob. Pierre and Athos were the only two who knew her whereabouts, but Athos would have never given out the secret. Death could not drag it from him. "So Pierre is safe?"

"Of course, and free to run wild like he always has. However, I'll make certain you never see him again."

"Perhaps not. God will decide." She steadied her hand on her lap. *But what about Athos?* "Did you collect on your bet?"

François sat up. "I see your thoughts wander so soon to another."

She glanced away, hoping to hide her feelings.

"My bet," he said, "the bet that had you running from my awful gambling habits. The same wager that should have also driven you away from our guest, Monsieur Athos, the real person behind the disgrace on your honourable head.

"Come," he said, a hand on the bed, "sit beside me."

"You were the one who pushed me here." *Into the seat, the city, the solitude.*

He didn't ask twice but drew her limp form to the bed and locked her next to him with his strength. "All the talk on the streets is that I won the bet. Those who matter most in Paris now know you as the woman who withstood the seduction of a Musketeer."

He slid a finger down her jawline. "You, Nicole, are a mystery to me. A gorgeous, confounding mystery. Do you know how much I think of you? I wonder every day why my love has never been quite enough, the perfect fit. See, I know, you think about it as well.

You can't fathom why I haven't satisfied you. I'll change that. *We* will change that."

His lips were wet on her neck, and his breathing sped up. The room was hot, and he whispered between tastes of her throat. "I know a different story altogether. My letter to Athos was all the excuse you needed to send the Musketeer away, but you didn't. He tried to leave, but you pursued him. You went after him like you should have gone after me." She squirmed, and he tightened his hold around her ribs. "No, Nicole. You won't escape me ever again. You will love me. You will be with me. There's nowhere else for you to go."

His kisses slid from her neck to cleavage, and he lowered her onto her back. Darkness closed in around her. She left her body as his words locked her in burning isolation. "Athos is dead. Dead and never to be yours again."

Chapter 51
Athos Lives

Athos anticipated his arrival in Paris might ease his mind, but trouble felt closer than the arm bandaged to his body. Every day on the journey north, he tried to move it. Up, down, sideways, any way. The listless limb refused to budge. He unwrapped the arm and imagined flexing the muscle. In his mind, he arm-wrestled, hunted and fenced. He ended the mental exercise at the château. He stretched his arms out to Nicole, walked through the tall grasses, welcomed her into the privacy of his embrace and undressed her piece by piece.

No use.

The gypsies outfitted him with a long cape to hide the injury. Wounds were his signature, but on this trip, he needed to appear strong. He rode directly to the abbey, and a few people in the streets recognized his face. He slipped away before a group of Cardinal Richelieu's guards doubled-back to confirm his identity. The news would travel in waves: the Musketeer was home.

A monk made Athos wait in the foyer of the church when he asked for Grignan.

Grignan drooped with fatigue. "I expected you."

He led Athos to the altar of the Madonna. The portrait was lit by candles. Hung high, her eyes were downcast.

"I want to see Nicole," Athos said.

Grignan tucked his hands into his sleeves and sat heavy-hearted. "I'm afraid she's no longer here."

"You let her go?" Athos took Grignan by the elbow.

"Her husband came for her."

Athos stumbled back and bumped into a low partition in front of the Madonna. He stood under her gaze.

"She confessed to me, Athos."

Athos turned to the painting. "Did she weep?"

"Many times, except at the end. When she left with her husband, she—Nicole wasn't well."

A hard spot formed in his throat. "When? Where?"

"He took her many days ago, almost a week. I don't know where he took her. He tried to extract her confession from me."

Athos followed the contours of the Madonna's face. *Could Nicole survive?* He heard the priest shuffle near.

"My son, your desire for her contradicts God's will. I can offer you guidance, if need be. I'm at your disposal as a servant of God. You can seek forgiveness as she has done. Please, let me serve to cleanse your sin."

Athos waited for a sign; the Madonna gave none. "She has already done so," Athos said. "Nicole restored my soul."

Grignan didn't try to stop him from leaving, but he wandered from the church aimlessly. He dragged his horse into the best and worst streets of Paris. She could be anywhere, easily found, but not to return to him. In Le Luxembourg district, another thought dawned on him. The Comte believed he was dead. Nicole had lost her freedom and her lover in the same day.

He stumbled from street to street. Though in forward motion, he felt immobile. Stuck in a labyrinth. Lungs full of poisonous vapours. Sealed alive in a mausoleum.

He squinted back tears and kept moving. *She will survive. She has thrived without me before.* He took what little comfort he could in her strength. Believing he was dead might help her make a clean break. The larger question was: Could he live apart from her?

Athos blocked a strong ray of light. In the Paris streets, the faces of men and women, aristocrats and peasants, circled around him. *How far have I walked?* He ducked into an alley to think. He was alive, and the spores of rumour would float into every crevice. He didn't want her to find out about him that way, and he needed François to go on believing he was dead. Even if he could never resume a life with his love, he wanted to tell her—and very few others—that he was alive, good of heart and still hers.

★★★

The landlord at d'Artagnan's apartment directed Athos to the tavern. Under a wide hat, Athos manoeuvred his horse through the evening street traffic. The Taverne Cheval seemed different to Athos, alive with hope.

The crowd was loud and full of unfamiliar faces. He interrupted a few small groups to inquire about d'Artagnan, only to have one patron recognize him. "Eh, it's the Comtesse's suitor!"

Athos begged off to a dark corner and, in relief, succeeded in his quest. Hidden behind a nearby column, d'Artagnan was snuggling up to a shapely courtier. She noticed Athos first and tucked under d'Artagnan's chin to whisper.

"Good God!" D'Artagnan came over like a rolling boulder. When he hugged too tightly, the dead arm beneath Athos's cape came between them. Athos urged him back to a quiet table, nodding at the mademoiselle, who took the hint to vanish.

D'Artagnan waved for a bottle. "The stories are wild! You're dead, you're alive, you're a ghost roaming the streets of Paris. Frankly, I haven't been this happy since I became a Musketeer." Boyishly, he grabbed the bad shoulder. Athos jerked back in his seat.

"What's happened to you?" d'Artagnan asked.

"My latest injury. Still healing." Athos bolstered the elbow to make the arm appear more normal.

"Who have you been fighting?"

"Gypsies and very old demons." Athos wiped sweat from his brow. "D'Artagnan, I need your help."

"Anything. You know that."

"I need to see someone without anyone else knowing. But she's probably confined to her premises, either by her own choice or because of her husband. I need to bring her out in the open, into a crowd. Can you help?"

"Of course. This person doesn't happen to be—?"

"Yes, the Comtesse. Nicole Rieux."

D'Artagnan almost landed an over-excited slap on his shoulder before Athos blocked his wrist. "My friend, this isn't a game."

"The Hell it's not. It's love. You fell in love with her. Pierre told us."

"Pierre? You've seen him?"

"Not for many days, but he came to Treville with your letter, and he and I spent a night around the city celebrating your revival. He was a little sullen, and now he's disappeared."

"Unfortunate. But Nicole is my first priority," Athos said. "I need her to see me alive and whole. I'm certain she thinks I'm dead."

"Getting her out in public shouldn't be too difficult. The King and Richelieu are hosting an art exhibit in three days. All the aristocrats are invited."

"But she won't go without a good reason. She'll need prompting or a clue. A message must be delivered by someone inconspicuous."

"Planchet?" D'Artagnan offered.

"No, too lowly, though I hold your servant in the highest regard."

"Treville?"

"Too busy."

D'Artagnan opened his mouth, then began to smile. His well-endowed companion peeked from behind the column, followed by a long curl. "That's a face likely to do the job." He jumped up and covered her bosom in kisses. "Now that we have the pigeon," he said, buried in her fragrance, "who will be writing the message?"

"Your friend may be able to help us in that effort, too." Athos looked the mademoiselle up and down and poured a glass to overflowing from the bottle deposited at their table.

***

Strategizing with d'Artagnan made the evening pass quickly. Athos realized he owed his friend as much as he owed Nicole. D'Artagnan's help after the near-fatal jump had saved his life. As they left the tavern at closing, Athos endured the ribbing d'Artagnan had held back all night, but it didn't last long. A ruckus drew them to a group of hecklers.

A dozen or so men crowded around a figure sprawled on the street, face down in the muck. The fallen man clutched a sword, which Athos immediately recognized.

"Stand aside!"

Pierre was bruised, smudged with mud and slobbering. Despite scratches on his face and bleeding knuckles, he grinned half-cocked.

"Athos," he said with a thick tongue. "You can't make me go home."

Athos and d'Artagnan draped Pierre's arms over their shoulders and headed back to the tavern. The crowd jeered, and several of the surlier onlookers recognized Athos and demanded the truth.

"The drunken boy says you won the bet!"

"I'd wager the young scoundrel is half-witted," another said.

"But see how the Musketeer cares for him. The boy must know the truth."

The tavern proprietor groaned when he answered the door. After he pocketed a shiny incentive, the Musketeers were allowed in, and the door was bolted. Athos pressed a warm rag onto Pierre's eye. "Picking a fight?"

Pierre set the sword aside and took over the dabbing. His head lolled after each wipe.

"Defending you, not that I have any reason to." Pierre's elbow slid off the table.

"Setting the record straight, eh?" d'Artagnan said to Pierre, then to Athos: "He must have been trying to convince them you truly had won Nicole over. It would keep the Comte from winning a sum larger than a year's worth of sugar."

D'Artagnan explained the news swirling about since the Comte's return to Paris—his wife's fidelity had become legendary and lucrative. Athos connected the links: No wonder François had abandoned Camille and the shipment.

Reunited with his sword, Athos cut the air with it. "Please, for Nicole's honour, as a gentleman, let the gossip run its course."

Pierre dropped the rag and flopped across the bench. "Then don't lie to me anymore."

"I've been as truthful as—"

"You said I was to become a Musketeer."

"And you shall, if you keep your head about you."

"Lie number one," Pierre said.

"It was the same for me," d'Artagnan told him. "Like I said, you can't step right in, sword swinging. You must earn a spot as a Musketeer."

"You're a good swordsman," Athos said.

"Lie number two." Pierre kicked a table leg.

D'Artagnan shrugged. "But what about Vachon and Henri?"

"You've seen François, haven't you?" Athos said and left Pierre's festering mood for another table.

Wobbly, Pierre followed and splintered a floorboard dragging his feet. "You could kill François. You're good enough."

"That idea is a prime example of why you ended up face down in the street. If you spent time thinking before you acted, good might come of it."

"He killed my father!" Pierre eclipsed the candlelight from the chandelier. He didn't need pity, and Athos was relieved that Pierre finally knew his origins. Athos drew the cape from his shoulder to expose the lifeless limb wrapped to his body.

Pierre blinked. "What happened?"

"Nicole would call it a miracle," Athos said.

"But you're … it looks useless."

"Someone saved me. A gypsy. A man I believe was your father."

A wrinkle chiseled Pierre's forehead. "Don't. Do you hear me! Don't!" He reclaimed the sword and tripped stalking toward the exit.

"I know it sounds far-fetched, but François told me himself that your father lives."

Pierre's reaction started low, between his hips, a raw animal response, that grew to a cry of devastation. Athos pulled d'Artagnan back. The crossbrace on the door kept Pierre from falling on his shins.

"Lies!" Pierre screamed. "My whole life is filled with lies."

"Truth is your divinity. You have the truth now. Use it. Make the life you've dreamed of." Athos held back. Pierre curled and uncurled, sobbing. After several minutes, Athos offered the damp rag again. "I need you. Nicole needs you, and we have a plan."

Pierre slumped and leered. "Does it involve François?"

"Most certainly," Athos said and lifted him to his feet.

By dawn, the three men swore to carry out their plan—all for one and one for all—and separated to set in motion each piece of the intrigue.

Chapter 52
A Message in Prison

Nicole began taking pleasure in the door-slamming. François controlled her schedule and their bedchamber, but she refused to speak. It drove him away several times a day and night in abrupt aggravation. In the short windows of solitude, she daydreamed.

The visions involved flight. She stood in a summer field and loose gauze covered her body. In a whirlwind, enormous wings erupted from her shoulder blades. At times, the wings were brown and striped, on other occasions, red and speckled with yellow. Most often, the wings, which spanned several feet beyond her fingertips, were white.

In quick bursts, she lifted into the air between the treetops and clouds. The sky was a blanket of soft blue. She soared steadily, buoyed by the wind and fearless of predators. From above, the landscape displayed its order and chaos, where one glide revealed beautiful pastures and the next, jagged mountains. Nature was unpredictable. The contradiction haunted her after the daydreams ended. All concluded the same; she flew into the sun and burned to ash.

She had lived with the visions once before—the year after Sibonne's death. They weren't painful or sad, simply impossible to control. She felt helpless to their repetition. She told no one, especially the priest, because she feared the judgment more than the dreams themselves. They overtook her, so she flew and burned, flew and burned, without end.

While mourning Sibonne, drawing distracted her. But this time, François withheld paper and charcoal until she spoke again. She didn't care. She couldn't draw what she wanted. François would forbid her rekindled interest in the human form.

His anxiety was most evident right before bedtime.

"Tell me, and I won't ask you again." He lay in trousers; she in her nightdress. "How many nights were you with him?"

She stared at the canopy.

"I'm your husband. He's dead, sucked into the caverns of Hell, most likely, for luring you into sin. Sin, Nicole! There's no love on earth that can redeem your act with him. God may have forgiven you, but it's beyond my capacity. Do you hear me?"

He clamped her cheeks and forced her face toward his. "You can't love him. You don't love him. You think I have no way of knowing about you two. You'll bring the consequences of this silence on your entire staff. One of them will know, and I'll scorch it out of them by bonfire or brand."

She closed her eyes, and he pushed her away. "And if they don't speak, then Pierre will."

White gauze covered her skin in the heat.

"He will know if Athos took you by force or with your willing consent."

Wings flared and beat the air.

"Whether he took you in your bed or in the sacrilegious confines of your chapel."

She lifted from the grass and hung suspended.

"One day, what you *will* tell me, is whether he sent you into ecstasy. To touch you that way is my privilege and none other. You will soar for me, and I'll never give up trying."

Up and up, into hot clouds, into light and flame, until her body scorched.

The door slammed, and a fresh set of wings unfurled.

★★★

A week into her silence, François insisted they take a ride in the carriage. He ordered the driver through the streets at a clip fit for royalty in peril. It was early, minutes after sunrise, when the city and its people were quieted by the night's mists.

François dressed formally, and his clothes stiffened his already hardened heart. She stared at her gloves but could feel his disapproval in stolen glances. He only spoke when the carriage stopped at the entrance of the abbey of Saint Germain-de-Prés. "Stay here. Do not move."

Nicole's extremities went from cold to prickly. *Dear God, does he come to confess? Pry forgiveness from me by seeking God?* All her disparate thoughts scattered like sea-swept pebbles as she saw Father Grignan follow François from the abbey. Any semblance of kindness François had used to convince the priest to come outside evaporated when the carriage door swung open.

"Get inside," François commanded. Sweaty, Grignan climbed clumsily into the coach and sat next to Nicole on the bench seat.

"Madame Rieux," Grignan said, finding her hands. "It's good to be in your company again."

"Hands off," François asserted and placed Grignan on the opposing seat. Anger pulsed from every pore of François, and he smelled rank. In twenty years of marriage, Nicole had seen him in this state just once, the time that he had interrogated her about the whereabouts of the mismatched lovers Sibonne and Remi after their disappearance.

"What's the meaning of this?" Grignan stuttered a few times.

"You're the keeper of some very important information, without which this marriage is worthless. I believe my wife to be an adulteress, and as her husband and the guardian of her fidelity, I demand to know whether her affair is only physical or if she also took this man into her heart." François braced a boot across her ankles. "So tell me, did she love him or just bed him?"

Nicole's collar choked her. Even if she had the courage to defend herself, the fabric strangled her windpipe.

"Monsieur? Comte?" Father Grignan waited several seconds to get François' attention, so rapt by Nicole that he refused to look away. "I believe you were born a Catholic and raised in our faith. Therefore, you know there's no mountain on earth that can be moved to make me repeat what is shared during the sacrament of confession. It's absolutely private and for God alone. I cannot accommodate. Any confessor would tell you the same."

"You live in a sheltered world, Father Grignan. I, on the other hand, live in reality, where a heavy coin purse can make the tongues of the pious wag with glee."

The point was lost on Father Grignan, but Nicole understood exactly. His gifts to her church were made for reasons other than her benefit. The colours of her sanctuary's stained glass bled together. François knew her every confession. Her wings had been clipped by the hands that fed her. *I have been caged and kept for years.*

"I won't abdicate my position for money," Grignan said.

"Your position is about as solid as my wife's faithfulness. If my sources are right, you've been denied a parish on account of unorthodox beliefs. If you have any chance for survival, I offer it to you. Wealth has a way of blinding eyes."

"Not all eyes," Grignan looked at Nicole, "and certainly not mine."

François pounded on the bench. "You're a small, small man doomed to failure!"

"I don't deny my miniscule place in the Kingdom of God." Grignan leaned forward, unafraid. "But God is my keeper, and I shall not want. You … you, I cannot promise as much."

"Your stoicism is meaningless." François grabbed Nicole by an elbow. "I want to know if she fell in love with him!"

"That's not my answer to give," Grignan said. "That can come from only one source. This I do know: sometimes words are unnecessary."

Grignan leveraged his ample body off the seat. "Such darkness." He shook his head and dropped his head and shoulders to leave. "May God be merciful."

Nicole covered her face with her hands after the carriage door closed, to have them immediately pried off by François. "Father Grignan will regret his refusal to cooperate for years to come, but his penance will be leagues behind your own."

François slammed his fists on his knees. "If you never speak again, it doesn't matter. The truth seeps out of every pore."

He exited the carriage, too, and stood at the abbey door. He yelled to the driver, sending her, his possession, back to the prison he called home.

★★★

A message arrived the next day. A servant announced a guest for Nicole. When the Comte heard it was a courtier of Queen Anne's, his vanity blossomed.

The bloom faded fast. "I suppose I'll have to do the talking."

Mademoiselle de La Trousse kept her introduction short. "Madame, I've been sent by the Queen to deliver this." She presented an envelope with a royal purple seal. "She's excited that you have returned to Paris after such a long absence."

Nicole took the note and returned to her seat. The paper was heavy and folded on four sides. It was Nicole's first personal message from the Queen. Bits of wax seal crumbled onto her lap. The script rivalled the most ornate wedding invitation. Obviously, the message was dictated. The signature, however, appeared genuine.

Comtesse de Rochefort,

Please join the Royal Court at the forthcoming exhibit of France's finest painters, the Le Nain brothers. The night promises to be memorable, enhanced by your return to Paris. In reminiscence of your last visit with us, please wear your green dress, which is both flattering and unforgettable. Your admirers in Paris welcome you back.

Anne

"Well?" the Comte asked and glanced with appreciation at the messenger. Nicole handed him the letter, and his initial delight became bewilderment. "She remembers what you wore two years ago?"

"The Queen," Mademoiselle de La Trousse answered, "is very observant. Madame has been missed."

"Yes, but I can't recall what you wore then. Can you? Nicole?"

We only stayed a short while. It was hot. I was never in her line of sight. Never.

"Well, of course, we'll go," the Comte said, taking the lady's hand and bowing. "Thank you and please carry our acceptance to the Queen."

Nicole continued sitting. The Comte demanded the servants search every cranny for the dress in question or summon a dressmaker. He rambled on in a mild tizzy.

"Green? How on God's Earth did she recall that detail?"

"An extraordinary impression," Nicole uttered when she was finally alone. "Dark green."

Chapter 53
The Way Back to Her

"Why couldn't it be a costume ball?" Pierre argued, midway through several bottles of wine in Athos's apartment the afternoon of the art exhibit. "I could go inside if there were costumes."

This time, d'Artagnan restated the plan.

"You're our first eyes and ears. Athos can't go in and wait for Nicole to arrive. We need a lookout. It's going to be dicey for him. Most of Paris believes him dead, and he can't go pacing around the hall awaiting their entrance."

"If, in fact, they make one." Athos worried the letter was too weak of a clue for Nicole. She hadn't been seen in public since the day Pierre brought her to the city. Gathering that information had been d'Artagnan's job.

"It might annoy the Comte to see you, Pierre, but if he sees Athos, he'll go straight for his sword," d'Artagnan said. "I'm the obvious person to approach Nicole because he won't suspect me. Remember, the Comte and I conspired to get Athos out of the city."

Athos threw Pierre a crumb. "If I'm able to speak with Nicole, I can give her a message from you."

"It's not Nicole I'll miss seeing," Pierre said.

"Confronting François is a ludicrous dream," d'Artagnan said.

"It's not him either."

Athos and d'Artagnan exchanged quizzical glances.

"It's the Queen," Pierre said. "I want to see the Queen."

"Are you serious?" Athos asked.

"How else am I to get ahead? You two have been little help in that regard."

Athos shared a nod with d'Artagnan and hugged Pierre's neck, placing the masterpiece sword back in the youth's possession. "If we are successful tonight, then I may have one favour left."

★★★

The borrowed clothes from Athos were roomy, and the slack in them filled with frigid air. The cold tightened Pierre's joints. He patted his middle with the long cuffs of the wool coat and blew puffs into the night. Guests for the exhibit started arriving at nightfall. Couples and groups rode in coaches the likes of which Pierre had never seen. One had glass windows. The women wore exotic feathers, and the men flashed gold timepieces and flamboyant silk scarves.

His job—to wait for Nicole's arrival and race several blocks with the news to the awaiting men—seemed beneath him. It felt like his chores at home. Belittling. Planchet could have done it. The valet was gladly drinking with the others.

Pierre had argued for a different job until Athos promised to request an audience with the Queen. He said the chances of seeing her tonight were small because Le Louvre was large, and she'd arrive a different way than everyone else.

Outside, Pierre was among the ordinary citizens along the streets. Events at Le Louvre attracted gawkers. Some cat-called; many gossiped; but most were like Pierre, awestruck by the wealth. The atmosphere became bawdy, and he fit in like potatoes in soup.

Coaches clogged the street within an hour, and before long, they idled right in front of Pierre's post, an archway to a milliner's shop. He dug his hands into his pockets and hopped from foot to foot. He learned the names of the coach owners from the chatter nearby. The conversations ran together.

"Ah, there's the Marquis, his son is a bit off," a brown moustache said.

"The Duc d'Orleans has sent his wife to the coast with a persistent cough," a fat woman told another.

"The Cardinal has a distinct dislike for Monsieur d'Luce," a rosy barmaid said in passing, "because his shirttails come loose."

A street vendor tempted Pierre with a handful of warm chestnuts. "Have you heard," the man said, "that the Comte there gambled a fortune on his wife's fidelity? The Musketeer never turned her fancy." The laughter that followed was not Pierre's.

The Rieux carriage, engraved with Rs on its side and rear panels, was bigger than the others, more ornate and required six horses. If the interior matched the drapery, it was blood red. It reeked of the wealth of a hundred nobles. Pierre's ego shrunk and morphed into a gnarl.

At the drop-off, two footmen arranged steps and opened the door. Nicole hid under a dark cape with a hood that tied in front with a wide ribbon. Black velvet gloves ran above her elbows. Though cloaked, her grace and poise were too potent for Pierre to mistake. The message had worked.

François was decked in so many layers that they hindered his ease of motion. A ruffled shirt and collar, a vest, jacket and overcoat made him larger than one man alone. His chest expanded like a strutting rooster, his pride six paces ahead.

Mesmerized, Pierre tripped over a small boy squatting in the street. Pierre nodded an apology and immediately left, annoyed by the Comte's showiness. But the boy, filthy and short for his head size, followed. After a corner, Pierre jerked him up by the collar. "Off with you."

"Would you like to know a secret?" The boy stuck out his hand, which was smeared with dirt.

"What could you know that's worth a coin?"

The boy winked. "A way in."

★★★

D'Artagnan forged ahead into the crowded exhibit hall, leaving Athos to hide. Their Musketeer uniforms and plumes got them past the door with little notice. Athos quickly found refuge at a wide column by the exit and wiped sweat from his brow. Planchet was outside playing sentry, Mademoiselle de La Trousse was mingling in the crowd and Pierre was left to anchor the apartment with numerous bottles of victory wine.

But Athos worried. He couldn't make a scene, otherwise he risked ruining Nicole, and if François discovered Athos, all bets were off.

Athos's injured arm hung free, dangling from his torso. He had wrapped it as best as he could to appear whole. Yet the dead weight on his shoulder caused a persistent thrumming behind his eyes, and he suffered episodes of double-vision. He needed his sight more than ever. He needed to see her—make a swift but renewed connection, and be gone.

★★★

Nicole reluctantly handed her cloak and gloves to an attendant. She shivered when François ran a hand up her back.

"Are you cold?" he asked.

She removed his hand from her waist.

"Will you speak tonight?" It was an awkward show of concern. She passed him and headed for the huge crowd.

Her dress, several seasons old, set her apart. The newer fashions favoured billows on top of billows. Her dress was simple, beautiful but plain. She looked down at her front. Had the letter from the Queen been meant to ridicule her? The thought scrambled her belief that the letter had contained a secret message: *Athos lives.* Because of her sorrow, hope had overshadowed the real meaning. She was being punished for shunning Court life.

Reversing to the coatroom, she ran into François. Her first words in weeks escaped her throat: "Take me out of here."

François pulled her close, his eyes shining like the fine buttons on his jacket. But his pleasure at hearing her voice faded to disappointment. She squirmed to get by him. François blocked the way and glowered. "I appreciate you breaking your silence, but choose your words carefully. You're here at the Queen's request. It pleases her. It pleases me. She'll expect you, and if I can speak with the King, I'll smooth over the mishap with the sugar. This isn't about you. This is anything but about you."

The cold from the granite floor shot up her legs. The stockings, the tulle, the garters and girdle encased her in frost. Music spun from the ceiling. It cracked in her ears. Tugging her along, François escorted his prize. She became a slab of ice chipped away by custom and expectation. The party pitched, the path tightened, and an unfamiliar guardsman approached.

"Why, François, wonderful to see you." In the little space left, a handshake was offered.

"Excuse me, d'Artagnan, we expect an audience with Queen Anne." François shook hands quickly and pulled Nicole closer.

"A moment won't matter." D'Artagnan captured Nicole's hand and, by doing so, started a friendly tug-of-war. "May I introduce myself? I am d'Artagnan of Gascony and a Musketeer. Your husband and I are mutual friends of Athos."

He kissed her hand, pinched her fingertips and released. His face sparkled with mischief. Her head thawed. "Athos?"

"Yes, Athos. You know of him, I take it?"

François gathered both of her hands and jerked forward, disturbing a couple in matching satin. "Some other time, d'Artagnan."

"Do you bring news of Athos to Paris, François? Did he help in your venture at Nantes? Many stories are racing about."

"You don't know?" Nicole freed her hands from François' grip. "François? Tell him what happened to Athos. This man is his friend."

"I said, 'Some other time.'"

"He's dead." Her lips tingled with sorrow. The words still felt raw; the hurt burrowed deeper. Bumping several patrons, she went to d'Artagnan expecting to find hurt, too. His reaction was sympathy and tenderness—for her. Toward François, anger.

"Is this true?" d'Artagnan demanded of François, calling above several heads. "Is Athos dead? Did you witness it?"

"Gypsies ambushed our caravan. He was shot by an arrow and drowned."

"You survived," d'Artagnan said, shouting above a convergence of party-goers and holding on tight to Nicole's hand. "How?"

François started toward them. "What are you implying?"

"Nicole," d'Artagnan said. "You need some air."

"Take your hands off my wife!" François threw his weight to make an opening.

D'Artagnan shielded Nicole. "You'll find rest by the first column, near the large canvas of the nudes. Be quick about it. Your time is short."

Then he pushed her into the torrent, a swarming wall of people unaware of the green dress slipping passed.

★★★

She trained her eye on the top of the first column. The crowd crushed the flare of her skirt. Tall men, beautiful women and servants with trays blocked the way. She side-stepped and pushed and reached for every opening. Breathing was impossible. Was she moving or being moved? The floor shifted like sand. The people, their buttons and starched folds obstructed every turn. Her escape from Henri flashed in her memory. She was fleeing again, taking her fate from God and into her own hands. Toward the unforeseen.

★★★

D'Artagnan was taking too long. Athos, dizzy from the pain in his shoulder, cooled his forehead on the tall stone column. Mademoiselle de La Trousse awaited his signal at the end of a semi-circle of people admiring two nudes in the large painting nearby. The piece was the last in a row of oil paintings close to the wall. Larger than the others on display, the canvas painting, the size of an impressive church window, sat on a sturdy three-legged stand. Athos darted behind the painting for better cover and tossed his hat and doublet to the marble floor. His chest pounded.

He concentrated on the sounds from the crowd. No disruptions. Women cackled and chirped compliments about fashion and friends. Men swapped boisterous stories about money and land. Servers padded between guests with platters of empty drinks, and champagne and wine flowed from bottles until emptied.

A tired servant with a platter scooted behind the painting. The tray rattled when Athos surprised him from behind. "Pardon me, Monsieur," the servant said, catching a tottering champagne glass. "It's just—"

Athos seized the server's lapel and shushed him.

"The Queen," the server whispered, the shakes setting in. "She's here, reviewing this painting."

Athos quickly drank a full stem. "Then go to her," he said, and the servant flitted back into the crowd. Athos didn't move. The crowd on the other side of the painting became quiet, and the courtiers awaited the Queen's verdict of the artwork.

"I believe it's one of Le Nain's finest," Queen Anne pronounced. "He calls it Allegory of Victory. Your thoughts, Muriel?"

Mademoiselle de La Trousse flapped a fan. "I believe you should ask Comtesse de Rochefort. She's a fine judge of art."

"Comtesse, what a delight. It's been much too long." Skirts swished like a small flock of birds before Athos heard the voice of a dove.

"It's most memorable because of your invitation," Nicole said.

"A confidante of your husband's is the one to thank," the Queen replied. "I would have never known you were in Paris. Welcome back, I hope it's for a long stay. And what do you think of the painting?"

"The wings are magnificent. Their proportion is perfect." Nicole paused, and Athos heard faint steps and whispers. Then, as if answering a question, the Queen declared: "One of the King's Musketeers informed me of your return to Paris, Comtesse. One of his finest. Athos."

Athos fell to one knee and gratitude filled his chest.

Sweet Anne of Austria. My sweet, forthright Queen.

He wished he could show himself to Nicole in this moment of resurrection. He couldn't imagine Nicole's shock or how she could keep from fainting. All he could do from his hiding place was raise a silent blessing. His concern for her reputation prevented anything else. In the midst of his prayer, Mademoiselle de La Trousse spoke in a low voice to the person he wanted most to share this moment.

"Comtesse," the lady said, "let me show you a piece more striking than this painting. It's certain to impress your heart."

★★★

Athos rested his head upon one knee. The painting hid his body in shadow. The tension in his back dissolved as he softened to reunite with Nicole, the triumph of a plan well played. The unfolding events or his wound, most likely both, weakened him. He was immobile, powerless to rise and bear witness to the beauty rounding the large canvas.

A warm hand brushed through his fair hair. Her fingertips skimmed his cheek, and he pressed them deeper. He absorbed her body heat and inhaled the things she had touched in her preparations. *Holy water. Tears.* He brought her hand from his cheek to his lips, and her spirit settled into his healed heart.

"You live," Nicole said.

"For you."

"For us." She cupped his chin and tipped it up. He smiled and rose to her lips. They kissed between her halting sobs and his tender affirmations. He whispered his love repeatedly, declaring words poets agonized for ages to write. The moment she wanted only his kiss, he knew her to be whole again.

Chapter 54
Glory Trumps Patience

Pierre watched the clandestine reunion through the spindles of a second-floor balcony. Having memorized the placement of the doors, windows and columns, he felt confident the early evening hadn't been wasted. A slight advantage was better than none. His heart skipped when he saw the Queen, fairer than any artist's rendering. She had spoken directly to Nicole. But that was several minutes ago, and the scene was changing fast.

D'Artagnan and the Comte began repelling the crowd with their continued argument. Pierre couldn't hear a word of it over the party and decided that if he was to make any impression—on the Queen, the King, France itself—he must act.

He entered the crowd from an area where the party thinned out. Without question, Pierre wanted to see the Queen, but his motive was to make a name for himself. A risky feat. Pierre's word against François' would be as dubious as an Englishman bearing gifts, so he brought proof.

He came at François' back. D'Artagnan saw him first. "Pierre, stop!"

The plea was in vain. He throttled the Comte around the throat, and the nobleman buckled in surprise, writhing and wheezing, yet Pierre's hold was solid. People shrieked and moved back.

Pierre laid the sword even with his rival's bowel. "Tell them!" Pierre circled the edge of the retreating crowd. "Tell them you lied!"

The Comte struggled for air. D'Artagnan waved back possible challengers from the crowd. "Let him go, Pierre. Remember who you're putting in jeopardy."

"I don't care. I want the truth out. The truth, François." He shook the reddening face of his captive. "The truth or I take your life here before everyone."

Men yelled in the outer ring for guards. The Comte dug his nails into Pierre's forearm and rasped. "Your father is alive. I can show you. You can be with him."

Pierre shouted into the crowd: "The truth is that this man took Paris for a fool—"

"Check your tongue before you ruin the people you care most about," d'Artagnan urged in a low voice.

"Tell them, François! Tell them about your wife. That your pious idol loves another and that your pride caused you to hide the shame. For greed, for fortune!"

Whispers started in waves from the closest onlookers. François tried resisting Pierre's chokehold. "I showed you mercy. I gave you freedom. Give me mine, or even God can't save you."

"Let God try."

Pierre brought the sword to the Comte's throat as the Musketeer whom Paris believed was dead stepped from the crowd and issued a single demand: "Drop my sword."

François and Pierre stumbled back in unison. Pierre squeezed tighter around François' neck and pointed the sword at Athos.

"He lives! Athos lives!" Pierre's shouts echoed. "You see! The Musketeer everyone thought had perished lives. And loves."

Pierre forced François on all fours and, like an executioner, positioned the sword on his neck. Women shaded their eyes and grew pale. Pierre tossed back his head wildly.

"Doesn't anyone understand?" At last, he threw a wad from his pocket toward a man protecting a companion.

"Drop my sword, Pierre." Athos was almost there.

"Stand back or you'll force my hand. You know I'm capable." Pierre squeezed the pommel, cagey as never before.

"For God's sake," François pleaded from the floor, "someone do something." His eyes darted from man to man.

No man intervened. The crowd parted, a murmur spread, and like a scenery change in a play, Queen Anne emerged from the opening.

"Athos," she said, serene on the surface. "Is this the young man you told me about?"

Athos bowed and nodded.

"You're Pierre Tremon of Bretagne Province?" she asked.

Pierre swallowed and glanced at Athos.

"Tell me your truth," she said. "If you must speak, speak before me."

Pierre steadied the sword and locked his knees. "This man, the Comte de Rochefort, told all of Paris that the Musketeer lost a wager to seduce his wife. The Comte lied because he thought Athos was dead and no one would ever know the real truth." He nodded to the courtier with the paper, who held it up, flattened out. Even smudged, the charcoal likeness of Athos was unmistakable. "The Comtesse drew that," Pierre said, "after she fell in love with him."

A lady in waiting retrieved the drawing for the Queen, who beamed over it. "Athos, her hand doesn't lie. The Comtesse earns her reputation as an accomplished artist. She places her entire heart in this one simple piece."

"I can't deny it," he said. Seeing Nicole's image of him for the first time filled him with awe and humility.

François reached up to the Queen, the sword still trained to his neck. "Please, I don't deserve this."

The Queen didn't have to say a word, for Pierre stood down and handed the sword to Athos, sending François skidding backward.

"Comte de Rochefort, you shall return every ounce of your winnings," the Queen said, "and Monsieur Tremon, if being a Musketeer is what you desire, you should listen and learn from Athos. An impulsive heart and head serve no one."

"But—" Pierre began.

"And to all three of you," she said, "the rest of your affair is private. This is neither the time nor the place to resolve your dispute. If I learn otherwise, the Cardinal's guards will take over. Now, I have a King, a Cardinal and two impatient painters waiting for me." The men bowed as she circled back and disappeared into the throng.

★★★

François' face turned red. "Outside. All of you."

"It's over," Athos said, pulling Pierre back.

"Over?" François unbuttoned his jacket and collar. "I'd sooner be impaled on the gates of the Bastille."

"Pierre's life isn't yours to destroy. Let him be," Athos said.

"I will. If you win."

D'Artagnan was at Athos's side. "I am your second."

★★★

Nicole trembled from the inside out. She promised Athos she would stay away from the commotion behind the painting with Mademoiselle de La Trousse. Nicole wrung her linen handkerchief at every odd noise from the centre of the hall. When it began to quiet, her promise unravelled.

"Take me to him," she demanded. "Now."

★★★

The betting was furious. Men widened the circle, and valets escorted several women outside. The Duc d'Orleans kept track on a tiny abacus. The odds favoured the Musketeer, until Athos removed his coat.

"Useless, isn't it? You'll be dead before I've broken a sweat." François jeered. Rebidding roiled from behind the human barrier. Then Athos raised his good arm and readied to *en garde*; the odds shifted again like mercury.

Unfazed, François smiled darkly with superiority. "No man is ever as skilled with both," and he lunged.

The duel broke every rule of convention. The challengers spun in messy patterns without regard to safety, forcing spectators to run for cover. Athos rebuffed several rounds and rallied with his good arm, but the dead weight on his other side prevented equal comebacks. Each of his attacks, weaker than the last, fell aimlessly. Every block sent bolts of pain down his back. His vision blacked in and out. The exertion slammed him with reality—his body wasn't healed. Though skilled at disguising his emotions, his hope disintegrated.

The only advantage worth exploiting was the hatred that spewed in his direction. François' weakness was his pride.

"You lost her long ago," Athos taunted, adding fire to the Comte's anger. "You know it, François. She hasn't loved you in years. Killing me won't change her."

François upped the intensity, raging in relentless attacks. Guards in the Cardinal's colours appeared in the periphery. D'Artagnan and Pierre shoved back onlookers, their faces flat with dread. Before long, Athos was only blocking, lacking energy for an offensive. He swung his dead arm wide and cursed the crowd to get out of his way. He grunted at every hack and flung sweat in all directions. The audience hushed, poised to witness the fall of an immortal.

A cry of agony from the crowd stopped the Comte's final momentum, and Nicole tumbled forward. The gasps in the crowd turned to silence. She scrambled between the men, breathless, and faced her husband.

"Stop this." Pale and dishevelled, she grabbed the Comte's sword by the blade. "This is the end. Let this go, and take me home."

"Stand aside." François stared her down. "Stand aside!"

"No. Kill me. Kill them all. It won't change our life together. We're not one, François. I forgive you, but we're not one."

"Let go of my sword!" He focused on her hand gripping the blade. Her face went white, and blood trickled between her knuckles.

"Nicole, let go," Athos said, a few steps from her side.

"You're hurting her," Pierre said and swiped a sword from the scabbard of a stunned aristocrat.

"Then so be it." François clamped down on her wrist and slid the weapon out.

She whimpered then screamed. Her blood made teardrops on the granite. Perfectly round. Stunningly bright. And soon, they were absorbed in a larger pool of crimson growing at François' feet. The strike had entered his lower back. It was a clean lunge, a move as precise as a guillotine. The sword plunged back-to-front and came out a darkened fate.

Pierre quaked, leaned back and pumped the bloody sword toward Heaven.

Chapter 55
Reconciling Fate

Nicole's written request to see Athos arrived at his apartment three weeks into her mourning. Grignan had offered her sanctuary at the monastery. Her note to Athos, a single handwritten line on a thin scroll, was tied in a black ribbon. Her message came by d'Artagnan, Athos's sole intermediary with her since the Comte's death and the only person Athos let into his rooms in Le Luxembourg district.

During the separation, Athos had drafted letters in the night with the curtains drawn in his apartment and candles blazing. Each encouraged her to reunite. At first, his pleas consisted of a few words, then grew into page upon page of promises of steadfast support. The writings, sometimes several a night, devolved into splintered poetry. Her replies came through his friend: "Not yet." Athos endured her distance without a thimbleful of wine.

Finally, she asked him to meet her in the abbey of Saint Germain-des-Prés at the quietest time of day, the hour following vespers.

After François' death, the abbey had held the funeral Mass in the church sanctuary. Every pew had filled to capacity. Most nobles attended out of curiosity—to watch her, the widow who had fallen from grace, wondering if she would show emotion, cry, demonstrate her regret. She withstood the shame alone. Pierre was locked in the Bastille. D'Artagnan reported to Athos that her composure at the funeral was bland as cream. But the eyes of society judged her. No grief on her part would repair her reputation.

At the hour of their rendezvous, Athos entered the abbey as the crowds from evensong dispersed. He found her sitting motionless at the statue of Saint Benoit. The murky grey light of the sanctuary was a sedative, one she appeared to have consumed to the point of addiction. Athos resisted drinking from the same draught. He wanted to be the rock she needed to survive.

"Have you read my letters?" he asked, keeping a distance but craving connection. "You're my love. I'm your servant."

"The letter." Her voice was atonal, and she wore black. "François' letter to you wasn't the whole story."

Athos realized he was entering the middle of a conversation she had begun with herself since her husband's death, a never-ending negotiation with doubt.

Her bloodshot eyes stared at the stone saint. "Tell me in plain words, what came between you and François."

"I thought you understood."

"*Make* me understand." For the first time he could remember, she sounded hopeless.

"When I found him in Paris, he was my last resort to an honourable death. He was the better swordsman. His skills at duelling were almost as legendary as mine. I wanted him to kill me."

"So you provoked him." She swallowed hard. "You boasted you could make me fall in love with you."

"I knew he would fight for your honour. His reputation was beyond dispute, except that I angered him beyond the limits of his better judgment. He was incensed when I suggested you could be unfaithful, and in the end, his anger kept him from winning the duel. That's when he proposed I jump from the tavern roof to keep the bet alive. He had no choice. My sword was poised to take his life."

"Would you have killed him?" She twisted the wedding ring underneath her glove. A bandaged covered her other hand.

"My actions were wrong." He reached for her, but she tucked her elbows in protectively. He drew back. "I also implied he had a lover, not thinking it could be true."

She didn't move. Her lack of a reaction proved his sad suspicion—that she knew of François' mistress. Another notch of shame on her years of unhappiness.

"But would you have killed him?" she asked again.

"I wanted *him* to kill *me*. I wanted to die."

"He saved your life," she said, still immobile. "He told me, and so did the letter he wrote to you. He brought you to me to cool off, so he could use you to satisfy his greed."

"He had other motives." Athos clasped his hands and considered keeping the last secret a while longer. He dropped his head. "He wanted to reunite Pierre with his father."

She finally looked at him. Tears streaked her cheeks. "Remi?"

"He's alive." He finally could look in her brown eyes. "I've seen him, and he knows about Pierre. I told Remi about his son and grand-daughter."

"Alive? Remi isn't alive. François told my sister he killed him. He can't be alive."

"He lied, Nicole. He wanted Sibonne to tell him how to find her baby. The lie was leverage. He thought if Sibonne believed Remi were dead, she would want the baby returned to her."

Nicole shook her head. "Remi can't be alive. If he was, he would have come after Sibonne and Pierre to save them. He would have rescued them. He would have crossed the River Styx for them."

"Sibonne didn't give him a chance." Athos hated telling her the hard facts. His words settled into Nicole like a dreaded disease.

"But Pierre came to us," Nicole said as if talking to herself. "Why would Remi give him up?"

"I don't know, but when I spoke with him, Remi hinted that he'd made a pact with the grave—he must have meant Sibonne's—to turn over his son to the only other woman who could be his mother."

Nicole's heart took its last blow, and she collapsed. Quickly catching her, Athos placed her in the hollow of his good side and rocked her. She sobbed like a mother for a dead child.

"Sibonne couldn't live without Remi," she wailed. "Is that what love is?" Then her fury ignited. "How could François lie! He killed her! How could he?" Several visitors in the church startled. Athos controlled his own heart from breaking by saying *I love you* to the question thick on her throat: *How could he? How?* Athos bore her weight and tried to calm her.

"I failed in so many ways," she said. "I didn't acknowledge Sibonne's love for Remi. I didn't keep their secret location to myself. I wanted her with me so I could be whole."

"I caused François and Pierre to suffer. Don't take the blame for that, Nicole. It will destroy you."

"I've destroyed myself." She pushed away.

"Pierre isn't a lost cause. His father still lives, and François wanted to reunite them. As long as I'm a Musketeer, I'll pursue that end, which begins with Pierre's freedom. I have influence, and I hope ..." he said, finding her eyes, "I hope I have you."

Nicole let him hold her hands, but he felt it was because she was too beaten down to stop him. He kissed the salty tears from her cheeks, but she moved away and wiped her face with the back of her glove.

"My path is clouded now." She wiped again. "I'm not ready for this. I'm not ready for ... "

For us, he thought.

"I'll wait." He extended a hand; she didn't take it. He went to a candle in front of the statue and lit it. The flame burned bright with his vow. "I'll wait because I love you."

She stood and left through a heavy side door. The stillness in the sanctuary intensified his dread. Silence and emptiness were friends of the weary. He needed sleep and her warmth. Or, a sympathetic ear.

Father Grignan sat down with a windy *harrumph.* "Will you pray with me?"

"Would it make a difference?" Athos's head felt full of stones.

"It never hurts." The priest began his low cadence. "God grant us grace. God grant us courage, in the facing of this hour—"

"Grignan," Athos said.

The priest opened his eyes.

"I believe you offered me the chance for forgiveness."

Grignan crossed himself and, repressing a smile, began to get up.

"Not in a confessional, Father. Let's stay here. It's been many years since my last confession, and I have much to say. This open place and your kindness will help me say it."

Athos joined the priest in a huddle around the statue of the saint. Blanketed by God's mercy, he told his story until the past was set free.

Chapter 56
To Live Again

Athos continued writing to Nicole. Grignan provided Athos comfort and his only company. D'Artagnan was sent to the military build-up to retake Montauban. Athos's bad shoulder kept him side-lined and sleepless. Days turned into weeks.

His requests to see the King on Pierre's behalf went unanswered. Like his pleas to Nicole, he kept writing them. He also wrote for help from Camille, whom Grignan tracked down. Relieved to learn his ally had lived to make it home, Athos lamented that even Camille's statesman-like support garnered nothing in return. In every effort, the scandal was too fresh to make headway, but Athos swore to fight on to free Pierre from the Bastille and restore Nicole to his side. As for the Queen, Athos had no more favours to ask of her, especially after the spectacle at Le Louvre. The only silver lining in his effort to save Pierre was that François had been a less-than-sympathetic character in Paris. No one missed him. Athos's reputation might suffer temporarily, but it wasn't tainted at all. His exploits made him an idol. The story grew grander with each repeating.

And so he wrote and waited.

In early winter, Nicole finally accepted Athos's escort home to Rochefort. Cordes, who had been summoned to Paris after the funeral, headed up the journey using François' lush Parisian carriage. Athos served as outrider, but his status to her was lower than a servant. Nicole only interacted with Cordes. The first day, Athos overheard her complain that the carriage smelled like a man, which turned her stomach.

At the end of each day, Nicole directed Cordes to find separate lodging for the two men. Athos knew it was not Cordes whom she wanted at a distance.

"A word," Cordes said one evening a few days into the journey. Cordes had finished feeding the horses for the night. In the cold stable, the puffs of air coming from Athos were the only sign he was still breathing.

They sat on a dry haystack in an empty stall. "She's fragile, my Lord. The worst she's ever been."

"Call me Athos." He patted Cordes' shoulder. "I wonder if she'll ever use my name again."

"She spent many days in silence after Sibonne's death."

"You were with her then?"

"Only just."

"She's faced with another heartbreak unless I can find mercy for Pierre."

"If I know his vinegar, Pierre will survive the Bastille." Cordes jabbed an index finger out like a sword into a body.

"The Bastille is worse than death," Athos said. "I'll keep asking for his release, but I'm not optimistic. I've heard nothing from the King."

"Nicole will need much more support when she arrives home. Coming back will either restore her or send her over the edge."

"Thank you, Cordes."

"For what, my Lord?" He cleared his throat. "Athos."

"For giving her what she gives to others, selfless care."

"To God's ears."

Cordes' prediction was uncanny. Over the next few days, Athos observed Nicole refusing food and traveling without blankets and scarves. The wind bit through Athos's clothes, and the carriage provided her cover but little insulation. Cordes began to spend considerable time trailing her to and from the carriage at stops for meals and lodging. She crept like the dead. The journey slowed to an excruciating pace. The days grew shorter. The long nights prevented swifter travel. A few days before Advent, Athos decided he had to talk to her.

During a full moon, he took a chance at an inn in Laval. Athos went to her upstairs room a few hours after she retired. He tried the knob when there was no answer to his knock. It was unlocked, and the door had not caught. She was lying on a sagging mattress, which appeared to further drain her body of its spirit.

"Nicole."

Her back was to him. He touched her shoulder. "Speak to me. Tell me what you're thinking."

"My heart is dead," she whispered.

"Your heart is in pain, but it beats on." Using his thumb and forefinger, he found her pulse on a wrist. "I feel it. It's strong, only disguised by sorrow."

"I pushed my husband away. I pushed François to his death. Pierre will be next."

"If I tell you something and it touches your soul, you must make me a promise to live again. What I have to say is personal and important. Only for your benefit."

"There's nothing you could say. My soul has washed away."

"Promise me," Athos said, squeezing her shoulder. "If what I tell you moves you, you must live again."

"For what? You'd be better off staying away from me."

"You so doubt your compassion. Let me tell you what I must, then live."

She flattened the side of her face into the pillow and tensed as if for a fall. He gently pulled a hair from an eyelash. He etched her beauty into his memory.

"Because of you," Athos found a reserve of courage, "Nicole, I confessed, before God and priest and Church. I'm absolved. I'm free. Grignan heard my confession before we left Paris."

She lifted her head. The moon's silver light outlined the disbelief on her face. "Did you do this for me?"

"No. I confessed for myself. My past is behind me. My future is reborn."

"Is it?" She turned her back again. He didn't mind. He ran a hand over her shoulder blade and felt blessed she didn't shudder.

"I'll be near when you need me. I'm yours," he said.

He made certain the door caught when he left.

★★★

The next day, all day, he felt her watching. The carriage curtains were drawn open a few inches wider on each side. He couldn't see in, but the energy of possibility shot sparks of hope through him.

If it was time she needed, he had it to spare. His arm tingled. It was not useful for necessities, to eat or wash, but he took comfort in increments of healing. He lived for increments. A few nights later, Nicole allowed Cordes to find them rooms in the same inn.

Athos couldn't sleep, not that his body ever cooperated, but her presence a few doors down sent his blood rushing like a thundering stampede. He waited for Cordes to start snoring before going out to check the hall, not fully comprehending why.

Smells of stew and potatoes from the evening meal wafted from the kitchen below. Stragglers' laughter covered the creaks his steps made on the planks of the open walkway. Approaching her threshold, he could tell her candle was out. Time clicked to a halt when her door opened, and Nicole, in the cloak she wore at their first kiss, backed out of the room and fastened the door shut. She darted for the stairs and never saw him.

He followed her outside, where her shoulders relaxed and her cape fluttered. He realized she was heading for the stables. Her strides lengthened, and the night air filled his head with fresh, invigorating promise. He breathed deeply, perhaps to catch her scent or feel what she felt. He could feel that she needed to be outdoors, in the natural world that suited her best.

An oil lamp hung from a peg in the stable, and he stood back while she stroked a horse. She spoke to it in whispers, calming the animal, calming herself, finding a center point in a storm. Her expression was masked by her hood. Athos might have stayed hidden had another horse's whinny not caused her to look in his direction.

"Hunting me again, I see." Her face was still obscured.

He gestured for permission to enter her circle. She nodded.

"You're lighter on your feet tonight," he said.

"Perhaps." The horse flicked an ear as her scarred hand passed near it.

"Some consider the night air dangerous."

"Only when the danger comes in the form of a man." She let the hood fall, and her expression invited his approach.

"I asked you once if my status as a Musketeer disturbed you. I'm not sure I got a clear answer."

The horse nudged her shoulder, and she went back to petting. "Being a Musketeer is an honourable life. What will you do when you return to Rochefort?"

He smiled. "Wait."

"To heal? For another day in the service of the King?"

"I'll wait to feel your love again."

She paused in mid-stroke on the horse's mane. She turned around and captured his grey eyes in gratitude. He encircled her, and his hands transferred warmth and calm. Her tears fell softly. He knew they were the first in months not from pain or regret.

"Despite the horror we have lived through, I believe a miracle has occurred," she said. "Your life is a miracle."

Her unexpected kiss bathed Athos in love. It was her life force upon him, a power of Heaven and Earth, saint and Creator, all the goodness of redemption. She wept in his arms then asked him to sit in the hay and listen. "I've rewritten my history since you came to me. Can you fathom the changes you've brought on? A few months ago I was a secluded wife trying to disappear into the landscape. I believe I have led a selfish life, and because I wanted it one way, I was working against God. François' death horrified me, and I will bear the shame for many years and seek forgiveness. But I question whether God meant for me to be François'. It never felt like love. It goes against everything in my faith to have fallen in love with you, Athos. You were angry and self-destructive when we met, yet I've always been drawn to people who wear their passion outwardly—my sister—and Pierre, too. So it makes sense that you would affect me. You are honour-bound and brutally forthcoming and allow your heart to love to the point of breaking. I want such a love, have always wanted it, and now it's mine. My life may be upside down and torn apart, but my heart lives with you. It is right. I love you, Athos. I have no fear now. I believe there's holiness in true love. It's pure. God is there."

She continued recounting her thoughts since Paris, the good and the bad. She was timid at moments in his arms, still hurting from circumstance, but she hoped for the chance of a new beginning between them. Her voice rang sweeter than an angel's hymn. She kept him near, talking, touching, for minutes and hours, until sunlight illuminated their rebirth.

★★★

Within days of their return to Rochefort, they moved to the chalet. They rode in with provisions for many weeks. A layer of snow covered the journey, and the chalet was surrounded by the tracks of stags and small prey. It was frigid inside, but they soon set it aflame.

The lovers craved privacy, and life at the chalet allowed Nicole and Athos to discover each other.

Their existence was primitive. Fires every morning, wood chopping, water boiling, all exercises in staying warm from the everlasting nights of winter. The chores were chores, necessary to prolong the single reason for their separation from the world—to indulge the heat of love.

She melted into him. Their movements became one. Every movement. The love-making, the daily meals, the poetry, the drawing, the baths. Their lives synchronized.

Like their love, their conversations deepened. They discovered similarities in beginnings and endings. His, before and after Milady. Hers, before and after Sibonne.

Their bodies flowed across each other like clear water over smooth rock. It tricked their minds into late, late wakefulness, believing their history was erased in the safety of their sensual exploration. They vowed to find harmony when the world called them back.

The cold and the crackling branches of ice-laden boughs isolated them. He stayed within her reach every night, separating the strands of her auburn hair with the seriousness of prayer. Many evenings they curled on a deerskin near the largest fireplace in the main room. The fire and layers of heavy blankets were necessary, but their skin-to-skin contact provided the heat.

"It will happen. In the spring," he said one night in February. He wove a fine brunette lock between his fingers.

A pop in the fire made her blink. She sat up and stared.

"Have you been inside the Bastille?" she asked.

"I haven't crossed inside." He nestled his bare chest against her back.

"Do people survive it? Escape? Find a sympathetic hearing?"

"Some. Not many." A flame shot through the flue.

Nicole wrapped a silk scarf around her shoulders and vanished to the bedroom. She brought back a thick, well-worn journal, its leather cover stained from use. She ran two fingers along its spine. "You should read this."

Athos crossed his legs and guided her to sit in them. He read the inscription.

"You kept a diary. You chronicled Sibonne's demise."

"And in reality," she said, "my own."

"You live whole now. With me." He brushed the back of her shoulder with his cheek.

"Do you believe God has a greater plan?" she asked.

"I believe his work is often concealed from our mortal eyes." The heat in the room ebbed with a gust of wind from outside.

"Read this, then take it to Pierre," she said. His arms were around her, caressing the book and her hands upon it. "Sibonne also wrote letters to Pierre in her final days. I haven't read them. They should be given to him when you secure his freedom."

As the days passed, the birds ventured out timidly, and the nights began to grow shorter. Finches and starlings weighed down branches dripping in the thaw. Athos tested his arm each day with physical exercise but was angered by its slow progress. Feeling was coming back. He yearned for a full recovery but not for the end of winter. He wanted this time with Nicole to last forever.

He had promised to go for Pierre by spring, but the pending separation from her agitated him. He was growing used to her presence, the warmth of her body, the feel of her blood churning next to his. He realized their time of rejuvenation had to end. Avoiding the real world seemed selfish, and it meant disregarding Pierre's fate. Thoughts of Pierre weakened her composure daily. Her mind was wandering. He saw it. The distant stares left him anxious. He took up the axe when he couldn't distract her, when her mood defeated his. She became more and more remote.

Leave us be, he told the demons, slamming the wood into splinters. He yearned for infinite bliss, for Nicole to be his and his alone, but Pierre had to be brought home alive. Otherwise, guilt would eat away her soul.

"You didn't hear me call." She was behind him, wrapped in a wool throw. He curled the axe in his good arm and buried it in the stump.

"I don't want to leave this place or you," he said.

"You'll always have me." She pulled the blanket around them both. She was naked underneath.

"Your boldness shocks me." He swivelled around and hugged her middle.

"I'm certain I'm pregnant."

He was speechless. How could his heart get any fuller? His hands smoothed over her belly, and his astonishment immediately switched to concern.

"Don't worry," she said. "I've prayed many years for a child. It's a happy coincidence that my failure to produce an heir wasn't my own fault."

"But our child will be a bastard," he said and scooped her up for the door.

Inside, he made straight for the bedroom and laid her across the bed and covered her in wool. "Are you warm enough?"

She laughed, threw off the blanket and rubbed her belly button in tiny circles. Her lack of modesty was another outcome of their time together. "You'll be a father."

He rested a chin on the edge of the bed, spellbound by the circular motions of her hand. Beyond a doubt, she was the most beautiful woman he had ever known. He moved his body gingerly over her, his chest nestled on her pelvis. He stared intently at her centre.

"When?" he asked, unable to think.

She ran her hands through the blond on his head. "In the fall. An autumn baby."

His smile grew in proportion to the widening of his heart. He framed her torso with his forearms, struggling with his weak arm, and began to kiss around her navel.

"Father Grignan will marry us," he said between kisses. He quit abruptly. "We can't delay."

She held him by the weaker arm before he could get off the bed.

"A moment ago, you were telling me how you never wanted to leave, and now you're rushing off?"

"For our baby." He smiled when she didn't let go.

"Show me why you wanted to stay." She angled her head teasingly.

Nicole's body was a delicacy, rare and satisfying like wine at its peak. He kissed her wide-eyed and brushed against the tips of her breasts with his bare chest. Her lips parted with his, and her tongue glided across his lower lip. He slipped a hand inside the soft triangle between her legs, and in the instant his exploration made her arch, he feathered his proposal across her neck: "Marry me."

Chapter 57
The Road to Redemption

The dappled light beneath the willow played in an early spring wind. Athos caught a paper crane from Nicole's palm when the wind blew it off. He handed it back, and the breeze repeated. Dirt stained the wing tips.

Athos rubbed her neck. "I'll be back."

"I know." She laid a cheek on her bended knees and looked back at him. He stretched out behind her, legs straight in the grass, loose clothes helping him relax. He glowed with health and love.

"How is your arm today?" She blew the crane instead of waiting for the wind.

"Moving, more and more." He wiggled his fingers and bent the elbow. He leaned in and kissed her. "You could come with me."

"You know how I feel about Paris." Her gaze went to the pond and the field beyond. "Did you kiss me?"

"Is that an invitation for another?" He nosed her shoulder.

"After the stag, when I fainted, did you kiss me then?"

"It was our very first. How did you know?"

"I sensed it," she said.

"So, love does transcend all states of being." He hugged her waist with his strong arm.

"All states?" she challenged. "Even guilt?"

"Especially guilt," he said.

They walked in silence to the front of the château, where she had left a bundle for his trip. It seemed light for its importance. Her journal, the stack of Sibonne's sealed letters to Pierre and a note to Father Grignan, wrapped in twine. Together, the package measured smaller than a Bible. Snug in a leather pouch, she gave it to Athos before he departed.

"You know it may be impossible for me to get these to him." He took the package and drew her near. "I'll miss you terribly."

They had said their personal good-byes in the night. In truth, they had been saying them for most of the late winter, aware that the trip could not be delayed past early spring. By then, enough time might have passed for Athos to bargain for Pierre's freedom. His life was at stake. Athos held the only card, his connection with the King and Queen. Nicole was an outcast because of the legacy of her husband. Wealthy but an outcast.

Only Cordes attended the departure to inspect all of Athos's equipment and prepare the horse. Hannah refused to speak to Athos, and Duchy barred him from stepping foot in the kitchen. He had not seen baby Sophia since his arrival. In some ways, the good-bye mirrored his new status—imperfect.

"Say it again," he begged of Nicole, his guardedness destroyed by the pending separation.

"I love you."

"Now, tell me once more about our baby," he said.

"You won't be needed back until fall."

He lowered an ear to her middle and touched the gentle bump with his fingertips.

"You need to pick a name if it's a girl," he said, a sigh at the end.

"It's not a girl," she responded in a playful tone. "Raoul will laugh one day when he hears you wanted a daughter."

He smiled and gave her a final kiss.

It was mid-morning when Athos rode out. Nicole, struck by a sudden chill, tightened her shawl and headed to the chapel.

Historical Notes

Reading *The Three Musketeers* by Alexandre Dumas isn't required to enjoy or understand *Blood, Love and Steel: A Musketeer's Tale*, and here's why: Athos is a symbolic character of bravado and heartache. Writing about him was the equivalent of breathing life into an archetype.

The fictional character of Athos came into being in 1844, when *The Three Musketeers* began to appear in newsprint instalments. *The Three Musketeers* was later released as a book and was quickly translated and distributed to several destinations across Europe. It has been reviewed, criticized, and researched. Scholars determined that Dumas wrote the book based on records from the era of King Louis XIII. Athos and his companions, d'Artganan, Porthos and Aramis, are fictional characters while the King, Queen Anne of Austria, the Duke of Buckingham and Cardinal Richelieu are real historical figures.

The new characters in *Blood, Love and Steel* are fictional, although a few of the names in the book are drawn from history. The Comte de Rochefort, François Rieux, evolves from a place and a name. The Rieux name is mentioned in the history of Rochefort-en-Terre, and a François Rieux appears to have held the title of sovereign there, but 200 years earlier than the time period of this book. A man named Rochefort is also a major player in the Dumas story, but, in my mind, the character of the same name in this novel is a different man.

The town of Rochefort changed its name to Rochefort-en-Terre in the late 19th Century and continues to thrive in southwest Brittany (Bretagne), having been established originally as a medieval fortress. I took liberties in describing the city's major land formation as a cliff. I selected it as a location for Nicole's château because the town has a large stock of 17th Century architecture. Similarly, the church Nicole attends faithfully, Notre Dame de la Tronchaye, still exists and dates back well beyond the time period of this story.

A guardsman for the King of France, or any military man for that matter, would have participated in the armed conflicts of the time. In *The Three Musketeers,* Athos and his compatriots go to the Siege of La Rochelle, which took place between 1627-28. I place Athos back in Paris the summer after the siege. I write that Athos also served at the Siege at Montauban, which occurred in 1621 and ended poorly for the French. Like armed manoeuvres tend to be, they were bloody, and Athos would have seen his share of carnage. The Redition of Montauban, when the Huguenots finally surrendered their stronghold of the city, is where d'Artagnan is sent at the end of *Blood, Love and Steel.* This occurred in August 1629 and essentially ended when the Protestant Huguenots gave the city to the French Catholics.

The time period of this book is after the Hundred Years' War but before France's direct involvement in the Thirty Years' War, both of which were propelled by religious friction. Catholicism was the predominant religion in France, though Protestantism and less-orthodox thought were part of the picture, as I indicate in the reference to the Ursulines, a group of nuns from the early 1600s who were advocating new ideas. Father Grignan would not have been alone in his unorthodoxy but more likely a subdued radical, as I tried to depict him.

Art was becoming a more important aspect of French life, due in no small part to the influence of Cardinal Richelieu. The painting Allegory of Victory, which Athos hides behind in the climax of Part Two, is a piece dating to 1635 by one of the Le Nain brothers, who were enmeshed in the aristocratic society of King Louis XIII. The original work is not nearly as large as I depict in this book, but the artwork fits the feel of the storyline. Le Louvre, where it could have been displayed and where it lives today, was the royal residence where many artists and nobles milled about in courtly life, shortly before Versailles became the centre of aristocracy under Louis XIV.

Books also would have been available widely to nobles, though large, private libraries would have been an anomaly and restricted to persons engaged in higher education and scholarship. Father Grignan quotes Shakespeare but in all likelihood he would not have seen the sonnets yet, though they were popular in England.

Most of my research for this book focused on socio-political aspects of life for both French aristocrat and peasant. Agrarian life predominated and provided the majority of the French their means of survival. Wine-making would have been widespread but rudimentary for the lowest classes. Aristocrats would have had the finest wines, food, art and culture. But as I indicate in this tale, an aristocrat who sought financial gain from a trade, as the Comte de Rochefort does, would have been frowned upon. It certainly would have painted him unfavourably. Also true to historical records, Pierre and Hannah at seventeen would have been young to marry and would have needed the consent of the sovereign, even before seeing the priest.

I always kept in mind the story of Dumas and strived for connections to be consistent. I favoured his telling, but made a few departures for dramatic affect. Chapters from the *The Three Musketeers* that I heavily relied on were "The Musketeers at Home," "Athos's Wife," "A Conjugal Scene" and, of course, the climax, "The Execution."

Blood, Love and Steel was written for personal pleasure. I did not presume to make it a Dumas copycat, either in voice or plot. I wanted Athos to live again. I wrote the book for the love of the character and a wish to see him find fulfilment. Any errors in historical accuracy are my own and a product of my enthusiasm for Athos to find love.

Jennifer Fulford
Summer 2013

CPSIA information can be obtained at www.ICGtesting.com
Printed in the USA
BVOW07s0944150714

358969BV00002B/10/P